ANNA BELFRAGE

RIP IN THE VEIL

ANNA BELFRAGE

A RIP IN THE VEIL

Matador
9 Priory Business Park,
Wistow Road, Kibworth Beauchamp,
Leicestershire. LE8 0RX
Tel: (+44) 116 279 2299
Fax: (+44) 116 279 2277
Email: books@troubador.co.uk
Web: www.troubador.co.uk/matador

ISBN 978 1780882 420

British Library Cataloguing in Publication Data.
A catalogue record for this book is available from the British Library.

Typeset in 11pt Bell MT by Troubador Publishing Ltd, Leicester, UK

Matador is an imprint of Troubador Publishing Ltd

Printed and bound in the UK by TJ International, Padstow, Cornwall

This book is dedicated to Sofia and Jeanette.

CHAPTER 1

The radio died first. Halfway through Enrique Iglesias'
Hero there was a burst of static and the display went black.
The dashboard lights gave up one by one, the steering
wheel locked, the engine coughed, and the BMW glided to a
stop by a crossroads.

"Hey!" Alex Lind said. "You're a high-class German car,
right? So don't go temperamental on me, okay?" She pumped
the accelerator and turned the key a couple of times.

"Oh, hell! I don't have time for this." She extracted the
key, wiped it against her jeans and reinserted it. "Come on,
come on, come on …" Nothing; not even a little whirr.

"Shit." Alex slammed the steering wheel and got out.

To her left the ground rose in waves towards the moors,
the heather shifting from dull brown through green to
deepest purple, while to her right the land fell away in
jumbles of rocks and sheer cliff faces. No signs of
civilisation, just the crossroads, very much empty space and
five sheep.

"It could be worse," she told the closest sheep. Yeah; a
boulder could have become dislodged from higher up the
slope to bounce down the hillside and flatten her into mush.
"Not that you care, do you?"

The sheep twitched an ear.

Alex dug her hand into her pocket and produced her
mobile phone, new since yesterday.

"See?" She showed it to the sheep. "The wonders of
technology." Somewhere among her contacts was the AA
number. Except that her phone was as useless as her car,
not a flicker of anything resembling electronic life flashing
across its display, no matter how many buttons she
pressed.

This was strange; first her car, then her mobile. It was
the same with her computer; dead to the world. It didn't

exactly help that it was unbearably hot as well. Sahara heat in Scotland – okay, that was an exaggeration, but it wasn't far off, with dark brooding clouds hanging like a lid over the moor. She kicked at the ground, sending a small stone to bounce over the tarmac. One of the sheep bleated, two more followed suit, and just like that they were off, five dirty heaps of wool scampering across the road and disappearing down the rock strewn incline.

"Right," she said and opened the bonnet. As far as she could see there were no disconnected cables, nothing to explain why the car had stalled. Alex slid back into the leather seat and took a deep breath; maybe the car just needed a little rest and now, when she turned the key, it would purr into life. Nope – and she couldn't even get the top back up. German junk. Next time she'd go for Japanese.

"I hate you," she told the convertible as she got out. If she – and in particular the PowerPoint presentation on her computer – wasn't in Edinburgh within the hour, Diane would probably fire her. Probably? She'd be out on her ear so fast there'd be skid marks all over Diane's new carpet. She did a quick calculation; walking back to the closest village would take an hour or more, but if she remembered correctly there was a farm a couple of miles ahead. At least they'd have a working phone.

A raindrop plopped down to hiss on the warm metal beside her, was followed by several more. There was a small stand of trees on the opposite side of the crossroads, and when the rain increased in intensity she put on her waterproof jacket, retrieved her rucksack from the front seat, and made for the stunted alders.

She never got to the other side. Immobilising pain – the mother of all headaches – had her coming to a halt, blinking in an effort to relieve the building pressure behind her eyes. Her elbows and the back of her neck prickled, she felt dizzy and nauseous, like she did the few times she tried the roller coaster rides down in Blackpool. Must be the heat, this goddamn heat that was making her sweat like a piece of cheddar left out in the sun. The first thunderclap made her flinch. The air tasted of iron and salt, and her heart was like a power hammer in her chest.

The road was flowing beneath her feet, a shifting mass of colours that swirled in tightening spirals towards the centre of the crossroads. Heat hallucinations; she closed her eyes for an instant before dropping them to the reassuring black of the asphalt. It wasn't there. The tarmac melted away before her eyes, replaced by strange bands of greens and blues, bands that rippled and twisted around her feet, dragging her in the direction of a ... a hole?

With a ripping sound a huge funnel opened at her feet, pouring out light so bright it hurt her eyes. And the noise! Chalk screeching over blackboards magnified a zillion times. She raised her arms to shield her face and tried to back away, but the road disintegrated below her, and she slid this way and that, like a drunken figure skater on a slope of ice. Shit! What was happening? An earthquake? No earthquake, just a ... a ... Alex screamed, scrambling back from the edge of the rapidly expanding void.

The next clap of thunder sent her sprawling into all that light and for an instant or two she hung suspended, before hitting the ground so hard the air was knocked out of her. The skies opened and in a matter of seconds she was drenched. She lay stunned, staring at the lightning that lit up the sky. Her hair bristled with static electricity, and her arms and legs were so heavy, almost detached from the rest of her. She tried to move her hand and saw the muddy fingers twitch in response. Mud? She swayed to her feet. How odd; no hole, no dazzling light, definitely no asphalt – just a narrow dirt road.

Thunder growled and roared, and she whimpered as she crossed the muddy track, making for the hillside. She had no idea where she was going, only that she had to... the road, it was dangerous on the road. A bolt of lightning flashed through the sky directly over her head. She screamed for her father when the current coursed through her body, lifted her up into the air, and flung her up the hill where she hit the ground head first.

* * *

"This is unacceptable," Diego Sanderson said, frowning in turn at John Orrock and Diane Wilson. "I've come a very long way for this meeting."

"I'm so sorry, Mr Sanderson." Diane looked flustered, the pale skin on her chest and neck mottling in reds.

John went over to the window, squinting through the curtain of rain to the trafficked street far below. Damn! Alex should have been here by now. He tried phoning her again, aware of their client's eyes boring into his back. Nothing.

"Huh." Diego Sanderson said. "So where the hell is she?" He sat back, looking cramped in the elegant wooden armchair.

Good question; where was she? It shouldn't have taken her more than two hours to drive across the moors, and now – John threw a look at his watch – it was almost four hours since he'd heard from her.

"She might have run into car trouble." Diane looked genuinely concerned, one cheek sucked in. That surprised John; Diane and Alex tolerated each other due to mutual benefit, no more. Alex needed the jobs Diane threw her way to get back on track after that unexplained absence three years ago and Diane knew a gift horse when she saw one. Still, once they'd been friends – best friends, even – and he suspected that every now and then they both missed each other.

"If she's having car trouble then she's going to be stuck out there for quite some time," Sanderson said. "Look at the way the rain's coming down. It sure doesn't seem as if it's going to let up anytime soon."

John got to his feet. "I'm going to look for her, something must have happened."

"Yeah; she might have drowned," Sanderson muttered.

John threw him a dark look; this wasn't funny.

Sanderson stood up. "I'll go with you. After all, without her there's no point to this meeting, is there?"

"Really, Mr Sanderson," Diane said, "you don't have to do this. Let me invite you to dinner instead."

Sanderson shook his head. "I'll go with John; that consultant of yours is travelling around with my new security network in her computer, and I plan on ensuring it's undamaged."

John frowned. "I'll manage on my own, I think."

"I'm coming with you," Sanderson insisted, eyeballing John.

"Fine," John shrugged. "I just have to call the babysitter first."

They were silent on the drive south. Sanderson had insisted on a quick stop at his hotel and was now dressed in jeans and Timberlands. He studied the landscape with an expression of dislike.

"Bleak, isn't it? Far too much space, you know?" He made a face. "Give me inner city Chicago any day."

They crested a small hill and in front of them the road ran in a straight line. No hairpin curves, no major obstruction, just a black line of asphalt that bisected the landscape around them as if it had been drawn with the help of a ruler.

It was growing dark and the rain was still coming down, but now in a relaxing patter. The clouds hung far too close to the ground and even with the AC on the heat filtered its way through the metal of the car.

"Jeez, it's hot." Sanderson flapped a map to create a fan effect, grunting when John braked.

"That's her car!" John pointed at a red shape standing halfway up the hill. He threw himself out of the car, slipping as he made his way across the road. "Alex? Alex!" he called, scrabbling up the hillside. What was the car doing here, almost twenty metres from the road?

"Maybe she miscalculated and drove off," Sanderson said from behind him.

"Alex is an excellent driver, and even if she'd driven off, this is uphill. She wouldn't have gotten this far."

Sanderson seemed to agree, his eyes narrowing as he scanned the vegetation.

"No tyre marks, no nothing. It's as if the car was thrown there."

The car was empty, the key still in the ignition. Sanderson's face paled when he put his hand on the leather seat.

"It's dry."

John didn't understand at first but leaned over to touch the backrest. Dry.

"But it can't be, it's been raining all afternoon. It's still raining."

"Not here, not here where the car is," Sanderson said.

John broke out in goose bumps and edged closer to Sanderson.

"How?" he stammered.

"I don't know," Sanderson said, colour flooding back into his face. "How the hell should I know?"

Sanderson staggered back a few metres from the car. He looked ill, all of him swaying where he stood.

"It seems kind of staged, don't you think?" he said.

"Staged? How staged? She's had an accident!"

"Yeah, right; look at it. Not a scratch on the paintwork, nothing's out of place ..." Sanderson seemed about to faint, sweat was beading his upper lip and hairline, and he hugged himself, half bent over as if he were in pain.

"Are you alright?" John moved towards him.

"We must go," Sanderson said, grabbing John's arm. "Call the police and have them look for her, but we have to go."

John wrenched himself free. "Now that we're here we might as well look for her. She must be somewhere close, perhaps she's hurt." He threw Sanderson a worried look; the man looked about to collapse. "Why don't you sit down?"

Sanderson shook his head. "It's just a dizzy spell, jetlag or something." He straightened up, unclenched his arms from around his waist. "I'm fine," he said, his statement very much at odds with his ashen face. "Let's get on with it, okay?"

They looked everywhere for her. John's throat was sore from calling her name, his jeans were wet up to his knees after wading through drenched heather and bracken, but he just couldn't stop looking. She had to be here, somewhere. At one point Sanderson held up a rucksack.

"Hers? It's badly burnt – look, the zipper has melted together."

John sank down onto the ground, clutching the black computer backpack. Sanderson crouched beside him and hid his head in his hands for a moment before raising his face in John's direction.

"It's dangerous here," he said, heaving himself back onto his feet. "We have to go. Now!"

"How dangerous?"

"It just is, okay? Can't you feel it, how the whole ground is heaving?"

"No," John snorted, "of course it isn't."

"But the stink!" Sanderson leapt down the hillside. John inhaled, surprised to notice Sanderson was right; a stench of heated, scorched metal, of tyres burning, hung in the air.

"Besides, you'll never find her," Sanderson called up from the road. "She's gone."

"Gone? She isn't gone," John bristled.

"Of course she is! As gone as that accursed mother of hers. *Ay Dios mío!*" He moaned and hunched together, hands pressed to the sides of his head.

"Mercedes? You know Mercedes?"

"No, I never had the pleasure; she sort of disappeared before I had the opportunity of meeting her. Oh, Jesus, will you look at that?" Sanderson pointed at the dark, roiling skies. John looked from the clouds back to Sanderson.

"Scared of thunder?" John couldn't help it; he jeered.

"Yes, yes! It scares the shit out of me. Now can we please, please leave?"

John frowned down at where Sanderson was standing. Something was happening to the road, it undulated round Sanderson's feet. He blinked a couple of times.

"I have to find her," he said, relieved to see the road looked normal again. The first clap of thunder rolled across the valley and Sanderson jumped.

"We can come back later, but now let's please go, okay?" There was a frantic edge to his voice and John took pity on him.

He only got halfway down the hill before the storm broke. No rain, just thunder and lightning that stood a stark white against the backdrop of clouds. Sanderson swore, kicked at something John couldn't see. With a tearing sound the crossroads cracked open, bright light streaming upwards. Sanderson screamed when he was yanked into the chasm. He clung to the edge, hollering for help. John ran as fast as he could, but before he could reach him, Sanderson was sucked down, still screaming. With a clap the hole snapped shut, the reverberations throwing John off his feet.

For the coming minutes he hung on, incapable of moving when the ground pitched below him, stones and boulders rolling and bouncing around him. Once the rain began to fall, the air quieted and John sat up. His car stood where he'd left it, the BMW was still halfway up the hill, and the crossroads was just as it had always been, the asphalt dark with rain. The hillside stood pungent and peaceful around him, but of Alex and of Sanderson there was no trace. No trace at all.

CHAPTER 2

Matthew Graham stumbled to his feet. Sweetest Lord! The repeated thunderclaps had thrown him to the ground, near on knocked him senseless. Still; everything seemed to be in working order, even though he tasted blood in his mouth.

He turned his face up to the rain, relieved that the uncommon heat of the last few days had broken. The air still smelled of dust and too much sun, but now there was the fresh scent of water as well, of damp earth and wet bracken. He rubbed at his wrists, running fingers over the visible scars that ringed both of them. Home; he was home, and weeks of looking over his shoulder as he made his way north were over. Here he was safe, able to melt into the moors and fells of Scotland so as to make him difficult to catch. It almost made him smile. Almost.

He looked about for his few belongings, settled his roll on his shoulder and stood for a while, taking his bearings. Further up the hillside he made out a darker splotch against the drenched slopes. A cave, no doubt small and damp, but far better than spending a night on the drenched ground.

He came to a stop at the sound of the birds. Large and black, they flapped and cawed, bickering over something that was lying further down the slope. A dead sheep? One bird landed on the ground, there was a piercing shriek – most definitely human – and Matthew lengthened his stride, yelling at the corbies to be gone.

A woman; on her front, with one arm trapped below her, the other extended by her side. He crouched, not quite sure what to do. She was in a bad way, one foot scorched around the ankle and down to her toes, and on her forehead there was an ugly contusion, blood trickling sluggishly from it.

From the way her breath hitched, each inhalation interrupted by a protesting whimper, he suspected she must have landed on her ribs. He looked down at the road, measured the distance with his eyes. Had she been thrown this far by the thunderstorm? He couldn't think of any other reason for a lass to be lying here in the heather, all alone.

The thought brought him up short and he spent a couple of tense moments inspecting what he could see of the hillside for her possible companions. Nothing. He chewed his lip; a woman travelling on her own was most unusual, and here, on the empty moor with miles and miles to the closest farm, it was not only unusual, it was puzzling – as was her whole appearance. His eyes flew up and down her legs; what was she wearing? The woman uttered a low, guttural sound. Her head rose a half inch or so from the ground, the eyes opened. Blue eyes attempted to focus before closing again.

"Can you stand, then?" He shook her shoulder. Her eyes snapped open, a wrinkle appearing between her brows. The woman lifted her head and stared at him, a sob escaping her when she drew in a deep breath.

"Oh shit!" she said.

Matthew retreated, eyes fixed on her.

She blinked. "At least it isn't orange," she said, waving her hand in the direction of his shirt.

Orange? He tilted his head.

"You know," she went on, giving him a faint smile. "Like those Hare Krishna people."

He had no idea what she was talking about, but nodded all the same. Her eyes lingered on his breeches, his bare shins and feet, they stuck on his belongings, returned to his breeches and flew up his shirt.

"Who are you?"

He had no intention of telling her that, at least not yet, so instead he mumbled something unintelligible. Despite an odd accent, the woman spoke good enough English, not Scots, but what did she mean with her comment regarding his shirt? And why was she gaping at him as if she'd never seen a normally dressed man before? To be fair he did look somewhat worse for wear. The shirt was old and the breeches were the ones he'd stolen from the drover a few weeks back, but at least both garments were whole and reasonably clean. The woman sat up too fast, groaned and clutched at her ribs. She vomited, standing on all fours.

"Jesus," she said, making him frown at her careless use of our Lord's name. "What's happened to me?"

"It looks as if you were struck by lightning, no?"

She stared down at the burnt foot, turned her head to the side and retched.

"My shoes," she said, "where are my shoes?"

"Not here."

She struggled to sit up. "I think I remember," she told him, "so much noise, so much light, and then I was flat on my face."

He nodded and helped her to stand, one arm round her waist to keep her upright. She leaned against him and was sick all over their feet.

"I'm sorry," she whispered afterwards. "I couldn't help it."

"Not to worry, but we have to get out of this rain. You're cold, and need to lie down. Up there." He jerked his head in the direction of the cave.

"Maybe we should call for help." She slid her hand into a slit in her strange breeches.

"Here?" He almost laughed. Who would hear them? And besides, he had no intention of doing anything to attract attention. He studied the bright red object she'd pulled out.

"It's brand new," she said, catching his look.

"Ah," he nodded, eyes stuck on the shiny metal casing. A wee enamelled box, but what might be the purpose of it? She glanced down at the object and made a face.

"Stuff never works when you really need it, does it?" She shoved it back out of sight.

He lowered her to sit, and she mumbled her thanks.

"Were you on the road as well?"

11

"Aye." He couldn't take his eyes off her legs. No shift, no covering skirts, only those strange elongated breeches, hugging tight around well shaped thighs and a round, strong arse. Christ in His glory! He hadn't been this close to a woman in several years, and his blood raced through him, making him ill at ease and elated at the same time. Where was she from, to dress in such an immodest fashion? He'd belt any woman of his before allowing her to so expose herself.

"What?" she demanded. "Do I look strange? Am I green all over?"

He muffled a laugh. "You look very strange, but nay, you're not green"

"Well, thank heavens for that, I would have hated being turned into a frog or something."

"A frog?" He shook his head. "You don't look like any frog I've seen."

A smile flickered over her face, held for a heartbeat or two before becoming a grimace. She raised a hand to her forehead.

"My head; it's killing me." She closed her eyes.

Alex rested back against the cave wall and concentrated on breathing without hurting herself. She studied him from under her lashes, irritated to find he'd gone back to gawking at her. What was the matter with him? Had he never seen a woman in jeans before?

She looked closely at him. Tall, broad in shoulders and chest, but thin and with an underlying pallor to his skin – as if he'd been ill, just recently allowed out of bed. His hair was cut unbecomingly short except at the back where some longer strands still hung on, his cheeks were covered by a dark, unkempt beard, like the one Magnus would sport at the end of his summer holidays – so far nothing alarming. His shirt though… Worn linen that laced up the front, mended cuffs – all of it hand stitched. Maybe his girlfriend had made it for him, or maybe New Age people believed in doing everything from scratch, in which case they needed a serious fashion update. She moved, scraped her foot against the rocky ground, and winced.

"Is it alright if I touch you?" he said. "It might ease somewhat if I wash the blood off."

"Sure, go ahead, touch all you want." Well, within limits of course.

He looked at her with a hesitant expression. "All I want?"

She made a huge effort to look him straight in the eyes, despite the fact that she could see two – no, three – of him.

"Help me, I'm not feeling too good, okay?" She turned her head to the side and retched, but this time it was just slimy yellow bile that burnt her throat as she heaved. "Fucking hell," she said afterwards, keeping her eyes closed to stop the whole world from spinning. "I must have hit my head really hard."

He spent quite some time on her forehead, close enough that she could smell him, drawing in the scent of sweat and unwashed male. She wrinkled her nose. Phew! How about some soap?

"What?" he said. "Did I hurt you?"

"No, I'm fine." She wasn't; her brain was banging against her skull, the broken skin on her forehead itched, her ribs were using her lungs as a pincushion and her foot... no, best not think about her foot, because it looked absolutely awful, blisters like a fetter round her ankle and all the way down to her toes. She flexed them experimentally. It hurt like hell.

He poured some more water onto the rag he was using and wiped her face. She liked that, opening her eyes to smile her thanks at him. He smiled back, teeth flashing a surprising white in the darkness of his beard. He sat back on his haunches, a worried expression on his face.

"What?" Did she need stitches? Because she really, really hated needles.

"Your ribs, I have to do something about them."

"Like what?"

"Bandage them, so that you don't shift them too much."

"You've done this before?"

"It happens, aye."

"Oh, so you're a doctor?"

"A doctor?" He laughed. "Nay, lass, I am no doctor. But setting ribs is no great matter, is it?"

"It is when they're mine." She shifted on her bottom. "It won't hurt, will it?"

"No, but I will have to … err … well, I must … the shirt, aye?"

"The shirt?"

"Well, you have to take it off."

"Oh." Where did this man come from? "That's alright; you won't be the first to see me in the flesh." He looked so shocked she laughed, but the pain that flew up her side made her gasp instead.

He pulled his bundle close and rummaged in it, muttering something about having to find something to bandage her ribs with. Finally he extracted what looked like a rag and proceeded to tear it into strips.

He was very careful as he helped her out of her jacket and her shirt, and at the sight of her bra his eyes widened, but he didn't say anything. She sat up so that he could wrap the torn lengths of cloth around her. His exhalations tickled her skin and she took short breaths, staring straight ahead as his big, capable hands worked their way around her torso, a gentle touch that sent surprising and quite unwelcome tingles of warmth through her body.

She was aware of his eyes on her skin, on her neck, but mostly on her breasts, quick glances that returned time and time again to the lacy red bra edged with cream that cupped her breasts and lifted them high. She sat up straighter, shoulders pulled back. She peeked at him, met his eyes and looked away.

"What's this?" He put a finger on the satin strap. Impossible; men that hadn't seen a bra didn't exist – not where she came from.

"It's a bra."

"A bra," he echoed, tracing it round her middle. She jerked back, making both of them gasp.

"My apologies." He raised his hands in a conciliatory gesture. "I shouldn't … But there, now it's done." He gave her the shirt and averted his eyes as she struggled to put it back on.

Alex closed her eyes, trying to come up with a label to pin on this strange man. Isolated goat farmer? Recluse? Maybe he was an old-fashioned – extremely old-fashioned – Quaker, or maybe the Amish had set up a little colony up here in the Scottish wilderness.

Her thoughts drifted; she wondered where her computer might be, considered crawling out to look for it, but couldn't find the energy. The meeting! Bloody hell, the meeting! And Isaac; she was due to pick him up before five today. Right; she had to, yes she had to … what? Walk? With a foot that looked like a barbecued piece of pork? She slumped against the wall. No; stay here. Yes, just … rest, sit still. John would sort it all out. John would come and find her – of course he would.

It was getting dark. The woman was shivering and after covering her with one of his threadbare blankets, he disappeared into the night. Everything was wet, and he had to go far afield before he had enough half-dry wood to even attempt a fire.

When he ducked back into the cave, she seemed to be sleeping, her head lolling to one side. He fumbled for his flint and kneeled down to start the fire, small sparks flying off the steel with little or no effect. Wisps of faint smoke uncurled and faded but no flames took hold, and Matthew evicted a long, very colourful string of curses under his breath, a worried glance in the direction of the woman. Her eyes were wide open.

"What are you doing?" Her gaze drifted from the piled wood to the flint and steel in his hands.

"I'm trying, no? But the wood's wet, and…"

"Give me my jacket," she interrupted, indicating the red garment. He handed it to her and she dug into one of the outer pockets, grinning as she brandished a small box. "I collect these." She threw it in his direction. He studied the little box, turning it this way and that. She sighed and crawled over to join him by the opening.

"Here." She took the box and opened it. "Matches." She held a brittle stick aloft.

His eyes never left her hands as she struck the head of the stick against the side of the box. He had to force himself to remain where he was when the flame sprung forth. Magic, this was magic, and behind his back he made a sign for protection against evil. No wonder he thought her strange, she was a witch or a fairy. She hadn't noticed his reaction, but was busy putting the flame to the little pile, smiling when some of the drier twigs caught. She raised her eyes to his.

"What?" She frowned, shoving her short, dark hair off her brow. She didn't look like a witch, her eyes wide as they met his. Still, he muttered a silent prayer – just in case.

"How?" he stuttered, pointing at the little box in her hands.

"It's just a box of matches."

"Matches," he repeated.

She put the box in his hand. "Try."

He wanted to refuse, and at first he just sat with the box in his hand. Finally, he did as he'd seen her do, pulling out one of those wee sticks with that curious knob on top, and striking it against the side of the box. He dropped it with an exclamation onto the floor when it burst into fire. She laughed and he scowled. He repeated the procedure and this time he didn't drop it, but held it until it singed his fingers before blowing the little flame into extinction.

"Bravo," she said. He handed back the box but she shook her head. "No, keep it. I've got more."

She smiled a refusal when he offered her a piece of his bread, muttering something about not thinking her stomach could handle it – not yet. She kept on blinking, pressing the heel of her hand to her forehead, and he suspected her head was hurting something awful. Every now and then she'd slide her hand into the side slit of her breeches, pull out that wee enamelled box, stare at it and frown.

"Stupid, worthless gadget," she said at one point, raising her arm as if she intended to throw it. But she didn't, returning it to its place before lying down, arms cradling her head. Matthew stretched out beside her. Too close, but what was he to do, given the cramped space?

"What's your name?" she asked.

"Matthew," he replied after a while, rolling over in her direction. "Matthew Graham."

"I'm Alex Lind." She eased herself up to sit. She licked her lips and he fumbled in the dark for his water skin, extending it in her direction.

"Alex?" he sat up. "That's a lad's name."

She snorted and drank some more. "No it isn't, last time I looked I was definitely female and it's still my name. Short for Alexandra." She twisted her head in the direction of the opening, exposing her nape, a bare patch of skin highlighted by the severe haircut. She had right pretty ears, tight to her skull and ending in a slight, pink point. Fairy ears...

"What are you?" he whispered, making her turn to face him.

"Just plain Alex; you know, an ordinary woman."

"No you're not; in my world women don't walk around baring their bodies like you do, their hair cut short."

"I'm not baring my body! I'm fully dressed, for God's sake!"

He winced at her careless blasphemy.

"Aye, there's cloth all over you, but it reveals more than it conceals."

"Tough, okay? You'd better learn to live with the times, mister; just because you've chosen to live in some kind of archaic religious context, it doesn't give you the right to judge the rest of us."

"Religious context?" he echoed. "Archaic?"

"Well, look at you! You dress like a cross between a Hare Krishna monk and an Amish person, you stare at me as if you've never seen a bra before. You must've been living in some kind of secluded all male community."

His mouth twisted into a wry smile; aye, that was very true. He leaned towards her, trying to see her eyes in the dark.

"What's a Harray krissna monk? And I haven't seen a ... bra is it? before. I would definitely have remembered."

She was staring at him, hands clenched tight around each other. Matthew gave her a wary look; the lass was gaping as if she'd seen a ghost.

"But you know what a car is, right?"

Matthew shook his head.

"A TV? Radio? A phone?"

He frowned; was this some sort of game? "Nay, I've never heard of any such things."

She gulped and scooted away from him, eyes flying to his bundle, the flint and steel he'd left discarded on the floor. She moaned, hid her face in her arms.

"No," she whispered. "No way. Stuff like that doesn't happen, not in real life."

"What?" He came after her, but she reared back and the expression on her face made him raise his hands, palms towards her. "I'm not about to hurt you."

"It's not you, it's just..." She broke off to stare yet again at him and his possessions. "Bloody hell, no, no, no." She crawled towards the opening. "The car. My car, it'll be right there, where I left it. This is just a bad dream, an effect of hitting my head too hard."

"What's a car?" he said. She laughed, and then she began to cry instead. He followed her outside, made a grab for her when she slipped.

"My BMW," she said, "it has to be here!"

He had no idea what she was looking for as she limped up and down the slope, but whatever it was, it wasn't where she'd expected it to be.

"A dream, it's just a dream, isn't it?" She looked at him beseechingly, and he had no idea what to say. This was no dream, unless they were both sleeping and dreaming the same thing.

"It can't be true," she said, and to his surprise she placed a hand on his arm. "Too solid," she moaned, "you're too damn solid, you hear?" She hit him, repeatedly.

"So are you, lass, but I don't take to hitting you, do I?" He wrapped his arms around her, pinned down her hands.

"Sorry," she hiccupped before breaking down completely, a warm weight against his chest. Dearest Lord, but it felt good to hold a woman this close, her hair tickling his nose. It was a near on perfect match, her body a collection of curves that fitted comfortably into his larger and broader frame, her head resting against his shoulder. With an effort he released her. She was still weeping, albeit silently, and he coaxed her back inside, unnerved by her dejection.

"What is the matter, lass?"

She just shook her head, mumbled something he made out as 'impossible', and sank down to sit before the little fire. She quieted, drew in a few shaking breaths and wiped at her face.

Alex dragged a finger through the dirt of the cave floor. Think, Alex, think! There had to be some sort of explanation to all this. Total blank. She snuck him a look, this man in old fashioned clothes who used flint and steel to light his fire, who'd never heard of things like TVs and cars. This couldn't be happening to her – to be precise, it couldn't happen to anyone. Time was a fixed dimension, no bloody variable! But her car; gone! Maybe she was looking in the wrong place, down the wrong hillside. A flare of hope rushed up her spine only to crash into the rational part of her brain, the part that was telling her all the evidence pointed in one way and one way only. Something impossible and incomprehensible had happened to her – but it had happened.

She glanced at Matthew, met eyes framed by a concerned frown.

"Better?"

"Not really." She took a deep breath; here goes. "What year is it?"

"What year? Don't you know?"

She hitched her shoulders. "I do, but I just want to check."

"It's 1658," he said, spitting to the side. "Three years since I was thrown in gaol due to the betrayal of my brother and wife, three years spent in chains."

She closed her eyes; 1658? Panic shrivelled her windpipe to the size of a drinking straw.

"Are you sure?" It came out squeaky.

He gave her an odd look. "Aye, I am. What year do you think it is?"

"Err…" Alex cleared her throat. What on earth did she tell him? The truth? "I'm not sure. It must be the blow to my head, right?" She fisted her hands to stop them from trembling, but it didn't help, the tremors shivered up her underarms instead. 1658! She had to get back! She had to …

"Oh, God," she said, "Isaac!"

"Isaac?"

"My son, and … " Just like that she was crying again, this time with loud sobs that tore at her throat. Matthew pulled her close, shushing her as she cried her heart out into his shirt.

"Is he dead?" he said a bit later. He was still holding her, one large hand stroking her over her back.

"No," she whispered, "he's just gone." All of them were gone; none of her people existed here, and the thought of never seeing them again tied her guts into a bundle of painful knots.

"How?"

"Not now, some other time, okay?" She sat up to see his face. "Do you want to tell me? You know, about your brother and wife and all that?" Not that she cared, but at present any distraction was welcome.

"No. I prefer not to think of it at all." There was a raw edge to his voice that made her suspect he did think about it – more or less constantly.

"Oh." She threw him a cautious look. He was rubbing at his wrists. "And now? Are you going home?"

"Aye; at last. Not that there's much to come home to." He leaned his head against the wall, a harsh sound escaping from his compressed lips.

"You okay?" Well, no, she could hear he wasn't.

"Okay?"

"Are you alright?"

"Aye." He turned his face away.

Alex snorted. "Men."

She rose to her knees and gave him an awkward hug – much more for her own sake than for his. He reared back, all of him stiffening. She insisted, drawing him close. A few moments and he made as if to sit up. She didn't want him to, she needed someone close, a breathing human warmth to dull the gnawing fear in her belly. So she patted at her thighs and after a long moment of hesitation Matthew allowed her to settle his head on her lap. Maybe he needed it too.

Alex knew the moment he fell asleep, the large body suddenly so much heavier. Through the small opening she could see the summer dawn begin to lighten the skies. She studied him in silence, running a finger over his head. What was she to do? And how would she ever get back? Hang around and wait for another thunderstorm?

CHAPTER 3

She shoved Matthew hard, giving him an apologetic smile when he threw himself backwards, his hands clenching into fists.

"Sorry, I didn't mean to scare you. It's just I have to ..." Her bladder was about to burst and it was either wake him or drench him – and that last alternative didn't seem a good one. It was quite enough to have thrown up all over his feet.

"Oh." He looked disoriented, staring at her as if she were a mirage. That makes two of us, she thought as she crawled out into the morning air, her head jangling with pain.

No car. She'd been hoping there would be, that all this stuff about this being 1658 was him being delusional. Insane. He didn't seem insane, but heck, you never knew – not these days. Still; no car. She blinked. She was having a nightmare. Or she might be in some sort of coma, maybe she'd had a car accident, and now she was drugged to her eyeballs with morphine. Not that it was working very well, because if anything her foot hurt more today than yesterday. Swollen and bright red, it was a bundle of shrieking nerves. She blinked again. And again. No car. Impossible; this was all impossible. Think again, Alex Lind, her brain jeered, look around you. Looks very possible, no? In fact, it doesn't look too much like a dream either.

"Nightmare, not dream," she corrected herself. Her head hurt. Her ribs hurt. Her foot hurt. An accident. A coma. Please let this be a coma.

When she managed to limp back from her secluded outdoor toilet behind a largish boulder, he was standing some feet from the opening, relieving himself in a steaming, hissing stream. Matthew threw her a look, shook himself, ordered his breeches, and gave her a small smile.

"Hungry?"

She nodded eagerly. For the last half-hour she'd been thinking fried eggs with tomatoes, sausages and crispy bacon – or toast, just heaps of toast with butter and jam. She swallowed back on the rushing saliva flow in her mouth. He grinned and used his bare toe to indicate what looked like a heap of feathers.

"Fledglings. I'll roast them."

Not exactly bacon. She stared when he proceeded to cake the dead birds in mud before putting them into the low burning fire.

"Mud?"

He gave her a surprised look. "Otherwise they burn to cinders before they're cooked."

Oh, she nodded, looking at the little dirtballs with certain wariness. What about the feathers? And all the lice and stuff that lived on them?

"They burn off," Matthew said.

Great; sounded fantastic.

By the time the birds were done, Alex was so hungry she no longer cared. Bones, innards and meat, it all went down.

"You want the last one?" Matthew held it out to her. Alex eyed it longingly, but after a quick assessment of their relative sizes shook her head.

"No, you go ahead."

She stretched out on the ground, pillowing her head on her arms. If she closed her eyes she could pretend everything was as it always was – for like five seconds. She heard him move, and twisted her head in his direction. He flushed and looked away when she intercepted his stare.

Alex took the opportunity to do some inspecting of her own; long legs, dark, strong brows and a nose that looked very nice in half profile. And the eyes… she had a thing about eyes, and this man had hazel eyes fringed with thick, dark lashes most women would kill for. He was close to six feet two, she reckoned, which must make him a very big man in the here and now, half a foot or so taller than she herself was. She closed her eyes, nostrils flaring as she tried to catch his scent. He did smell very ripe, but more of sweat than of actual grime. She sniffed at her own shirt and made a face; not only sweat but blood and dirt and... ugh, she needed to wash.

"There's water there, right?" She pointed at the copse of trees that stood down by the crossroads.

Matthew inclined his head in affirmation. "It's a small spring and the water is considered very good."

"It is? Why?"

"I'm not sure, mayhap because it's Scottish?" He said it lightly, almost disparagingly, but she could hear he meant it. Alex smiled at his archaic patriotism. But then, she wasn't Scottish. She was nothing, a mongrel of Swedish and Spanish ancestry raised respectively in Seville, Milwaukee, Stockholm and Edinburgh, their polyglot home full of strays from all over, the occasional Spanish visitor and a substantially higher amount of Swedish cousins.

"I'll just go down and wash, okay?"

He nodded and Alex turned to him, inundated by a wave of gut clawing panic.

"You won't go, will you? I mean, you won't just leave me here?"

Matthew studied her for a moment before giving his head a slight shake.

"Nay, lass, I'll not leave you behind."

He ended up having to help Alex down the hill, supporting her as she limped towards the burbling sound. She shivered in her jacket – the wind had a cooler edge today than yesterday. Yesterday? It couldn't be yesterday, could it? Shit, she didn't even exist yet, but a quick run of hands down her body assured her that she did.

It was good water; Alex drank, washed hands and face and was doing a rudimentary tooth brushing when a hand closed over her nape, squeezed hard into her flesh. She reared back, ignoring the way her ribs squealed in protest.

"Agh! Let go!" It came out rather muted, given the

pressure on her neck. Psychopath! No goat farmer, no monk, this Matthew guy was a raving beast, and now ...

"Alexandra Lind, right?" the man holding her said. What? So she had her name tattooed on her nape? And it was definitely not Matthew, because this was a Yank – a horribly strong one at that.

"Do I know you?" She tried to twist loose.

"Indirectly, and now, you little bitch, you're going to ..."

Who was this maniac? She flapped an arm at her unseen attacker, heaved and twisted. Jesus! His fingers dug into the tendons of her neck and the pain was paralyzing. The water ...closer and closer came the surface, and Alex realised he intended to duck her. Drown her? She cried out when he increased the pressure, and then she was underwater. Nightmare. Definitely a nightmare. Nice pebbles. Bubbles, many bubbles. Air. Lovely, lovely air. Alex gulped and gulped, raising a dripping head to stare at Matthew, who was fighting with an unknown man. A grunt, a heave and the man was thrown to land a few feet away. The man screeched at the impact.

"Are you alright?" Matthew asked Alex.

"Yes," she said shakily.

"Do you know him?" He cocked his head at the groaning shape.

"No."

"Yes you do!" Two penetrating light eyes fixed on her.

Alex shook her head, taking in a battered face, a dirty flannel shirt and jeans that seemed to have burnt off at calf length. He looked awful; the skin on what she could see of his legs was blistered and raw, made even worse by a large flesh wound. But he was here, an undoubtedly modern man – however big an arsehole -and the sight of him had her heart twisting in hope. One person dropping through a time hole she could, with a gigantic stretch of mind, contemplate. Two doing it at the same time was so improbable as to be risible, so obviously this Matthew character was the odd one out, not she. Yes! Not a coma, not a nightmare, just a freak thunderstorm, and poor Matthew needed psychiatric care.

"Who are you?" she asked.

"Don't give me that! You've seen my picture often enough on my homepage."

"I don't think you resemble any likeness of yours," Matthew put in. "You're somewhat worse for wear, no?"

Alex peered at the man. "Sanderson? Oh my God, you're Diego Sanderson! What on earth are you doing here?"

Sanderson sat up and his hand strayed to his neck, rubbing it.

"I could ask you the same, right? What have you been doing? Some spontaneous camping?"

"What do you mean?" she said.

He gave her a piercing look. "Well, you didn't make it to the meeting, did you?"

"Nor did you, from the looks of it." And why had he almost killed her just now?

"Yeah I did; but then I went looking for you. No point to the meeting without you, hey? After all, Hector couldn't care less about this new security setup, no, what Hector wants is you."

"Hector?"

"He dislikes untidy ends, my dear Hector. And he hates it when his plans backfire – like they did in Italy some years ago. But you know all about that, right?"

"I have no idea what you're talking about."

Her brain was trying to make some sense of what he was saying; he knew about Italy? And who was Hector? The name tugged at her brain cells, an insistent niggling that yes, she did know this name. Oh my God; that Hector!

"*No me mientas* ! Don't lie! Ángel disappeared down there, and Hector wants to know how." He lunged at her, was blocked by Matthew

"Who?" She half closed her eyes at the memory of Ángel. No, she wasn't going to think about him. She ducked her head to avoid the pale blue eyes fixed on her with apparent dislike. Without a word Matthew hunched down beside her, placing himself between her and Sanderson. Alex exhaled.

Sanderson's eyes stuck on Matthew, travelling up and down the worn linen shirt, the woollen breeches and the heavy leather belt. His eyes widened, his mouth fell open, he cleared his throat and gawked some more, his Adam's apple bobbing like a cork.

"Where the hell am I?" he said. "Where the fuck have I ended up?"

Matthew regarded him, mouth pursed. "Am I to assume you don't know what year it is?"

"1658," Alex supplied, "and yes, we're still in Scotland." She very much wanted Sanderson to break out in contemptuous laughter, but instead he groaned and shook his head, a long string of dejected 'no's' bursting from him and effectively killing the flaring hope she'd felt at the sight of him.

Matthew stood, shielding his eyes as he looked down the southern road.

"Something's wrong," he said. "We have to go."

She scanned the surrounding landscape; heather, more heather, even more heather. Nothing that looked in anyway sinister.

"It's too silent," he said, and she obligingly listened so her ears hurt at this too silent. Insects buzzed, leaves rustled, the water trickled across its pebbled beds and the birds... no birds! Alex got to her feet and Matthew put a restraining hand on her arm, pointing in the direction of flashing reflections and an accompanying cloud of dust. Still a mile or so off, she calculated, squinting as she tried to count the reflections.

"Soldiers." His fingers sank into her flesh. "I have to go. Will you be coming with me?"

"What about him?" Alex inclined her head at Sanderson. Not that she wanted him anywhere close – not after those comments about Italy and Ángel – but she still had to ask.

"Can you walk?" Matthew asked him.

"No, not with this." Sanderson waved a hand at his leg.

"Best you hide then." Matthew pointed at a huge stand of brambles. Sanderson gave him an incredulous look.

"In there? And what do you think I am? A knight in armour?"

Matthew's mouth twitched. "I see no other alternative. Here, I'll hold up the lower branches for you as you crawl in, aye?" Sanderson scooted into the hiding place, cursing when he pricked himself on the thorns.

"Do you know how to get back?" Alex hissed just as they turned away.

"Get back where?" Sanderson hissed back, a dark shape barely discernible against the undergrowth.

"To our time – you know, cars, TVs, appliances…"

"No. I have no idea. I don't think you can. You're stuck here, forever, just like I am." He exhaled unsteadily and Alex felt her heart do yet another acrobatic manoeuvre in her chest – this time out of fear, not hope.

"There must be a way back!"

"Yeah, right, people leap back and forth through time on a regular basis." He eyed her with dislike. "This is all your fault. I wouldn't be here if it wasn't for you."

Matthew dragged a limping Alex back up the hill. Her head throbbed, and round and round echoed Ángel, a small knot forming in the pit of her stomach. On purpose she hadn't thought about him for nearly three years, and she wasn't going to think about him now. Ha! Liar, liar, pants on fire. The damned man popped up in her head far too often – like every time she saw her son. Isaac. Alex blinked, gasped. Isaac. Her knees buckled, her feet stumbled to the point that it was difficult to move, let alone keep up with Matthew's punishing pace.

"The cave, let's just hide in there." Her ribs were killing her, every breath an agony.

"Not if they have dogs." He heaved her in front of him up the hillside.

He darted into the cave to retrieve his bundle, and then

he pushed on upwards, half carrying Alex across the uneven ground.

At the top they stopped to look down. Below them stretched the road, the crossroads, and the small copse of trees in which Sanderson lay hidden. They dropped flat on their stomachs, and she felt as you do when you play hide and seek, wanting to giggle with nerves.

"You're a runaway, aren't you?" Very unnecessary question, it didn't exactly take an Einstein to work that one out. He nodded but didn't elucidate further, his right fist clenched round the handle of his knife. Dirk or dagger would be a more correct term, she thought, eyeing the twelve inch length of steel with respect. Alex dug into her jeans, searching for her pocketknife, but instead her hand closed on her phone and she pulled it out. The display blinked into life and three bars appeared on the left hand side, indicating connectivity. It made the hairs on Alex' arm stand up straight.

"What?!" She sat up. Matthew pushed her back down with an angry frown. Alex looked at the display, and yes, the three bars were still there. But how? Ignoring Matthew's glaring eyes she dialled John's number, jerking back at the static that coursed into her ear. Of course not, she snorted to herself, how could that possibly work? Matthew studied the mobile, his brows raised in an inverted "v".

"What's this?" He extended a finger to poke at it.

"It's a phone, you use it to talk to people that are far away."

He was staring at her again, flickers of fear and incomprehension darting through his eyes. Light hazel, she noted, much more green than brown, with small golden flecks in them. He widened them under her open inspection and covered her hand, giving it a little squeeze.

"You have to tell me the truth, lass, because there's more to this than meets the eye."

"I don't think I know the truth, but I'll tell you what I know. And you'll tell me."

"About what?" he hedged, and his eyes went an even lighter shade of green.

"About why you're a runaway."

"Aye." His hand tightened on hers in warning and they watched as a swarm of men appeared on the road below.

They did have dogs, a whole pack of dogs that bayed loudly, all of them scrabbling in the direction of the little grove of alders.

"Sanderson!" she raised herself on her arms, only to be brutally pushed back down. "They'll find him." They already had, and she watched him being pulled from his hiding place, his voice loud as he protested at their rough handling.

"Let me go." She twisted under Matthew's hard grasp. "I have to help him. Look! They're hitting him." Alex filled her lungs with air to call out, surprised into gasping by the pain in her side. Matthew clamped his hand over her mouth and pushed her flat against the ground.

"If they find me they'll drag me back in chains. I'm never going back, you hear? Never! " His voice was tinged with desperation. Alex struggled, but he easily held her still. "If I let go, will you promise to be quiet?" he whispered in her ear.

The bloody hell she would. He was hurting her, his hand pinching tight around her mouth. Alex tried to bite him, wanting to open her mouth and yell until the soldiers found them and they could cart this huge oaf away into captivity for all she cared.

She had to help Sanderson, however much a potential lowlife he might be. He was one like her, flung down unaware into a new and frightening existence, and maybe they could help each other find some way back, even if he didn't seem to think so. Back to normality and a life where the road in front of her was paved instead of being a dirt track. She tried to heave against him, attempting to buck him off.

"Like that, aye?" Matthew said and rolled on top of her. Alex could barely breathe, protesting squeaks escaping from under his hard hand.

She refused to speak to him once he let her go, shrugging off his helping hand when they made their way back down to the cave. Her ribs hurt like hell after his ungentle treatment, and she was still clutching her phone, the other hand stuffed into her pocket. He'd let her raise her head enough to see when they took Sanderson away, his agonised screams as he was dragged across the ground echoing in the wind.

Alex brushed a hand across her face, blinking back on tears that made her vision blur. She didn't want to be here, please let her wake up, please let this be a dream! She frowned down at her phone and texted a message to John. "*In the cave*," she wrote. Maybe he could somehow push himself through time to find her. When Alex pressed the send button the phone surged with pulsating energy, red-hot against her skin, and she dropped it with a muffled expletive. Matthew bent down and picked it up, handing it to her before he busied himself coaxing life back into the little fire.

"I'm sorry that I had to hurt you, but there was nothing we could do for him." A tremor ran through him as he stared off towards the south. "But there was plenty they could do to me."

The thought obviously had him sick with fear, so Alex gave him a nod and sat down, stretching her legs in front of her. Her brain was turning somersaults and she'd managed to scratch the scab on the forehead open, a trickle of blood oozing its way downwards. She was exhausted and very, very hungry. Never get back, Sanderson had said, there was no way back. Oh God; she bit down hard on her lower lip to stop herself from bawling. And Isaac wouldn't even remember her, growing up alone in the world without father or mother.

The phone beeped to inform her it had delivered the previous message. It made Alex tingle all over, imagining electronic sound waves bouncing back and forth across the fourth dimension, time. Maybe those wormhole things did exist, random points in universe connecting distant times and places. She wrote a goodbye message to John and sent it off. The mobile vibrated, there was a sizzling sound and the display went black.

CHAPTER 4

"Impossible," Diane said, "people just don't disappear." John scrubbed his hands through his hair and shook his head in agreement.

"I know. But he did." He nudged the rucksack with his toe. "Look at it, as if it's been in a fire or something. Hit by lightning, hey?" He gave a shaky laugh. "Maybe that's what happened, a freak storm of such strength that it sort of buried them both or something."

"On the same day? Two people?" Diane snorted with disbelief. "There must be a logical explanation."

John hitched his shoulders and yawned. Driving back had been a trial, his eyes blinking shut with a weariness that was more driven by terror than exhaustion. The man had disappeared before his eyes; the expression on Sanderson's face as he was sucked into the abyss was one he'd never forget. It must have been the ground splitting open and the poor bloke had fallen into a crevice or something. But the light, the noise … Diane handed him a cup of tea and sat down beside him.

"Of course there's an explanation," she said, light green eyes meeting his.

"I'm all ears. I can't wait to hear how you explain all of this."

"I'll have to see it first, won't I?"

John yawned again and nodded. "We have to call the police. They might be able to find them." He made a face, a tremor running through him at the thought of Alex lying dead and crushed under tons of moving earth. He felt nauseous with loss and shoved the dawning understanding that she might in fact be gone, for good, away from him.

Next day, Diane looked at the road and then back at John, two brows striving towards her hairline.

"It's just as it always was."

"I know, I told you, didn't I?" No wonder the police had been irritated; nothing here corroborated his story. He stared at the bucolic surroundings, at the undulating hills and the straight, undamaged stretch of road that flowed from the crossroads and onwards. Yesterday hadn't happened. He must have imagined it, but he knew that he hadn't. He crawled with fear. What the fuck was going on?

Diane gave him a quizzical look and got out of the car.

"Well, come on, now that we're here we might as well take a look." She tied her trainers and stood waiting for him. At first he was incapable of getting out, his body trembling with remembered fear. Diane tilted her head and studied him, her face pulling together in concern.

"It's alright," she said, jumping on the tarmac. "Look, it's perfectly safe." John edged towards her, trying to control the shivers in his legs.

"Her car was standing over there." John waved his hand towards the hillside. Nothing wrong with it according to the tow truck driver. Diane began to walk in serpentines up the slope, her eyes on the ground. He followed her with reluctance.

"Have you tried her phone?" Diane asked over her shoulder.

John looked at her with exasperation. Of course he'd tried her phone.

"Try again, if she's anywhere close we might hear it."

He stuck his hand in his pocket, stopped by her soft exclamation of surprise. She sank to her knees beside a large outcropping of stone.

"What?" John scrambled in his haste.

"It's still red Converse, isn't it?" Diane used a stick to lift something off the ground and turned to face him. The blood drained away from his head so fast it left him dizzy; one burnt red Converse, the sole a melted mass, the canvas black from toe cap to heel.

"Oh God," he said, his voice shaking.

Diane handed him the water bottle and patted him on the back.

"It could be someone else's," she said. "We don't know that it's hers."

He wiped his mouth, avoiding her concerned eyes. It was hers, and whatever had happened to her must have been pretty awful to leave her shoe so badly burnt.

"Can lightning do that to you?" he said.

She shrugged in an I-don't-know gesture.

"I've heard of people being killed by lightning, but I've never heard of someone being obliterated by it."

He held the shoe gingerly, staring at it in an attempt to find a connection to Alex. Maybe if he concentrated hard enough, the shoe would feed him some kind of image. He heard himself how ludicrous that sounded. Not even Mercedes, Alex' long gone mother, would have believed in something that silly. Or maybe she would, he shuddered, remembering a night several years ago when Mercedes had been well into her cups.

Very strange, was Mercedes, an intense woman who mostly seemed to paint – weird pictures heaving with contained colours. A small canvas signed by Mercedes hung by their bed and he generally avoided looking at it, feeling a disquieting tug in the pit of his stomach when he got too close. Mercedes had disappeared three years ago, coincidentally the same day Alex resurfaced after three months of unexplained absence in Italy. And now ... he bit down on his lip.

"What?" Diane said.

"I was just thinking ... poor Magnus, hey?"

"Yeah ..." Diane sighed and looked away. "Poor, poor Magnus. First his wife, then his daughter."

"He knew." John chucked the shoe to the side.

"Who knew what?" Diane sounded confused.

"Him; Sanderson. He knew about Mercedes having disappeared. He said so, just before he ... well ...oh God ..." John pressed his hands flat against his legs to contain the trembling that surged through him. People just don't evaporate into nothingness, he reminded himself, there's always a logical explanation. In Mercedes' case maybe her brain caved in, making her throw herself off some crag or other. And in Alex' case ... well, he had no idea.

"He did?" Diane shrugged. "Not that strange, is it? It was all over the papers for a couple of weeks."

John's phone beeped and he pulled it out, his heart lurching when he saw the sender ID.

"From her," he said and opened the text. "*In the cave. A.*" He stumbled to his feet. "There's a cave, somewhere here there's a cave." Maybe she was hurt, her foot burnt off her, and if he didn't find her she'd die of exposure and thirst and gangrene or something.

Diane looked at him as if he'd gone mad, but stood up and began to beat her way up the increasingly steeper incline. Flies buzzed, clouds of butterflies rose disturbed as they waded through the gorse and heather.

It was well into the afternoon before John found the opening, almost invisible behind a creeper of some kind. Diane came over to join him and they both peered into the gloom.

"No one's been here recently," Diane said.

John agreed, pushing his way into the small, enclosed space. It smelled of damp and a vague scent of mulch. Heaped debris, twigs, leaves, the carcass of what looked like a desiccated hedgehog lay in the opening. John did a slow turn. In one corner something caught his eye and he moved closer. Very faintly on the uneven wall he could make out words, written in faded capitals with some kind chalky rock. "ALEX WAS HERE." An arrow pointed downwards and he dug at the earth, ignoring Diane's worried voice.

"Jesus," he groaned, staring down at what he had uncovered. "What the hell is this?" A small, rectangular object lay wrapped in what looked like a faded cloth pouch.

"Outside," Diane said. "We can't see anything in here."

John followed her out into the sun and closed his fingers

round a rusted metal object, still a clear red in streaks. It was her phone, and when he lifted it up to show Diane, bits and pieces flaked off to crumble into rusty dust.

"What has happened to her? How can you logically explain this?"

She sat down beside him. "I can't. I have absolutely no idea."

They sat in silence on the hillside.

"She just sent me a text," John said, shaking his head. "How can she have done that if her phone lies buried in a cave?" Diane gave a helpless shrug. "And look at it," he continued, "it looks as if it's been in the ground for centuries."

His phone beeped again. A new text. From her. Impossible, he thought, feeling sweat break out along his spine. *"Take care of Isaac. Love u. A."*

John lay back against the ground and closed his eyes to stop the spinning sensation in his head. Alex was here, she even texted him – from a phone that lay in pieces in his hands. People don't just disappear, he told himself, and then he saw Sanderson drowning in that funnel of light. His hand groped for something, someone. Diane took hold of him and squeezed.

"It'll be alright, we'll find her. Somehow we'll find her."

He turned towards her and hid his face against her jeans clad thigh. "I don't understand."

"Who does?" Diane sighed, running her hand through his hair. "Come on," she added a few minutes later. "We'd best get going."

Diane drove all the way back to Edinburgh, with John sitting stunned beside her.

"There must be a logical explanation," he said, twisting in his seat to face her. "There must be, right?"

"Of course."

"And if there is, then she'll come back, won't she? People don't just disappear, do they?"

"I'm not sure," she said, keeping her eyes on the road ahead of them.

"But you said! You said there had to be a logical explanation."

She sighed and glanced in his direction. "Even if there is, I don't think she's coming back."

"Of course she is!"

Diane looked away. "She might be dead, no?"

John folded his arms over his chest and decided not to say another word.

She parked outside the office and turned to face him.

"You want me to come with you?"

Yes, he really wanted her to, but this was something he had to do on his own. Oh God; pick up Isaac and tell him his mother was gone; call on Magnus and inform him Alex had disappeared into thin air.

"No, I'll be fine," he said, releasing his seatbelt to scoot into the driver's seat.

"You sure?"

"Yes." He drove off before he begged her to come with him.

John hesitated in front of the bright red door. He loved this little street in Stockbridge, lined with similar row houses in unprepossessing grey stone, all of them with doors that attempted to give them a touch of individuality, exploding in reds and greens and blues and even, unfortunately, in yellow.

Isaac tugged at his hand. "Offa?"

John smiled down at him. "Yes, let's see if your Offa's home, shall we?"

He was, a bright smile appearing on his tanned face when he saw his grandson, mirrored in Isaac's face. John watched them hug and felt something twist inside. They had each other, they were of blood. He was just a random man, with no biological ties to either of them now that Alex was gone. If, he reminded himself furiously, if she was gone. He followed them into the house, stepping over Magnus' as yet unpacked suitcase.

He walked down the passageway, stopping at every framed photo down its length. All of them were of Alex; from chubby babyhood through long legged angular pre-pubescence to self-conscious teenager hiding her swelling chest in bulky sweaters.

"What's the matter?" Magnus said.

John swallowed. "Was the conference any good?" he said instead.

Magnus made a dismissive gesture, his bright blue eyes boring into John. "Has something happened?"

"Yes, I'm afraid it has." John inhaled. "Alex seems to have gone missing. Again." He caught Magnus as he stumbled, supported him over to an armchair and poured them both a very stiff whisky before sitting down beside him.

"How? When?" Magnus was pale, his blondish grey hair a mess after he'd run his hands through it. "Holy Matilda; you think ... you think she's been kidnapped again?"

John took a deep gulp, savouring the burning feeling that travelled down his gullet to land in his gut. Kidnapped? None of them really knew what had happened to Alex down in Italy. She had refused to talk about it, clamming up completely whenever he tried to raise the issue. And now he'd never know. He shook himself, aware of Magnus' eyes hanging off him.

"Yesterday, it happened yesterday. She got caught in a lightning storm out on the moor. At least that's what we think, and then she just..." John hid his head in his hands. "Oh God; oh God, oh God, oh God."

Magnus sat back, with his glass held like a lifeline in his hand.

"She just went up in smoke; the car, all her stuff was there, but she was gone." He wasn't telling this well, he could see that in Magnus' face. So he pulled up his knees, clenched his arms around them and told him everything, from the moment when he started to worry about Alex being late, to the moment Sanderson disappeared.

"And I don't know what to do," he finished. "How do I go about finding her again?" His hand strayed to his pocket and the remains of her phone, still wrapped in that old piece of cloth. He pulled it out and put it on the table. "I found this, but I just don't understand."

Magnus poked at it but didn't unwrap it. Instead he walked over to the shelf where he kept his whisky and brought the bottle back with him.

"Tell me again," he said, once he had topped up both their glasses. So John did. When he drifted to a stop Magnus bent forward and undid the little package, staring down with an aghast expression at the worn and rusted remains of his daughter's phone.

"She just bought it."

"I know," John said and his whole hand was shaking.

Any further discussion at that point was interrupted by Isaac, who came to lean against Magnus, complaining that he was hungry.

"Well, we can't have that, can we?" Magnus said, tousling Isaac's dark hair. No, Isaac agreed seriously, his tummy hurt.

A few hours later and they were back in the study, after having fed and put Isaac to bed.

"It's just like with Mercedes," Magnus said, "an inexplicable disappearance."

"I know. And we'll never know what happened – just like with Mercedes." John leaned forward to clasp Magnus' hand hard in his. "I'm so sorry." Magnus nodded, looking drawn.

"Mercedes…" He raised his drink to his mouth, one quick gulp before he slammed the empty glass back down on the table. "I'm still hoping, you know?"

"It's been three years," John said.

Magnus shrugged and stared into the empty grate. "Still; I hope." He smiled slightly, shaking his head. "Thirty years —more than that. I met her in Seville, in 1968. I was there to study Spanish, a tall gawky Swedish boy. She saw me on one of the bridges across the Guadalquivir and flirted with me. I was twenty-two. I have no idea how old she was, only that she was quite a lot older."

John's skin puckered; Mercedes had always seemed so young, ten, even twenty years Magnus junior.

Magnus nodded. "I know, she didn't age much, did she? And … " He tensed and cocked his head. "Did you hear that?"

"No."

"Shh, listen!" Magnus said, getting to his feet.

John rose as well. From above came the soft but unmistakeable sounds of something moving stealthily across the floor of the room upstairs – Mercedes' studio.

"Didn't you have it all wired a few months back?"

"I don't have the alarm on while I'm in the house, not after setting it off twice by mistake in one month." Magnus handed John a cricket bat, armed himself with a golf club and jerked his head in the direction of the stairs. "Come on."

They tiptoed up the stairs, crossed the small landing and stood for a while outside the door.

"Why in there?" John whispered.

"No idea," Magnus murmured. "Maybe it's a crazy art collector."

"Very crazy and very persistent."

Magnus had been plagued by break-ins over the last few years, always directed at the studio.

"This time he isn't getting away, this time I'll bash his knee in or something. Ready?" Magnus said, one hand on the doorknob. John gripped his bat and nodded. Magnus opened the door and threw himself inside.

John had but the vaguest impressions of the man they surprised in the darkened studio. Black clothes, a black ski mask, and in his hand a heavy torch. The window stood wide open and the whole room smelled of rain. Magnus said something – in Swedish, John assumed – the man wheeled, and for a moment it was like a live tableau, all three frozen into position. And then the burglar vaulted over the table, making for the window, and behind him came Magnus, golf club raised high.

Crash! The intruder sent one, two, three filing cabinets to the floor in his wake. Impressively strong, this guy, and John hesitated in his approach, his hold on the bat sweaty. What was he supposed to do? Swipe at the head? An arm? Magnus clambered over the remains of the cabinets and charged. There, he had him! The burglar heaved, twisted loose. A scuffle, a shove, and Magnus staggered back. John rushed to help. All he could properly make out was the square of light that was the window and silhouetted against it, Magnus and the burglar. The stool caught him mid shin and John fell, landing hard on knees and hands.

From across the landing came Isaac's voice, raised in sobbing shrieks. Magnus grabbed hold of the burglar, grunting with the effort of restraining him. In one swift movement the black clad man turned, brought the torch down on Magnus' head and jumped through the window, for all the world as if he'd been a cat. There was a loud clatter and a muted yelp, and by the window Magnus groaned and clapped a hand to his head.

"Magnus!" John was torn between his crying son and his hurting father-in-law.

"I'm okay," Magnus said, "go and check on Isaac."

Two hours later Magnus sank down to sit in his chair, an impressive plaster covering the left side of his forehead.

"Three stitches, and yet another bloody book of paper work to complete for the police and the insurance company." He shook his head when John raised the whisky bottle. "Painkillers; they don't mix well, do they?"

"As far as I can see nothing was taken," John said. "But he's made a mess up there, small canvases scattered all over the place."

"Just like all the other times, although I wouldn't notice, would I, if he made off with a couple."

"No, probably not," John said. "I tried to clean up." A hasty shoving together of the paintings no more, because even if he had no intention of ever admitting it, John drowned in nausea whenever he handled any of Mercedes' pictures. "I couldn't get the cabinets back up, though, and one is mostly matchwood anyway."

"I'll do that later." Magnus sighed and closed his eyes. "*Herre djävlar*; what an awful day this turned out to be." He opened one eye and nodded at the glass held in John's hand. "I'll have one of those after all. I bloody well deserve one, don't you think?"

CHAPTER 5

They came from the east, two men that crested the hill, stopped for a moment, and began to make their way towards them. Matthew rose, eyes locked on the approaching men. One was carrying a sack, had a brace of hens thrown over his shoulder, while the other was holding a staff of sorts – a long stout stick. They went barefoot the both of them, with mended, ragged breeches and dirty shirts.

Alex scrambled to her feet. "More soldiers?"

He shook his head. Nay, not soldiers, but fighting men none the less. Matthew frowned; armed, he'd warrant, and he had nothing but a dirk to defend them with. He stooped, closed his hand on a heavy branch and felt somewhat comforted. Not much of a defence against the staff, but he was not an inexperienced fighter – not by a long reach.

"Stay in the cave," he said.

"Why? I can …"

"Do as I say, aye? Those two have their sights set on something, and I reckon it's on you."

"But …"

"Go! I don't want them looking too closely at you."

Alex hobbled off, ducking into the small opening just as the two men reached them. The older of the two nodded a greeting and gestured for his companion to set down his burden.

"Nay," Matthew said, "I'm in no mood for company." Father and son? Brothers? Related at any rate, both men sharing dark, coarse hair, lumpy noses and receding chins. After a quick inspection, Matthew dismissed the younger of the two as essentially harmless. No; it was the elder, the man with the staff that was the one to watch out for.

"Oh, aye? Is it the lass you're worried about then?" the older man said. "Don't worry man, we won't touch her – not unless you invite us to." His dark eyes leapt from

Matthew to the cave opening, to the branch in Matthew's hand, small mouth curling into a contemptuous smile. He handled the staff with assurance, and now that there was only a yard or two between them, Matthew could see the top end had been sharpened. A stake then, not a staff, and from the matter that clung to its tip well used. Matthew shifted on his feet, ostentatiously weighed the branch in his hand.

"I won't. She's not for the likes of you."

The younger man snickered, keeping his eyes on Matthew's hands.

"Strange looking lass," the older man said. "We saw her as we came over the moor, before she hid away in yon cave."

"Strange? How strange?"

"Odd clothes," the younger man piped up, pointing at the bright red jacket, left behind by Alex in her haste. He made as if to set down the sack and the fowl.

"Go," Matthew said. "I already said, no?"

The older man laughed. "I think not."

Out of a capacious pouch he produced a flintlock pistol which he aimed at Matthew. Matthew took a step back. Pistols were fickle things, even at close range, and from what Matthew could see this particular weapon was not well maintained. But a loaded muzzle was always a danger and Matthew was not quite sure what to do. The ruffian grinned, hefted the pistol higher. His stave fell to the ground beside him.

"Get the lass," he said to his younger companion. "She'll be worth a pretty penny or two."

The young man dumped his load on the ground, took a few steps in the direction of the cave. Matthew sidled away, putting a further yard or two between himself and the pistol. The younger man ducked into the cave. Matthew tightened his grip on his dagger. Should he throw it? The muzzle wavered, the man's interest distracted by the loud yells that emanated from the cave.

"Incompetent," the man muttered. "What is taking him

so long? A few slaps and she'll come along nicely – they all do." Matthew took the opportunity to launch himself at him, moving like an enraged viper over the ground.

"Stand! I'll shoot, aye?" The man swung the pistol back, squeezed the trigger and … nothing. Wet powder? Worn flint? Matthew didn't care. The pistol was thrown to the side, the man lunged for his staff, and Matthew flew the last few feet, tackling the man to the ground.

He was screaming now, the brigand, and even more when Matthew flipped him over, dagger raised. Something glinted. Matthew cursed, retracted his head; a knife, a wee blade that narrowly missed his neck. Matthew brought the dagger down. Once, twice and the man shrieked, raising a hand to defend his face. Matthew changed his grip and brought the dirk's handle down so hard the man flopped and went still, subsiding mid-scream.

From the cave came the younger man, dragging a struggling Alex with him. She did something; her free hand flashed down and with a howl the man let her go, cradling his arm. Not entirely defenceless then, this strange lass.

Matthew pushed himself off the ground, strode over to the younger man and collared him, dragging him choking and gargling to join his companion, sprawled on the grass.

"I said, no?" Matthew said. "We have no wish for company, aye? Now go, before I do you more harm."

A few minutes later they were gone, the younger supporting the elder who was bleeding profusely from his face – as he well deserved. Matthew picked up the staff, worn shiny after years of use, and with a grunt swung it at a nearby boulder. The stave bounced off. Again, and it splintered. Matthew threw it to the side.

"Will they be back?" Alex said, appearing by his side.

"I reckon not."

"You're bleeding." She pointed at his hand.

"No lass, not me. Them."

"Oh. How hurt are they?"

"They won't be coming back in a hurry." He looked over

to the two hens left behind by the two rogues. "You like chicken?"

Matthew was surprised by her reluctance to help with the birds, her face going pale under her tan when he suggested she gut them now that he'd plucked them. After watching her clumsy attempts he sighed and took over, and a few minutes later the air filled with the scent of roasting meat. Alex didn't look overly impressed.

"Bread would be nice, and some vegetables, you know, tomatoes."

Nay, he didn't know, and he gave her a long look. She stared right back and to his irritation Matthew broke eye contact first, thinking he'd never seen eyes of that particular shade of dark blue before.

"So," she said, once they'd finished eating. "Tell me." He studied his hands, his fingers tracing his wrists.

"I couldn't stand it any longer, so I escaped and here I am, almost home."

She huffed and shook her head. "Oh, no you don't. You tell me the whole story, from the beginning."

He didn't want to. Margaret, Luke, they'd betrayed him, allowing him to be condemned for something he hadn't done.

"Start from the beginning," she said. "You know, once upon a time…"

He gave her a crooked smile. "This isn't a fairy tale, this is my life."

"It's still a good beginning. That's what Magnus says."

He picked up on the yearning tone, inclined his head and began to talk.

"I'm the eldest of three brothers and one sister," he said. "Matthew, Mark, Luke and Joan."

"Very evangelical."

"Aye, but that's how it is with my family."

"So, no Roberts or Richards?"

"Nay, good, biblical names, aye? John, Peter, Martha and the like."

"Salome?" she teased, but he just shook his head, irritated by her interruption.

"Do you want me to tell you?"

Alex dragged a finger across her lips and nodded for him to go on.

"Mark died when he was ten, of the measles." He fell quiet and rubbed at his thumb.

"The measles?" Alex echoed. "You die of the measles?"

Was she daft? Everyone knew people – and in particular bairns – were carried off regularly by the measles.

"Aye; it's a nasty disease, no?"

"Oh. Not very common where I'm from."

"Really?" He leaned towards her, noting that she'd shoved her hair back behind her ear, exposing the slightly pointed tip.

"Later," she said, "we talk about me later. So, go on."

"There was only a year between Mark and me, and now that he's dead, Joan is closest to me in age, and then there's Luke, bastard that he is." He snuck her a look, distracted from his story by the way a few tendrils of her curling hair lifted in the evening breeze. "I found them in bed," he abbreviated, deciding he didn't want to tell this strange woman everything. "I rode in late an April afternoon meaning to surprise Margaret, my wife, and I did, but she surprised me even more."

He gave her a very brief description of events, from the moment he threw his gloves and hat on the kitchen bench to when he entered his bedchamber to find his wife naked with his own brother.

"I swear, had I had my sword at hand I would have gutted him there and then. Instead I just stood there, like a gaping fool, and she... well, she ..." he broke off. Margaret had laughed, told him she no longer needed or wanted him – not now that her Luke was back.

"So what did you do?" she asked.

He gave her a black look; what did she think he'd done?

"I dragged my brother naked from my bed and I didn't

let her get properly dressed before I threw them out in the yard. And when she stood there in the dusk, with her body shamelessly exposed, she asked me to bring down her son, telling me he wasn't mine, because Luke had fathered Ian, not me."

Alex moved close enough to pat him on his arm. He flinched and scooted away, uncomfortable with the compassion he saw in her eyes.

"Four weeks later a company of soldiers rode into my yard, and I was arrested for treason and tied like a common criminal before they threw me onto my horse."

"Had you? Committed treason, I mean."

He chewed the inside of his cheek, considering how much to tell her.

"I'm for the Commonwealth," he said. "I don't hold with kings and the like, but believe all men to be equal in the eyes of our Lord."

"Oh my, a Founding Father."

"A what?"

"Never mind," she said, waving for him to continue.

He looked up at the darkening August sky and sighed.

"In this specific case I was tried for treason against the Commonwealth, for supporting the king and partaking in the Glencairn rising. I did no such thing, but Luke did, and yet he stood in the witness stand, a solemn look on his face as he damned me to hell with his detailed descriptions of what I'd done. They called me a spy, a turncoat, and I was none of those, for I have only ever fought for the one side, the side of free men ranged against a despot king."

"But…" she gasped. "How could he do that to you? First your wife, then your freedom; this Luke character needs someone to give him a big fat kick up his arse!"

"Oh, aye," Matthew said. "I wouldn't mind doing it myself – or worse."

"And anyway, why did they believe him? You wouldn't have told him about your treasonous activities, would you? Not unless he was on your side."

"They believed him because they wanted to. And I was sentenced to five years in gaol because the judges decided to be lenient and not hang me – on account of my years in the army." And thanks to wee Simon, his lawyer and brother-in-law, his manor was still his, safe from Luke's grasping hands.

She stared at him. "And you escaped after three, which makes you a fugitive, an outlaw."

Matthew shrugged and looked away, uncomfortable with her blunt statement. "I'll be safe, here in Scotland."

"How? Scotland's part of the Commonwealth too, no? Didn't Cromwell make it a Protectorate, under him?"

"Aye, but he's ailing, he's been ill with the ague most summer." He stared off at nothing for a while. "There's no one to replace him. He's a great man, is Oliver Cromwell, but men that are strong leaders cull out their potential successors as they go. And that son of his... no, he won't last, and the Protectorate will be no more."

"Still," she said, "wouldn't it have been better to sit through two more years and then be truly free?"

He looked at her for a long time. "You've never been in gaol, I take."

No, she agreed, she hadn't, and she wasn't planning on going there either.

"Nor was I." He sighed and sat up straighter, extending his arms to her. Round both wrists ran a bracelet of chafed, irritated skin, half healed gashes that had abscessed and been lanced, leaving ugly pox like scars behind.

"Imagine doing everything with a weight of iron between your hands and down your legs. When you turn in your sleep you wake of the chains, when you want to scratch your head you have to raise both hands, because otherwise you won't be able to reach. And with every movement you make, the chains clink."

She encircled his wrists, her thumbs caressing the soft inner skin. It made his blood thud and he retook his hands.

"Sorry," she mumbled.

"For what?" he said with a faint smile. "Don't mind me. I'm not much used to company." Especially not that of an attractive woman with a gentle touch. "It's very lonesome, you know, being in prison."

His eyes fixed on the moon that hung like a golden cheese just above the horizon. Lonely in the midst of so many people, but that was how it was, a constant shrieking solitude. All of them, every single one of his cellmates, as lonely as he was, staring up at the minute patch of sky they could see through the ventilation hole, dreaming themselves elsewhere –anywhere but where they were.

It had been pure chance, him being in the yard when the men dead from the fever were to be carted away for burial. It hadn't been a conscious decision; he'd just lain himself flat in the bottom of the cart, gritting his teeth at the proximity of all those dead bodies, a silent prayer ringing round his head as the cart creaked to a stop for a final inspection before starting up again.

"Euuw! You hid under the corpses?"

"As far down as I could get, I didn't want to be prodded by a sword, did I?"

The drover had squeaked with fear, eyes bulging with incredulity, when Matthew rose to his knees a few miles down the road.

"I stole his clothes." And his horse, riding the broken backed nag as hard as he could all that night. "He went lame on me, so I left him in on a village green and continued on foot, stealing what I could."

"And now I'm almost home," he finished. What home? A house, aye, and his lands, but no wife, no son, and towards his only brother a deep and burning hate. Alex leaned forward, one warm hand coming up to rest on his cheek.

"I'm glad for you, that you'll soon be home. And I'll keep my fingers crossed that you'll live in peace there." She sounded very forlorn.

"Thank you," he smiled, and covered her hand with his own.

She shifted on the ground and swore when her burnt foot scraped across the grass.

"You won't walk on it for some days," he said, peering at the damaged skin. It was swollen and hot to the touch, and his gentle probing made her flinch. "We'll have to wait until you can put weight on it." He frowned at that; those ruffians might well decide to return, as might the soldiers. He'd move their camp on the morrow.

"You don't have to stay," she said. "I don't want you to be caught. I'll be fine on my own."

He snorted at this total untruth, shaking his head. "I can't leave you alone, lass. We'll wait until you can move. Mayhap I can see you on your way."

She bit down on her lower lip. "I don't think you can, I don't think I have anywhere to go. My home is lost to me."

He considered various reasons for this; mayhap she'd dishonoured her family, or was running from an abusive husband. Or maybe she was from somewhere far away and had set out for new lands. She was not from here, of that he was certain, letting his eyes travel down those blue clad legs. She noticed and gave him a tight smile.

"Jeans; everyone wears them where I come from."

"Djeens," he repeated, "well, you must be from very far away, aye?"

"You could say that again," she mumbled, hunching together.

With a little sigh their fire collapsed into a heap of smouldering embers and for some moments Matthew busied himself with adding some more fuel to it.

"So," he said once the fire had recovered from its near death experience. "Your turn, aye?"

Alex chewed at her lower lip, wondering how to explain.

"I was born in Seville, Spain." She looked at him and decided to tell him in one fell swoop. "In August, 1976."

He blinked. "What?"

"Yes, 1976." Okay, maybe she shouldn't have told him

quite so abruptly because if his mouth fell anymore open she'd not only fit an apple but a whole melon into it. She could totally sympathise with his reaction. She cleared her throat, fiddled with a loose button on her shirt.

"What day in August?" he said, surprising her. She counted days in her head. Today was the eleventh of August, and in thirteen days she'd be twenty-six. Probably more or less ancient in these times, she shuddered.

"The twenty-fourth, but that's okay, I don't expect a cake and gifts."

He laughed, a dark, soft sound, and moved to sit a bit closer, his eyes intent on her face.

"How?"

Well, at least he was still sitting beside her, not running away from her in panic – that had to be a good sign, right?

"I have no idea." She told him of the car and the thunderstorm, of the hole that opened below her. He gawked at her.

"But…" he began, closed his mouth and exhaled before trying again. "But, no, you can't do that! It's impossible!" He swallowed. "Unless…" he broke off.

"Unless what? You think I'm some sort of witch?"

"Are you?" He averted his eyes and she could swear he was praying under his breath.

"Of course not! And this is just as unbelievable to me as it is to you, okay?" She hugged her legs hard to her, looked at him from under a curtain of hair. "I keep on hoping it's some sort of dream, so will you please pinch me hard enough to make me wake up?" He did, and she yelped, glaring at him. "Ow! I already knew I was awake – unfortunately."

Matthew took a deep breath, took two, his eyes never leaving hers.

"It's true! Who would ever make something like that up? God's idea of a joke, right?" She laughed shakily and to her relief he joined in, before leaning towards her, eyes alight with curiosity.

"Tell me then, what's it like, there in the future?"

So Alex did, spending the coming half hour describing a life that made him at times gape and just as often laugh, insisting she had to be pulling his leg.

"No plague?" he asked, impressed.

"No," she said, "and people don't die of the measles."

Matthew threw her a sharp look. "And him? The man by the spring? Is he from your time as well?"

"Obviously," she muttered. "What will they do to him?"

"I don't know. He didn't speak Scots, did he, and his clothes..." He looked at her jeans.

"I should have helped him." Not that she'd really wanted to, not after his comments regarding Italy.

"How? One lass against a troop of soldiers? And he didn't seem to care much for you, had I not been there I think he would have hurt you – badly."

"Probably." Alex suppressed a tremor or two.

"Why?"

"I have no idea." Which was, after all, the truth.

"But he said, no? About Italy and ..."

"Look; I don't want to talk about it, okay?" She stared him down, eyes never leaving his until he shrugged and went to find some more wood.

"Matthew?" Alex got to her feet. "Is that you?" She scanned the outer rim of their weak circle of light, certain she'd heard something. There; a shape grew out of the slope, transforming into a man when he came closer. At his heels tagged another man, and Alex recognised them both from before. Shit.

"Where is he?" the older man hissed.

"Who?" Alex backed away from the brandished knife.

"Your man, the one who did this to me." He pointed at the long, slashing wound down the side of his face.

"Not here." Alex bit back on an exclamation when she put too much weight on her injured foot. Well, at least she had two good arms, should it come to that. She raised them, hands like blades. The younger man scowled and rubbed at his arm. She'd gotten him good with her previous Karate chop and she'd guess he had a bruise the colour of an aubergine all across his biceps. Still; she'd prefer it if Matthew were to come back A.S.A.P. She shuffled backwards, keeping the little fire between her and the two men.

"Grab her," the older man said to the younger. "Take her and we'll be off, aye?"

"Try," Alex growled.

The man laughed, clearly unimpressed.

"But …" the younger man said, throwing worried looks into the darkness that surrounded them.

"Do as I say; once we have the lass, he'll not risk us hurting her, will he?" He leered in the direction of Alex. "And we won't; not as long as she's accommodating."

You wish; she'd poke his eyes out before she let him touch her. With a reluctant mutter the younger man moved towards her, carrying a length of rope. Alex licked her lips.

A stone hit the older man squarely on the back of his head and he fell to his knees.

"Da?" the other man rushed towards him. Yet another stone came whistling through the night and landed with a dull 'thonk' on the father's head, making him topple forward. He keened when his hands sank into the embers of the fire.

"Da!" the young man said. "Da, your poor, poor hands!" He batted at the smoking sleeves with his hands, yelping when he burnt himself.

"I told you, no?" Matthew roared from somewhere up the slope. "I told you to get yourselves gone and not bother us." He strode into the light, loomed over the two ruffians. "Go, and this time don't come back."

"No, no," the younger man stammered. "We won't, aye?" He helped his father up to stand and without a backward look disappeared into the August night.

"Bloody hell," Alex said. "Is life always this exciting round here?"

"Nay, in general not." He scowled in the direction of

where they could still hear the would be robbers' progress. "Such as them should hang, attacking lonely travellers and women."

"Well, they picked the wrong guy to mess with this time, didn't they?" Alex sank down to sit.

"We should get some sleep," Matthew said. "Do you need help back into the cave?"

She shook her head. She'd buried the leaking phone in a feeble attempt to leave some trace behind should John in the future get her text, and she didn't want Matthew to see her stark writing on the wall – she'd more or less gouged the letters into the surface. She'd even stolen a holey stocking from his bundle, hoping that the wool would protect the fragile metal casing from the vagaries of time.

"I'd prefer to stay outside. Will that be dangerous?"

Matthew laughed. "No, I don't think so. They'll not be back, will they?"

"Not unless they're very, very stupid," Alex said.

Alex lay with her back to him, eyes lost in the dark skies above. One day, and it felt like an eternity. How was she to stand a whole life here?

"John," she whispered to the night. "My John." No; don't cry, Alex Lind. She stuffed her hand into her mouth and bit down. Hard.

CHAPTER 6

The receptionist looked up with relief when Diane and John entered the office next morning.

"Thank heavens you're here," she said in what was meant to be a discreet whisper but carried far too well. "There's a gentleman here to see you. He's been here since eight – and he was here yesterday afternoon as well. I think he's upset."

"Upset?"Diane rubbed a hand across her face.

"He says he's Mr Sanderson's partner."

"But ... why didn't you call me? Yesterday?"

"I tried," the receptionist said.

Diane pulled out her phone. "Shit. It's gone flat. Stupid battery, I charged it yesterday morning."

"I'll just ..." John pointed in the direction of his office. "I have a backlog of e-mails to get through."

"Oh, no you don't; we talk to him together."

"Yes," the receptionist nodded, "he specifically said he wants to see you both."

"Bloody hell." John threw a glance in Diane's direction. "Well, come on then, let's get this over with."

The man who was waiting for them swivelled when he heard them enter. Where Sanderson had been big and bulky, along the lines of a rugby player gone to seed, this man had the looks of a ballet dancer or a fencer, thin and graceful with startling blue green eyes in a tanned and well cared for face. His skull was shaved and his upper lip was bisected by a hairline scar, creating the impression that his thin mouth had two cupid bows, one overlapping the other.

"What happened?" he said. "Where's Diego? He's been gone for two nights! And I've tried to contact you, but ..."

"I'm sorry," Diane said, "but who exactly are you? Mr Sanderson has never mentioned that he has a partner."

The man's scarred mouth twisted. "Why should he? But trust me, I'm his partner, both in life and in business. " His voice was like smooth chocolate, cultured and without an accent. He regarded them with what could have been amusement if it hadn't been for the assessing look in his eyes as they rearranged their faces into expressions of commiseration.

"I'm Hector, Hector Olivares. So, what happened?"

His eyes never left John as he retold what had happened, from the moment they got to the crossroads to when Sanderson disappeared. Afterwards he tented his hands in front of him and stared out the window with an unfocused gaze.

Hector cleared his throat, turning those disconcerting turquoise eyes back to John.

"Where exactly did this happen?"

John frowned. "How exact?"

"As exact as you can make it."

John went over to Diane's desk, indicating that Hector should come along.

"There," he said after a while, pointing at a zoomed in map on the computer screen. "It's a very odd crossroads, with the little track bisecting the road at an exact ninety degree angle."

Hector nodded, mouth setting into a grim line. "Yes, they're always very exact, the time nodes."

"Time nodes?" Diane scoffed. "What would they be?"

Hector raised his brows at her tone and directed himself to John.

"Time nodes are points at which every now and then the fabric of time rips apart, through earthquakes, freak weather or volcanic activity." Hector made a dismissive gesture. "The volcanic activity generally precludes anyone actually falling through the holes. You burn to death instead. Of course," he added in a tone as casual as if he were discussing the price of milk, "there are other ways to travel from time to time, but they require magic − black magic − while the time nodes, well, they're natural cracks in time."

"Natural?" John croaked. Was he supposed to guffaw? Call the closest mental asylum?

"Don't worry," Hector said with a crooked smile. "It only happens to one in a million or so."He tugged at the sleeves of his dark cashmere jumper and walked over to the window. "*Porqué?* Why did this happen to you? I told you to be careful."

"Be careful?" John said. "He knew this could happen?"

Hector levelled a dark look at him. "Diego didn't fully believe me." Hector sighed and turned away. "And now he's fallen into somewhere else."

"And Alex?"

Hector made a disinterested gesture. "She's obviously dropped through time as well." He put a hand on John's shoulder in a brief pat. "Don't expect her to come back. They never do."

"Well," Diane cut in, "first of all Mr Olivares, we don't know what has happened to either Alex or Mr Sanderson, and secondly, I must say I find your theory entertaining but totally incredible. Time nodes – really!"

Hector shifted his shoulders under his jumper; one moment he was a slight, somewhat effeminate man, the next he looked as dangerous as a starved tiger. Diane stood her ground.

"And anyway, how on earth would you know one can fall through time? Unless you've done it yourself, of course." She threw John a triumphant look, as if saying *See? Got him.*

"Oh, I have," Hector said. "Several times, as a matter of fact, flung from one time to the other." Something dark settled over his face. "And all because of Mercedes Gutierrez Sanchez, time travelling witch that she is."

"Mercedes?" John took Diane's hand in his; he didn't like this, not at all. He tried to laugh, but somehow it got stuck halfway up. "That's ridiculous!"

"Is it? Is it really?" Hector shook his head. "What would you know?"

Hector left shortly after, having wheedled a promise out

of them to drive him out to the crossroads the day after, insisting he had to see the place where Diego had disappeared.

"I'll pay you of course," he'd said, bowing with certain irony in Diane's direction. "Just as we'll pay for the work you did for Diego – assuming you've got something to deliver."

John sank down onto the sofa and stared at Diane.

"Please tell me you still believe there's a perfectly rational explanation to all this, please, please, tell me you're laughing your head off at what that rather sinister man just told us."

"Of course I am," she said, "but he was very matter-of-fact, wasn't he?"

"Yeah, he was. And what was all that crap about Mercedes flying through time?"

"I wouldn't put it past her," she said with a teasing grin. "I've thought for years that there was something very strange about her. I suppose dropping through time nodes would have a disruptive impact on your sanity, no?" she said sarcastically.

John gnawed at his lip. "She was pretty ageless, wasn't she?"

Diane shrugged. Good genes, she told John – and a skilled hairdresser.

The silence lay like a smothering blanket in the car as John drove it back towards the crossroads the next day. Hector sat in absolute stillness, hands folded over crossed legs, and studied them from his position in the backseat. Diane was keeping up a constant conversation with John, no doubt in an attempt to distract him, but as far as Hector could see it wasn't working very well, John's shoulders square under the red wool of his sweater.

He wondered how much of the previous night Diane had spent verifying his identity and mentally he tipped his hat at her; Diane Wilson was thorough and not easily intimidated, and those were qualities he appreciated – particularly in people working for him. He met her eyes in the rear view mirror, sharpened his gaze until she looked away. Hector went back to regarding the speeding landscape. In the front seat Diane was saying something in a low, intense tone and without turning his head he tuned in.

"… so of course there must be some sort of explanation," she said to John. "It's just that we haven't found one yet."

Good luck to them; he'd spent most of his extended life attempting to unravel the logic behind his own fate. He'd thought he'd found it when he met Diego, a divine compensation of sorts for all the previous fruitless years. He sighed; the only reason Diego had hired Diane Wilson's company had been to get at Alexandra Lind, an opportunity to get her alone and browbeat her into telling them what had happened to Ángel. Now it had all gone wrong: no Alexandra Lind, and no more Diego. Hector fisted his hand, caressed the thick gold ring that adorned his ring finger.

Hector took his time studying the barren surroundings. There was nothing here, nothing that would help him learn where Diego had ended up. Ignoring his audience of two, he walked out to stand in the exact centre of the crossroads, and there he crouched to lay his palm against the warm asphalt.

"*Adios*, Diego." Poor bastard, he'd never cope in a world without fast food and modern amenities. He straightened up and rubbed at his bruised thigh, courtesy of that panicked jump out of the studio window a couple of days ago – stupid thing to do, he'd been far too distraught about Diego to make much of a cat burglar. Still; he had to try, no? He needed one of those paintings, and even more now that Diego was gone from his life.

He turned to look at them, two rather apprehensive young people standing very close together.

"Strange isn't it? First Alexandra goes missing – is apparently held somewhere against her will for some months – and on the day she reappears, her mother vanishes, never to be heard from again. Unfortunately."

It had been one of the happier days in his long, long, life, the day Ángel called him to tell him he'd found her – not the witch herself, but her daughter, an Alexandra Lind. Was he sure? Yes, Ángel had yelled – well, he was almost sure, like ninety-nine percent sure. So what did Hector want him to do? Well, that had been easy, no? At last; a golden opportunity to snare the witch once and for all, and if the daughter was somewhat battered as a result, well, so be it – blame it on the mother, not on him. Hector's brow creased together; damn Mercedes! Somehow she'd evaded his elegantly baited trap and in the process taken Ángel with her. How?

"You don't really like her much, do you?" Diane said.

"Who? Mercedes? No, her I don't like, but then why should I? She's a witch; this is all her fault, she's the one who started it, dragging me out of my time."

"Oh dear." Diane made a tut-tutting sound. "And why, one wonders, no? What did you do to her?"

"That, Ms Wilson, is none of your business. Let's just say that she has utterly destroyed my life, and for that I would dearly want to make her pay." She made a derisive sound that Hector chose to disregard. At times it was better to ignore than punish – the aftermaths could be so tedious. He did one last, slow turn, bidding Diego a mental farewell. And now who would share all his secrets? Hector sighed; years of companionship left one very vulnerable to the darker sides of solitude.

"We might as well drive back," he said. "There's nothing to see here, is there?"

"What were you hoping for? A neat little sign post saying *Time Node*? An open hole to another dimension in time?" Diane said, her voice loaded with sarcasm. "You know, something – anything – to corroborate your rather weird story."

"Are you calling me a liar?" Hector sank his eyes into her.

"Yes, I suppose I am – or delusional, take your pick."

"I am not delusional," Hector said through gritted teeth. This young woman was beginning to annoy him. He forced himself to un-claw his fingers.

"None of this time travelling stuff is true!" Diane said.

"No, of course it isn't," John broke in. "There must be a logical explanation."

"Of course," Hector sneered. "I can't wait to hear it. How will it explain the dry car in the middle of the downpour? Or her rusted phone? Or my poor Diego?"

"I don't know," John mumbled.

"No of course you don't, because there isn't one."

"There must be," Diane said.

"There isn't; trust me." Hector turned to look at a deflated John. "Get over her, she'll never come back." John moaned, and Hector gave him an irritated look; what did he have to whine about? It wasn't him who had been thrown out of his time, was it?

She'd tricked him. Hector shoved his hands into his pockets. Fucking witch! Hector pressed his lips together to contain the rage that roared up from his belly, clogged his throat and filled him with the desire to rip someone's heart out. Now.

He turned his back on them, struggling to calm down. The landscape rose and fell in soft swells around him, muted greens creating a soothing backdrop to the odd purples and pinks – so different from his homeland, a land of dusty heat, of faded browns and dull yellows. *Sevilla, mi Sevilla...* And the year was 1480 or thereabouts, and he was young, an up and coming man at the court of *La Reina Isabel*, handpicked by Her Most Catholic Majesty to help in that most sensitive of tasks – cleansing the newborn Spain of all heretics.

He followed them back towards the car, sunk into his memories. So much power; a bright future stretching before him, a life of wealth, of influence, a servant of the Inquisition, a man who came and went unhindered through the gates of the Alcázar of Seville – and then Mercedes ruined it. Witch! To stand there and curse him, to tell him she would make him pay and for what, hey? For doing his job! Was it his fault her father was a false convert? Benjamin ben Isaac became Benito Gutierrez only to avoid expulsion from Seville– everyone knew that. Well; not until he, Hector, told them so, nodding gravely as he described how Benito settled the prayer shawl around his shoulders.

"Hmm?"

"I said, do you want us to drop you off somewhere, or is the office fine?" Diane twisted to look at him. "Are you alright?"

Hector strangled a guffaw. Alright? Of course he wasn't alright! He was living a life he shouldn't be leading, in a time he shouldn't be in. Damn you Mercedes! He stretched his lips into a smile, told Diane the office was fine and sat back.

He'd lied. Benito was no false convert, and nor was his pretty youngest daughter, Dolores. But what was he to do, trapped in a mess that threatened to explode in his face? He had no choice! But his biggest mistake had been to let Mercedes live – he should have dragged her before the Inquisition as well, and then she'd have been yet another woman roasted to death on the central plaza and he could have gone on with his well ordered, happy life.

His hands knotted together. Instead … She'd yanked him out of his time, the witch. Years – endless years – thrown from one age to the other in his desperate attempts to get back, to go home. Mercedes had cackled with laughter when she told him she'd cursed him – never to die, always to roam, unless he made it back to medieval Seville. He crossed himself; please let me die, strike me with a heavenly bolt and obliterate me, hang me upside down and slice me open, throw me into an erupting crater, but please, please let me die – don't leave me to rot to pieces.

He cleared his throat, met John's brown eyes in the rear-view mirror and busied himself finding a piece of gum. A painting; he needed to get his hands on one of

Mercedes' paintings. That was how it all began, no? With a picture the size of a postcard, and he'd looked at it, unable to tear his eyes away from the growing funnel of bright, bright light. So much noise, so much pain ... he shuddered.

Hector leaned his brow against the window, and in his head danced Dolores, pretty, pretty Dolores. He wondered at times if, once he found himself at rest, he might see her again. It almost made him laugh. If Dolores got the opportunity, he was sure she'd tear his balls off and feed them to him. In his more introspective moments he admitted he deserved it.

CHAPTER 7

On the seventh day of this her new existence, Alex walked downhill in the direction of the spring, compiling a new list of things she missed the most from the twenty-first century. As the effects of her concussion waned, the enormity of her predicament became increasingly clearer to her, leaving her with an urge to dig a hole somewhere and hibernate, sleep her way through this extended nightmare. Totally unproductive behaviour, the logical part of her brain remonstrated, and so instead she made lists.

"Lemon meringue pie, or maybe a cappuccino with a brioche?" She was constantly hungry, her stomach protesting in long, angry rumblings at this sudden and brutal change in diet. In the end she decided none of these made the shortlist – after all, she wasn't starving. "Toothbrush," she nodded, "toothbrush, soap, clean underwear, toilet paper and …" Hmm. Sanitary pads, she added some minutes later. Talk about inconvenient.

She hesitated by the road on her way back. Every morning she'd hurried to look at it, hoping that it would have resurrected itself in its modern form overnight. It hadn't. So far, she'd avoided setting foot on the crossroads itself, having to ward off vivid memories of that churning hole whenever she got too close. But today she took a deep breath and shuffled to the middle, forcing her legs to remain straight.

She closed her eyes and raised her arms. Please; take me back. Nothing happened. Of course nothing happened! What had she expected, a revolving door through time? John. He swam before her, blond hair flopping over his forehead. She folded together around his name, cradling it to her. She fell to her knees, clasped her hands as her grandmother used to do, and prayed, a gabbled stream of words in Swedish –the only language she'd ever heard used to invoke God. Maybe if she did this long enough something would happen, taking her back to her world and her John.

"What are you doing?" Matthew's voice recalled her to the empty moor and the dirt track that went for a road.

"Nothing." She stood, feeling ridiculous.

"You were praying, no? Begging the Lord to whisk you back to your time, I reckon."

Alex shrugged. "I guess I thought it worth a try at least." She made an effort and smiled at him. "If wishes were horses, hey?"

"Ah well; I wouldn't much mind a horse myself, but one has to make do with what one has, not yearn for what one doesn't."

"Easy for you to say." She had absolutely nothing here.

"But true none the less." He adjusted his bundle and smiled at her. "Ready?" They were leaving today, Matthew having pronounced her foot was good to go.

"All set." She threw one last look at the crossroads before following him up the hill.

The sun was directly overhead by the time Matthew decided to stop. Alex sat down under a stunted tree and lifted her feet to inspect the soles.

"It's been years since I walked barefoot. Look, I have bruises."

"No you don't, that's dirt." He handed her the water skin and tilted his head at the soft murmur of water. "Would you eat frogs?"

"Frogs?"Not if she could avoid it.

"They can be quite tasty, mayhap not the sort of food you're accustomed to, but all the same." He did a quick scan of their surroundings. "I don't think we'll find any — what was it? Chocolate?- anywhere close."

"No, probably not." All morning she'd been telling him of the food she was missing. Frogs seemed a poor substitute for hamburgers and tandoori chicken, and it definitely was a far cry from one of Magnus' chocolate cakes.

"It's food, no?" he said, a sharp edge to his voice. "Better than walking on an empty belly."

"As long as you cook them."

Alex tore into the frogs with determination. Chicken, pretend it's chicken. She'd picked dandelion leaves and tried to convince him to try some. He did, but told her such green stuff was best left to horses and cows. But he ate more than his share of the raspberries she'd found, laughing at her when she tried to keep her own hoard safe from his raiding hands, laughing even more when she jumped him in a playful attempt to get her berries back. Matthew stuffed them in his mouth and flung himself down beside her.

"I haven't laughed like that for many years."

"Well, I suppose being in prison does that to you," she smiled. He nodded and closed his eyes. Long, long lashes and she liked the way his eyes shifted colour, from not quite gold to muddy green.

She woke with a start some time later, her head pillowed on his chest, and sat up so fast she woke him up as well. How had that happened? He got to his feet looking as embarrassed as she felt, and they kept their distance when they resumed their walk.

"You said you were born in Seville," he said once they were back in stride.

"Yes. I'm half Spanish, half Swedish, although Magnus insists I ended up French given my temper." She smiled at the thought of her father. "I miss him, and I'm so sorry that he'll never know, maybe he'll think that I just took off, you know?"

"Why would he think that? You have a bairn, don't you?"

"Yes, but still; what else is he to believe?" And now Magnus would be all alone; no wife, no daughter.

"Mmm," Matthew nodded. "So what's he like then, your Da?"

"He's the best," she said, stooping for a moment to study a small flower. "He's a botanist, like his father was, and his grandfather and his father before him… you get the picture, right? According to Magnus, one of his forefathers actually was a disciple of the great Linnaeus." That drew an absolute blank and she frowned, trying to remember when Carl Linnaeus was born. He wasn't in the making yet, it was fifty years at least before he'd be born.

"He has a thing about roses," she went on. "You should see our garden in the summer, at the last count he had over forty varieties, and in spring he'll spend weeks cutting them back, talking to them in Swedish."

"He talks to his roses?"

Alex laughed at his incredulous expression. "He talks to all his plants, he says it's good for them."

He laughed. "Fortunate he isn't a farmer; he'd have a right dry throat."

"He used to tell me stories when I was little, scary Swedish stories about trolls and goblins and fairies, and then I'd wake up crying in the night, and he'd take me down to the kitchen and we'd sit and talk over milk and cookies." It had always been Magnus; Magnus who walked her to school that first day, Magnus who'd spend hours helping her with her science projects. And now she'd never see him again. She cleared her thickening throat; get it together, Alex Lind. But why the hell should she? She drew in a long, shuddering breath; *Pappa; min Pappa.*

The following days they walked more than Alex had ever walked in her life before. They rose at dawn, ate whatever they could find, and walked until late afternoon. Sometimes Matthew snuck down to isolated farmhouses, procuring an odd loaf of bread, some eggs and the occasional chunk of salted pork.

"Do you steal it?" It seemed an unnecessary risk.

"Nay, I buy it." He held up a worn leather pouch and shook it, letting a soft jingle of coins leak through. "But this I stole."

"Oh well," she said, eyeing the very small pouch. "I'm sure he doesn't miss it."

He looked at her sternly. "Of course he does. I took two months' wages off him."

Not only did they walk, they talked – long rambling conversations about this and that, although mostly it was about her life in the future, because Matthew couldn't get enough of hearing about it. He bombarded her with questions, and Alex talked and talked, about everything from showers to television. This last had him fascinated; a wee box filled with people? Whatever for? And when she laughed and talked about entertainment he shook his head; how entertaining could it be to gawk at other people's lives? Why not live your own? But most of all he liked all these new games she taught him – in particular as he consistently won.

"You cheat," Alex protested one evening, giving him a sullen look.

Matthew grinned back. "No, I don't; I'm just better than you are."

"I taught you this; of course you're not better than me!"

"The tally board proves differently."

"Huh; again." She wiped the sand clean of noughts and crosses, handed him a stick. "And this time we have to get five in a row."

"It won't help," he laughed, "but you get to start."

"Of course I do; you won the last time. But this time I'll win." She shook her head, making her curly hair dance around her. In the light of the setting sun it glinted bronze and gold.

"Nay you won't." She committed the same mistake every time, but he had no intention of telling her that.

"And if I do?"

"Then you'll get the last egg." He shifted somewhat closer to her. "And if I win?"

"The egg?"

Matthew pretended to think. "No ... if I win I want you to dance for me."

"Dance?" She'd gone a very bright red.

"I saw you, no? How you danced yesterday." She'd been singing something strange, doing dance steps he'd never seen before, many of them quite provocative.

"That was private!"

"You knew I was there, didn't you?" He laughed out loud at the wave of pink that flew up her face, making her glower at him. "Anyway, if I win, that's what I want."

"I'm going to beat you silly!"

But she didn't, and Matthew made her dance for a very long time. But he did give her the egg.

On the fifth day she insisted she had to wash. "Not only me, but my clothes as well." Matthew sighed but found her a small pool, retiring further upstream to fish while she washed.

When he came back, she was sitting chastely wrapped in her blanket, and he kept his eyes off her bare shoulders and the soft hollow at the base of her throat where he could see the pulse thud. She was attempting to untangle her damp hair, and he followed the movement of her arms, her hands. Finally he couldn't stand it and moved closer.

"Shall I help you?"

She just nodded and Matthew kneeled behind her, sinking his fingers into all those curls. He took his time about it and she sat stock still. Neither of them said a word.

"There," he said once he was done. He got to his feet and turned his back on her while he adjusted his breeches. "I caught us some fish; hungry?"

"So, what is it today?" he said once they'd eaten. His ragged spare shirt was spread to dry and his three stockings hung like garlands from the branch above him. He still wondered what had happened to the fourth stocking. He scratched at his beard, now somewhat less bristling after a long session with his knife, and looked down at her where she lay in the grass.

"Huh?"

"What makes the top five today?" He liked these lists of hers, yet another opportunity to hear about a world so different from his it made his ears want to drop off with incredulity.

"Number one is still the same," she grinned.

"Toothbrush," they choroused.

"Shower," she went on, "phone, car and trainers." None of them were new things and he settled back with his head pillowed on his arms.

"Who do you miss the most today?" He heard her sigh, and without opening his eyes he knew she'd be sitting with her knees drawn up to her chin, arms wrapped hard around them.

"Isaac, today it's Isaac."

He wasn't sure if he believed her, because it seemed to him that while she spoke very much about her father and now and then about her son, she rarely mentioned her man, John, and in his experience the one you didn't speak of was the one you missed the most.

After a long nap, Alex stood up and dressed, grimacing at the dampness of her jeans. She packed together her stuff, and seeing as Matthew still lay half asleep, she shook out his blanket before bending down to roll it back up around his things. The folded paper looked like a deed of some sort and she spread it flat, trying to decipher the curling handwriting.

"What are you doing?" Matthew sounded very cold.

"Nothing." She attempted a smile.

He took the paper from her, folding it back along the original creases before stuffing it inside his shirt, eyes never leaving hers.

"I'm sorry. It isn't as if I could read it anyway."

"It's not for you to read my private matters."

"I know, I just said I'm sorry. And as I also just said, I couldn't read a word of it." Except for the one word in the heading that had stuck out like a neon sign; divorce.

Matthew obviously didn't believe her, throwing her angry looks as he rolled his blanket round his belongings and shoved his feet into his worn shoes. He didn't even stop to make sure she was ready to go before he strode off along the stream, leaving her to make her way best she could.

"You're doing this on purpose," she yelled an hour or so later. "You know it's going to be hard going for me, barefoot as I am, right?" She rolled up her jeans and splashed into the stream instead.

He didn't reply.

"Well fine! See if I care." She came to a stubborn stop and limped over to sit on the bank, holding her breath as she pulled out an evil looking thorn from her big toe. The thin skin over her healing burns was irritated and one of her ankles was covered in a nettle rash.

"Bloody sadist." She threw a concerned look around her. The woods stood thick, and she had no idea in what direction she was heading. Well, she wasn't going to follow him, that nasty brute, instead she'd walk back to the clearing. From there she could see the hills and she much preferred sleeping up there, however bare, than here in this teeming, buzzing green. She paddled her feet in the water, hoping that he'd come back before it grew too dark. When she pulled her legs out of the water, three leeches hung like curling decorations on her calf and she regarded them with disgust.

"Okay; no fainting, no wimpy shrieks. Just get them off." But that would mean touching them and they looked very slimy. "Where are all the men when you need them," she muttered, and then she did just as Magnus had taught her, she slid her nail in under the front end – or what she assumed to be the front end, she wasn't about to try and check – and felt the thing loosen its hold and drop to the ground. She was quite proud of herself a minute or so later and turned to share her pride with Matthew, belatedly remembering that he was an insensitive jerk who had left her alone in this threatening environment.

She got to her feet, and in her gut fear bloomed. What was she to do? She trudged back the way she'd come, and for the first time since all this had happened to her she realised just how alone she was. No one would miss her, not on this end of the time chute. No one even knew she existed, and she had no family, no friends, not one single person who cared if she lived or died. It almost made her cry, but she knuckled herself hard in the eyes and increased her pace. She didn't want to get stuck here for the night.

Sheer instinct had her coming to a stop several metres away from the clearing. She crouched down and peered through the bushes. Someone had kicked life into the remains of their earlier fire, and she counted to a total of six men sitting round it, four in what looked like leather tunics topped by breastplates, two more at ease in only their shirts. Helmets had been lain aside, she could make out the outline of horses on the further side, and her eyes flew to locate the cameras and the rest of the film crew before she recalled that this was no movie, this was her new life – lucky her.

Alex' calves were beginning to cramp, gnats settled on her uncovered neck and forearms and still she didn't dare to move. One of the soldiers – roundheads, real life roundheads, down to their cropped heads and rather dashing leather boots – poked at the fire.

"He said, no?" he said in a loud voice, running a hand through his bristling ginger fuzz. "A woman, dressed just like him in those outlandish, blue breeches."

"Oh come on, Smith," one of his companions said. "The man's a fugitive royalist. Why believe one word he says?"

"But he says he isn't," the first speaker said. "He insists he's from somewhere in the Colonies. And he did say he had a female travelling companion, wearing breeches similar to his."

"Pfff! A woman in breeches! Who's ever heard of that, hmm?"

Alex wiped her palms up and down her jeans. It must be Sanderson they were referring to. Slowly, slowly, she began inching away, casting about for a better hiding place.

"But he said…"

"He said a lot of things, Smith, the tenor of it being

that he was innocent and should be set free." The other men snickered, making Smith glower at them.

"Why would he invent something as far-fetched as that?"

"Well he would, no?" a rather fat man said. "Admitting to being an escaped convict would be stupid."

"I'm just saying…" Smith began but was interrupted by a lanky man with no hair at all.

"It's your fault we're here, Smith. It's you and your big mouth that has us riding up and down these damned moors on the off chance that we'll encounter a woman in breeches."

"Because he said she ran off with a man. And what's a woman …"

"Smith," the fat man groaned, "give it a rest. Do something about the fire instead, we need more wood."

Still muttering, Smith heaved himself to his feet and made straight towards where Alex was hiding.

She didn't know what to do; she didn't dare to break and run, and the bushes were far too scraggly to offer adequate protection should he come close. She crawled backwards, wincing at every snapped twig. The soldier came to a standstill, cocked his head in the direction of the sound. Alex muffled a whimper against her arm, tried to stop herself from breathing. She relaxed when the roundhead shrugged and veered off to her right. She slid even further back, aiming for the protective thickness of the woods. Almost there… More twigs breaking, yet another interminable minute holding her breath, and one more slithering movement. She took a relieved breath. A metre, no more, and then she'd be safe. A foot came down on her back, pressing her hard into the ground.

"And what might we have here?"

Rough hands turned her over, and in the fading light she couldn't properly make out the features in the face staring down at her.

"My, my," Smith crowed. "He was right, after all. A woman – in breeches!"

CHAPTER 8

She got as far as the closest tree before he brought her down. She'd kicked herself free the first time and now this Smith character was angry.

"Take your hands off me!" Alex squirmed like a worm under the roundhead's hard hold.

"I think not," Smith panted, the sound cut short when Alex landed a punch on his mouth. He hit her back. Hard. It stunned her, and by the time she'd regained her breath and her anger, he had flipped her over onto her front, one arm wrenched up high behind her back. Something was looped round her wrist; a belt? He reached for her other arm, and she dug her fingers into the dirt. Had to ... yes, she tried to heave against him, but the man was the size and weight of a walrus, soft blubber squashing her flat.

"Smith? What's taking you so long?" someone called from the direction of the fire.

"I'll be right there," Smith called back. "And then we'll see who was right," he added in a satisfied undertone, securing his belt around Alex' arms at elbow level.

"Let go! Get off me, you ..." She rolled, kicked and bit, and there he was, a ton of stinking male pressing her to the ground, one hand groping her breasts. The agony to her trapped arms was such that she froze, unable to move.

"What's this?" Smith's fingers were inspecting her bra. She replied by sinking her teeth into his underarm, which made him yelp.

"Smith?"

"I'm fine," Smith hollered. "I just caught myself a vixen. You'll pay for that," he said viciously.

"A vixen? Here?"

Alex could make out the sound of several men moving towards them, but what was she to do, pinned under this man whose fingers were now struggling with her jeans. A wave of rage surged through her; no way. Disgusting creep of a man, and what the fuck did he think he was doing, sticking his dirty fingers into her jeans. So; dig your heels in, tense your goddamn thighs and buck, now.

Smith grunted with surprise, sliding off to her right. Ha! Her shoulders were on fire, her arms pulled so tight behind her it felt as if the sockets were about to give at any moment, but she was back on her feet, poised to run, when from the direction of the fire came four more men.

"Well, well," the fattest of the men said. "Look at that."

"See? I told you, no?" Smith got to his feet, one hand holding up his breeches.

"It might be a lad," one of the soldiers said, squinting at what he could make out of Alex.

"Definitely not a lad," Smith grinned. "I've made sure."

"Oh have you, now? Well, we'd best make sure as well, no?"

They converged on her; Alex leapt away, but the men just laughed.

"Run, lass," one of them urged, "we could do with a bit of sport."

Alex considered her situation; with her hands tied behind her she had one option; run and run fast. No way would she be able to kick all five of them to the ground, and her foot was far from healed anyway. Smith lunged, Alex twisted out of range, brought up her knee. Too bad she missed his balls, but the effect was pretty good anyway, with him collapsing like a pricked balloon.

"Feisty, no?" one of the other soldiers said. "Are you alright down there, Smith?"

Smith scowled at Alex and heaved himself upright. Alex turned and ran. They came after her, whooping like boys playing at Indians. Unlike boys, they weren't playing, and Alex was cornered. She licked her lips. Bambi meets the wolf pack. Except that Bambi was better at running. One of the men snickered.

"Me first," he said.

"In your dreams," Alex spat, trying to sound menacing. Her voice squeaked. They laughed.

From the campsite came a blood curling shriek. Again. The soldiers turned.

"What was that?" the fat one said.

The obvious leader shook his head. "Will? Are you alright, Will?" he called.

In reply came wild neighing, more shrieking.

"Moss-troopers!" the leader said. "They'll steal the horses."

He rushed towards the clearing where fire seemed to be spreading in wild, uncontrolled tongues through the closest bushes.

"Come on!" he barked, and all but Smith hurried after him. Powder exploded when the fire found the pouches, a horse broke free of the hobbles and charged off into the night, and Alex took off.

"Oy!" Smith rushed after her, but Alex had no intention of stopping, crashing through the undergrowth like an aggravated boar. A hand came down on her arm, she screamed, yet another hand clamped down over her mouth and she was lifted to the side, pressed hard against a tree trunk.

"Shush," Matthew whispered in her ear. Alex wanted to cry.

Matthew undid her bindings, threw the belt to the side. From the campsite came shouts, from some metres away came the sounds of a man running through the woods. Smith, she supposed, knees wobbling.

"Quickly." His breath tickled her skin. Alex needed no further telling. She slunk after him into the protective darkness, mimicking the way he was running, torso bent at an almost ninety degree angle to his hips.

An hour or so later they stopped, and Alex sagged down to sit.

"Are you alright?" Matthew asked.

Alex nodded, still out of breath.

"He didn't hurt you?"

"A bit, but nothing too bad." She massaged her aching shoulders one by one, rearranged her clothing. She slid him a covert look; he'd come back for her, saved her, so maybe he did care a little, however big a bastard he'd been earlier.

"They're looking for me," she said. Damn Sanderson; probably his idea of an adequate little payback.

"Mmm, I heard." He remained where he was, crouched over his fire making efforts, his eyes darting in her direction.

"I'm sorry," he said after a few minutes. "I shouldn't have left you alone."

"It would feel more sincere if you said it while facing me."

He turned. "I'm sorry," he enunciated clearly. He sat down beside her, waiting.

"So am I, but I did apologise already before."

He nodded a gruff agreement.

"My brother-in-law helped me," he said without any form of preamble. She must have looked confused. "With the divorce."

"What divorce?"She did her best wide eyed look – not that it worked, given how his mouth twitched.

"Mine. And I disowned the child as well, in view of her telling me in front of witnesses he wasn't mine."

Alex scratched her head vigorously. The bloody midgets had eaten their way across her entire scalp.

"I didn't know you could."

"Could what?"

"Get a divorce. I thought you needed some kind of papal dispensation."

Matthew raised an eyebrow. "The Pope? What would he have to do with us?"

Alex hitched her shoulders. She had absolutely no idea.

"I thought you'd gone for good," she said with a quick glance in his direction. She blushed at the intensity of his gaze. "It made me realise, twelve days too late, that here I'm totally alone. It scared me." She sighed and looked away, fiddling with her blanket roll. He could say something, not just sit there staring at her. She cleared her throat and got to her feet, muttering something about a human break. His hand closed round her ankle and she looked down in surprise.

"You're not alone," he said, before gracefully standing up. "Not unless you want to be." His eyes were very close. Somehow she got the impression she was answering a much bigger question than the one actually expressed, and she licked her lips before replying.

"I don't."

"Good," he smiled, and his hand rested briefly on her head.

"So, do you get gifts for your birthday, then?" Matthew asked a couple of days later. Alex smiled at his transparency, but was touched by the fact that he'd actually remembered.

"Oh yes − and for Christmas. And of course wives expect gifts at anniversaries and such as well."

"And it would be the one gift, no?"

She grinned up at him. "It tends to get a bit wild and crazy, at least for Christmas − mountains of gifts. Quite disgusting really, commercialism at its best."

He clearly didn't understand, and she tried to explain about Christmas shopping and after Christmas sales, and all the commercials winding kids up weeks in advance with expectations.

"But why?" he said. "Why would anyone buy something before Christmas, if you can buy it at half price after Christmas?"

"Because everyone expects gifts for Christmas, not New Year's Eve."

He made a small sound of astonishment at this incredibly stupid behaviour and dug his fingers into the waist lining of his breeches, struggling to extract something.

"Here, happy birthday, aye?"

Alex turned the small piece of wood round and round in her hands. It was exquisite, a miniature, faceless baby, spine curved shrimplike and small legs pulled up to meet equally small pudgy arms. It fit into the palm of her hand, and yet the detail was fantastic, down to small toes and fingers and wisps of hair on its skull. And he'd made it himself, for her.

"Look, it's sucking its thumb!"

"Aye, and it's a he, not an it. So that when you feel the need to touch Isaac you can at least run your fingers over this little one, and maybe he will feel it."

"How did you know? That sometimes it aches in me to touch him?" Sometimes? Like a hundred times a day.

He looked away. "It was the same for me – with Ian."

"Thank you." She let her hand rest on his arm longer than necessary. He smiled down at her, raised his free hand as if to tweak her hair. She wanted him to.

He stopped halfway through the movement, turning in the direction of the small grove further down the slope. Alex narrowed her eyes; among the stunted trees she could make out horses, more than one, and she could hear the murmur of voices as well.

"What?" she whispered made nervous by how tense he'd gone. Two horses stepped into the open, the sun shot sparks off a breastplate, and when two more horses appeared Matthew wheeled, dragging Alex with him.

"Run!"

She didn't need a second telling. Soldiers – even she could see that. He rushed them through the undergrowth, and Alex had to wade through bracken and heather. From behind came the unmistakeable sounds of pursuit, loud voices telling them to stop.

Gorse tore at her arms, her hands, the tender skin on her unhealed foot broke open, and still she ran, struggling to keep even pace with him. Which was bloody difficult, given the length of his legs. But not even Matthew Graham could outrun a horse, and how the hell would they get out of this one? The ground shook with the approaching horses, a dull throbbing that vibrated up her feet and legs to close like a fist of ice round an unidentifiable point in her belly.

A swift assessment of the terrain and Matthew turned them sharply to the right. What, up there? He shoved her towards the scree slope and she stumbled and fell flat on her face on the slippery, shifting rock face. She was up again, scrabbling on all fours. When a shot went off she squeaked, ducking for an instant before increasing her efforts up the steep incline.

Agh! She hopped for a couple of steps, anything to keep weight off her foot. She had a stitch up her right side, she could taste iron in her mouth and her breath was coming in short gasps. Breathe normally! One, two, one, two. There, much better. Her foot – it was killing her, but she was too frightened to even consider stopping, dodging like a hare between boulders and shrubs.

A long stretch of grass, a horse that came at them from the side, and Alex redoubled her efforts. Arms up, arms down. Feet, move your feet. Extend your stride, pretend you're Michael Johnson or someone. Michael Johnson? He only did four hundred metres, the wimp, this was uphill and much longer. But she tried, pumping legs up and down. Useless; the ground dragged at her feet.

The horse came closer and closer, and when she threw a look over her shoulder she could see reflections dancing off a long blade. Bloody hell; she was going end up sliced to bits. She hiccupped, moved her arms faster – or tried to. The man cheered as he shrank the gap between them.

"It's her, it's her! See? She's wearing those breeches!"

Oh shit; not him again.

She tried to count them; two behind them, one on the far right, and then this enervating Smith character. Yet another shot and Matthew yelped, limping for a couple of steps before regaining pace.

"They got you?" A wheeze no more, but she had to know. He shook his head, but there was trickle of blood flowing down his calf. A ricochet of sorts; her brain grappled with this, happier to be solving this particular dilemma than the one of how to evade all these damned soldiers.

Matthew pulled her along, plunging down one slope, up the other. It made Alex dizzy. She lost her footing, her hand slipped from his grip, a few decimetres became metres, and the horse was upon her. She tried to run, tripped and landed hard on hands and knees.

Alex made an incoherent sound; it would kill her, those huge hooves would crush her back, her head, her everything. I'm going to die! No, I don't want to, please, no, no, no, *Pappa*, help me, *Pappa*! No Magnus, but Matthew, leaping back towards her.

The sword flashed, Matthew twisted out of range, rose to strike the horse across its head with his roll. The animal reared and Matthew pounced, grabbing the soldier by his booted leg and pulling him off. The man landed with a dull thud, flopped and went still.

"Get up! Move," Matthew gasped, heaving Alex back onto her feet.

Yet another incline, more stones, more gorse, and Alex' teeth ached with the effort, her lungs protested at every panicked breath, and still she could hear the soldiers behind them. She rushed up the last few metres, treading hard on Matthew's heels.

"Shit!" Alex came to a swaying halt, arms thrown wide to stop herself from falling down the sheer drop that yawned at her feet. She swallowed and looked at the small body of water, an uninviting black far below; what was this, ten metres?

"I hate heights," she said, and then irrationally began to laugh. He took her hand, motioning back to where the soldiers were urging the horses up yet another shifting scree slope.

"We have to jump."

"I know."Without further thought she closed her eyes and leapt straight out. She landed with a splash, thrilled to discover she was still alive, her limbs intact.

"Can you swim?" Matthew's head popped up beside hers.

"A bit late in the day to ask, no?" A shot whizzed by and from above came angry shouts. Another shot, this one uncomfortably close and Alex squawked, her mouth filling with water.

"Dive, swim for the willow." And just like that he was gone.

The willow? She was in a state of panic and he expected her to recognise a bloody tree? Well, wasn't she the lucky one to have a botanist for a father. She submerged herself and swam for the further shore.

"Matthew?" She surfaced under the trailing branches, gulped down air. "Matthew?" Oh God, oh God. They'd shot him and he was by now floating dead in the middle of the pool, and then what was she to do?

"Here, Alex, I'm here." He boosted her up the tree, urging her to climb higher. "We stay here until it's dark," he whispered once they were safely astride a branch that hung out over the water, his body like a protective layer round her. Alex nodded and unclenched her hand from around her little wooden doll.

"They must be here somewhere!" There was an irritated tone to the voice Alex recognised as Smith's. Persevering bastard.

"We've looked, no? Where do you think they're hiding, under the gorse?"

"No, but perhaps up a tree, no?"

"A tree?"

Alex bit her hand to stop herself from whimpering. And if they came looking, then what? Behind her Matthew had stopped breathing. Well, she hoped not, but it felt that way. His mouth came down to her ear.

"Your feet. Pull up your feet." So she did, and he whispered that she should stand, press herself against the trunk. With the agility of a monkey he clambered over to another branch, rose and flattened himself against the gnarly bark. Alex wanted to giggle – alternatively pee. Her toes, her calves, her thighs – all of her cramped with the effort of holding herself upright and still. She didn't dare to look down. She didn't dare to move her head, keeping her cheek and ear squished against the tree. She could hear her own pulse, loud but surprisingly steady. From below came sounds. Someone was shaking the lower branches, banging at the trunk. There was a loud curse.

"Now what?"

"I slipped. This tree grows more in the water than out of it."

"Afraid of water, Smith?"

"I can't swim, can I?" Smith sighed, did some more branch shaking. "Not here."

It was probably no more than five minutes before Matthew decided they could sit back down. It felt like half a century. Besides, there was no way she could sit down. Her limbs had gone rigid, shivers of tension rippling through the muscles of legs and arms. She'd sunk her fingers so hard into the bark the joints hurt. If she moved she'd overbalance and plunge to her death. She peeked down, swayed. Well; perhaps not death, but close – unless she landed in the water.

"I've got you, aye?" A large hand grabbed hold of her arm. Slowly, centimetre by centimetre she slid down the trunk. Something tore at her cheek. With a little sob she resumed her previous sitting position. The branch swayed when he moved over to sit behind her.

By the time they made it down from the tree they were stiff with cold.

"Do you think it's safe?" she breathed.

"Aye, it's hours since we heard anything last." He straightened up and looked with disgust at his sodden roll. "We'll walk, we need to get warm anyway."

Alex just nodded, fell into step with him. "They nearly caught us."

"But they didn't, did they?"

"What…" she broke off, took a steadying breath. "And if they'd caught us, what would they have done?"

Matthew looked away. "I'm not sure about you, but me they would have clapped in irons – or hanged."

"Ah." She didn't feel like talking much after that.

"How's your foot?" he said a bit later.

"Okay," she lied. Every step was agony, and she was quite sure she'd cut herself on the scree, but she had no intention of slowing them down. Matthew pursed his mouth but left it at that.

All through the night they walked, Alex setting one foot before the other despite the constant, throbbing pain. She had to work hard not to limp, and it was with relief she sank down to sit once they stopped. He set water to boil and knelt before her to wash her feet. Just as she'd suspected there was a deep cut on her instep, and he spent extra time on it, ignoring her little sounds of protests.

"Thanks," she said once he was done.

"My pleasure." For an instant the back of his hand rested against her cheek.

It took a long time for Alex to relax sufficiently to even consider sleep. All in all, this birthday had been excessively exciting. She closed her hand around her little doll and wondered if John was thinking as much of her as she was thinking of him.

CHAPTER 9

"John?" Diane shook him. "It's almost six. Aren't you supposed to pick up Isaac?"

He tore his eyes away from the blank computer screen and hitched his shoulders.

"He's with Magnus." A pathetic attempt to distract Magnus from the fact that today was Alex' birthday. He picked up his Rubrik cube and sat turning the faces. "Do you believe him?" he asked, keeping his eyes on his toy. It was the constant question in his brain these days, from the moment he woke to the second he fell asleep.

"Who? Mr bloody Hector Olivares? Of course I don't! Do you?"

"I don't know, but he definitely seemed to believe himself, don't you think?"

Diane exhaled and shook her head. "Maybe, but what worries me is that you don't dismiss it as being totally impossible. Time nodes don't exist, of course they don't."

John swivelled on his chair and looked at her.

"How would you know?" In fact, he'd come to the conclusion over the last fortnight that he did believe Hector's time node theory, however borderline crazy.

"Come off it. You can't seriously believe anything he said was true. He's a sick man with an overactive imagination."

"He's a man who just lost his partner," John corrected harshly.

Diane looked away. "Sorry." She reached over and took hold of his arm. "She's gone, John. We don't know how, but she's gone."

John swallowed, ashamed of even thinking this, let alone voice it.

"She isn't coming back, is she?"

Diane sighed. "No, I don't think she is."

John was on the verge of asking her if she thought Alex was dead, but desisted. He didn't want to know what she thought – he had no idea what he himself thought. Now and then – now and then? Who was he kidding? More or less constantly – he pondered the possibility that this disappearance might somehow be linked to those months when she'd been gone last time, and at times it filled him with surging hope, because if she came back once she could come back twice, right?

Mostly it made him hope there was no link, because he never wanted to see Alex as extinguished as she'd been the autumn of 1999. Pregnant and silent, almost inhumanly silent – during the days, that is, because at night she dreamed and screamed. Jesus; it had been a trial, for them both. A trial that grew exponentially worse with the advent of baby Isaac, fathered during those lost months by a man Alex refused to talk about, except to say his name was Ángel Muñoz.

Those were the only two words she'd ever uttered about her experiences, and only because Magnus had insisted the boy had a right to know – someday. Isaac; all he had left of her now.

"If ..." Diane's voice jerked him back to the here and now. "... if Alex is gone, what happens to Isaac?" What was she, a mind reader?

"To Isaac? Why should anything happen to him?"

"Well, he's not yours is he?"

For a moment John considered slapping her. Not his? Of course Isaac was his, had been from that dark December day when he'd been born. A hell of a lot more his than Alex' – at least to begin with, because Alex had refused to feed him, touch him, have anything to do with him those first few months. Post partum depression, the doctors had said, but John wasn't that sure. Even now, with Isaac pushing three, there were moments when John would find Alex watching her son with speculation, an odd glint in her eyes. He frowned at Diane.

"Of course he's mine. I'm the only father he's ever had."

"But as per the letter of the law ..."

"What letter of the law?" He could hear it, the panic in his voice. "I'm his dad – no one else. No one, you hear?" He slammed the door on his way out.

John was still seething as he walked his way across the Princes Street Gardens, making for Fredrick Street and the shortest route to Magnus' house up by the Botanical Gardens. He was behaving irrationally and a small voice inside of him was telling him that he should phone Diane and apologise, because none of this was her fault. He stopped by a bench, sat down, and all energy drained away from him so fast it left him spinning inside. Alex, he groaned, rubbed his hand across his face and began to cry.

The odd passerby gave him concerned looks and one elderly lady pressed a paper napkin into his hand, but mostly people hastened by the man who sat crying his heart out in the August dusk.

John cried until his eyes hurt, wiped his nose, cried some more, and finally felt the sobs subside. He jumped when his phone rang, bringing him hurtling back to the here and now and the fact that it was eight o'clock, and he'd totally forgotten Isaac.

"John?" Magnus' voice sounded hollow, and John pressed the phone harder to his ear.

"What?" He closed his eyes as he imagined scenarios where Isaac had also disappeared. "Is Isaac okay? Is he there?"

"Yes," Magnus said, still in that strange voice. "He's fast asleep." He breathed heavily, a soft sound whooshing down the line. "Will you please come?"John had never heard Magnus sound like that, so he promised he'd be there in twenty minutes, rang off and set off at a run for the closest taxi stand.

"Keep the change." John got out of the taxi at the entrance to Magnus' street. He had his hand on Magnus' gate when a sudden movement made him stop. He peered into the shadows. There; something moved, leaves rustled. A cat? John squinted in an effort to see. No cat; a man was standing below the window to Magnus' study, most of him hidden from view by the huge rhododendron. The man grabbed hold of the sill and heaved himself upwards, as graceful as a Russian gymnast. Light spilled out of the window to illuminate his face.

"Hey!" John broke into a run. Quick as a flash the intruder dropped back to the ground, rushing for the fence with John at his heels. The door banged open.

"John?"

John didn't – couldn't – reply, driving the intruder towards the wooden fence. He widened his arms and attempted to grab the man. Hector Olivares sneered and kicked him straight in the gut. John folded together like a penknife, and Hector scaled the fence and vaulted over to the other side.

"Hector Olivares?" Magnus helped John to stand. "Are you sure?"

John scowled in the direction of where Hector had disappeared.

"I'd know that face anywhere." He straightened up and waved Magnus off. "I'm fine, perfectly capable of walking on my own, alright?" But he was glad to sink down into one of Magnus' armchairs, a huge mug of milky coffee in his hands. "Thanks."

Magnus sat down opposite. "Why would he do something like that? Why ..." He broke off. "Perhaps it's him! That's my burglar!"

"You think?" John tried to match his indistinct memories of the burglar with Hector. Both of them slight, both of them agile and strong. Maybe. He sipped at his coffee, gave Magnus a concerned look. The tall man looked tired and irritated. He kept on looking out the window, as if expecting Hector to materialise there.

"So what was it you called me about?"

Magnus picked up a small, battered note book and held it out to John.

"I found it, in the studio. It was hidden under one of the drawers in the broken cabinet."

John took the book from him. Black waxed covers and rounded corners – the old-fashioned kind his gran wrote her recipes in.

"What is it?"

"I have no idea. I haven't read it yet, I … well, I couldn't." Magnus' voice creaked with emotion, eyes glued to the notebook.

John looked from Magnus to the little book and back again.

"Why not? It's just a notebook." He flipped through it; most of it was blank, here and there the odd sketch, now and then page after page filled with Mercedes' distinctive, scrawled handwriting. Fountain pen, never ballpoint with Mercedes, and here the ink varied from a fresh black to a faded brown.

"Look at the first page." Magnus' eyes were extraordinarily blue in the lamplight.

John opened the book to the first page. *The Book of Ruth* it said, but Ruth had been crossed over in red, replaced by a wobbly *Mercedes*.

"Not that one! The next one."

John turned the page. A family tree. Isaac ben Daoud, Jacobo ben Isaac, Isaac ben Jacobo, Benjamin ben Isaac, Ruth bat Benjamin.

"Strange names," he said, "Jewish, no?" He frowned at Magnus. "Mercedes was Jewish? Is she this Ruth person right at the end?"

"I have no idea; I bloody well hope not, given the dates."

John had to squint to properly see the numbers. "Fifteenth century? So not Mercedes then. Maybe this was just a new idea of hers – to write a book."

"I don't think so." Magnus retook the book, turned a few pages, cleared his throat and read.

I am Mercedes Gutierrez Sanchez. My husband is Magnus Lind. And once I was Ruth bat Benjamin, but that was very, very long ago.

"Jesus …" John said. "What is she saying? That she used to be a Jewish girl born in the fifteenth century?" He quelled an urge to laugh; sophisticated, cosmopolitan Mercedes a medieval Jewess? No, totally impossible.

"It seems so, no?" Magnus handled the book gingerly.

"Should we read it?" John's eyes hung off the notebook.

"I'm not sure." Magnus fidgeted in his seat. "I need something to eat first."

It was well over an hour later. No matter that Magnus had cooked, done the dishes, wiped down the counters and insisted on more coffee, they were now back in his study, the little book a tantalising presence on his desk. Magnus wasn't sure he wanted to read it, in fact he was regretting not having burnt it when he found it.

"So," John said, nodding at the book.

Magnus made for the shelf where he kept his whisky. In silence he poured them both a drink, returned to where John was sitting.

"I can read it if you want," John said when Magnus made no move to pick up the book.

"No." Most reluctantly Magnus opened the notebook. He took a deep breath and began to read.

My brain is like a sieve these days. My memories, they dribble from me. I no longer remember it all – don't want to remember. My fingers tighten round the pen. My story. Must write it down, before it slips away from me. Magnus always says to start at the beginning. The beginning? Let there be Light, He said. Well, no, not that beginning. My beginning.

I remember I was born in Seville. No; I know I was born on the third day of Pesach in 1461. Or was it 1462? I'm not sure. But my mother was Miriam, my father was Benjamin, and I, I was Ruth. The house we lived in was tall and narrow, squeezed into a corner of a small plaza in the Judería of Seville. Lovely, lovely ochre walls, like honey in the afternoon sun. Sheltered, green courtyards, trickling water, heat, always so much heat.

On the first floor lived my grandparents and... no, I don't recall. Irrelevant. On the second floor I lived with my parents and my sister, the third floor was my grandfather's workshop, and on the ground floor, in a little room off the storage rooms and the kitchen, lived Geraldo. Yes, I remember Geraldo.

Geraldo was old. He talked all the time, and most of it was nonsense, but some of it was not. My grandfather had taken him in one night very many years ago, pitying this man who walked the streets in charred, odd clothing, speaking of thunder and lightning, funnels of bright, bright light, and of falling and falling. If he hadn't done so, grandfather would say, well then poor Geraldo would likely have burnt as a witch, and all for the sin of being out of his head.

My father was a doctor. He had but to taste a drop of his patient's urine to be able to diagnose them, and mostly he cured them as well. My mother was a chameleon, a woman who shone like the sun when my father was close, but wilted and faded when he was not. My sister was younger, happier, prettier, but I was the chosen one – oh, yes I was.

I remember paint. Colours. Amber, carmine, beautiful sienna red, cobalt and vermilion. Brushes arranged by size, easels and half primed canvases, laughing sitters and on his stool my grandfather, eyebrows pulled together as he concentrated.

He was no ordinary painter, my grandfather – in my family we rarely are. No; we have magic in our fingers, and my grandfather was a painter of things unseen, evoking desert storms out of canvases the size of a hand palm, waterfalls from painted walls. But these were hidden skills, things we never spoke of. I'm not sure my mother ever knew.

"What? Like a family of weirdly talented painters?" John laughed. "No one can paint like that."

Magnus hitched a shoulder. There was a painting in his

bedroom that was very much like that, in palest whites and greens, here and there a dash of yellow. At times, if the light was right, it glowed into life and it was him and Mercedes naked in a long gone Seville afternoon. But he didn't feel like telling John this.

I was three — only three? no, that can't be right -when my grandfather decided it was I that had inherited his talent. Blood red squiggles and my sister cried, long strokes of greens and browns, and my mother nodded to sleep. I was the wizard's apprentice. I was taught to see and capture all the things most people never notice. The imprint of a hand on a surface of water; the rush of air that precedes a rainstorm. He tried to teach me his own special trick — painting his way into people's heads — but I never mastered that; perhaps I didn't want to.

When I wasn't painting, I helped my mother — all little girls helped their mothers. I baked and cooked, sewed and washed, and swept the house clean before Sabbath. And when I had a moment over, I was mostly with Geraldo, begging him to tell me one more story, one more time.

He told good stories. About girls that fell down bunny holes and boys that grew up with wolves. But my favourite was the one about the thunderstorm — the one that made the adults laugh and say poor Geraldo was truly out of his head. Geraldo would scream it was true, all of it. I believed him.

One day he was out walking, he'd say, and just as he was trying to decide which way to take in the crossroads before him, a huge storm broke above his head. Terrible, he'd whisper, lightning and thunder but no rain, just very, very hot. And then ... he'd swallow, shake himself ... and then rose around his feet bright bands of greens and blues, they wrapped themselves around him, and those horrible colours tightened into a vice around him, propelling him towards a hole in the ground.

Like the bunny hole Alice fell through? No, of course not! This was a bottomless pit, a hole streaming bright, bright light, and he didn't want to, but there was no way to avoid it, and so he fell. He fell and fell — and landed here.

John made a strangled sound, looked as if he intended to say something. Magnus shook his head; no more interruptions.

So easy, no? Just like Geraldo described it. A swirl of blues and greens, a dot of burning white, and there I was, leaning expectantly towards this bright point of light. My grandfather yanked me away, screaming that what had I done, I had near faded away before his eyes. He burnt the painting. I didn't paint one like it for very many years.

When I was eight, my grandfather choked to death on a plum stone. No more painting. Don't know why. It made me angry. To distract me, Father brought me along to see a patient, promising he'd buy me a pet on the way. A magpie. I danced by his side. That was the day I met Hector Olivares — eyes like aquamarines, hair like gilded copper. He took my bird! He opened the cage and set it free, laughing at me when I cried. My father offered me a new pet but I shook my head. I wanted my bird.

At fourteen I was María de las Mercedes, no longer Ruth, no longer Jewish but Catholic. No choice. My father was Benito Gutierrez, not Benjamin ben Isaac, and my mother stopped shining at the sight of him — she cried. And died.

At seventeen I met Hector again, and I stuck my tongue out, still angry at him for my bird. But this Hector was not a nasty boy, he was a young, handsome man, and he laughed and offered me a white rose in compensation for the lost bird. To Dolores, my sister, he offered a red rose. She blushed.

Ay, ay ay! Dolores and Hector, always together, and Dolores grew secretive and smug, disappearing for hours on end. Two years, a few more months, and Dolores was bright eyed and rosy, whispering to me that soon, yes very soon, Hector would ask for her hand.

He never did. He laughed, and said he couldn't marry a marrana, *a Jewish convert. But he liked his little mistress, his hot-blooded little Jewish bed mate. Dolores cried when she told me this. Never again would she see him, never, ever again!*

But one afternoon she was out, sent by me to buy marzipan

from the nuns, and it grew dark, and still she didn't come. And when she finally did, there was something wrong with her face, with her eyes, and she smoothed at her skirts, all the time her skirts.

My father found out. He cornered Hector and dragged him off his horse, beat him, kicked him, leaving the young grandee covered in mud and chicken shit. People laughed. Hector got to his feet and promised revenge.

The coming years were calm and peaceful. I married an older man, a prominent Christian. He was kind to me, indulged my fascination with paints and brushes. Long, orderly days, no Hector, just a steady roll of weeks and months. Until the eve of Dolores' wedding.

They scaled the walls, they came through the gate, and we were dragged into the patio, all of us – my father, Geraldo and me. And Dolores, God help me, Dolores as well. She was undressed by these men, and Geraldo might have been old, but he loved us, and he picked up a spade and hit one of the men. They killed him. And they laughed, forcing Dolores down on her back.

I recognised Hector behind his mask, and when they were done with her I thought they might turn on me, and I almost hoped they would, because it was unbearable to stand and watch. But they didn't. My pregnant belly and my husband's name protected me. I was shoved into a room, tied and gagged.

Next morning the house was empty. No father, no Dolores. No Dolores! My father, I looked everywhere for him, for them, I knocked my way round all the houses in the neighbourhood but all I got was shaking heads and hastily hooded pity in their eyes. Hector; I ... yes, I would go to the queen, to the Inquisitor himself, tell them what he had done. Geraldo dying in his blood, my sister ravished, and my father ... My husband wouldn't let me. What proof but my testimony?

Two months later and we were standing on a balcony overlooking the plaza. A festive occasion – an auto de fé no less – and the square below was crowded with people, the air heavy with the scents of fried pork, of bread and too much sour wine. And there they came, the penitents, a straggling line of men and *women that filed silently after the chief Inquisitor himself, Alonso de Hojeda. By his side rode Hector. And among the penitents ...* No! Dios mío, no! *I don't want to remember this, but I must, I must. My sister, my Dolores, but she was no longer a happy, pretty girl, she was a hairless waif, dressed in rags. And there was my father, and I wondered what they'd done to him to make him stagger along as he did – but I didn't want to know.*

They burnt my father next morning and I stood as close as I could. For an instant I met his eyes. He roused out of his stupor, drew in a lungful of scorching air and screamed that he was Benjamin ben Isaac, and that hear all, hear all that the Lord our God is one. Only one. I hope God heard him.

Dolores they burnt a week later, and it was awful, awful, awful. And to one side was Hector, and I walked over to him, spat in his face and promised him he would pay. My husband dragged me away, but not before I saw Hector pale.

My son was born. I didn't care. I painted. All day I painted, and one day I heard that Hector Olivares was tied to his bed, stricken by an inexplicable burning disease. I smiled and added further touches of red and black to my picture.

I recalled Geraldo's story, and I painted exquisite swirls of blue and green, and in the centre a point of beckoning, soothing white. I went to visit Hector, bearing my painted canvas as a gift of sweetmeats on a plate. He looked awful; no youthful radiance, only a suffering husk, eyes sunk so deep into his grey cheeks they shone black, not blue. Did he hope I'd come to forgive him? Heal him? He took the extended painting and looked. Before my eyes he vanished away, and I was filled with black joy – until something clawed at my legs and dragged me along.

So many lives, so many places; these I don't remember nor recall. Not important. I painted. Oh, God how I painted. I fell, and fell, but always to new places, new lives, never back to where I belonged. At my heels was always Hector, accursed, angry Hector, no longer ill and weak, but full of life and purpose; to find me and punish me.

One day I realised one fell towards what one saw at the bottom of the funnel of light. I had painted myself to a dull, dreary place, had to leave, hurry, go, before Hector grabbed me and had me burnt like a witch. I locked myself into my little attic, they banged up the stairs, pounded on the door. I held my painting between my hands, closed my eyes, and in my head rose the image of the previous place – Greece somewhere? Two seconds later I was there.

But no matter how I tried, no matter how hard I prayed, I have not once been able to bring forth the image I need to take me back home. God's punishment, I think. I don't always like God.

Yet another fall through time and I was overjoyed at the sight of the Guadalquivir. This was my river, my city. But not my time. For days I wept. So close, so damned close! And then on a bridge I met him. Magnus. I knew immediately he was meant for me. Did he feel the same? Hands hovering millimetres from each other, eyes that met, darted away, met again. My man. A new life, a new beginning. My past receded, my hunger to return was dulled. And no Hector. For years and years no Hector.

One day I woke, looked into the mirror and screamed. Not my face, but an old, old face, shrivelled into an elongated raisin. I blinked. The image returned to normal. I began noticing other things. How if I was angry fire rushed through my veins, scalding my fingers.

I spent hours in the shower, before my mirror, looking for signs of my real age. I splayed my hand against a sheet of paper, thought about Hector, and the paper crackled under my touch. And in my brain it grew; a clamour to go back, to die. Maybe that's the way it is; life becomes tedious after years and years of living. But not my life, not my precious days with Magnus.

I fought these whispers. I closed my mind to the alluring sounds and smells of my childhood city that seemed to float constantly around me. One day I succumbed, squeezed out ultramarine and azure on my palette, added dabs of forest green and lime, and began to paint. That is five – no, six years ago by now. My studio is littered with my magic swirls, and not all of them work, most of them don't, they lie flat and lifeless on the table. My magic is dying and exponentially my anguish is growing. What if I don't make it home? Will I ever die, or have I cursed *myself as well as Hector? And where is he? I sense him close, and at the thought my fingers, my toes begin to burn. So much anger, so much hate. I set my digit to an empty canvas and it sizzles and turns black. Oh my God; what have I become?*

Sometimes I sit in my studio, surrounded by all my paintings, and I can hear them; my people, my family spring to life for an instant. My mother laughs at something my father says, my grandfather whistles as he paints. Magic. Dangerous magic. I should burn them all, every single one of them. But I can't. I have to go home, I want to stay here. Magnus. Does he know I love him?

I am Mercedes Gutierrez Sanchez. Once I was Ruth. When I hold my hand up to the light, I see the flames that curl inside my fingers. I must go home – or self combust.

Magnus closed the book. He rested a trembling hand on it, fingers caressing the cover. Why hadn't she told him this before? Now he'd never have the opportunity to hold her hand, comfort her with his presence. I wish you'd trusted me enough to tell me, he thought. In his head rang her laughter. Trust you? My sweetest, sweetest man, I'd trust you with my life. But you would never have believed me. He sighed; no, he probably wouldn't.

"*Herre djävlar.*" He tried to smile at John, hoping to see something in the younger man's face that would relegate all of this to the make believe. Instead he saw shock. Magnus groaned, large hands wringing the note book. Why, oh why, hadn't he thrown it out with all the other rubbish in the cabinets?

John extricated the notebook from Magnus' hands.

"It's late," he said, "let's go to bed. We can talk about it tomorrow."

With John's arm around him, Magnus made it up the stairs. And Alex? His little girl, where was she? Had she been catapulted down a funnel just like the unfortunate Geraldo?

CHAPTER 10

"This is beautiful," Alex murmured a few days later as they stood on a crag. He didn't reply, his arms open to embrace all that openness. "Where exactly are we going?" She shaded her eyes as she looked towards the south. He took her by the shoulders and turned her southwest.

"There." He pointed into the hazy distance.

"And how much longer will it take us?"

He shrugged. "A week? Two? I don't want to walk straight back." He smiled down at her. "If you release a homing pigeon, where will you look for her?"

"At home."

"Precisely."

"They will always come looking," she said.

"Aye, but once I'm home, I'll get fair warning."

"Not if that bloody Luke is still around."

"He isn't, and if he is, he'll rue it. Hillview is closed to him. "

He turned her back south and drew a half circle to indicate how they had walked, moving vaguely northeast for some days before beginning the long turn west. He stood with his hands on her shoulders and sniffed her, inhaling her scent. He tightened his hold on her shoulders, and she leaned back against him. He let his hands slide along her arms and sat down, pulling her down to sit beside him.

"My mother hated this," Alex said. "She said it felt like the heavens were planning to fall on her and squash her flat. Magnus always laughed when she said that, promising he'd stand and hold the sky above her head should it happen. It didn't comfort her in the least, and she'd sigh and tell him that she was a city girl, and that to her nature at its best were the planned gardens in Seville, her home town."

"Well, to each his own, aye?" Matthew laughed.

"A cada uno lo suyo," Alex nodded, "one of my mother's favourite expressions."

Matthew lay back against the warm rock, staring up at the nothingness above. Should the sky fall down he imagined it would be like being smothered in a featherbed, a slow drowning in an enveloping softness.

His mind leapt from one kind of enveloping softness to another, and he lay in the sun with his eyes closed and felt his cock stir. He wondered what it would be like, to undo those glinting buttons in her djeens and slip them off her, and if she'd want to keep that bra thing on or not. Not, he decided, sinking into a far too pleasurable daydream, one hand moving downwards. He sat up so fast it made his head spin, looking down at Alex who lay beside him, a contented expression on her face.

"So, you're a Catholic." Unfortunately; all papists were destined directly for hell.

She opened one eye. "I am?" she sounded very surprised, and Matthew swallowed back on a chuckle.

"Well, aye; if your mother's Spanish, she's a Catholic, and then so are you."

Alex made a very disinterested sound. "I don't think I've even been baptised, and I've definitely never been to mass or confession or all those other things you'd do if you were a Catholic."

"You're not baptised?" He was scandalised.

Alex opened both eyes, raising herself on her elbows. "I don't think so. My parents weren't that much into religion."

"But..." He cleared his throat. "That means you're a heathen!"

"No I'm not! Heathen are people living in primitive countries that have never even heard of God. If anything, I'm agnostic."

"Agnostic?" Matthew said. "Do you mean to tell me you don't believe in God?"

Alex regarded him with obvious caution. "Of course not, it's just that I don't think you need to be part of a church to believe in God. I can just as well pray to Him here, out in the open, as in a dark and smelly little chapel, right?"

"Hmm." He decided to drop the subject — after all, her spiritual welfare wasn't his concern. But deep inside he knew that he wanted it to be, every facet of Alex' life he wanted to be his concern. It shook him to the core to admit that.

"You don't speak much of your mother." Matthew broke an agreeable stretch of silence.

"No," she said, all of her signalling that with this very short answer the subject had been broached, discussed and closed.

"Why not? You talk so much about your father. Is she dead?"

Alex sighed. "As far as I know she isn't even born yet, is she?" She looked away, hands clenching into fists.

"You know what I mean."

Her reticence was making him curious. He let his eyes travel over her, wondering if her mother had bequeathed the strong bones, those tight, pointed ears with no earlobes to talk off, and that wee dimple in her cheek. He narrowed his eyes, trying to recall who she reminded him of. He was inspecting her far too openly and she frowned.

"I hate it when you do that," she said, levering herself over the side of the crag. She dropped to the ground and stood waiting for him.

"Do what?" He landed beside her.

"Look me over as if I'm a choice piece of steak." She sat down at the base of the rock. Matthew muttered an apology and lowered himself to sit beside her. He snuck a look at her, his brain snatching at several half baked comparisons. Sweetest Lord! He reared back from her, muffled an exclamation.

"What?" she asked.

"Nothing." Margaret! She could be Margaret's sister!

"Why are you looking at me like that?" she demanded, brows pulled into a frown.

"It's nothing, I sat down on a thistle or such." He made an affair of looking for this thistle, all the while peeking at her.

Slowly he relaxed; aye, there was a resemblance, even a strong resemblance, but it was no more than that. Both had blue eyes, both had the same well defined, arched brows and similar facial structure, but Alex' hair was a vivid, curling brown, here and there threaded with strands of treacle and honey, glints of deep, dark reds. Not like Margaret's waves of black, a rippling pelt of shiny silkiness that fell like a waterfall down her back when she pulled out the pins. He leaned back against the crag, cleared his throat and smiled at her.

"So, your mother."

Alex closed her eyes and pretended to sleep. She didn't want to talk about her mother. Even leaving aside that last, horrifying afternoon – no, don't go there – Mercedes had been uncomfortable to grow up around. Too intense, too ... well, weird.

He kicked at her foot. "Alex!"

"Why do you want to know?"

"Why don't you want to talk about her?" he asked back.

She hitched her shoulders.

"Ah, lass, I'm sorry. Is she dead then?"

Alex shook her head, feeling an uncomfortable rush of heat up her throat and cheeks. She had no idea; she supposed Mercedes was dead – she should be – but she wasn't sure, not anymore. Alex pulled her legs close and studied the barren landscape. No cars, no distant tractors, no distorted music from a passing vehicle. She missed that, all those sounds that she belatedly realised had tied her to her time.

"Mercedes," she said, "her name is, or will be Mercedes."

"Mercedes, aye? And that's a Spanish name?"

"Well it certainly isn't Swedish or Scots," she replied with irritation. "Her first name was really Maria de las Mercedes, but as every second woman in Spain is called Maria in one form or other she was always known as

Mercedes. And her sister was Dolores, but I never knew her. She's dead." And taboo; Mercedes clammed up whenever Alex asked her about this unknown aunt.

"She's an artist," Alex went on, smiling at the memory of her mother in front of her easel; smudges of crimson and cobalt on her hands, emerald green streaking her arms, and that ubiquitous cigarette, lying forgotten in the ashtray as Mercedes bent forward to add yet another miniscule dot of zinc white to her latest masterpiece.

"She painted the occasional cat or horse for me, but mostly she painted..." Her voice drifted off as she tried to think of how to explain the disturbing canvases that flowered from her mother's hands. "I think she painted grief, grief and loss, you know?"

"How'd you do that?" he asked.

"I don't know. But when you looked for too long at her paintings it was as if a silent scream built inside of you."

Matthew looked pale and Alex laughed dismissively.

"Silly, right? I guess she was good with her brushes, twisting those columns of colour so that they pulled your eye in; always red and orange, always like a huge fire that surged and struggled against the constraints of the frame." Alex stared off across the faded greens and browns that stretched in silence all around them. "Sometimes she painted small canvases, blues and greens with the odd dash of white. John always complained that they gave him a headache, made his stomach heave, and he's right, they were rather weird, disconcerting somehow."

She felt a sharp twist inside at the thought of John. What was he doing now? Would he believe Diane when she insisted that she, Alex, had decided to go AWOL, or would he know that she'd never do that?

"You don't speak much of him, John, either," Matthew said.

"Well, you don't speak too much about her, Margaret, do you?"

"No, but if you want me to, I will."

"It's not really any of my business, or is it?" Her eyes caught his and held them, and they sat like that for some time, green locked into blue.

"Mayhap it is," he smiled, and stretched out a finger to run down her cheek. All of her thudded, wanting him to touch her some more, but instead she sat back, forcing him to drop his hand.

"Maybe; and if you tell me about her, I'll tell you about him."

He splayed his hand so that his little finger touched hers. She closed her eyes and concentrated on her breathing.

He helped her back onto her feet, holding on to her a bit longer than necessary. Blood was flowing so swiftly downwards it left him lightheaded, and his fingers tightened round her hand as he struggled to bring himself back under control.

He couldn't walk like this, with his privates a coil of aching tension and throbbing blood. For an instant he saw himself pulling her back down onto the grass, saw how he struggled with her odd breeches and ... He snaked an arm round her waist and pulled her close, ignored her little "oh" of surprise, and kissed her.

She stiffened at first, hands flat against his chest. But then an arm slid round his neck, the other followed suit, and he drew her even closer. She opened her mouth to his, and she tasted of tart, unripe blackberries, of the grass stalks she'd been chewing as they walked, and, very faintly, of smoked fish.

He just couldn't let her go, and she didn't seem to mind, grinding her hips against him in a way that made him groan. Ah, Jesus; he was on the verge of losing all restraint, and so, seemingly, was she, a pliable warmth in his arms.

He released her so abruptly she nearly fell. She stepped back, an unreadable look in her eyes.

"I'm sorry," he stuttered. "I shouldn't ..." His chest was heaving, as was hers, and in silent consent they turned away from each other, a moment in which to collect their thoughts and regain a semblance of control over themselves.

When they began to walk he took her hand and she let him, opening her fingers to braid them close with his. All that afternoon they said nothing at all, but their intertwined hands seemed to fuse together and it was with reluctance he let her go to set up their camp for the night.

"Is it safe?" Alex nodded at the little fire.

He gave her an amused look; ever since their run in with the soldiers she was constantly scanning their surroundings, and now she half rose, doing a full turn before sitting down again.

"Like a bloody neon sign," she muttered, kicking in the direction of the fire.

"Neon sign?"

"A huge, illuminated signpost. Maybe we should put it out." She glowered at the cheery little blaze.

"Why? We've not seen any sign of them for days, have we?"

"No, but still…"

Matthew produced cheese and bread and she subsided into silence while they ate. But she kept up a constant vigilance, eyes flying from one outcrop of stone to the other.

"Alex," Matthew sighed, "you need not worry – not now, in the dark. They'd never risk their horses over this terrain at night." When she continued to look unconvinced he placed a hand on her leg and gave it a little shake. "Trust me."

"Huh," Alex said, but he could see her relax. To further distract her he rummaged in his bundle, extending something to her.

"Here; it must be cold with nothing but a shirt on you at night."

She unfolded the woollen shawl and beamed at him.

"But what about you? Those ratty blankets of yours have more holes than threads in them."

"I got me a plaid." He didn't intend to tell her he'd stolen it – and the shawl.

"Shall I tell you then?" he said. "About Margaret?" She nodded and scooted closer. "I first met her when she was six and I was eleven," he began, and Alex slipped her hand into his, making him think of very many other things than that far gone day when Margaret was brought to live with them, perched in front of his father on his big grey. He sternly told himself to concentrate.

"She was an orphan, and my father had been given wardship over her, him being an elder of the Kirk." Da had been present at the hanging of Margaret's father, and seeing as the lassie was left destitute and alone he had offered to take the girl in and raise her.

"Poor her; both her parents were dead?"

"Aye." Well; as far as they knew, the mother supposed dead. "She was quite wild, and it took Mam time to tame her, to make her comb and braid her hair, to say her prayers and stop trying to run away. Poor wee Margaret, she was always crying for her mother." He looked at Alex and tugged on her hand until she was sitting close enough that he could feel the warmth of her along his side. She smelled of green wood and winter apples, sweet and somehow soft.

"Margaret and Luke were of age, and over the coming years those two ran Mam and Da ragged with one wild prank after the other. They were much younger than me and I didn't notice them except at mealtimes. And then for several years I was gone from home, and when I came back they were no longer wee, but still doing everything together. People talked, but Da chose to wave it off, reminding the speaker that those two, Luke and Margaret, were like brother and sister, nothing else."

"Why were you away from home? Did you go to University or something?"

"University?" Matthew laughed. "Me? I'm a farmer. No, I was in the wars, for four years I was a soldier of the Parliament."

"But… you can only have been a boy!"

"I was fifteen when I joined, nineteen when I rode back home." And by then a king was dead, his son in exile, and the dawn of a new world stood bright around him, he thought ironically.

"Anyway, one night Da found them in the hayloft and he had Luke beaten to an inch of his life and sent away the next day, leaving a weeping and desolate Margaret locked up in her room."

"What; he threw Luke out for sleeping with her? That seems kind of harsh, no?"

"Aye well; Da and Luke had not been seeing eye to eye for quite some months by then."

"But he was a child! You don't just throw your son out like that."

"He was all of fifteen, fully capable of making his own way in the world." He could hear himself how defensive he sounded.

"At fifteen?" She shook her head.

"At fifteen I was serving as a soldier," he said sharply.

Da had mayhap been hasty in throwing Luke out, and Mam had been distraught for days, a constant shadow at Da's heels as she pleaded with him to reconsider. Too stubborn at times, was Da, and Mam's nagging had, if anything, set his mind even more. And Luke had it coming; months of open defiance, far too many complaints regarding his carousing ways in Cumnock, and then that time when he'd told Da he was old enough to make up his own mind, and that he, Luke Graham, was for the king, no matter that Malcolm Graham was a Covenanter. Youthful bragging, no more, but blasphemous in a household where the eldest son had served in the Commonwealth armies.

"And then what happened?" Alex said.

Matthew hitched his shoulders. Margaret had wept for days, but once she emerged from the chamber she shared with Joan she had concentrated all her attention on him. It had surprised him to discover that the lassie had grown into quite the swan, and he had spent several evenings watching how she moved, how blue her eyes were and how bonny she was when she laughed. He sneaked a quick look at Alex, so uncomfortably similar to Margaret, and just as quickly looked away.

"She was a very pretty lass, aye?"

"So you fell in love with her," she said, a smile tugging at the corner of her mouth.

"I did," he sighed, leaning back against the rock. "Mam tried to warn me, Joan as well, but Da ... well, the thought of his ward having been despoiled by his son stuck in his craw, so he was glad to see the way I began looking at her over the coming months, encouraging me to do the right thing by the lass. And she seemed to enjoy my company, spending all her time with me."

Long evenings out in the stable, him sweeping and currying, her sitting talking to him; summer afternoons when she'd appear on the edge of the field, her hand shielding her face from the sun as she looked for him. The way his heart leapt at the sight of her, how her hands would leave him trembling with want, and him taking at face value what he now recognised had been a desperate struggle to survive in a world where the people she loved were all gone.

"I think she did love me, a little. And had Luke not come back, mayhap it would have been a good marriage. But he did, bastard that he is, appearing on our doorstep five years ago come December."

"That was the winter Da died in the mill race, and no one could understand how he came to be there – he was afraid of water, always kept his distance from the millpond. And as we came back from burying him, Luke rode into the yard, all in flashing silks, his hat decorated with white ostrich feathers." He sighed and disentangled his hand from hers, leaning forward to add another piece of wood to the fire.

"Do you... nay, no matter."

"Do I what?" she said.

He kept his eyes on his twisting hands and cleared his throat.

"Do you at times deny your man your bed?"

"I don't understand, how deny? Do you mean are there times when he wants to but I don't?"

He mumbled something in agreement, looking at her from under his lashes.

"Of course there are, but John's pretty persistent, and, well, I like to, you know, so mostly he manages to convince me even when I don't want to." She took his hand. "Did she?" she said gently. "Did she deny you?"

"She was ill, or she said she was, and when she asked me to please sleep elsewhere, troubled as she was by pains and aches, well I did." He threw Alex a look. What a fool he'd been! "Not always, though," he hastened to add, "and I was tender and careful of her, gentle so as not to hurt her, but she would lie unresponsive in my arms, not at all the lass I wed. When she told me she was with child, I thought that maybe that was it, so I did as she asked and didn't touch her like that... didn't want to force myself upon her, you know?" He looked away into the night.

"I was gone a lot during her pregnancy. There was unrest and I was called to fight, riding back and forth across Scotland to stamp out the royalists. Luke remained mostly at home, and only afterwards did I learn he slept where I should sleep – at her side." His mouth dried up with acrid bitterness; cuckolded, in his own bed, by his own brother.

He intercepted a pitying look from Alex and turned away, all of him flooding with resentment at reliving these feelings. Night after night in that damned hell house of a gaol he'd relived it, day after day as he was worked as a dog, the only thing he'd seen had been that devastating image of them twisting together in his bed.

All the way from the south to here, it had been that memory and the rage it woke in him that spurred him to go on. But for the last few weeks the image had faded, and he'd slept nights without once dreaming of it, all because of her, the woman sitting by his side as he tore off the scab on this painful wound and retold it all again.

"But... what about your sister? Your servants? Why didn't they tell you?"

"Joan was married by then, and they were discreet. Well, they would be, I suppose." He fell silent and stared into the flames.

"I loved him so much. From the first moment I held him in my arms, I loved my wee Ian, and it was all a lie. When she told me he wasn't mine, I wanted to kill her, but instead I threw her out and kept the bairn, but I couldn't hold him like I used to, and all I saw when I stood by his cradle was her and him, as they were the afternoon I found them." He sighed and hugged himself. "So I sent Ian to her, because how could I keep him and not love him as he should be loved? But sometimes I miss him, and there's a gaping hole in my heart where he used to sit." He busied himself with the fire, anything to keep his face hidden from her.

"Who do you think killed your father?" Alex said, breaking a strained silence.

"Killed him? I told you, he drowned." Matthew looked at her in astonishment.

"But you said, didn't you? That you never understood what he was doing by the water to begin with."

He stared at her, swallowing so hard his throat ached. "Merciful Christ! You think she did? Or him, Luke?"

"I have no idea, but it all seems a bit strange, doesn't it?"

He nodded, recalling the grey, ice cold body of his father and how water ran out of his mouth, his nose and ears when they got him out.

That was the first night they slept spooned together. Fully dressed, wrapped in plaid and shawl but very close, and Matthew fell asleep with her hair tickling his nose and her bottom pressed against him. Too close, he thought ruefully, inching his aching crotch away.

CHAPTER 11

"Your turn," Matthew said the next day. They were walking briskly, both of them huddling against the cold. It was drizzling, a foggy rain that sank through everything, and after only an hour of walking Alex could barely feel her feet. "It's still August," she'd grumbled earlier. "Not bloody October."

"My turn what?"

"To tell me about John." He threw her a quick look and pulled his plaid tighter around himself.

Alex didn't reply at first. The intimacy of yesterday had been difficult to recapture when they woke up cold and wet, and she hadn't known if to take his hand or not when they started off, and now it felt as if it was too late.

"He was the new kid at school, come all the way from London, and we made life hell for him." She laughed, seeing a very confused John standing in the middle of the school yard trying to understand what everyone around him was saying. "I don't really speak Scots," she went on, making Matthew smile. "But I can, if I want to. And I did, playing along with the rest, all of us doubling up with laughter when he misunderstood."

"You went to school?" he said.

"Didn't you?"

"Nay, not really. Da was a fine one for the letters and such, so he taught all his bairns to read and write early on. And I was sent to Glasgow for a year of schooling, but I didn't like it much. I was the new lad, aye?"

She frowned at the implied criticism. "I only did it for the first two weeks and then I ran into him at the disco. Like a dance," she clarified.

Alex looked away, hugging the memory of that particular evening close. She'd been what? Fifteen? And John had shown up in tight, tight jeans and a Ralph Lauren shirt open over an equally tight black t-shirt. When he asked her to dance she'd nodded, and they'd danced all that night and she never spoke bastardised Scots to him again.

"Love at first sight?" Matthew teased, his hand snaking out to take hers. She liked that.

"No," she lied, "he was great and I liked going out with him, but I had other boys to dance with and go out with as well."

"Several lads? At the same time?" Matthew sounded disapproving.

"I danced with them; okay, so I kissed some of them as well, but that's all."

"That's all?" He grinned down at her. "How many lads have you kissed then?"

"I don't know; twelve?" She shrugged in an offhand way. "But I've only slept with…" She made a big show of counting in her head. "…four, including John."

Matthew came to a stop and the look in his eyes made her drop his hand.

"What? Why are you looking at me like that?"

"You've been married four times? You must have been very young, no?"

Alex threw back her head and laughed. "Of course not," she assured him once she'd gotten herself back under control. "I haven't been married even once." If anything his face became even more forbidding.

"Oh aye? So you take lads to bed without being wed?"

"Hey! I live in the future, Mr Prude. I come from a time when women are recognised to have sexual needs, okay? And if I like a man a lot, and I want to and he does too, what's the big deal?"

"Our women don't do that," he said severely.

"No, they seem to sneak behind your backs instead."

For an instant his whole face collapsed, and she saw just how much it all still hurt him before he rearranged his features into a mask of absolute indifference.

"Mostly they don't, and when I wed again it will be to a

woman who will be true to me, only me." His voice ached with yearning and he turned away and walked on up the track, leaving her standing alone and rather ashamed.

"Shit." She sank down to the ground. "John," she whispered, and her eyes filled with tears. "John," she gulped, and began crying in earnest. She'd never see him again, or Magnus, or Isaac. "My son," she moaned, clutching at herself. She wasn't sure if what she felt was loss or guilt, but she closed her eyes and pretended she could stick her nose into Isaac's hair and draw in his scent, that complex compound of baby shampoo, Johnson's Baby Oil and crisp, clean, cotton t-shirts.

"I do love you," she said to the mirage image of Isaac that was skipping before her. Of course she loved him – even if she had at one point wanted to put him up for adoption. Yes, of course she did, even if both Magnus and John loved Isaac much, much more than she did.

It took him some time to notice she wasn't following, all of him concentrated on keeping the rage inside of him under control. He'd told her, and she'd flung it back in his face, and he had to clench his hands not to turn and slap her. Slap her and take her, because she wasn't the woman he thought her to be, and he didn't need to show her consideration, did he? He prickled with shame. He had more or less called her a whore and now he wanted to treat her like one.

"I'm sorry," he said. No reply, and when he threw a look over his shoulder she was not to be seen. With a low curse he retraced his steps.

She was sitting on the grass, her head hidden in her arms.

"Alex?" He sank down beside her, tried to put an arm around her but she shook it off.

"Leave me alone! Just let me stay here and die, okay? I never asked to come here, did I, and now I'm stuck in a time where I'm an immoral freak and all I want is to go back. I want John, I want Magnus and oh God, I want my son." She snivelled and wiped her runny nose with the back of her hand.

Matthew tried again, his arm coming round her, and this time she sat still under his touch.

"I'm sorry, lass, it's a terrible thing to lose a child, in whatever way."

She nodded, resting her head against his shoulder.

"Isaac," he went on, unnerved by the way all of her seemed to be curling inwards with dejection. "It's a bonny name. Wee bit Old Testament." His mild teasing made her smile, albeit weakly. He hugged her and stood up, using both hands to lever her back onto her feet. "Look at you, you're all wet from sitting in the grass."

She looked down at her wet jeans. "I'll live."

"Aye, of course you will." He wasn't referring to the damp. When he held out his hand she took it, her fingers twisting hard into his.

The skies cleared, wild gusts of wind drove fog and clouds away, and a warm sun was steaming wet off the ground.

"Won't his father take care of him?" The laddie was a bastard, born out of wedlock, but such children were often recognised and cared for by their sires. And from the way she said his name, this John seemed a decent man, no matter that they had lived in sin.

"He doesn't have a father."

He struggled to look unperturbed. Not John's son. He couldn't help himself.

"All bairns have a father. But mayhap you don't know who."

She slapped him. "What is it you're insinuating, that I'm a whore? Some sort of irresponsible cow who sleeps around and just gets herself pregnant for the fun of it?"

"Cows would in general be considered irresponsible." He rubbed at his cheek. "I won't have you raise your hand to me again."

"And I'll not have you casting doubts about my character! That's the second time today, you oaf."

They walked in silence up the steep incline.

"He's dead, my son's father is dead."

"Ah." He threw a look at her tight features. "I'm sorry to hear that."

"I'm not. I hope he rots in hell."

He raised his brows in surprise. "I take it you didn't like the man then?"

"You take rightly, I saw him die and I was glad."

He came to an astonished standstill.

"You did what?"

"You heard me," she said, still walking. Her fists were clenched so tight the knuckles stood white against her tanned skin.

He caught up with her and put a hand on her arm. "Won't you tell me? It may be that the telling of it can help."

She looked at him from under tear hung lashes. "How can it help?" She wound her arms tight around her midriff, looking so desolate it made him want to cradle her, whisper words of comfort into her ear. "How will a boy of two grow up without his mother?"

"I don't know," he said, extending an index finger to catch a tear that slid down her cheek. "But doesn't he have other people that love him?"

She hung her head, dug her bare toes into the grass. "Yes, my father loves him. And so does John."

"Well then; that's not so bad, is it? Two men that love him; surely they'll care for him." They began to walk again. "So, will you tell me?"

"Tonight," she said. "I'll tell you tonight."

They were making their way up a low ridge when Matthew drew her to a stop.

"Look!"

At first she thought it might be more soldiers, was already preparing to flee, but when he pointed through the screen of shrubs she saw a stag and a hind, the male deer dancing behind the passive female who had politely lifted her tail out of the way.

"He seems kind of new to this," she whispered, having watched the stag mount and dismount several times. Matthew chuckled, shook his head.

"That's the way they do it," he said in a low voice. "Mayhap it ensures the female is more welcoming."

"Welcoming? If you ask me she looks bored stiff, all she's doing is standing still."

"A good start, no?"

She licked her lips, very aware of the warmth of his thigh where it pressed against hers.

"Although most males can outrun the female and corner her," he added, "make her stand still."

"Really? Are we talking deer or in general terms?"

In the glade before them the stag had gotten it together, and they were silent.

"He looks exhausted," Alex commented once the stag was done.

"He has several hinds to serve, aye?" The deer bounded out of sight and Matthew stood. "Shall we see, then?" he said, helping her to her feet.

"See what?"

"If it applies only to deer." There was a green sheen to his eyes.

He's flirting with me, Alex thought, and her blood fizzed in her veins.

"I'll give you a head start, but mayhap you don't dare to?" He pointed up the slope to a collection of granite boulders. "If you get there before me you're safe."

"And if not?" Alex said, trying to sound casual.

Matthew winked. It made him look very young, and with a little jolt Alex realised that he hadn't done much playing or flirting the last few years. So she nodded, whirled and set off, flying like an arrow in the direction of the stones – after all, she didn't want to make it too easy for him.

He caught up with her halfway up the slope, leaped ahead with the grace of an antelope, and Alex slowed her pace to enjoy the sight of him. He ran effortlessly, long legs striding over the ground. He jumped up to stand on one of the stones, jiggled his hips in a triumphant dance and stood there, grinning at her as she walked the last few yards. He dropped to land before her.

"A forfeit," he said, and his hand rose to touch her hair.

"A forfeit?"

He was standing close enough that unless she tilted her head back all she could see was his shirtfront.

"Aye," he said and then he kissed her.

He was quite good at this, Alex decided, even if it would've been nicer had he brushed his teeth. But what the heck, nor had she, and his tongue was warm and strong, his lips just wouldn't let her go. Alex' arms were round his neck, all of her she pressed against him, and with a surprised squawk he overbalanced and sat down, with her still in his arms.

"Oops," Alex grinned, and she was back on her feet, not quite certain what to do. "We could do it again, but this time you get the head start." She pointed back towards their discarded bundles. "And if I win, I claim a forfeit, right?"

Matthew's long mouth curved into an expectant smile.

"And what would that be?"

"That, Mr Graham, is something you'll find out afterwards – unless you win of course."

They were still arguing amicably as to who had won the race when three men appeared from the surrounding shrubs. Dirty and ragged, one of them barefoot, the others in clunky boots, and all had daggers in their hands. Like rats they emerged, silent and fast. Matthew was sitting with his back to them, but must have seen something in her face and whirled – too late.

Three against one makes for nasty odds, and before Alex had gotten her wits about her they'd pinned Matthew to the ground, laughing at his angry protesting yells. Alex backed away. Not soldiers, but she wasn't all that sure that was a good thing. And those knives ...

They kicked Matthew, telling him to shut up. He curled together. They kicked him again, and Alex' hands tightened into fists when blood spurted from Matthew's nose. It was all she could do to stop herself from flying at them, but what good would that do? They'd probably stab him if she did. No; better wait – lure them away, improve the odds.

She wiped her hands against her jeans. She wiped them again. Stop sweating, goddamn you! One man sat on Matthew while the others rifled through his bundle, muttering with disappointment at the meagre pickings. And then they turned to her.

She saw the gleam of interest in their eyes, uncertain if it was because of her or because of the rings she wore on her fingers. She tensed, a slight shifting as she raised herself onto the balls of her feet, bouncing lightly up and down to find her balance. Breathe; long, deep breaths through your nose. Her pulse steadied.

She let the shawl drop to the ground and one of the men laughed, nodding at the discarded garment.

"Aye," he said, taking a step towards her. "'Tis better if you're willing. Not that I mind if you're not."

He reminded her of an overconfident fly facing a spider – except that she didn't like the idea of herself as a spider. A mouse and a cat? Yes; she could do the cat. He studied her jeans with curiosity and took another step in her direction, his eyes locking on her chest, her mouth. Keep on dreaming, mister.

She swallowed. She hadn't done much real fighting, only once before had she used the full range of her martial skills outside the mat. Big no-no, that. The man's eyes did a cursory run up and down her legs, lingered yet again on her chest and stopped at her hands and ears.

"Give us the rings; the rings, the earbobs, and the pretty link around your wrist."

She shook her head, making him smile in anticipation.

"I'll get it off you anyway, and I don't much care if your finger comes off with it."

"Arsehole," she muttered, loud enough for him to hear. The smile vanished and he moved determinedly towards her.

"You need to be taught manners," the man said. What? He expected her to curtsey and simper while he tried to rob her?

"Really? I would say exactly the same thing about you. Bastard. Son of a bitch." Come on, she urged silently, come on then.

She cast a look in the direction of Matthew; not dead, not even unconscious, but angry like hell, trying to heave his human fetter off his back. The man in front of her took two quick steps, she skittered away. The idiot grinned. Horrible teeth.

"Fearful, are you?"

"Of you? Don't make me laugh." But she sidled away, head twisting as if she intended to run, and the other man snickered, moving to block her escape.

"She won't be quite as loud when we've finished with her, will she?" he said to his companion, waggling his tongue.

She spat at him. "Come closer and you're dead," she threatened and they laughed.

"Give them the rings, Alex!" Matthew yelled. "Just give them the rings and your wee trinkets. It's not worth your life, is it?" He strained against the hold on his neck, raising a bloodied face in her direction. "You can't fight them, they've got knives!" He struggled, but the man on his back sank a knee into his kidneys, there was a glint of metal as the bastard brought his right hand down hard on Matthew's upper back. With a grunt Matthew slumped back onto the ground and Alex wanted to rush to his aid, but her way was blocked by the other two.

"Wise man," one of the ruffians told her, indicating Matthew with his head. "Why fight? It will only mean us hurting you the more."

"You wish, we'll see who gets hurt." Sheer bravado. She gulped; concentrate Alex. One mistake and you're dead – or wishing you were.

She let them get very close, spitting obscenities at them. They laughed, promising her she wouldn't forget the coming afternoon. No, she probably wouldn't. She licked her lips, had to swallow a couple of times. Aim for the head – or the balls. Or both. Oh God; here they come.

When they were within reach she exploded, a kicking dervish that flew at them. Thwack! A head jerked back. An astounded gasp, hands that grabbed at her arms. Aah! What was that? Alex stumbled back. He'd kicked her in the shin, the bastard.

Only one of them was standing, the other was trying to get back up. She yelped when the dagger swished by her face. She crouched; the man sneered. Two steps to the right, he mirrored her. She raised her arms, hands held straight and stiff. He jabbed at her with his dagger. His eyes slid over her shoulder, at the last moment Alex threw herself to the side and the other man stumbled to his knees with his own momentum, the dagger digging into the moss.

She wheeled and kicked, did it again. And again. And again. Again. Again. Air whooshed, spines sagged. There was a dull tinkling as an unhanded dirk landed on a stone. Alex turned towards Matthew and the third man stood and fled.

Matthew stared at her. "What was that?"

"I kicked them," she whispered, and collapsed to her knees. "Shit," she said, hiding her face in her hands.

"You kicked them? You killed them!" He groaned as he sat up. His shoulder!

"They're not dead – at least I hope they're not."

"I don't, I hope they're very dead. Scum." He got to his feet and scowled at Alex. "You should've given them the gold, you shouldn't have tried to fight them. What if they'd knifed you?"

"But they didn't, right? I knew I could take them out."

Matthew mouthed 'take them out' a couple of times, eyeing the two prone bodies.

"You were lucky, they could have hurt you."

"I couldn't give them this ring, it's my engagement ring, John's ring."

He was washed by a wave of jealousy for this unknown John, but restricted himself to a tight nod. He bent down to study the two men.

"They're dead," he pronounced, giving her an admiring look.

"Oh God, I'm not allowed to do that." Alex paled, looking so greensick he worried she might vomit.

"What do you mean?"

Alex gnawed at her lip. "My mother insisted I had to learn self-defence, she said all women had to know how to fight their way out of tight corners."

Matthew nodded his reluctant approval, dabbing at his bloody nose with the tail of his shirt.

"You should leave it to your men, but I'm glad you could fight for us both today."

She hitched her shoulders. "I'm not supposed to kill, only defend myself. Not hurt someone else."

Matthew laughed. "You think your mother sent you to learn to fight with the intention that you never use it?"

"Yes, I think she hoped I wouldn't have to." She inhaled and held her breath for a couple of heartbeats, did it again. "Let's get out of here," Alex said in a breaking voice. "I don't want to stay close to…"

Matthew followed the way her eyes darted back and forth between the two dead men.

"Sit here, I'll take care of it. We can't leave them out in the open. Even dogs deserve to be buried." He ignored the burning sensation in his shoulder and right arm, working one handed to heave the bodies down a small crevice and cover them with stones.

Once he was done he came over to where she was sitting.

"We'd best get going, I'd prefer it if we were well away from here before nightfall."

She stumbled to her feet, eyes a very dark blue. "Will they hang me?"

"Hang you?" Matthew shook his head. "They'd have to catch you first, no?"

"Oh," she squeaked, clearly not comforted.

"They won't. No one will ever know."

"But he ..."

"The third one? I dare say he keeps well away from the long reach of the law."He choked back a gasp when he settled his roll on his mangled shoulder and succeeded in giving her a small smile before leading the way up the closest slope.

CHAPTER 12

"Hi." Diane looked very energetic, appearing at John's door well before nine. She laughed at John's bleary face. "The early bird catches the worm, remember?"

He swung the door wide. "Any particular reason for your visit?"

"No, not really." She detoured to greet Isaac.

There was something so natural in how Diane approached Isaac, genuine liking colouring her voice as she talked to the boy- none of that cautious reserve with which Alex often treated her son. Isaac grinned up at Diane, handed her a piece of his crumbling Duplo tower, and scooted over to make room for her when she knelt down beside him.

"Coffee?" John asked.

Diane gave Isaac a parting pat and moved over to where John was looking for clean mugs.

"I just wanted to say I'm sorry," she said. "I didn't mean to upset you the other day."

"Upset me?"

"You know; about Isaac."

"Oh, that." Eons ago. When he was still trying to convince himself both Mercedes and Alex might one day resurface.

"And when you didn't come in to the office yesterday or the day before, I thought ..." Diane shrugged.

John blinked. He'd spent the last few days in Magnus' garden, more or less zonked out of his mind.

"I was with Magnus," he said, pouring them both some coffee. "In fact, I'm going there later today. Want to come?"

"Is he alright?" Diane sounded concerned. He threw her a look, wondering if her eyes had always been this green or if she was using contacts to enhance the colour.

"Alright?" John shook his head. "No, I don't think he's

alright – and especially not after finding that notebook."

"Notebook? What notebook?"

So John told her, deciding that Diane was an exception to the never tell rule they'd agreed on. Diane heard him out in silence, scepticism shining out of her eyes. She clouded when he told her of his run in with Hector.

"I don't like him," she said, "there's something off about him."

"But he does seem to be telling some sort of truth, no?"

"Truth?" Diane raised her brows. "Just because Mercedes has written something down, it isn't necessarily the truth, is it? Let's face it; there were days when she was very, very weird."

No wonder, given her life, John sighed.

"We're going to burn them," he said. "The paintings. Today. Magnus wants to – just in case. I don't think he'll mind if you come along." John had no idea really, but somehow having Diane's cool intellect beside him helped.

Magnus seemed glad to see Diane, his eyes crinkling together when she hugged him. He was looking worn, the unshaven cheeks bristling silver in the sun.

"You've not been eating," she frowned, poking him in the gut.

"No, it hasn't seemed that important lately."

Diane huffed and strode off to the kitchen, a very loud clatter indicating that they were all going to eat, soon.

Strangely enough, it was a relaxed meal – very much due to Diane, who pulled out all the stops and was a constant cheery presence, ensuring the conversation stayed well away from the subject of Alex and Mercedes.

Only once they'd finished their dessert did she ask to see the notebook. With a sigh Magnus went and fetched it, handing it over to her in silence.

"Well." Diane closed the covers, looking rather pale. "Forceful."

"You can say that again," John said from where he was

stacking the dishes into the dish washer. He straightened up and wiped his hands. "We'd best get started, no?"

Magnus nodded and led the way to the studio.

Isaac looked round the large, light room, small hands reaching out to caress paint tubes and brushes and the prepared but as yet empty canvases that stood stacked to one side.

"I want," he said, grabbing a tube of cadmium yellow. He lunged and crowed happily at the tube of cobalt now also in his hand.

"Do you mind?" John asked Magnus. "Is it okay if I sit him down somewhere with paints and a brush? I'll promise I'll clean up afterwards."

Magnus gestured at the paint spattered floor. "One more dash of yellow won't show up. But these are oil paints and it will be quite the chore to clean him off."

Isaac gave Magnus an offended look. "I know," he said importantly and waved a brush at him.

John and Magnus shared a look; John shook himself. Fancies; all children liked to mess about with colours.

Once Isaac was settled at the large table, they turned towards the furthest wall and the long line of finished paintings, all facing inwards.

"How do we do this?" John said. "It's not as if we can light a bonfire in your yard, is it?"

"Why not?" Magnus said. "Who's to know?"

Diane looked at the paintings and back at him. "They're very many, it'll take ages to burn them." Magnus just nodded and loaded his arms, making for the large windows. The pictures fell with splintering sounds as they hit the flags below.

"Well get on with it," he snapped. "We haven't got all day, do we?"

"Magnus?" John went over to him. "What's wrong?"

"Nothing's wrong! Everything's great. My wife's some sort of witch, and my Alex has apparently dropped through time. How can you possibly think that something's wrong?"

He glared at John, at Diane, and even at Isaac, before stalking out of the room.

"Oh shit, maybe we should do this some other time." John looked at Isaac. "Come on then, Isaac. Let's go home."

"Don't want to," Isaac said, busy squeezing blue paint onto the table.

"But I do. Come to Jojo."

"And what's with that Jojo crap?" Magnus yelled, reappearing in the door. "Jojo, it makes you sound like a toy. You're his father aren't you?"

John stared at him. He'd never seen Magnus this upset, hair on end, blue eyes narrowed.

"That was Alex' idea," he said. Her way of getting her own back, jealous as hell of Isaac's obvious preference for John.

"But she's gone!" Magnus rammed his fist through one of the canvases, "She's gone and she'll never come back, and the only parent that little boy has is you. You're his Dad, you hear? Not some fucking stuffed animal!" He sucked at his bleeding knuckles.

"Okay, fine; I'm his Dad," John said soothingly. "Isaac, come to Daddy."

Isaac shook his head. "No. Want to draw." He held up one very blue hand and grinned. He looked at Magnus and then at John. "Offa," he said, "Offa's mad."

"No," John said, "I think Offa's sad."

"Huh." Magnus wheeled away to stare out the window. "I want to do it now," he said in a controlled voice after a while. "I'm sorry about just now, it got a bit too much."

"Sure," John said, "I understand."

They started with the larger canvases, and Diane insisted that they should at least look at each picture before throwing it out the window in some sort of belated gesture to Mercedes. Their sense of discomfort grew as canvas after canvas depicted the same thing; fire, heaving blood red fire with something twisting at its midst.

"Her sister?" Diane asked.

"Or her father, calling out to his God," Magnus said.

John had problems tearing his eyes away. "Don't you feel it? How it sort of calls to you?"

Diane nodded.

"No," Magnus said. "If I hadn't read the notebook I wouldn't even have seen it as a bonfire, more like someone experimenting with surrealist sunsets." He bent down to drag a huge, framed canvas to stand. "Ugh!" he grunted, "this bloody thing weighs a ton!"

John came over to help him and together they manhandled the painting upright.

"Hector," John said, "it is, isn't it?"

"Yes," Diane agreed.

They studied the picture in silence; a serious man, fiery hair falling to his shoulders. Arched brows, a mouth that seemed undecided as to whether to smile or press itself together further, the upper lip bisected. And those eyes, hard and forbidding they stared back at them, gemstones on the point of exploding. His hand rested on the table beside him, a glove held casually in it, and on his head sat a magpie, beak half open as if it were laughing.

It was a strange picture; when they moved closer the image dissolved and reshaped, and suddenly Hector was naked, his face an anguished scream, small fires flickering around him. They drew back and the calm grandee stared back at them.

"Bloody hell," Magnus said, "how does she do that?"

"I don't know," Johns said, shaken by the agony in that contorted face. Together they picked up the portrait and walked over to the window. "Poor sod; may you find some peace however big a bastard you are," John said as they flung it down to join the pile below.

"Why thank you." They whirled to find Hector leaning against the door, one hand resting on Isaac.

Hector eyed them with amusement, threw a look at one of the large bonfire paintings, and tightened his grip on the boy. He scanned the room; several times over the last few years he'd sent men to this address to do some discreet breaking and entering, but each and every one of the canvases they'd brought back had been useless.

Twice he'd been himself, but ever since that idiot Charlie had bungled it so completely back in January, Magnus Lind had upped his security, making further trespassing somewhat difficult – as he well knew after his own attempt a few weeks back. Still, now he was here, and all of him quivered, his body straining towards the stacked canvases.

"Take your hand off my son!" John was halfway across the room.

"Now, now," Hector said, producing a knife. "Let's all calm down. And if we're to be quite correct, this little bastard isn't yours, is he?"

John snarled, baring his teeth in a primitive gesture of defiance. Hector laughed and swung the boy up into his arms. The child yelped, a high pitched sound that irritated Hector's auditory nerves.

"What are you going to do? Burn them?" Hector said, holding the squirming boy under his arm.

"Yes," Magnus said, "all of them. You know, like you made sure Benito and Dolores did."

Now how on earth did Magnus Lind know that? Hector frowned at him.

"Benito Gutierrez was a false convert, crying out to his father's God at the stake. It was just that they died, he and his daughter, and how unfortunate both daughters didn't burn. I was only doing my civic duty, protecting my faith."

"Of course," Diane said. "How silly of us not to understand; raping young women is always an indication of high religious values."

Hector glared at her. The only person who knew about that was Mercedes. Had she left them some sort of message?

"Dolores was a little whore," he said viciously. "For almost three years she met me in secret, received trinkets and flowers, shared my wine cup, my bed. And then..." He just shook his head. He had no reason to retell that long gone afternoon when Dolores had realised he had no intention of wedding her, or the subsequent fight. He fingered his upper lip, recalling just how close her eyes had been when she sliced the paring knife across his mouth.

"Let my grandson go," Magnus said, advancing over the floor. "Set him down and leave before I rip your heart out." Once again the blade shone in the lamplight, freezing Magnus to a standstill.

"You want the child, I want a painting. I'm sure we can reach an amicable agreement." Hector turned the boy the right way up and studied him briefly. "He looks just like his grandmother."

"Yes, and we can imagine just how much that thrills you," Diane muttered.

"I can't say it does." Hector glanced at Diane, at the two men, and retreated a pace or two, making for the paintings. He moved quickly, the screaming child dangling under his arm. "I don't even know if I have grandchildren."

"Hopefully not," Magnus said.

Hector gave him a cold look, changed his grip and the boy spluttered, legs kicking.

"Fragile, no?"

"Stop! Please stop!" Diane begged.

Hector released his hold and used his knife to beckon John forward.

"You," he said, "I need you to flip through all those paintings." He pointed at the stacks of postcard size paintings, hundreds and hundreds of them.

"Me?" John croaked, eyes hanging off his crying son.

"You." Hector watched him stumble towards the small canvases, noted his reaction to each and every one. The young man looked about to faint, all of him trembling as he handled those squares of beckoning blues and greens. Interesting; like a human antenna. Hector took his time choosing, but finally he selected three and had John place them right side up on the huge table.

"I would suggest you back away, unless you want to be dragged along as well."

"Isaac," John said, "my son…"

Hector looked down, surprised at seeing the boy who still dangled from his arm.

"Go and stand by the door." Once they'd complied he released the child, a small shape that flew towards the safety of his father's arms.

Magnus was already moving to grab Hector, but Diane latched on to his arm.

"No, don't get too close!"

The air around Hector shimmered, strands of colour dancing round him. Hector seemed to be praying, leaning towards the painting. A bright, white light poured out of the picture, and before their shocked eyes he sort of dove into the little square of twisting greens and blues and faded away, piece by piece. His head, his shoulders, one arm, the other… and all the time they heard him shriek, a disembodied sound that echoed through the room. With a rush of air he was gone, and on the table the bright turmoil of oils lay beckoning, whispering that they should come and look, look and drown in that white, elusive centre.

"He's gone," John said. He gulped air, kissed Isaac's head. Magnus nodded and approached the table, step by careful step. He swept together the paintings by touch alone, keeping his face averted.

"They burn," he said "and no more looking at them, okay?"

John backed away, still clutching Isaac. "I can't, I'm sorry, but I can't bear to be close to them."

Diane patted him on his arm. "Just sit there."

John leaned back against the wall. What on earth had he witnessed? Impossible, he tried, entirely impossible. Diane filled her arms with small, brightly coloured canvases and John could swear he could hear them whispering, begging him to come closer and look. He closed his eyes and all along his arms and back sweat ran in small rivulets, ice cold trickles against his overheated skin.

"Do you think he made it?" Diane dumped her pile out of the window.

"Made it?" Magnus asked, breaking a canvas over his knee.

"Well, yes; back to his time."

Magnus gave her long look. "Frankly Diane, I don't give a damn. I hope he rots in limbo forever."

* * *

Hector landed with a painful thud, had to lie still for some moments while he forced air back into his lungs. All of him seemed whole, but he knew from past experience that he would be covered with bruises, the odd burn. Not that he cared, because at present his major concern wasn't his health, it was where he was.

All around was silence, an unthreatening lack of sounds that indicated he was miles from any human habitation. Still he sniffed, hoping to be assailed by the scents of trapped summer heat, the stench of the Guadalquivir mudflats. Nothing. He was surrounded by grass and shrubs, a landscape devoid of anything that resembled his city.

With a groan he rolled over to hide his face in his arms. This wasn't Spain, nor was this his time. This was where Diego was, it had been Diego's face he'd seen just as the funnel closed over his head, and now he was as elegantly trapped here as a fly in a spider web.

"Please God," Hector said out loud, "please just let me die."

CHAPTER 13

It was dusk when they found somewhere to settle for the night. Matthew had been walking in silence for the last few hours, hurrying her along dwindling paths and through thickets where gnats swarmed like blankets round their head. She followed him like a sleepwalker, so immersed in the guilt of having killed two men that she didn't register how he faltered, even stumbled.

"Here?" she said when he stopped. A miniscule stream and only a stand of twisted junipers as protection against the rising wind.

He sat down with a grunt. "I have to rest, this'll do." He closed his eyes. His nose was a swollen mess, encrusted runnels of blood running down into his beard and down one side of his mouth.

"Are you okay?" She put a hand on his forehead. He was clammy to the touch and she sat back on her haunches. "What's the matter?"

"It's just a scratch," he said, moving his shoulder. His shirt must have been stuck to his skin, because there was a tearing sound and a hurried intake of breath from Matthew. She stood up, gnawing her lip.

"First things first, fire and water." She wrapped him in their combined blankets and left him sitting, telling him in no uncertain terms that she'd flay him if he as much as wiggled a toe.

"You've done this a lot, no?" he asked a bit later. A small fire was burning at his feet, the dented kettle set to boil with the aid of some largish stones.

"It happens," she said, concentrating on washing his nose. For an instant her palm rested against his cheek and he leaned into it, closing his eyes with a soft exhalation through his mouth.

"Right," she said once she was done with his face. "Let me see."

"Nay, it's no matter."

"In which case it doesn't matter if I see it, does it?"

He undid his plaid and she put a hand on the dark stain that covered the right hand side of his back.

"Jesus! You've been bleeding like a pig."

Matthew twisted, trying to see.

"Sit still." A strong grip on his shirt and she ripped it clean off him. It made him yelp, and the shivering increased when the cool night wind swept down his bared back.

"*Djävla skit*," Alex said, "*Helvetes djävlar.*"

"I know you're swearing, even if it isn't in English."

"I'm only doing that to spare your sensitive male ears." She'd never seen a knife wound before. Well of course she hadn't; she lived in a world where people got shot rather than stabbed – no major improvement really. "When did he do this?" Her hands traced other scars, faint welts up and down his back.

Matthew raised his good shoulder. "I don't rightly know, mayhap when he was on top and I was struggling to get back on my feet."

She washed him and sat back to think. The wound was still seeping, and now that it was superficially clean she saw that it was deep, having sunk into the uppermost part of the back, just below the shoulder joint. She tore off a huge piece of lining from her jacket and drenched it in scalding water, almost dropping the burning cloth.

If it hurt when she washed the open wound with the dripping cloth he didn't say, but his shoulders dropped when she decided she was done, pressing a piece of dry, soft cloth against the red skin. She found his spare shirt for him in his bundle, tore strips out of the discarded one to tie her primitive bandage into place, and sat back to survey her work.

"Does it hurt?"

He shook his head. She helped him pull the shirt over his head and motioned for him to sit closer to the fire. He closed his hands around the wooden cup of hot water and drank in gulps. He looked much better now that his face was washed, but it worried her that he shivered so.

"Talk to me," he said through chattering teeth. She nodded and helped him lie down with his head on her lap, heaping as much plaid and blanket as she could over him.

"I never finished telling you about John, did I?"

"Nay, you didn't, but you don't have to."

"You told me." She ran her hands over his head, down his back, lost in thought. "We were one of those off and on couples, you know, for some months we'd go out, and then we'd break up, and I'd be really mad at him, so I'd go out with someone else, and so would he, then one day he'd call and we'd get back together again." She decided not to go into too much detail regarding these reconciliations – after all, it was none of his business. Plus he was kind of oversensitive when it came to the sex thing.

"When he asked me to marry him it wasn't a surprise for anyone. We'd been living together for two years and it sort of seemed the natural progression of things, you know?" Alex smiled, caressing the ring on her third finger. "And then he went and ruined it." And if they hadn't fought so bitterly, if she hadn't flung his ring in his face and stalked off, she'd never have met Ángel and …

"What did he do?"

"He screwed my best friend." Stupid John, stupid her, and stupid, stupid Diane.

"Screwed?"

"Fucked."

"Oh, aye,"

"Okay, so it wasn't entirely his fault, we'd had one of our regular fights, this time it was him being mad at me for spending so much time at work, and I tried to explain to him that what with the Millennium looming, I stood to make the killing of my lifetime."

Matthew twisted his head to look at her and she realised she'd totally lost him.

"You work?"

"Of course; all modern women work."

"And the bairns? The home?"

Alex shrugged offhandedly. "Day care for the kids, and most men help out at home nowadays. Well, in the future."

"I stormed off back to Magnus and Mercedes, telling John he could stuff it, I wasn't about to let his insecurities hamper my career, and for a whole week he didn't call or drop by. So come Saturday I decided to go for a night out with Diane, and I ended up in a bar down in Leith." She smiled at his raised brows. "Somewhat gentrified in my day, not the dump it probably is now. Anyway, John was there as well, and he was still angry and hurt, so he said something about not knowing if he wanted to marry a power woman in a power suit, and that pissed me off so I threw my drink at him and left."

"Power woman," Matthew murmured, and she could feel him laughing. He turned his head to face her. "He didn't like that, did he?"

"No, I flung it in his face."

She'd stood outside the bar waiting for Diane, but the twofaced bitch hadn't shown up, so she'd made her way home. Once there, she was so inflamed with anger at John she decided to have it out with him that same night, so she'd rushed over to their apartment, thrown open the door and stood stunned at the sight of John and Diane tangled together on the sofa.

"He just stared, you know? And I wanted to cry, but instead I turned and ran, and the next morning I took a plane to Stockholm, not wanting to risk running into him."

He had come after, trying to explain, but it had all gone very wrong and she'd yanked off his ring and thrown it on the table in front of him and then she'd walked out, vowing to never, ever talk to him again – or Diane.

"My life unravelled a bit," she said, grimacing at the understatement. "And one day I found myself back home with an unwanted child in my belly." By the time she'd made it home, it had been too late for an abortion, and she'd felt so trapped, hating the invasive growth inside of her. Matthew raised his hand to where hers lay on his shoulder and squeezed it.

"John was very stubborn. He rang, he dropped by, he insisted on coming with me for all my appointments. And when Isaac was born I think he loved him from the first moment he held him. I didn't." She hunched with shame, recalling waves of resentment washing over her as she stood staring down at her newborn baby.

Matthew was silent for a while.

"He loves you a lot," he finally said in a rather grudging tone.

"Yes, and I love him."

"What happened to you?" he said later. They were pressed close to each other, she holding him tight to her chest in an attempt to stop his shivering. She didn't reply, and he thrust his backside against her.

"When?"

He made a very irritated sound and twisted round to face her, his breath hitching when he moved his shoulder.

"You know when; when your life 'unravelled'."

She sighed, swallowing back on the gut ripping fear that clawed its way up her throat.

"Some other time, okay?"

He placed a hand on her face, his thumb caressing her cheek.

"I'll hold you to it, lass," he breathed and then he shifted even closer and kissed her, a soft feathery brush that made her lips tingle with want.

He was burning with fever next morning, huddling under his plaid. She had him sit up and drink some more hot water and then she stood and scanned their surroundings, wondering what to do. Further away she could see smoke, and when she stood on tiptoe she could make out a roof.

"Would it be dangerous for you if I got help?" she asked

him, crouching down beside him. He opened bloodshot, watering eyes and squinted at her.

"Aye," he croaked. "I wouldn't want to be like this with strangers." He groped for her hand. "And you, it might be dangerous for you, what with your clothes and hair."

Not her major concern at present. She smoothed a nonexistent lock off his forehead.

"Stay here, I'll be right back."

Alex approached the little cottage on her toes, an eye out for dogs. Everything was silent, a small garden dug at the back, some hens clucking in the yard. She sneaked as close as she could, tensing to turn and run, but there were no movements, no sign of life except for that plume of smoke. Someone had to be there, she thought, inching towards the door. She knocked. No response, and she knocked again, louder. Nothing.

She considered trying the door and stepping inside but decided not to, overwhelmed by fear of being trapped in the gloom. Instead she raided the garden, found eggs in the little coop, but as she turned to leave she felt a twinge of unease. She shouldn't steal, not from people this poor. So she took off one of her earrings and placed it on the stoop, a small stone laid on top of it.

"Thanks," she said, and sped away.

Late that afternoon she understood she needed help. He was shaking with cold, and lying in the damp was not making it any better. She tried to make him eat some leek soup but he turned his face away, a racking cough making him bend double.

"This won't work. If we stay here you'll get pneumonia or something." She heaved him to his feet, ignoring his protests, and half dragged him down in the direction of the cottage.

By the time they reached the door she was as shaky as he was, and she lowered him to sit against the wall before knocking, calling for help. This time the door opened and a small, round woman stepped outside, peppercorn eyes regarding them both with interest.

"Aye?" she said, eyes travelling up and down Alex. Her eyes stuck on the jeans, they flickered over to Matthew, returned to the jeans and locked down on a wheezing Matthew.

"He's ill," Alex said, taking in the starched white collar and equally pristine cuffs. A white cap completed the ensemble, covering most of the grey, braided and coiled hair. It made Alex feel scruffy in comparison.

"Aye, I can see that." The woman leaned forward, and raised a stout finger to Alex' bare earlobe. "You were here before."

"Yes. I'm sorry, but I did try to knock, and I had to find us some food."

The woman shook her head. "You paid, aye?" she said, a twinkle in her black eyes. "You didn't steal. Not like some. You'd best come in," she smiled, showing a row of white teeth. "Get inside before someone else passes by." She stood aside to allow Alex to help Matthew inside, threw a look down the dirt track, and closed the door.

The inside of the cottage surprised Alex, not at all the cluttered dirty interior she'd expected, but a tidy, very bare home. Matthew was bedded down beside the hearth, and after inspecting his shoulder Mrs Gordon sighed and set water to boil.

"It isn't clean."

Matthew barely stirred when they rolled him over on his front, but he gasped when Mrs Gordon sank her knife into the half scabbed wound, slashing it wider than it had been before. Alex sat on him while Mrs Gordon poured hot water over his shoulder, finishing off the procedure by upending a small flask of what smelled like cheap brandy on the raw flesh. Matthew bucked, shrieked, and slumped into a dead faint.

"Ma…!" Alex caught herself in time – Mrs Gordon had insisted she didn't want to know their names.

"It's the pain," Mrs Gordon said with a shrug. "No great

matter, aye?" She produced a curved needle and stitched him together, patted him on the cheek and creaked herself upright.

"Wow," Alex was very impressed by her handiwork.

"I'm a midwife," Mrs Gordon said, "and I do some healing on the side. Stitching is more or less the same wherever you do it, no?"

"So, what are you running from?" Mrs Gordon handed Alex a bowl of what tasted like salty porridge. Not entirely unpleasant, and Alex could make out bits of carrot and parsnip, the odd piece of salted pork.

"We're not running."

Mrs Gordon shrugged. "You'd best be careful. The countryside is swarming with soldiers. It's a dangerous fugitive they're looking for." She threw sleeping Matthew a glance. "Not that he's much of a threat -about as dangerous as a newborn babe in his present state – and just as vulnerable." Her eyes drifted over to Alex, who squirmed under her slow inspection.

"He isn't a fugitive."

"No, of course not; and I'm the Queen of Sheba." Mrs Gordon laughed, apparently very amused. "They had a hanging planned some days back in Lanark, aye? Big, burly fellow with a bad leg. He gave them the slip and now they're looking everywhere for him."

"Well, he's not got a bad leg." Alex tilted her head in the direction of a sleeping Matthew.

"Nay, that he doesn't. But his wrists have been fettered recently, and his back has been scourged and you seem to be travelling very light." Alex opened her mouth, but Mrs Gordon patted her hand. "Nay lass, you don't have to tell me. But you must be careful."

Alex nodded, thinking about Sanderson. It could be him, big and burly with a wounded leg, but why would they want to hang him? She felt a chill in her gut and sneaked a look at Matthew. From what she'd overheard several days ago, the soldiers were convinced Sanderson was Matthew, and on the surface there was some similarity, both of them tall and with dark hair.

"Is it a hanging offence?" she asked in a casual tone. "To escape from prison – err – gaol?"

Mrs Gordon looked at Matthew and sighed.

"Not always, but right now it might be, with all turned upside down as we all sit and wait for the Protector to die. Especially if you're an escaped royalist." Her mouth pursed together as if she'd bitten into a sour rhubarb.

"He isn't a royalist."

"Well, that's good, no? I don't hold much with them myself."

Alex didn't sleep at all that night, Matthew's head pillowed on her lap, his dirk held in her hand. He sweated and shook, and his breathing was loud and raspy, coughing fits racking his body. Alex tried to muffle the noise as best she could, conscious of Mrs Gordon in her bed, however tightly closed the bed hangings.

"Is this my fault?" she asked next morning, "because I didn't manage to clean it properly?" She stroked his head, strong fingers massaging the base of his skull in a way that made him groan and burrow closer, still fast asleep.

Mrs Gordon shook her head. "He's not been well fed for a long time, lass. Look." She picked up Matthew's hand and let her fingers close round his wrist. It looked very fragile, all knobs and tendons, and as Alex ran her hand up his arm, down his back she could count his bones, feel the ridges of muscle and sinews but very little else. "He's been on starving rations for months, poor lad."

Matthew slept through most of the day, but Mrs Gordon seemed unconcerned, assuring Alex that this was in the normal order of things. She did however prod Matthew out of sleep long enough to have Alex help him to the privy, plied him with a large mug of willow bark tea, and watched Alex turn the blankets up tight around Matthew's sleeping form. She was knitting, her needles flying back and forth at an astonishing speed.

"What's your middle name?" Mrs Gordon smiled down at Alex.

"Ruth."

"I'll call you Ruth then, shall I? I can't go on calling you lass." She extended her knitting in the direction of Alex. "Can you knit?"

Alex realised this was some kind of test and nodded.

"My grandmother taught me, but I haven't been doing it much." Actually not at all, not since that Christmas when her single gift to her father had been a narrow but very long muffler, in orange and purple stripes.

"It's restful," Mrs Gordon said and handed Alex needles and a ball of yarn, studying her as Alex clumsily cast the first knots.

"I haven't done this in years."

"Ah," Mrs Gordon nodded.

Early next morning Mrs Gordon came rushing into the house, the full chamber pot still in her hand.

"Quick, soldiers!"

"Soldiers?" Alex got to her feet, throwing a panicked look through the half open door. Yes, she was right. The small yard was filling with mounted men – tired, drawn men that must have been riding half the night to show up here this early.

"Hide, you have to hide."

"But where?" Alex was close to tears, trying to wake a grumbling Matthew. One room, no back door, and in the yard someone hawked and spat. Mrs Gordon set down the chamber pot by the foot of the bed, rushed over, grabbed Matthew by the legs and began to pull him in the direction of her bed.

"Underneath," she panted, "and let us hope he doesn't wake up halfway through, aye?"

Together they succeeded in rolling Matthew out of sight, and at Mrs Gordon's curt command Alex got into bed. A male voice called a greeting, booted feet moved towards the door. A lace cap was crammed on Alex' head, a pillow was shoved into place above her stomach.

"Squeal, aye? Weep and cry, lass, sound like a birthing woman."

"A what?" She clasped her hands over the pillow.

Mrs Gordon didn't reply, busy at the hearth with water and herbs.

"Scream!" she hissed over her shoulder, and Alex complied. "Good, good," Mrs Gordon said, "keep that up, regular like, aye?"

"I'm telling you, we have no fugitive hiding in here." Mrs Gordon stood like a bulwark in the doorway and in the bed Alex squealed like a pig.

"We have to look, mistress," the officer insisted, sounding apologetic.

"Look! How look? And if the lass dies in childbirth while you're at it, what then?"

The officer stuck his head in, bobbed his head at Alex who gave up an extra little shriek. The little officer jumped, his head retracting from the doorway with the speed of a cobra.

"Alex?" Matthew mumbled, sounding very groggy. Not now! "Alex? Are you hurting?"

"Shit, shit, shit," Alex hiccupped. She made a puking sound and hung over the edge of the bed, sounding as if she was dying. "Soldiers," she hissed, sticking her hand in under the bed to squeeze down hard on whatever body part it was she got hold of. Oops! He gasped. She scrambled back up, and when the whole room filled with soldiers she pulled the quilt up as high as it would go. Mrs Gordon came to stand in front of her, arms akimbo as she glared at the soldiers.

"Make haste, I will not deliver a babe with a room full of men, aye?"

Alex did some very credible grunting and whimpering, and when a hand came wiggling up between the bedstead and the wall she shrieked for real before realising whose hand it was. She gripped Matthew's hand and squeezed, eternally grateful for Mrs Gordon who stood like a rock by the bed.

One of the soldiers approached the bed. Alex squawked, eyes on the drawn sword in his hand. What was he going to do? Jab it through the mattresses? Even worse, swipe it under the bed? She screamed, clutched at her make believe belly, and the soldier jumped, retreating a few steps.

Alex panted, didn't even have to pretend panic when the soldier moved closer. He knelt down. Oh God, oh God. He set a hand on the floor. Alex couldn't breathe. There was a loud clatter.

"Now look what you've done!" Mrs Gordon said, and the room filled with the stench of piss.

"Me?" The soldier scrambled back from the spreading puddle. "No, it wasn't me, I …"

"Of course you! Clumsy dolt. And who will have to clean it up, hmm? Who?"

"I'm sorry mistress," the soldier mumbled. "I was just trying to look under the bed."

"Look under the bed," Mrs Gordon snorted. "Here, let me show you, aye?" She grabbed hold of a broom and jabbed it repeatedly under the bed. Every time she hit Matthew, his grip on Alex' fingers tightened, but he didn't utter a sound. Alex did.

For a further few minutes the soldiers remained in the room before the officer sent them off to inspect the outhouses. The officer sat down with a grateful nod at the table to sip at a mug of beer.

Alex counted in her head, screamed and moaned, cursed, counted in her head, and did it all again. Hard work, this giving birth thing; her shirt stuck to her back, but she wasn't sure if out of exertion or fear. The officer drained his mug, bowed and exited the room. Alex fell back against the pillows. Matthew gave her hand a reassuring squeeze.

By the time Mrs Gordon decided things were safe again,

Alex was so hoarse she could barely speak, and quite convinced they should leave –now.

"That would be foolish," Mrs Gordon said. "The countryside is swarming with them, and anyway, your man is in no shape to do much walking, not for a day or two at least."

Her man? A liquid warmth flowed through Alex. Her man? She slid Matthew a look; yes, her man. Soppy idiot, she remonstrated with herself, trying to stop herself from smiling. He was smiling too, a slow smile that lit up his eyes and did strange things to her knees. Back to business; Mrs Gordon was right. No matter that Matthew insisted he could walk, was right fine, it was patently obvious he wouldn't make it far before collapsing.

"They'll not be back," Mrs Gordon said, "not after near witnessing a birth."

"And if they come looking for the baby?" Alex said.

"Well it died, no?" Mrs Gordon shrugged. "Happens all the time."

When they left, two days later, Mrs Gordon handed a wrapped bundle to Matthew and stood back. She refused the matching earring, assuring Alex that she should keep it.

"It may be that we run into each other again, aye? And then we'll know each other by the earbob."

Alex laughed and hugged her, which surprised Mrs Gordon so much she nearly fell.

"Go with God," Mrs Gordon said, a quick pat on Matthew's cheek. "And you child," she added, smiling at Alex. She put a restraining hand on Alex' arm and waited until Matthew had moved away.

"Your middle name fits you, lass. You're truly his Ruth."

CHAPTER 14

"Matthew?"

"Hmm?"

"Who's Ruth?"

He glanced at her. "Haven't you read your Bible?"

"No," she said, irritated by his tone. "I'm the heathen, remember?"

"So you know nothing of the Good Book?"

"Of course I do! I know about Abraham and Isaac, and the twelve tribes of Israel and..." she snapped her mouth shut at his amused look.

"And the New Testament? About our Lord Jesus?"

"Oh, like when he turned water to wine or walked on the lake of Galilee? Yes, I've heard them too." She'd seen a couple of very explicit movies about the life of Jesus Christ – and in particular his death.

"Well that's good then," Matthew smiled, "you're not an entire heathen." She swiped at him and he laughed, swiping back, the laugh becoming a wince when he moved his shoulder.

"I'm sorry," Alex said, "I shouldn't have..."

He waved away her concern. "I'm okay, lass." They shared a quick smile; he'd used her word.

"Okay," she repeated and took his hand.

"Ruth," she said, reverting to her original question. He stopped and took both her hands in his.

"I like Ruth, but why do you ask?"

She squirmed a bit. "It's something Mrs Gordon said." He stood waiting and she was very aware of how her pulse hammered through her wrists and into his thumbs, or was it from his thumbs and into her wrists? She was woozy with his proximity.

"It's my middle name, and as she didn't want to know our real names she asked me for my middle name. And when we left she stopped me in the door and she said ..."

"What?" he prompted.

"That it was an apt name," she mumbled, "that I was indeed your Ruth."

His eyes softened to a golden green, his hands tightening around hers.

"That would make me very glad," he said, kissing her on her brow before turning to walk away from her.

"Hey!" she protested, catching up with him. "You can't just say something like that and then leave me hanging. It makes me feel as if I'm left out, somehow."

"I could find you a copy of the Holy Writ, have you read it for yourself."

Alex looked round. "Where? Unless you think those sheep over there might have a book or two squirreled away under a gorse bush."

Matthew laughed, stopped. He looked down at her and cupped her chin.

"Wither thou goest, I will go; and where thou lodgest I will lodge; thy people shall be my people, and thy God my God. Where thou diest, I will die and there will I be buried. That's what Ruth says."

"Oh." Alex didn't know what else to say, but she was certain she would fall if he took his hand away.

This was getting far too serious, she reprimanded herself as she followed Matthew. She saw him shift his shoulder and wanted to rush to him, place a hand on the sore and itching wound. Bloody Florence Nightingale, she grinned. Except that prim Ms. Nightingale didn't go round with designs on her patients, while Alex, well, she was drowning in want.

Over the last few days she'd grown increasingly more aware of him, to the point where she'd considered turning towards him and just... She swallowed back a gust of nervous laughter. She wondered what he'd do if she did that, if he'd be surprised should she place her hand on his crotch and fondle him. He would probably be horrified at her forwardness, but she was pretty sure she'd be able to take his mind off that rather quickly.

His Ruth. A wave of heat washed up her neck and face. Those words, the way he'd said them, making her heart beat so hard it made her nauseous, and she'd known every single syllable to be true. Poor John, she sighed, never had it felt this way with him. Luckily Diane would be there, standing in the wings with broom and shovel to sweep up the pieces and glue them together.

A strand of bright green jealousy swirled through her head as she saw the two of them laughing over a glass of wine, Diane perched on a stool to watch John cook. Diane settled Isaac on her lap and he leaned back against her chest with a contented smile on his face, and Alex felt a knife tear through her gut. She came to a standstill as she dug for her little doll. She couldn't find it, and she turned out her pockets, rifled through her roll.

"Alex?" Matthew stood beside her. "What's the matter?"

"I can't find it, my baby, your gift. And I need it, because I miss him so much, and I want to pretend that I still can touch him." Matthew fell to his knees and helped her look through the few things again. No miniature wooden baby. "I saw him, I had an image of him sitting in Diane's lap, and he was happy and safe, and I want him to miss me! But he won't, will he? He'll have other adults in his life, and I'll fade to be nothing but his biological mother, the woman who gave birth to him but never saw him grow."

"Of course he'll miss you, but not yet. Later when he grows and starts wondering about who he is, he'll think about you. But right now he's a wee lad who's lost his mother, and it isn't a bad thing if he has others to love him, is it?"

No, she conceded, that was not a bad thing, even if she would have preferred it to be somebody else than bloody Diane.

"He's John's child, much more than mine, in the beginning he was only John's, because I couldn't bear to touch him."

"Because of his father?"

She nodded and dragged a hand across her face. "I was so afraid I'd see him in Isaac's face." She sat down, crossing her legs. "I've never told anyone what happened to me, not even Magnus or John. I just couldn't."She raised her face to meet his eyes. "But I think I have to tell you."

He lowered himself to sit beside her and took her hand in his.

"Why do you think that?"

She nailed her eyes into his and swallowed. "I have to tell someone; and it has to be you."

"Aye," he said, and swallowed just as audibly as she'd done. "It has to be me."

She followed the acrobatic antics of a swift with her eyes. He put a hand on her nape, rubbing slow circles over her skin.

"I told you, didn't I, about that time in Stockholm when I threw John's ring at him and stalked out, right?" Out of the corner of her eye she saw him nod, and she sat for a bit trying to sort her memories from those months into some semblance of order.

She'd been in a foul mood, but four hours and several shopping bags later, she'd decided to treat herself to a real night out on the town.

"So I ended up at Spy Bar, and who should I meet there if not Ángel." She shook her head; not at all a random meeting. Ángel had been following her for a fortnight or so by then, since their first meeting in Dusseldorf, but she didn't know it at the time. All she knew was that she wanted to party and Ángel was a fun guy, however unexpected his presence here in Stockholm.

For a couple of hours they'd sat and talked, mostly about Ángel and his career as a photographer, but also about Seville – their common ground.

"Photo what?" Matthew asked.

"It's a way of making pictures," Alex said, deciding it would take far too long to explain this in detail.

"Anyway; after a couple of drinks, Ángel took me dancing." He was a fantastic dancer and when the music slowed, he held her close, crooning along with the text. He had wonderful hands. Gentle and warm as they floated up her spine, down to graze her buttock, up along her flanks.

He'd made love to her there, on the dance floor, and it was only hands, nothing else. So when he asked her if she, well, would she like to, Alex nodded. They didn't talk on their way back to his hotel room.

It was midday before she managed to leave his hotel — she had to, she had a flight to catch. When she told him she was going to Italy he brightened. So was he, he told her, now wasn't that a coincidence? Coincidence my arse, but she didn't know that at the time, did she?

"I still don't understand how I could be so ... well, naive." She threw Matthew a look; he'd grown increasingly darker as she'd told him about Ángel. Now he nodded somewhat curtly, eyes very green.

"And John?" Matthew sounded censorious.

"He'd left me like a hundred messages. So I wrote him back, telling him I was off to do three weeks of installation work at the Banca Popolare in Milan, and then we'd see."

Three — almost four wonderful weeks with Ángel. Days spent in the dusty offices of the bank, evenings and nights with this experienced and creative lover, doing things she'd never done with anyone before. But she didn't tell Matthew this.

"I think ... well, now I think that he slipped me things, you know?"

Matthew shook his head.

"So much wine, so many colourful drinks, and every now and then he added something to them," she said. How else to explain just how fuzzy those weeks were? And anyway, she'd never have agreed to unprotected sex had she been all there — at least she didn't think so.

In retrospect, this was what confused her the most. Why had he played happy couples with her for those first initial weeks, was it to rub it in just how gullible she'd been? She gnawed her lip; maybe it had just been a delaying tactic while they found the right location, sufficiently isolated to ensure no questions were asked, no matter what goings on.

The day she was supposed to go home, he'd pleaded that she stay a bit longer – he had borrowed a place down in Calabria, and wouldn't she please, please come? So she did, and it was a fantastic house, set in splendid isolation with only the sea and the rocky landscape surrounding it. Not a neighbour in either direction for as far as one could see, and the last stretch of road was mostly gravel and crushed stone. And Ángel dropped her phone by accident into the pool.

On their second day there, two men had showed up. Ángel introduced them as Franco and Roberto, his assistants. Assistants? Oh yes, Ángel was going to utilise this beautiful place to take a whole series of photos – with her as his model. She hadn't liked the way he said that.

For the first time she'd felt a warning drumbeat at the base of her brain, but tried to look unconcerned and told him he'd have to be very quick, as she was only here for two more nights. Ángel just smiled. She'd ended up staying in that damned house for eighty-six more days.

That night Alex was led into the vast dining room, unfurnished except for a large oak table, and on the table was a picture of her mother. Ángel had tapped at the photo.

"Is this your mother?" he'd asked, and Alex had replied that yes, it was.

"And her name?"

"Her name?" Alex had looked at him; given that he had a picture of her, he should know, no?

"Tell me her name."

So Alex had said that this was Mercedes Lind.

"Her real name," he'd said, "not her married name."

"Mercedes Gutierrez Sanchez," Alex had said, not understanding at all. Ángel had punched his fist in the air, shouting that yes, it was the witch, they'd found the witch.

"Witch?" Matthew interrupted.

"That's what he said." She tried to sound dismissive.

"And is she? A witch, I mean?"

She shook her head, disconcerted by how Matthew had latched on to this one thing. Once she would have laughed out loud at his preposterous question, but now she no longer knew – not after the last time she'd seen her mother.

She coughed, trying to clear her throat; they were still executing witches in the seventeenth century, and she had an uncomfortable sensation that being branded the child of a witch wasn't good for your reputation. She decided to continue her story.

After a quick but loud phone conversation with someone called Hector, Ángel proceeded to explain why Alex was here. Bait, he'd said, a juicy worm wriggling on a hook. And tonight … he'd handed her a mobile. She was to phone her mother, give her the first in a long line of instructions. Instructions? Ángel had laughed. Didn't she understand? Hector wanted her to bring her mother here, to them. So that they could kill her, tie her to a stake and watch her burn.

"Burn her?" Matthew stared at her, aghast. "So she was a witch?"

"Ángel was off his head, okay? All of this was some sick, horrible game to him, a game he chose to extend for as long as he could." Three eternal months, to be precise.

Ángel had laughed at her shocked refusal. She was locked into a small room and as he left Ángel leaned forward to caress her cheek. She spat in his face. An hour later she succeeded in breaking the window, clambered out through the narrow opening and jumped. Two hours later she was back, unable to walk, or talk. They'd been waiting for her, and Ángel had beaten her with as much passion as he'd previously shown her in bed. His last blow broke her nose.

Matthew groaned. "But why didn't you…" he mimed a kick and a jab.

"Oh, I tried; but Ángel was just as good, if not better, than me." Reflexively she covered her nose. He'd played with her the bastard, making her think she had a chance to fight free.

"I used to think I was one of those people who'd be really brave, you know?" Alex fiddled with her ring, her bracelet. "It turns out I wasn't."

"Very few are," Matthew said.

Whatever.

Next morning Alex had been supported out of her little room, still in her bloodied clothes from yesterday, and Ángel had sat her down by the large oak table. In his hand he held a hammer. Franco grabbed her hand, pressed it down against the table. Ángel smiled and asked which finger. Which finger? Well, he said, he'd start with her fingers, then her toes, and after that ... he threw a look at a huge set of pliers that lay on the table. Alex swallowed, pressed her knees together, ashamed of the warmth that ran down her legs. So, which finger? Please, she'd said. Ángel had shrugged, and the hammer came down on her pinkie.

"See?" Alex held up her left pinkie. The upper joint was flattened. "He never hurt me again. He never had to." Matthew's hold on her hand tightened.

Over the coming months he reduced her to a nonbeing. She was underdressed and underfed, never allowed one full night of uninterrupted sleep. Roberto would scream her awake at two, Ángel would pour a bucket of water over her at four, and Franco... Alex took a deep breath.

For hours each day Ángel would photograph her, in one more demeaning pose after the other. And while Ángel never raised his hand to her, now and then Franco would, a hard slap when she wasn't fast enough in complying with Ángel's screamed directions. Worst of all was the day he tied her to the stake and ... Alex couldn't go on, gulping a few times.

"I thought he was going to set me on fire," she whispered, "and when he threw the match into the pile at my feet I screamed and screamed. He took photo after photo." And each and every one he sent to her mother .

Everything he told her to say to her mother she did,

from that first phone call in which Mercedes was told not to contact the police or Magnus, to the last ones when she begged her mother to hurry and find her, solve the goddamn clues and find her before these men did something really, really bad to her. Not that she needed a script to say that – she was quite convinced that Ángel would kill her.

"I should have …" she shook her head.

"What? Tried to fight him? And what do you think he'd done then?"

Alex nodded, seeing yet again that hammer, those pliers.

Finally one day Mercedes appeared in a cloud of dust, astride a motorbike. She planted her hands on her hips and yelled for Ángel to come out, come out and be done with her if that was what he wanted, but first he had to free her child – except she had called him Hector Olivares, not Ángel.

"When Mercedes showed up, Ángel flew to the phone and rang this unknown Hector, asking him what he was supposed to do, now that he had the mother standing in front of the door." She hadn't heard the reply, but Ángel had laughed and walked over to the open door. What he'd actually said had been in Spanish: "*Si no entras a buscarla te la devolveré muerta.*"

Mercedes had gasped at his threat to kill Alex and stepped inside. When Franco produced a rope to tie Mercedes with, Alex flung herself into instinctive action. Suddenly Franco was dead, Roberto was screaming, and Mercedes stalked across the room towards a terrified Ángel. Roberto had slammed into Alex who crushed his larynx with her first blow, the following kick throwing him back against the wall with a sickening thud.

"And then it was all over, well, except for the fact that in my belly grew a little stranger, and I didn't want him there." She burst into tears and when Matthew opened his arms she nestled in as close as she could.

Much later she sat in front of the fire and played the closing scenes through in her head. Mercedes had hissed in hatred at Ángel, promising him he would pay for every humiliation he'd put her daughter through. Ángel had stood stock still, incapable of moving as Mercedes sat Alex down on a chair and kissed her farewell. Her touch had singed Alex' skin, leaving blistered imprints on her upper arms.

Mercedes inhaled and stepped up to Ángel, wrapped her arms around him and in one tremendous surge of white heat they'd burst into flame, a silent, intertwined couple that twisted in the fire before evaporating, leaving nothing behind but a sooty sill.

Alex had sat stunned on her chair, and she had no idea who had tied her to it or who notified the police. Neither did they, although the switchboard operator insisted it was a woman, a woman who spoke Spanish, not Italian.

"Oh God," Alex muttered, blinking in an effort to re-consign these awful, awful images to the darker recesses of her mind. It didn't help. With a little groan she rolled towards Matthew, pushing against his solid warmth. An arm snaked out to draw her close, a misdirected kiss landed on her ear.

"Sleep, aye?"

Her last conscious thought was that mostly he smelled of water – cool, clear water burbling over a mossy bed.

* * *

The moment the cretin opened his mouth, Hector knew where he was; Scotland. A few more questions, most of them met by an 'eh?', and he'd gleaned this was sometime in the seventeenth century, and after a wearisome hour, he'd gathered they were closer to Glasgow than Edinburgh.

Hector scowled at nothing in particular, scanning the endless miles of moor that seemed to surround him. How was he supposed to find Diego here? He shook his head at the offered bread, but decided he wanted the knife, the cloak and the cheese. The idiot was still gasping when he left him.

CHAPTER 15

After a couple of days of erratic weather it was blissful to wake in a warm, golden sunbeam. Alex stretched like a cat, limb by limb, and unrolled herself from shawl and blankets, her stomach echoing with hunger. Matthew was busy at the fire, giving her a good morning before going back to watching his birds. She disappeared behind a nearby bush, returned some minutes later with a small twig in her hand that she was chewing into a brush. She frowned at his amused look.

"I told you, no? Unless you clean them they rot and fall out."

In reply, Matthew produced a well chewed twig of his own.

"I heard you," he grinned, running his tongue over his teeth. "They're clean, very clean."

Alex burst out in laughter before going over to kiss his cheek.

"I don't have any teeth there," he said, clearly disappointed.

"Tough." She gave him yet another peck and danced out of range. She threw a quick glance in his direction, meeting eyes that had gone an emerald green. Deep inside of her something contracted, a delicious ache that sent sparks of heat flying through her. This man was driving her nuts; days of kissing, of casual caresses – it made her blood boil. Hell, at times she worried he might see the steam leaking out through her ears or something.

"Are they done yet?" she said, pointing at the sooty birds.

He chuckled. "Soon enough."

"He would've loved this," Alex said as they walked their way through the woods that gathered in the folds of the hills. She had no real idea where they were, but they seemed to be walking west, and they'd crossed the Clyde a few days ago.

"Who?" He took her hand.

"Magnus," she said, feeling a twinge of loss. "He liked trekking, and he'd beg and wheedle and generally be a nuisance, until Mercedes and I caved in and went with him to Sweden or Switzerland or wherever he suddenly decided he wanted to walk." She laughed, shaking her head. "Mercedes wasn't an outdoor person, and she'd complain about everything: it was too hot, it was too cold, too wet. The wine was too warm and why weren't there any decent hotels out in the wilds. Secretly I think she liked it. Well, except for the 'Oh my God, the skies will cave in and squish me flat' bit. At least they seemed to enjoy themselves quite a lot at night, and I would hold my hands hard over my ears. Bloody embarrassing they were, always holding hands and kissing…" She shook herself free of her little reverie. She didn't want to think about Mercedes. Instead she turned to face Matthew and grinned.

"Magnus always used to say that there are three elements to good health; keep clean, eat and drink in moderation, and have as much sex as you can with your partner."

"Sex?"

"You know, make love." She was aware of a wave of blood washing through her and kept her eyes on the meandering pathway at her feet.

"Hmm," Matthew said, clearly as embarrassed as she was. "Well, at least we seem to be eating and drinking in moderation."

She laughed out loud. "I could do with getting clean," she said, sniffing at her shirt. "I haven't had a proper bath in what? Ten days?" Mrs Gordon had offered water and a pewter basin, and she'd washed hands and face, wiped herself as well as she could or wanted in that cramped little space. But that was four, no five days ago.

Now that she thought about it, she noted that she did smell; a ripe earthy smell with traces of smoke and grass.

She scratched at her head. Her hair was greasy and heavy, and she longed for a hot shower and her favourite shampoo to be followed by someone swaddling her in a bathrobe and rubbing her dry. Not likely to happen anytime soon.

I could do with making love, he thought, feeling his balls tighten with want. Near on four weeks with this woman, long evenings talking to her about everything in his life and hers – he knew her better than he'd ever known another person before in his whole life. He sneaked a look at her, at the way her arse moved in those tight leggings, the way her neck rose slender and uncovered from her shirt.

"There's a spring further up this hill, if you want to bathe."

"A spring? Ice cold water or hot water?"

"Of course cold," he grinned, "but very clean."

"Go on," she said, waving her hand at him. "Lead me to it."

By the time they got to the top they were both gasping for breath and sticky with sweat.

"There," Matthew pointed at a wide pool. Alex clapped her hands together, making him smile at the childishness of the gesture. She hurried towards the water, bent to scoop some up to drink.

"It tastes a bit weird."

He kneeled down to taste it, shaking his fingers so that drops flew like glittering sparks through the air.

"It's the peat," he said, taking off shoes and stockings to paddle his feet in the water. She sat down beside him, tugged at her mud caked jeans.

"I'd better wash these as well, and my shirt. Well, all my clothes." She gave him an inscrutable look, and Matthew felt his face heating at the thought of seeing all of her naked. He got to his feet.

"I'd best leave you to it, then." He handed her a piece of lumpy lye soap. "Don't get it in your eyes, it stings, aye?"

"And itches."

He laughed. "I'll be on the other side of those crags. Call if you need me."

He didn't mean to. Ha, of course he did. It was as he was coming back from taking a piss that a sudden movement from the pool caught his eye. He was mesmerised, crouching down in the shade of the closest crag, incapable of tearing his gaze away from her.

She'd taken off her breeches, exposing the full length of her legs, the roundness of her arse, and he could swear that even at this distance he could see the light, downy hair on her thighs. He could definitely see the triangle of pubic hair, glints of bronze in all that dark, and he wondered what had happened to that little scrap of red he'd glimpsed covering her privates some weeks ago. He slipped his hand inside his breeches.

He should leave, he shouldn't sit like this and watch her, but down by the pool she unbuttoned her shirt and pulled it off, and he wanted to be the one that undid that strange contraption that held her breasts in place, letting them spill into his hands. He rubbed himself, his hand moving rhythmically up and down. She was fully naked, kneeling by the edge of the pool as she scrubbed her shirt and those wisps of lace.

Something about the way she held herself made him suspect she knew he was watching, and that made it less of an intrusion, because surely she would have covered herself or stood to yell at him had she really minded. The way she rose to wring her shirt out, how she turned in his direction to shake the clothes before draping them over a sun warmed boulder – she was showing herself off to him. It made him smile and he shifted from foot to foot, his head ringing with her name.

Alex had by now finished with her clothes, turning instead to the business of washing herself. It was like watching a complicated dance, every one of her movements a silent demand that he come closer, take her and possess her. But he remained where he was, wanting to extend this moment for as long as he could, his eyes never leaving her. She lathered her hair and he laughed at her creative expletives when she got soap in her eyes. He'd told her, no? She rinsed herself, used handfuls of grit to polish herself, leaving her a rosy red, and Matthew moaned when she stretched, rising onto her toes with her arms extended high over her head.

She twirled, sank down to sit, and eased down onto her back, her face to the sun. Her hand brushed at her breast, it rested for an instant on her belly. It drifted lower, hovered over her pubic mound, and when her fingers threaded themselves into her bush Matthew inhaled. Her legs shifted apart and her hand slid in to rest between them. Matthew stumbled to his feet, his cock a thudding magnetic needle pointing him towards her.

He didn't undress, he just undid his lacings and fell to his knees between her legs. She opened her eyes and smiled, running one finger first into herself then over his lips. One thrust, and he was so deep inside he felt her brace, her heels scrabbling for purchase on the moss as she tried to put some distance between them.

"You're... err... quite big," she gasped when he flexed his hips again, but he was beyond hearing, all of him taken over by the raging heat in his balls and the fire that burnt through his cock as he drove himself deeper and deeper into her.

It was one long, endless afternoon, a succession of orgasms, of half-uttered sentences, of choked gasps. His fingers ... oh yes! There, there! She undulated under him, he loved her, she kissed him, they stumbled over to the spring to drink, to wash, and her hands on his penis, his hands on her breasts, was enough to make it all start again.

She was sore but she didn't care, lying spread-eagled under him, relishing his weight, his size, the surging strength that pounded into her until she no longer was – she just floated on a wave of sunlit colours. He collapsed on top of her, laughed out loud. Below him she fidgeted, squashed and breathless, and he moved to the side. Through half closed eyes she looked up at him.

"Wow," she said in a cracked voice. She raised her hand to trace the shape of his brows, his eyes. He captured it, nibbled her fingers one by one.

"Take it off," he said, indicating the ring on her third finger. She looked at him and then back at her ring. What did he mean, take it off?

"You're mine now," he said into her hair. "So take it off." Matthew rolled off her and held out his hand.

She sat up. His? Who did he think he was? She frowned at him, but the look in his eyes and the vulnerable curve to his mouth made her relent. He's old-fashioned, she reminded herself – very, very old-fashioned. He was still holding his hand out, eyes hanging off her. Talk about reverse commitment; by placing John's ring in his palm she was telling him she was his. It made her feel hollow somehow, her heartbeat echoing inside the cavity of her chest. It would mean accepting that she would never see them again, not John, not Magnus and not her baby.

Matthew's eyes locked into hers and for a long, long moment she held her breath. Finally Alex nodded, expelling the air in a rush. She had to tug a bit to get the ring off, and she held it in her closed fist in a silent farewell before she dropped it into his waiting palm.

"He gave you that as well." He touched the golden bracelet round her wrist. She took it off, dropping the chain links into his hand. He smiled, a soft sheen in his eyes as he pulled her down to kiss her.

"Mine, aye?"

She shivered in the evening breeze and huddled closer to him. "Yours," she said, and found to her surprise that she meant it.

He drew her close, he whispered her name, kissed her ear, her nose, the corner of her mouth. His hands were warm on her skin, his fingers touched and teased, and Alex wrapped her arms around him and took him inside. She gasped; he froze. He nuzzled her neck, she shivered and locked her legs around his hips. He took his time, and now it was Alex that laughed, her head thrown back.

He snickered at her gait when they walked up to the top, a self-satisfied note in his voice when he told her she was walking as if he was still between her legs. She huffed and brought her thighs together, feeling them sticky and sore. Despite all her washing she reeked of sex, of him, and her lips were swollen and tender. He stopped her beneath one of the crags .

"You'll be my wife then," he said, not quite a question, nor yet a statement.

"Yes," she swallowed. "I suppose I will."

He raised her hand to his mouth, uncurling her fingers to kiss her palm and then fisting her hand closed.

"It's you and I now, aye?"

"You and I," she echoed. And in her mind she turned her head to look at Isaac, John and Magnus for one last time

CHAPTER 16

They'd fallen asleep naked and sticky, with shawl, plaid and blankets wrapped around them and woke to sudden shyness, fumbling with buttons and lacings. Matthew snuck Alex a look and her ears turned a delicate pink.

"What?" She turned her back on him while fastening her bra thing. He ran a finger down her spine, smiling at the way she shivered under his touch. "What?" she repeated, twisting to see his face.

"We could stay for a few days," he said, his mouth quirking at the responding flash in her eyes. "We could do with some days of rest, no?"

"We could," she smiled. She grew serious. "Would it be safe?"

"Oh, aye; it may even be wise to keep low to the ground for some time." They'd seen far too many soldiers the last few days, riding in groups of six – no doubt still searching for yon fugitive, after all they were not that far from Lanark. Up here they were relatively safe, difficult to come upon by surprise.

He just couldn't get enough of her; three days on and he ran his hands up and down her body, marvelling at the curve of her hip, how her thigh flowed to meet her knee, how well her round breasts fit into his cupped hands. The smoothness of her, the taste of her skin, the sounds she made when he took her – all of it was wondrous.

He sniffed her, making her laugh when his breath and beard tickled her, he just had to stroke her again, nibble her nape, kiss her ear. And somewhere halfway through they fell asleep, his leg thrown across hers.

He woke a bit later, only to find her studying him, eyes travelling over every inch of his naked body. It made him uncomfortable, too aware of the scars that decorated him, and he attempted to sit up only to have her push him down.

She shifted closer, and his skin seemed to rise from him as she smoothed her fingers down his arms, his chest and legs. Soft lips on his neck, teeth that bit gently on his nipples, a wet mouth that trailed further down, and his breath was loud and ragged, his head filled with pulsating reds.

When her mouth closed round him, Matthew moaned, arching towards her, a small part of his mind wondering where on earth she had learnt to do something this… oh God, this… For a brief moment he was insanely jealous of John, for surely she had done with John what she was now doing with him, but then the sensation that filled him swept everything else aside, and he sank his hands into her hair to hold her where she was, with her mouth and her tongue making love to him as no one had ever done before.

"Merciful Father!" he exclaimed, and he didn't care that he was taking His name in vain – or was he? Alex laughed against his skin, her tongue flicked out to lick his balls, his cock, and there was that mouth again and with a strangled sound he came, and he came and he came and he came. When she released him, Matthew was a boneless heap of sated happiness, incapable of moving as much as a finger.

"Sweetest Lord," he croaked.

"Sweetest Alex would be more correct," she said, curling up against his chest.

"Aye." He raised his head an inch or so to peer down at her. "Thank you."

"You're welcome," she said and settled herself for an afternoon nap in his arms.

He was almost asleep, registering with half an ear the sounds of insects and birds that surrounded them, when a far more regular, manmade noise startled him wide awake. In an instant, Matthew was up on his toes, knife in hand, while he signalled for Alex to be quiet. He sat in absolute stillness, listening to the huffing sounds of someone making his way up the steep hillside.

"A soldier?" Alex whispered in his ear.

Matthew shook his head. Soldiers rarely went about

alone, and whoever it was that was coming their way was limping badly.

"Fucking hell," someone swore, and Alex clapped a hand to her mouth.

"Get dressed," Matthew said, jerking his head in the direction of a stand of shrubs. She grabbed at her clothes and darted off, leaving Matthew to glower at a very surprised Sanderson.

"What are you doing here?" Matthew said, waving his knife to show Sanderson he should sit.

"Taking a hike," Sanderson said. "You know, beautiful weather and all that. What the fuck do you think I'm doing? I'm trying to get away from those jerks that want to hang me!"

"Hang you?" Alex appeared so abruptly Sanderson nearly fell over backwards.

"Oh, you," he muttered. His eyes travelled over Matthew's naked body, back to Alex and her messy hair. "Interrupting something, was I?"

"No," Matthew said, "we were done – for now."

Matthew retreated a few paces to dress, keeping a vigilant eye on them. Alex stiffened under Sanderson's cold, scrutinising stare.

"Bitch," Sanderson said, making Matthew frown. "This whole mess is your damn fault."

"My fault? How can it be my fault?"

Sanderson fisted his hands and Alex shoved her shoulders forward, legs sinking into a crouch. Sanderson sneered.

"Karate Kid, hey?"

"Black belt. Want me to show you?"

"No," Sanderson said, dropping his eyes.

My power woman, Matthew grinned, tightened his belt and rejoined them.

"So, why do they want to hang you?" Alex asked.

Sanderson shrugged. "Apparently, I'm a royalist, kind of ironic given where I come from, huh? And even worse,

I'm a fugitive royalist called Matthew Graham, and so…"

"But you're not," Alex said.

Matthew's hand closed over hers, squeezing down in warning. He didn't want her saying too much, not to this man who was eyeing both of them, but in particular Alex, with dislike.

"Unfortunately, I can't prove that, can I? And somehow I suspect that telling them I was born in 1959 will just change the mode of death – from hanging to the stake." He paled when he said that, and for an instant he shared a look with Alex who'd gone just as white.

"The stake?" she echoed.

"We don't always burn witches," Matthew told them, striving to sound matter-of-fact. "Sometimes we hang them."

"Oh, well that's a relief," Alex said. "And anyway, I'm not a witch."

"Me neither." Sanderson's eyes walked up and down Alex, pausing at her chest and her mouth. Matthew leaned forward and raised a brow in warning. To his satisfaction, Sanderson averted his eyes.

"Your mother is Mercedes Gutierrez Sanchez," Sanderson said.

Alex flinched, cast a glance at Matthew. "Yes, my mother's name is Mercedes, but if you knew, how come you didn't tell me last time we met?"

"It sort of slipped my mind, my attention being otherwise occupied." Sanderson shifted his leg, groaning with the effort. He loosened one of the makeshift bandages and Alex reared back at the resulting stench. Matthew studied what little he could see of the leg; gangrene, he'd hazard.

"Does it hurt?" Alex asked.

"Do you care?" Sanderson said.

"No, not really," Alex said with a shrug.

"How did you make it up here?" Matthew asked with frank admiration.

"There's nothing quite as motivating as a waiting

gibbet," Sanderson said, flicking at something that moved up his dirty breeches.

"Nay, it tends to concentrate your mind, like."Matthew was intrigued by how tense Alex became at the mention of her mother, and with the pretext of getting more wood he stood and distanced himself the better to see her reactions.

"So; why this interest in Mercedes?" Matthew said, his curiosity further tweaked by how Alex scowled at him.

"Unfinished business," Sanderson said. Matthew fed a few branches and twigs into the fire. Sanderson gave Alex a malicious smile before going on, obviously enjoying her discomfort.

"My partner, Hector Olivares, has been looking for her for ages – in various different times."

Matthew felt the hairs on his arms sprout.

"Hector Olivares?" Alex frowned. "What does he want with her?"

"As I said; unfinished business. A permanent weariness, a wish to end this protracted agony called endless life."

"What?" Alex croaked.

Sanderson ignored her, turned to face Matthew. "Now Mercedes, well she's a real witch, the type one should burn – at least according to Hector." He smirked at the look on Alex' face. "She's cursed him, and unless Hector destroys her he will never die."

"Cursed him?" Matthew repeated, staring at Alex.

"Bullshit, you're talking absolute crap." She spat at Sanderson's feet. "Hector Olivares is a kidnapper and so are you. It was you, wasn't it, the two of you were in on what happened to me in Italy. I'm right, aren't I?"

"And so what if we were? That was three years ago, get over it," he sneered, but cringed back when Matthew loomed over him.

"Get over it? You held her against her will, no?"

Sanderson licked his lips, tried to back away from him.

"What were we to do? Hector had to be creative to snare the witch, and what better bait than her daughter?"

Sanderson leaned back from Alex' angry face and raised his makeshift crutch in warning.

"My mother is no witch!"

"You think? So you never noticed anything strange about her?"

"Of course not." She'd gone a very bright red, and Matthew wasn't sure it was solely due to anger. For an instant she met his eyes, hastily looked away, and Matthew's gut clenched. Dear God, this man was telling some sort of truth.

"Alex?" he said. "Is it true?"

"True? Is what true?"

"Is this man telling the truth about your mother?"

"Oh for God's sake!" She threw her arms up in the air. "How can you…"

"Yes I am," Sanderson interrupted. "I'm telling you, man; her mother is a dangerous witch, and whenever Hector gets too close she just disappears, dropping into a new time and place. Generally she yanks him with her, poor bastard."

"You're so full of shit!" Alex exclaimed, voice breaking with anger. "Don't listen to him," she said, turning to face Matthew. "He's lying."

"No I'm not! Mercedes Gutierrez Sanchez is a witch, you hear? A real, badass witch!"

Matthew backed away from the fire, and in his head he recited the Lord's Prayer over and over again. If the mother was a time travelling witch, what was the daughter? Definitely a time traveller … He sneaked a look at Alex' white face and then he turned and ran, wanting to put as much distance between her and him as he could – at least for now.

"Matthew!" Alex was on her feet. "Matthew!" She glared down at Sanderson, lifted her foot and kicked Sanderson's swollen leg – hard. "Son of a bitch," she said, ignoring his writhing pain. "Get out. Unless you want me to kill you right here and now. "

"You wouldn't!"

"Are you sure?" she said with quiet menace. "After all, why not make you pay for Italy?"

Sanderson tried to shift away. "It wasn't my idea, it was Hector, and…"

"I don't care," she cut him off. "I just want you to leave. Now. Can you imagine how much I can make that leg hurt? For how long?" She kicked him again, and Sanderson yelped. "Go." She pointed down the hill, and Sanderson got to his feet and limped away.

Afternoon was shading into dusk by the time Matthew came back. For some time he'd stood watching her as she paced back and forth, and even at the distance of several yards he could see she was crying, one hand wiping at her face. When she saw him she flew at him.

"If you ever do that again, I swear I'll take off and you'll never see me again, I had no idea where you were, or if you'd hurt yourself, or if you were ever coming back, and it's not fair, you hear? You know it frightens me, you know how alone I feel here, you… you… bastard!"

"Why didn't you tell me?" he snapped, cutting through her explosion.

"Tell you what?"

"That your mother is a witch."

"She is?" her voice squeaked into a high octave. "And how the fuck would you know, seeing as I myself have no idea at all? I've lived with her for twenty odd years, and guess what? I've never seen her spell someone, or walk backwards around the church at midnight, or milk the neighbour's cat, or have sex with Satan, or do any of those things a witch is supposed to do. Instead, I've had a mother who's cared for me, who loved my father so much it sometimes hurt to watch. So, Mr Knowall, tell me; how the hell do you know she's a witch?"

"Well, that's what he said, wasn't it?"

"And you believe him over me?" she hissed, running a hand through her hair so it stood on end.

Matthew pursed his mouth. "I don't know, I really don't know."

"Fine." She moved over to pack up her few belongings. In less than a minute the roll was tight against her shoulder and she stood to face him.

"Give it back," she said extending her hand to him. "Give me back my ring and my other stuff, because you obviously didn't mean what you said the other day."

"Alex, please Alex, sit down and we can talk this through."

"Talk what through? That you think my mother is a witch, and per definition perhaps I'm one too?"

"I haven't said that, of course I don't think you're a witch."

"My ring," she said, "and I swear I'll never bother you again." She leaned forward and caught his eyes. "And in the future, don't say things you don't mean. 'It's you and I now' you said, and then you just disappear for hours on end without caring how that might make me feel. Who knows, maybe Margaret was smart enough to fall for the right brother, the one who actually cares."

He hadn't meant to slap her quite that hard, was shocked when she stumbled and fell. He reached down to help her up, she flapped her hands at him, long hiccupping breaths whistling through her open mouth. She shoved at him, struggling to push him away, tried to rake her nails across his face. Without a word he wrapped his arms round her, gathered her to his chest and sat down on a nearby rock to hold her on his lap.

"Better?" he asked much later. She nodded, pressing her ear to his shoulder.

"I promise," he said. "I'll not do as I did again, leaving you all alone. And I did mean it, aye? All of it."

"I'm sorry for saying that stuff about Margaret. That was very underhand."

He kissed her head. "Forgiven, sweetheart. Will you forgive me for slapping you?"

"This time, but if you do it again, I'll brain you with something."

He laughed, and after a couple of moments so did she.

"I'm not sure," she said, keeping her cheek pillowed against the rough weave of his shirt.

"You're not sure of what?" Matthew looked up at the night sky. It was dark by now, and he could make out the uneven 'W' of Cassiopeia straight above.

"If she's a witch or not; I didn't tell you the whole story about Ángel."

"I noticed; do you want to tell me now?"

"She burnt him to death," she whispered. "She stepped up to him, wrapped her arms around him and they went up in flames."

Matthew didn't know what to say, his throat working uncomfortably.

"She was a good person, so if she's a witch, she must be a very light shade of white, right?"

"I'm sure she was," he said, but behind her back his fingers made the sign against the evil eye.

He shook her awake in the grey of the predawn, and put a finger to his lips. Matthew moved like a ghost as he packed together their camp, ears straining in the direction of the sound of approaching horses. He took her hand and rushed her down the slope, and a few moments later they were sitting huddled in the midst of a thicket, a blanket drawn over their heads.

He heard the creaking first, and then the soft thud of something heavy hitting the ground. From where he was crouched he could only make out the legs; sixteen legs, four horses. The men sitting on them were silent, no talking, almost no shifting in their saddles. Matthew's hand tightened on Alex' at the telltale scrape of steel on steel as swords were loosened from their scabbards, and it tightened even more when one of the men laughed.

"Got him," a voice said, and for an instant Matthew was certain it was him they meant, and that any moment now he'd feel a sword ram through his back. But then he heard the screaming and sank back. One of the horses stamped and the party moved further downhill. Still too close for comfort, and Matthew glanced at Alex to make sure she understood she had to keep quiet. She nodded that she did.

It was Sanderson, an enraged Sanderson who protested at how he was being treated and demanded to be taken to a senior officer, not a lieutenant barely out of the nursery. The lieutenant in question was not amused.

"And this is?" he asked one of the soldiers.

"Matthew Graham, sir."

"How many times must I tell you this?" Sanderson exclaimed, wincing as his swollen leg hit the ground. "I'm not Matthew Graham. I'm Diego Sanderson." He threw the officer a desperate look. "I think I know where Matthew Graham is, he's up there, in the dell with the spring in it."

"Good try," the officer said, "but we came down that way, and there was no one there." He scratched at his crotch and then looked at Sanderson again.

"What was it he'd done?" he asked, stifling a yawn.

"He's a royalist sir, an escaped fugitive at that. He's a horsethief; he's stolen money and food on his way north. Most dangerous, quite the hothead; spent a fair bit of time in chains or in the hole. Flogged a couple of times, but mostly cudgel work."

Matthew's pulse was racing, a loud thudding behind his ears that he was certain had to be audible to anyone within a furlong's distance. Alex was trembling beside him, and he didn't dare to turn his head to look at her, he just braided his fingers hard, hard round hers, just as much for his sake as for hers.

In the clearing the officer had dismounted and was inspecting Sanderson's leg. He kicked at it, recoiling at the muffled yelp, and then stood back to study the closest tree.

"A bit low," he muttered. "Watson," he called, waving over one of his men. "Will this do?"

The soldier studied the tree dubiously. "Not that high, sir, and the bough looks weak."

Sanderson was trying to stand, his eyes darting from the tree to the officer and back again.

"You can't be serious! I'm telling you, I'm not bloody Matthew Graham!"

"Well you would say that, wouldn't you?" The officer took off his hat to scratch at his short hair. "Damned lice, I'm crawling with them." He scratched his groin again and shook one of his legs, making the breeches flare out. "No, it'll have to do, I'm not going to cart a fugitive in that state all the way back to England. He'd hang anyway." He pouted and braced his hands behind his back, looking at his men. "Well go on then! We haven't got all day. We have orders to ride back today and you all know that."

"But…" said Sanderson, and the officer stalked over to him and slapped him in the face.

"One more word from you, sir, and you'll die gagged as well."

"But you can't!" Sanderson bleated. "I haven't done anything! I'm innocent!"

The officer snorted. "No man is innocent, and if you hang for the wrong sins then I'm sure you've done something to merit hanging. Look at you, ruffian every inch of you."

When Sanderson opened his mouth to protest, the officer produced a grimy handkerchief from his sleeve and stuffed it into Sanderson's mouth.

"There."

A rope was slung over one of the boughs, a struggling Sanderson was hoisted onto a horse and a noose fitted round his neck.

"I'm still not that sure, sir," Watson said, shaking his head. He tightened the noose and slid off the horse. Sanderson shrieked through his gag.

"Dear God," Matthew whispered. "Oh Lord, have mercy on his soul." He put his lips to Alex' ear. "Don't look, close your eyes."

"I can't" she whispered back. "I've already tried."

The officer stood himself at a distance from the tree

and nodded in satisfaction.

"Good. Mayhap it will gladden the Protector's soul to know that yet another royalist lies dead. One less to worry about now that the Protector is dead."

He inclined his head in command and the man behind the horse brought down his whip on the hindquarters, making the horse set off. Sanderson was jerked back by the noose, he fell towards the ground and Matthew noted that Watson had been right. The drop was too low, and Sanderson's feet scraped at the ground in an effort to keep the air whistling down to his lungs.

"Heave him up a bit!" the officer said, and the toes danced in the air. They danced for a long time, the stink from his vacated bowels hanging in the air.

* * *

Hector woke with a start, his mouth filling with acid. Diego! Something had happened to his Diego. He sat up, disoriented, trying to clear his head of what he hoped was a dream. He massaged his neck, a sensation of burning rope making his skin tingle. They had hanged him... Diego's eyes, frozen into an expression of permanent surprise.

Hector rolled out of the straw, an urgent need for a cigarette rushing out to his fingertips. But there were no cigarettes, not here, not in this dark hovel that stank of pig shit and mould.

He stepped outside, avoiding looking at the dark splotch of blood from where he'd killed his unsuspecting host. His hands smoothed down at the unfamiliar clothes, fidgeted with a frayed cuff. He took several long, steadying breaths. He was utterly alone, he was in the wrong time, the wrong place, and the family he had lay inaccessible in the shrouds of time. He had to find a portal; but how on earth was he to do that here, on a godforsaken moor in Scotland?

CHAPTER 17

They sat where they were for a long time after the men had disappeared down the slope. Before them, the swinging body twirled, tongue protruding from a blue face.

"Oh God, oh my God…" Alex leaned over and threw up, her whole body shaking. The rope creaked, fibres stretching so that Sanderson's feet scuffed at the grass.

Matthew crawled out and stood. Alex followed him and stuck her hand into his, needing to touch him, make sure he was alive.

"We can't leave him like that," she said, "the birds…"

Matthew licked his lips. "He's dead."

Alex threw him a sidelong glance. Of course he was dead. For ten minutes he had struggled to stay alive, harsh guttural sounds escaping the makeshift gag, eyes bugging out of his head. Matthew sank down to sit, keeping his back to the hanging man.

"I'm dead as well," he whispered, rubbing his hands through his beard. "Matthew Graham was hanged today."

Alex kneeled down beside him. "But you're not, you're sitting here."

"You don't really know, do you? If I am who I say I am."

That stumped her, and she sat back on her heels to look at him.

"Aren't you?"

"Aye I am. But you have to take it on trust, because I can't prove it."

"But others can, right? You sister and her husband, your brother…" her voice tailed off at his sardonic smile.

"I think Luke will have no reason to recognise me, after all, if I'm dead, he's the new master." He put a hand on her thigh and squeezed. "But there are others, lass; he'll not cheat me of what is mine. Not this time."

It was hard work. Alex' hands were raw with digging,

and her shoulders ached with the weight of Sanderson's body as they cut him down and dragged him across the slick grass to the hole they'd dug behind a thicket of brambles, a fair distance away.

"It's too shallow!" she gasped, once they began filling it in. So far she'd managed to keep her eyes from Sanderson's face, but now she glanced at the head end and his nose was still visible through the dirt. A small beetle scurried across it and Alex stumbled to her feet. She drew in a gulping breath and looked at Matthew.

"If you hadn't woken up that would have been you, and I, oh my God, I would've had to watch!" She wheeled and ran, away from the tree and the shallow grave, tripped over a stone and fell, all air knocked out of her. Her chin hurt, and she could taste blood in her mouth. Matthew put a hand on her shoulder.

"Are you alright?"

"No." She ran her tongue over her teeth to check they were all there. She sat up, frowning at the blood that seeped through her jeans.

Matthew hunched down and extended his hand towards her, index held aloft.

"Can you bend it?" He crooked his finger in demonstration. There was a soft light in his eyes, halfway between amusement and tenderness as he watched her raise her own finger and bend it.

"Good," he smiled, "then you'll be fine."

Alex looked from her forefinger to him and back again.

"How can me bending my finger have anything to do with my skinned knee or my bitten lip?"

"I have no notion, but Mam did that when we were bairns."He leaned forward and kissed her on the cheek. "She did that as well, and that always helped."

Alex wiped her hand across her face and smiled unsteadily.

"Smart woman."

They made very little progress that day. After their third near encounter with a troop of southbound soldiers, Matthew decided it was best to lie low for the remainder of the day. Only once the sun had set did they venture out of their hiding place.

"He's dead then," Matthew said out of nowhere. "The Protector," he clarified, "the soldiers, they said he was dead." He sighed and used a branch to dig at the small fire, sending sparks flying in all directions. "He was a good man – harsh, mayhap, but good – but he leaves an unsteady legacy behind."

Alex looked up from where she was scrubbing at the bloodied knee of her breeches.

"They'll invite the king to come back, you know."

Matthew looked at her in surprise.

"They will?" He laughed at himself. "Well, he's been the King of Scotland for some years already, quite the spectacle that was, with his royal person being fought over by the Covenanters and the Engagers." He grew serious. "So the Commonwealth will die then?"

"Yes. The British have a thing about their kings; you're stuck with them." She spread the djeens to dry and wound her shawl round her bare legs before coming over to join him by the fire. She leaned her head against his shoulder.

"They'll dig Oliver Cromwell up and cut his head off," she said. "Seems a bit overboard to do that to someone who's already dead, don't you think?"

Matthew didn't reply, but inclined his head in agreement. They'd do far worse than that, he reckoned, to the Commonwealth leaders left alive.

"Is it important to you?" Alex asked, startling him out of his thoughts.

Matthew looked down at her. "What?"

"The not having a king, being part of a republic."

"Aye. But the republic has been dead for some years, no? These last few years..." He broke off to shake his head. "... it has been one man, and one man alone, at the helm."

"Like a dictator."

"Aye – a good dictator."

"A contradiction in terms if you ask me," Alex said.

"It doesn't greatly matter now, does it? He's dead, and as you say it, things will revert to how they were – before men like Cromwell and Fairfax. A kingdom, not a commonwealth."

"And you don't care?"

"I do," he said, "of course I do. But…"

"But what?"

"I've lost so many years of my life to this conflict already," he said, "and now I just want to live in peace, tend to my lands, my beasts."

"Oh." Her blue eyes were very close to his and there was something in them that made him flush, an insinuation that he was going back on his beliefs.

"Maybe that's what happens when for one thousand, one hundred and thirty-nine days you've lived like an animal in a cage." He shoved her aside and stood up, his back to her.

They hadn't believed in him when he'd protested his innocence. Men who'd known him, fought with him, had chosen to listen to Luke instead. It tore like a canker at his gut, even now, three years on.

"You counted?" She placed a hand on his back.

"I counted every hour, every day." He wheeled to face her and she backed away from him. "I never want to live through something like that again, it near killed me. I just couldn't bend, and instead I was broken, and the pieces don't fit together as they used to."

He rubbed at his wrists. "Of the men I was locked up with, more than half died the first year. We were all beaten and underfed, cold and constantly ill of one thing or the other, but the ones who died were the ones whose inner light failed them, who woke one day to a hollow chest and the despairing knowledge that there was nothing worth the effort to keep on living for."

He was silent for a while, overwhelmed by memories of long, endless days. "My light still burns, but at times it gutters on the brink of extinction. I wouldn't survive another time in gaol; I'd just curl up and die. And so..." He shrugged, giving her a crooked smile. "I still hold to my beliefs, but I'll be far more selective as to what battles to fight. It's called adapting to your circumstances, no?"

"Adapting is good, that's what all of us have to do to survive." She cleared her throat, hugged herself. "And if you don't, you die."

"Aye," he said, realising she was talking just as much about her own situation as his. "I'm here, I'll be here for you, lass." She brushed at his face, stepped up close enough to meet his eyes.

"And I'll be here for you and two lights burn much, much brighter than one, right?"

"They do, no?" he agreed hoarsely. When she rose on her toes to kiss him, he kissed her back. When her arms came round his neck, his arms wrapped themselves around her waist. No more talking; not tonight. He lifted her into his arms and carried her over to their makeshift bed.

Alex woke to find him already awake. She rolled in his direction, stretched, and gave him a lazy smile.

"Did I?" A gentle finger traced what she was sure was a bright red love bite on her throat.

"Well, no one else did, I would definitely have noticed."

"I hope I wasn't too ..." he said, inspecting a blue spot on her breast.

"Oh, you were, but I didn't exactly mind." And he did sport a few bruises of his own, she smiled, a puddle of warmth expanding through her at the thought of last night.

"Hoyden," he murmured, using his long toes to caress her shin.

"Well, aren't you the lucky one?" She sat up, ran her hands through her hair in a useless effort to comb it into some sort of order.

He got to his feet, eyes narrowing as he studied his surroundings.

"We're nearly home."

She came to stand in front of him, and at their feet the landscape shifted from greys to gold and brilliant green wherever the sun touched it.

"It's as if there was only us," she said, her eyes on the threads of fog that glistened and glowed in the returning light. She drew in a breath of cold, clear air and held it in her lungs before letting it out. Never had she felt as alive as she did in this minute. Behind her stood her man, before her stretched a new, unfamiliar world, and with a twinge of guilt she realised that she hadn't thought about John, not like that, for the last few weeks. Matthew chuckled and leaned forward to bite her ear.

"Like man before the fall from grace," he said, his hot breath tickling her. "And this is our Eden spread before us." He turned her to face him. "This is your life now, here, with me. It's time, Alex, to let the old life go."

She didn't understand, but Matthew let go of her hand and extracted the bundle that Mrs Gordon had given him and placed it on the ground. He threw some more wood on the fire until it burnt a ferocious blue and beckoned for her to come close.

"Here." He handed her the jeans.

She looked at her pants and back at the fire.

"What do you want me to do?"

"Burn them, they don't belong here, they belong there, and you're not going back are you?"

She laughed nervously. "I suppose not, not unless I sit around and wait for a new thunderstorm."

"If you could, would you?" His eyes were very, very green and very, very close.

"No," she breathed, and threw her jeans in the fire.

All of it he made her burn; the jacket, her shirt and the bra. She had the sensation of performing some sort of sacrificial ritual, watching as the remnants of her old life went up in smoke.

He smiled at her as she stood naked in the chilly wind,

her skin stippling into goose bumps, and bent his head to kiss her on her nose.

"So, my little heathen, I think it's time you're baptised, no?"

"But you're not a priest, and this isn't exactly a church."

"It'll do, God is as present here as He is in a church, and I don't think He'll mind if I give you a name in His presence."

"And what were you planning on? Edwina?"

"No, I was thinking of Alexandra. Alexandra Ruth."

"And now what?" she asked as he helped her into what he said was a petticoat and handed her a skirt in dark brown wool. "How am I supposed to dress myself with all these lacings at the back?"

"I'll help you," he grinned, standing back to give her an appraising glance. "You look very nice," he said before pulling on his shirt, adjusting the worn cuffs and neckline. Alex gave him a doubtful look. She felt padded, her breasts kept in place by the lacings of the bodice, and when she moved her hips the skirt swung around her. She liked that, trying out different walks to make the heavy cloth dance.

"Why did she give you all this?" Alex pinched at the skirts. "That was very nice of her, no?"

Matthew rolled his eyes at her. "I bought it. We can't go down to Cumnock looking like tramps, can we?" It had been Mrs Gordon's idea, he explained, her insisting that the lass couldn't very well go about looking like a wee lad. And she hadn't taken much money either, saying the ear-bob well covered the cost.

"Cumnock? Why are we going there?" She didn't like the idea of going into a town, what if there were soldiers? He adjusted something at her waist, rolled their few belongings together and gave her his hand.

"To get married. I can't go on bedding you without giving you my name."

"Oh," said Alex Lind, and gripped his fingers hard.

CHAPTER 18

It was a shock to walk into the little market town. From a distance Cumnock had looked quaint, if very small, but as they got nearer, all Alex could think of was the stench. The privies, the animals on the street, the people – all of them smelled. In comparison she felt like a rose in a pigsty.

The few paved streets were covered in filth; discarded bedstraw, contents of upended chamber pots, the odd dead cat. Women in dirty, mended skirts hurried by, tagged by equally dirty children, a piece of burnt bread was lobbed outside and immediately a fight for it ensued between several dogs and two boys, all of them rolling round in the muck.

"What date is it today?" She held on tight to Matthew's hand, disgusted at having to walk barefoot through the stinking slurry that coated the streets.

"September twelve, I reckon." He helped her as they crossed a muddied stretch. It had begun to rain when they were halfway down the hill, and Alex pulled the shawl tighter round her shoulders, longing for the weatherproof qualities of her jacket. Matthew more or less ran up the streets, nodding in passing at the odd, curious shopkeeper.

"Matthew?" Alex hated having to puff. The bloody lacings were cutting her in half and things weren't exactly helped by Matthew's pace.

"Mmm?" Matthew threw her a quick look.

"Why do we need to get married?"

He came to a standstill. "Don't you want to?"

"That's not what I meant." She wasn't sure she did, things were happening at a pace that frightened her. "What I meant was, how come you feel you can baptise me just like that and wham! I'm no longer a heathen, but that a marriage has to be conducted formally. Why can't you and I just promise we'll be together?"

Matthew gave her a serious look. "A marriage is a legal

contract, it must be properly registered. Unless it's legal, any child of our union would be branded a bastard."

"What's the big deal? A child is still a child, no?"

"A bastard has no rights," Matthew said harshly, his eyes tightening as he studied her face. "You don't want to, do you?"

Alex sighed and looked away. "I'm scared, things are spinning way too fast. Look at me," she indicated her skirts. "This isn't me, not yet. I'm a girl from another time where being married or not isn't really that important, you know?"

Matthew tweaked her cheek and smiled. "But here and now it is important – very important. So will you have me declare myself to you here in public, or will you come with me quietly?"

Alex looked around at all the people. "Quietly, but I'm still scared."

"Of course you are," Matthew laughed, "but I promise to be gentle with you, aye?"

It was a relief to escape off the street, Matthew's hand firm on her waist as he guided her towards a door above which swung a wooden sign: Simon Melville, lawyer.

"Simon? Is that the Simon who's married to your sister?" Matthew nodded and opened the door, almost lifting her across the threshold. The office was very dark – dark and dusty, with huge leather clad tomes covering shelf after shelf in a creaking bookcase.

"Simon?" Someone moved in the inner corner. "Simon? It's me, Matthew." The shape picked up speed and Alex backed away as a small but very massive man threw his arms around Matthew, issuing a string of enthusiastic noises, among which Alex could make out idiot, wee fool, daftie and clumsy dolt, the last when Matthew trod on Simon's foot.

"We heard you were dead," Simon said once he'd calmed down. "But it seems those reports were somewhat exaggerated. Poor Luke will be heartbroken at seeing you alive and well." He laughed, a staccato sound that made

Alex recall summer evening spent playing at war with her Swedish cousins, all of them imitating machineguns. Simon grew sombre and punched Matthew on the arm. "What were you thinking? To run off like that... It may be it's dangerous for you to return."

"Not if I'm officially dead."

"Ah, but officially you're not. Not until it has been proved it was you they hanged. And there was no body to collect or bury when we got to the tree. Just a cut rope." Simon eyed Matthew and stood on tiptoe to examine his throat. "Well, it wasn't you at any rate, was it?"

"Nay," Matthew said, "it wasn't me."He took Simon by the shoulder and turned him in Alex' direction. "This is Alexandra, Alex Lind – my soon to be Swedish wife."

"Hi," Alex said, giving Simon a sketchy little wave.

"Well, knock me dead with a feather." Simon sat down with a thump.

Alex wasn't sure whether to take Simon's reaction as approval or apprehension, and she remained standing where she was, feeling very much like an object on display as Simon gawked at her.

Matthew looked amused. "She doesn't bite, and she does speak English."

Simon tilted his head to one side, a mischievous glint in his light blue eyes.

"She's right bonny, Matthew. What would such a pretty lass want with a lout like you?"

"Sex appeal," Alex said, which left both men nonplussed, even if the gratified expression that flew over Matthew's face showed he could work that one out.

"Sex what?" Simon asked.

"Never mind," Alex grabbed Simon's hand in hers and gave it a firm shake. "Pleased to meet you."

Simon retook his hand, giving her a surprised look.

"Your servant, ma'am," he said, standing up to give her a bow.

Curtsey, she told herself, that's what you're supposed to

do. Not pump a strange man's hand up and down, just curtsey and flutter your eyes. She nearly laughed, feeling like the proverbial bull in the china shop.

Matthew gave Simon an abbreviated and entirely false description of how Alex and he had met, involving highwaymen, a helpless Swedish lass and a dead father.

Simon clucked and shook his head, apologising for the brutal treatment the poor lass had received at the hands of his countrymen, and generally made an effort to look as if he believed a tale he obviously found incredible. Well, Alex thought, the truth would be even more unbelievable, but it was evident that Matthew and she had to work on their story before spreading it to a larger audience.

"So you're marrying the lass out of civic duty, aye? Not wanting to leave her unprotected in the world," Simon summarised once Matthew was done. He handed Alex a mug of cider, poured some for Matthew and himself.

"If that's his reason, I'll brain him before I marry him," Alex said, making Simon choke on his drink. She waited until he had stopped coughing before smiling sweetly and continuing. "I can take care of myself, thank you very much."

"Ah," Simon smiled. "So then why? Is there any particular reason for this haste?"

Alex shrugged. "As for him, you'll have to ask him, not me. As for me, well…" She grinned at Simon. "… I fear I've taken advantage of the poor man."

Simon laughed for so long and so hard that Matthew ended up whacking him between the shoulders, all the while glaring at Alex.

"I have errands to run," he said. "Will you promise to sit here and wait for me?"

Alex nodded but put a hand on his sleeve as he stood to leave.

"If you promise to be careful – very careful."

He ruffled her hair and assured her he would.

Two hours later he was back, safe and sound. Alex' mouth dropped open at the sight of this clean shaven, well dressed stranger. Her Matthew? Wow … He smiled when she ran the back of her hand down his face, his hand closing over hers.

"Have you got the contract ready?" he said. Simon nodded and extended the document for Matthew to read.

"I heard you've arranged for a room down at the inn," Simon said.

"Mmhm?" Matthew sounded disinterested.

"In your own name."

Matthew straightened up. "Don't you think I should?"

"I think that if you sleep there tonight, you'll not see the morning," Simon said, matter-of-fact.

"Hmm," Matthew nodded, exchanging a long look with Simon. "That way, is it?"

Simon hitched his shoulders. "Even shites like Luke have friends. And there's a few that would want to see him as master of Hillview."

"Hillview is mine," Matthew said, his voice very cold. "He's taken my wife, he took my freedom, but damned if he'll take my home."

Simon regarded him evenly. "You need a pregnant wife; it's one thing to plan the murder of a convicted royalist, it's quite another to consider murdering an innocent child." Simon turned a speculative eye on Alex. "I wouldn't go back until she's showing."

Alex sat down, closed her eyes and counted very slowly to a hundred. Then she opened her eyes and looked straight into Matthew's bright hazel ones.

"It'll be alright."

"Yes, you'll be dead, but fortunately the people who have no compunction in running you through, will stay their hand when it comes to your unborn child. So what am I worrying about? Let's just get married and work ourselves into a right sweat while we start that baby, hey?" With a jolt she realised that they might already have started a baby, and in his eyes she saw that he was thinking the same thing.

I hope not, she thought fiercely, I hope yes, she thought just as fiercely, and put her fingers to his lips in a soft caress.

"We don't have to go back, not just yet."

Matthew shook his head. "I do, Alex. I have tenants to care for, a manor to run, and my heart aches for the feel of my land under my feet."

"But what about Luke? What if he kills you?"

"He won't, and at Hillview my people will keep me safe." He got back off his knees and helped her up to stand. "Will you still…" He indicated the unsigned document with his head and his heart stood in his eyes, making her gut twist in response.

"I've burnt all my ships, remember? All of them but one; you."

He nodded and took her hand.

"Just so you know," she said once she'd signed the document, "I'll personally castrate you if you get yourself killed – especially by that unsavoury brother of yours."

Simon laughed at that. "Now that's a threat to take seriously, my man," he said to Matthew, "so you'd better keep yourself safe, aye?"

The minister was a tall, austere man that eyed Alex with some misgiving.

"What happened to your hair?" he asked, leaning over to study her.

"The fever," Matthew said, "it was the healer over at Lanark, who said it was best to cut it off."

"Hmm," Minister Crombie voiced. "Well, you look to be in good health now." Alex nodded that she was. "And you're not from here?"

Alex shook her head, letting Matthew do the talking. Much better story this time, about a Swedish lass left orphaned in the care of some distant relatives of Matthew, and him coming to take her to Edinburgh to see her on board a ship back to Sweden, but well, the Minister would understand aye, that sometimes …

The Minister listened with interest and then smiled, exposing a rather unhealthy set of yellow teeth.

"Matthew Graham, I've known you all your life, and you're a most incompetent liar – you always have been. Somehow I don't think people escape from prison merely to chaperone an unwed lass to a ship, hmm?" He shook his head and gave Matthew an appraising look. "It was wrong what was done to you three years back. We all knew you were no royalist, but those were turbulent times, and men will at times be more feared for their own skin than their immortal soul. I think you'll find that there are many that will want to atone, and Luke may find things a wee bit uncomfortable should he do something rash." He gnawed at his lip and let his eyes wander up and down Matthew. "Now about the lass," he continued, a peremptory hand stopping Matthew from interrupting. "The important thing is that you found her, not how, aye?" He turned and smiled down at Alex. "Do you wish to wed this man, lass?"

"Yes."

"Well then, we'd best get on with it."

"I didn't like the 'obey' part," Alex grumbled as they walked back to Simon's office. "I mean the love and to hold and all that, fine. But to obey? It makes me feel like a dog." Matthew didn't reply, he just grabbed her hand and began to run as the rain came pelting down.

"I'm just saying," Alex went on once they were back inside, "that I might have a bit of a problem with the obey thing. No, wait, I have a huge problem with the obey thing. Why should I obey you?" She glared down at her feet, now just as dirty as they'd been before she washed them.

"Because I'm your husband," Matthew explained with exaggerated patience. "And you're but a mindless wife." If it hadn't been for the light in his eyes indicating that he was, at least to some extent, teasing, she'd have kicked him.

"Hmph," Alex said, crossing her arms over her chest. "I'd like to see you make me."

"Oh, don't tempt me," Matthew grinned, "because I'm sure I could make you obey if I wanted to."

"We'll see about that, okay?"

"So, Mrs Graham," Matthew said next morning, planting a kiss on Alex' cheek. "Shall we see then?"

"See what?" she yawned. It had been a comfort to sleep indoors instead of out in the rain, but Simon's cramped office was not the ideal environment for wedding night activities, resulting in Alex sleeping on the narrow but padded bench while Matthew stretched out on the floor.

"If you'll obey." He twisted her so she ended up thrown across the bench, a firm hold on her nape keeping her still as he ruckled the shift up her legs.

"Oaf," she laughed. "Horrible wife beater," she added when he slapped her playfully on her rump. "Unngh," she said when he muffled her mouth with his hand, the other slipping under her to hold her still when he entered her.

"Do you think," he murmured against her neck, "do you think there's someone there?" His hand slid down across her belly in a gentle cupping motion.

"I don't know," she said, all of her melting at the tone of his voice. She turned in his arms, guided him back inside and for a long time they moved slowly and together. Very, very slowly, long fluid movements that impaled her on him, made her shudder and hold on to him, her teeth sunk into his shoulder.

"I think there is," he said, brushing a damp lock off her face. "I think we made it already that first time."

She let her finger run across his brows. "I hope he has your eyes," she whispered.

"I hope she has your mouth," he whispered back.

CHAPTER 19

Simon was crowing when he came through the door to his office, bringing with him a basket from which emanated the smell of warm bread. He kept his back turned as Alex and Matthew scrambled into their clothes, all the while humming under his breath.

"Someone tried to set the inn on fire," he informed them once they were decent. "And the innkeeper is right sore about it. Well, he would be, no?" He raised innocent blue eyes to Matthew's. "Now who would do a thing like that?"

"Simon!" Matthew sounded very displeased. "You haven't!"

"Me?" Simon shook his head. "How can you possibly think that I would?" He bent forward in a conspiratorial gesture. "Nay, word is out that a certain Luke Graham did, in view of him not finding his dear brother where he had hoped to, stark naked in his marriage bed."

"He did?" Alex said, and both men turned to give her an exasperated look.

"Aye, of course he did," Matthew sighed, a very green eye on his humming brother-in-law.

"At least it will force Luke to keep low to the ground for some time," Simon said in a satisfied tone.

Several hours later, Alex stood beside Simon, studying a huge beast.

"Are you sure it's a horse?" she said. "It looks like an elephant."

Simon laughed. "No trunk, aye? It's a horse."

Matthew was glowing when he came back to them.

"Look at him! Isn't he magnificent!"

"Hmm." She supposed it was good looking for a horse, grey and with enormous hooves. Nice hair though, the mane fluttering in the wind.

"Uncut," Matthew said to Simon. "I hope he isn't too

tempered. That might explain the price."

"Bad tempered?" Alex backed away, certain that the horse was eyeing her with the express intent of sinking those big yellow teeth into some part of her anatomy.

"He'll easily carry two," Matthew went on, "and with those legs he'll have a mighty stride."

Simon nodded his agreement and cocked his head in the direction of Alex.

"Don't you have horses in Sweden?"

Alex gave him a wavering smile. "Of course we do. But they're much smaller." She went back to studying the stallion; she'd need a ladder to get on, not that she particularly wanted to.

It was far more comfortable than she'd expected, a rocking motion that made her drowsy where she sat behind Matthew, her arms around his waist. She leaned her cheek against his back and rubbed affectionately, hearing a contented rumble in response.

"Will they think me strange?" she said, trying to keep the twinge of unease from her voice. He just nodded and she tightened her hold round his waist. "Will they like me, do you think?"

"I like you."

She could hear the smile in his voice.

"I sincerely hope so, but that wasn't what I asked, was it?"

"Nay. Simon liked you, didn't he?"

"I liked him." Alex laughed under her breath. How someone could be so … so …spherical was beyond her.

"Joan will surely like you as well," Matthew said, and she felt a slight tension drain away. She was nervous about meeting his sister. "And as to the rest," he shrugged, "I think they will. Not that they'll clasp you to their bosom right away, but once they get to know you, of course they will."

"Where'd you get the money?" She was only mildly curious, but wanted the distraction of hearing his voice. For the last half hour or so, Matthew had ridden in silence, his eyes drinking in the landscape around him in a way that made her think of thirsting men finding a well.

With every plodding step he was getting closer to his place, his roots, and inside her grew a sensation of sadness tinged with jealousy, because she'd never see her home again. All she had in the world was him, and the thought undressed her, leaving her naked in a strange and frightening place. What would happen to her if one day he woke up and found he no longer loved or even liked her?

She shifted; what had begun as an agreeable experience was now getting a bit old. The insides of her thighs were beginning to chafe, and she was certain that she'd never be able to pull her legs together again, sitting splayed as she did on the huge roan back. He hadn't replied and she repeated her question.

"I sold the bracelet."

She almost fell off the horse and instinctively dug her heels into its sides, making it squeal and buck, close to a ton of irritated horseflesh.

"You're tickling him!" Matthew barked. "Let up on your heels."

"Easy for you to say! You've got stirrups!"

In the end she slid off, landed with a thud, and sat glaring up at him.

"You could have asked. I would probably have said yes, but it was mine, not yours." Matthew remained astride, not replying. "I said you could've asked."

"I heard you."

"Well then why don't you answer? You had no right to sell it, you hear? It was mine, goddamn you!" She kicked in the general direction of the horse.

"Not anymore," he said, "as of yesterday your goods are mine to dispose of as I see fit."

"Fantastic, what a great start to our marriage to have you go behind my back and sell my, I repeat my, bracelet."

"I didn't go behind your back!"

"No, you didn't bother to tell me at all."

"I needed the money, Alex. You know that."

He needed the money to come home in style. Good broadcloth breeches, new linen shirt under a short, dark green coat with wide sleeves showing off the cuff ruffles of his shirt, and a gigantic horse. Ugly, a huge ugly horse named Samson with hooves you could use as soup tureens. She on the other hand, she looked like a church mouse. Brown skirt, brown bodice and still no shoes.

"You should still have asked; I would've said yes." She got to her feet and ignored him when he bent down to help her back up. "I'll walk, I don't feel like riding my horse." She emphasized the pronoun and set off at a brisk pace in what she assumed was the right direction.

"Alex!" He wheeled the horse around her, forcing her to a halt. "Get on. It's a long way to walk, aye."

"No, but never mind me, why don't you just gallop off or something so that you can show off your flashy horse – sorry, my flashy horse – to your grovelling tenants. God help us if the returning master were to show up on foot and in worn clothes, right?"

He flushed, turned the horse and dug his heels in, leaving her to watch as he raised a cloud of dust in his wake.

"Bastard, idiot, bloody, bloody man." He was gone now, disappeared from sight, and she was blindingly angry with him. Did he expect her to follow, like an obedient little dog? "Obey, my arse," she said, and stepped off the road and onto the grass. She walked along for some time, assuming that he'd soon come back, but by the time the sun was beginning to dip behind the trees, and he'd still hadn't shown, she was on the verge of tears.

"What the fuck am I doing? Why do I do something as stupid as marrying that… that… old fashioned jerk!" And why was he doing this to her, again? He'd promised that he wouldn't go charging off, and then he just did. She felt a small jolt of fear. Maybe he'd hurt himself, been attacked by highway men and was at this moment lying bleeding in a ditch minus coat, horse and purse.

He wasn't, and a moment later he came trotting up the road and rode over to where she had sat down in the shade. He could see she was angry and hurt in the way she refused to meet his eyes or in any way acknowledge he was there, and he sighed inside.

With every mile he got closer to home, he was starting to question the wisdom in marrying this strange woman. He could have offered her the safety of his house without pledging himself to her, and these niggling thoughts left him with a sensation of deep shame. He'd bedded her, he'd promised he loved her and he did, just seeing her sitting in the grass brought that home to him, but still... would she be the wife he needed? He couldn't picture her doing the rounds of the tenant's cottages like Mam had done, and she had none of the skills or the experience needed to run a house the size of Hillview.

It shamed him even more that she'd been right in her accusations; he did want to ride in on a good horse and in new clothes, a shield against all the whispered comments and worried eyes he was sure he would meet.

He drew Samson to a halt and looked down at her, thinking she was the prettiest thing he'd ever seen, rosy with anger and with dirty, dusty feet. He should have bought her something new as well, had even fingered a soft shawl embroidered in blues and greens, but it had stuck in his craw to use her money to buy her presents. Not to buy himself things though... Time to grovel, he decided, and dropped off the horse to sit beside her.

"You're right, I should have asked."

"Too right, you should." She raised her eyes to him, and he saw such disappointment in them he flinched. "You promised," she said, not allowing him to drop his gaze. "You swore you'd never barge off and leave me alone again."

There was no other word for it; he squirmed. "I wasn't far, not far at all."

She filleted him with her eyes. "I didn't know that, did I? You made me feel abandoned, when you'd promised me you never would." She sighed and looked away. "And you do it on purpose."

There was nothing he could say, because she was right. He knew, the moment he'd spurred Samson on, that it would scare her to see him ride away, and the thought of her dependency on him thrilled him. It made her weak where he was strong, and he could choose to protect her from the fear of losing him or not, as it pleased him.

"Oh, Jesus, Alex." He kneeled down in front of her. She wouldn't lift her face, but kept her gaze on the pebbles she was rolling round in her palm. He tugged at her hair until she raised her eyes. So blue, he thought, blue like forget-me-not's at dusk. "Today it's thirty- three days since you dropped into my life, and I can no longer imagine a life without you. And it's the same for you, no?"

She nodded grudgingly.

"So when the anger hits me, when I do what I just did, how can you doubt that I'll come back for you?"

"You took your time about it," she said, a slight wobble to her voice. He bent forward and kissed her, tongue flickering for an instant against hers before he sat back.

"I'm like a homing pigeon, and you're my dovecot. Without you I'd be homeless, so wherever I go, for however long, I'll always come back. Always, you hear?" He smiled at the waves of pink that washed up her cheeks, and held out his hand to her. "Now; let's get on *your* horse and go home, aye?"

He had placed her in front of him this time, and as he rode up the last stretch his hand slid down to hold her close, a nervous shiver running up his spine. Would she like it? Would Hillview seem the paradise to her it was to him? He nudged Samson on over the top and released his held breath at the view that opened in front of him.

The small valley bathed in afternoon sun, golden light danced over the damp grass and glinted off the shingled roofs. The crops were mostly in, the denuded fields dark splotches against the green of the sloping meadows. The late barley still stood man high, and on one of the closest corn fields Robbie was loading sheaves onto the flatbed cart.

The stables, the barn, they were just as they had been when he last saw them, that day when he was hauled off to stand trial for something he hadn't done. Someone had painted the stable doors, and the henhouse had been reroofed, the wooden shingles still a whitish green.

He saved it until last, but finally he turned his eyes to his house. Pride fizzed through his veins at the sight of the two storey building, a grand modern house built by his grandda just before the Bishops' Wars. His eyes flew over the weathered stone walls, the slate roof with two chimneys, one at each end. He heard a surprised shout, and there in the door stood Mrs Brodie. He sighed; he'd hoped Joan would've been here to receive them, but she was staying with their Graham cousins, helping tend Aunt Moira who was ill.

Alex hadn't said a word, taking in his world, his home. She sniffed; there was a tang of manure and a man came out of the stable, pushing a wheelbarrow full of what she assumed to be soiled straw, and dumped it onto a pile just off the side. A cloud of flies buzzed up, but settled just as quickly.

She hoped he wouldn't ask her what she thought, because right now she had no idea. It was so much smaller than she'd imagined from his descriptions, the main house not much more than a normal sized cottage in her days. Well, perhaps a bit bigger, she conceded, but no way close to the half timbered Tudor manor house she'd pictured. People burst from doors, women and men congregated in front of the main entrance, and Matthew's hold on her tightened before he clucked Samson into a walk.

She counted them as they got closer; four men – one not more than a boy and one positively ancient – three women and two girls. There was absolute silence as Matthew held in Samson, all eyes glued to Alex, an astounded whisper flying between the women before they reverted to staring at her. Alex didn't want to get off the horse, made uncomfortable by this scrutiny, and considered yanking on the reins to turn him and somehow ride away, but Matthew deposited her on the ground and dismounted, one hand immediately at her waist.

His hand trembled where it lay, and Alex suddenly understood his need for horse and clothes, how important it was to him to return an apparent landowner, not a convicted felon. She moved closer to him in an attempt to give him reassurance, wanting very much to take his hand, because just the feel of it would stop her heart from beating like a jungle drum inside her chest. As he made no move to take hers, she supposed it wasn't on for men of certain standing to hold hands with their wives in public.

"Mrs Brodie," Matthew inclined his head. "Ewan, Sam." Short muttered responses, a general shuffling of feet. It made Matthew nervous, and his eyes slid across the assembled faces, wondering which one of them would run like a hare to advise Luke he was back. He cleared his throat and urged Alex forward. "May I present my wife then? Alexandra, Mrs Matthew Graham."

"Hello," Alex said brightly, "nice to meet you." She'd exaggerated her outlandish accent, and it made Matthew suppress a grin to see the surprised reaction of Mrs Brodie et al. But at least they were smiling now, a swift chatter as they inspected his wife, a softening in their eyes as they looked from her to him and her again.

"Welcome home, master," Mrs Brodie said, "it's been far too long, aye?"

"Yes, very much too long." Matthew turned towards the

hill. He was filled with a childish urge to spread his arms wide and rush up through the woods but instead he offered Alex his arm and led her inside.

Matthew wasn't sure if he wanted to take his new wife to bed in the same room where he'd been so cruelly deceived by his first spouse, but in the event he was given no choice, and that evening Mrs Brodie ushered them both into the main bedroom with a satisfied expression on her face.

The feather mattress had been aired and turned, clean linen brought up from the closet, and Rosie had plumped the pillows into welcoming white mounds, giving the bed hangings a discreet shake to clear them of some of the accumulated dust.

"Will you be wanting anything more?" Mrs Brodie asked, eagle eye sweeping the room to make sure there were candles, towels and water.

"No, this is fine," Matthew said, closing the door in her wake.

He stood to the side and watched as Alex wandered round the bedchamber. She trailed her fingers over the mule chest, rubbed at one of the two pewter candlesticks, and looked somewhat flustered at the sight of the chamber pot. She went over to the small window, inspected the pitcher and basin, did a slow turn round the bed and sat down on it, her hand gliding over the soft sheen of the worn linen sheets. She bounced up and down a couple of times, making the rope frame creak.

"It's quite narrow."

"It is?" Matthew shook his head. This was the biggest bed in the house, a bit more than four feet in width. He hung his breeches on one of the clothes pegs, draped his stockings over the stool and took a hesitant step in the direction of the bed, all of him overwhelmed by images of a long gone April day. Something must have shown on his face, because Alex got to her feet and moved towards him, brows pulled together in a worried frown.

"Is this where they..." she coughed, "you know, where you found Margaret and Luke?"

"Aye, this is the bed where I was conceived, where I was born. It's the bed where I bedded my wife and thought I conceived my son, except that I didn't, did I? Instead I was cuckolded in it." He looked at the bed with distaste.

"We could burn it."

"Burn it? It's a fine bed, no?"

"Yes, but if you're uncomfortable sleeping in it ..."

"It's not the bed's fault," he cut her off.

He didn't speak as he helped Alex undo her lacings, his eyes on her as she hung up her clothes and went over to wash. For an instant he imagined her Margaret, and only when she turned, her short hair haloing her head, did he relax into the certainty that this was Alex – his Alex. Still he hung back, reluctant to cross the few yards that separated him from the bed.

"I don't bite, remember?" Alex settled back against the pillows and grinned. "Well; unless you want me to, of course."

That made him laugh, and he resolutely shoved all memories of Margaret aside and went to join his wife in bed.

* * *

Hector threw up, wiped at his mouth and sat back.

"I'm sorry," he said, which was both inadequate and unnecessary given that Diego was dead as a rock. But someone had taken the time to bury him, had dragged him to this shallow resting place behind the brambles – too shallow, not enough to disguise the scent of rot. Which all in all was a good thing, because otherwise how would he ever have found him?

He was inundated by a spurt of anger. If Diego hadn't gone looking for the Lind woman he'd have been safe back in Chicago. The thought brought him up short; could she be here too? Well, why not? They'd disappeared in the exact same place, on the same day and due to the same weather phenomenon. It didn't require a gigantic leap of imagination to assume they'd ended up in the same time.

He stood; he had no clear idea of where he was, but in the distance he could make out a huddle of houses and supposed that would be the closest thing to a town he'd find. He needed funds and clothes and cigarettes. He laughed, studying his trembling fingers; maybe he could find some tobacco at least. And maybe he could find Alexandra Lind.

He sighed; so he finds Alexandra and then what? Would it help him at all? At least she'd be able to tell him what her damned mother did to disappear so completely three years ago. And should she not want to... Well, he had ways of being most persuasive so he'd have her telling him the truth in a matter of minutes. The thought sent a little frisson up his spine; he liked making people talk.

He held out his arms. His body was changing, the smooth and tanned skin wrinkling at a worrying pace – as if this latest fall through time had released an ageing agent previously held at bay. He turned his hands this way and that. For a man pushing one hundred and ten he was in pretty good shape, he comforted himself. He clenched his fists; it wasn't right! He shouldn't be here, he should be dead and buried in Seville, and all of it, yes, goddamn, all of it was Mercedes' fault. And if he couldn't make her pay, well then maybe he could have some fun with her daughter. Hector's fingers clawed in anticipation. After all, did not the Bible state that the sins of the fathers revolve on the sons?

CHAPTER 20

The following few days were very confusing. Alex woke that first morning to a bed already empty of Matthew, and when she made her way down to the kitchen, eyes crusty with too much sleep, she was met with silent disapproval from both Mrs Brodie and Rosie.

"I didn't know there was some kind of eleventh commandment, Thou shalt not sleep late," she quipped during a brief run in with Matthew. "One would think I was at minimum one of Babylon's whores from the looks they gave me."

He laughed and assured her that in the future he'd make sure she was well and truly awake before he left her. That sounded promising, and she tried to look cheerful as he hurried back to the barn.

Alex had never felt so out of place in her whole life. The differences between this time and her own were much more evident here, in a functioning household, than they'd been on the moor when it was only Matthew and her- after all, hiking and camping were in many ways unchanged over the years. But here... All these people, all of them expecting her to know what to do and how.

She was submerged in questions, from what did she want for dinner to did she think they should perhaps slaughter the hog now. How should she know? She had no idea, she had never shelled peas, never wrung the neck off a hen, and as she wandered around her new home she began to realise that she had a huge uphill in front of her.

The linen closets were opened for her inspection and she wasn't sure if what she was seeing was good or bad. All she saw were rows upon rows of neatly stacked sheets, of pillowcases with embroidered edges and piles of folded linen towels.

"Lavender sachets," she said, needing to make some kind

of comment. "I like the linen to smell of lavender." Mrs Brodie pursed her mouth, but nodded and promised she'd see to it.

The house was moderately clean, but Alex frowned at the dust on the skirting boards and very pointedly looked into the corners, making Rosie blush and mutter something about being only one, aye, and it was a big house.

"Hmm," Alex said in a tone that had Mrs Brodie throwing a black scowl at Rosie before assuring Alex all the floors would be scrubbed thoroughly within the coming week.

"Good." With an internal sigh Alex wondered when her elusive sister-in-law would show up, because she was sure Joan knew how to run this home, and maybe she could teach her.

It was a segregated little world; the farm labourers were welcome to enter the kitchen and there sit at the trestle table laughing and jesting with Mrs Brodie and the two lasses. If needs must, they'd go and find the master in his study, a small room just off the main hall where Matthew, just as his father, now had to struggle with bills and accounts. But none of the men ever entered the parlour, or ventured upstairs. Mrs Brodie and Rosie of course went everywhere, but they would knock before entering, and Rosie scurried away like a mouse if Alex entered a room.

"I don't think she understands me," Alex said to Matthew. "She just looks at me with those huge cow's eyes of hers."

"She understands you, but she might be a bit shy, aye?"

"Right." She wasn't about to tell him that she suspected Mrs Brodie very much on purpose spoke an almost unintelligible brogue, nor did she intend to share all those moments when she was certain they were all laughing at her behind her back.

Instead, she persevered, smiling brightly at them, conversing stubbornly with Rosie and Sam, Mrs Brodie and Gavin, a half grown boy who wouldn't do more than nod or shake his head in reply – alternatively flee when he saw her approach.

Whenever Alex entered the kitchen, a silence the thickness of a bear pelt descended until she left again. She stood in the passageway and heard the conversation and the jesting resume, and she felt lonelier than she had ever felt before.

She cheered up when she saw the orchards. This was an area she knew something about, having spent several summers with her apple loving grandmother as a child.

"Applesauce, and maybe dried apple rings." This was a novelty she could see. "We do them in Sweden, you peel and core the apples, slice them very thin and hang them up to dry."

"These apples we use for cider and winter apples," Mrs Brodie informed her, sounding unimpressed by dried fruit and apple sauce.

"Some we'll use for apple rings," Alex said, needing this one little victory to confirm that she was not only nominally mistress of the house.

Mrs Brodie made a small guttural sound but desisted from further comments – to her at least. Apparently she decided that the master needed to be informed of his wife's whimsical ideas, and later that afternoon Matthew strolled across to where Alex was sitting in a ray of sunshine and dropped down beside her.

"Apple rings?"

"Yup. Apple rings."

He smiled and kissed her on the cheek. "Okay."

By the time Matthew came indoor in the evenings, Alex was exhausted after her day spent in a silent trench war, and all she wanted to do was to curl up in his lap and cry, because how was she ever to cope or fit in? But she didn't let on; he was so happy to be here, and his eyes sparkled over supper as he told her of this or that tenant and how bonny the bull calf was, and did she know his favourite mare was still here?

He fell asleep the moment his head touched the pillow, a hand on Alex' waist, and beside him she turned and tossed, staring for hours into the dark while her head buzzed with jumbled images of her lost life and this her new, unfamiliar existence.

She was inundated with homesickness, stuffed the pillow in her mouth to muffle her sobs. She didn't belong here; she longed for days in the office, evenings with John and Sundays with her father; for leisurely meals, good wines and conversation about other things than the weather and the goddamn animals – things like politics and business, casual gossip about the latest scandal, tips about movies to see.

Matthew hadn't felt this alive in years. He bounded up in the mornings to hurry off and oversee the work for the day, not noticing how difficult things were for Alex. Or rather he did, but expected her to manage on her own.

He sat on the roof of the barn and repaired it, and when he raised his eyes off the closest crossbeam he was filled with a curling cloud of happiness at being back where he belonged. Sometimes he'd hurry up the hill towards the moor, dodging between oak and alder saplings, and when he was far enough from the house he'd throw himself down on the fading grass and lie spread-eagled with his gaze lost in the deep blue high above. He felt the world turning below him, his blood surged and roared in his ears, and all of him prickled and sang with the joy of being alive.

He woke early on the Sunday to a room that was hazy with the soft light of dawn and a cock that stood with urgent want. Matthew turned and smiled when he saw Alex beside him, her curved back towards him. His wife. Apart from that first night he hadn't bedded her since they got here, exhausted after days spent on catching up on three lost years, and now he spooned himself around her. She grunted and shifted away, a very clear not now. He pulled her back.

"Uh." She sounded very irritated, brows pulling together in a frown. He lifted her shift out of the way. "Matthew, I want to sleep."

"Well, I don't."He flexed against her and she tried to move away. He flipped her over on her back, and her eyes snapped open, two slits of blue glaring up at him. He lay on top of her, pressing his stiffening cock against the soft warmth of her uncovered belly.

"Get off, I don't feel like it."

"I do. You're my wife, and there are some things my wife doesn't do."

"Like what? Sleep late in the morning?"

"Aye, that as well, but that's not what we're talking about, is it?"

He raised himself to undo the fastenings of her chemise, baring her breasts to his hands. He cupped one and squeezed, just a bit too hard, making her hiss in surprise and attempt to shift from under him. He held her still and studied her face, his hand still holding her breast.

"She doesn't say no. When I come with my need, my wife doesn't turn me away. Never again. "

"But…"

He kissed her into silence. "No buts, no buts at all."

She shook her head and tried to sit up, he grasped her by the shoulders and held her down. Come on, he urged her wordlessly, come on then and fight. So she did, her eyes spitting flames, and he took hold of her wrists. There was no way she could win, but she tried anyway, a silent heaving struggle that ended with her lying still and panting beneath him.

He kissed her, his tongue following the contour of her upper lip. She tried to say something, but he was in no mood for talking, so instead he kissed her, kissed her until she opened her mouth to his and kissed him back. He brushed his fingers over her breast, down her flank, he slid a hand under her waist and held her still, pinned against the bed by his weight and strength.

She set her hands to his chest and shoved, but it was a half-hearted shove, a token resistance, no more. He kissed her again, a kiss that had very little to do with gentleness or courtship, far more with a need to show her who he was, and who she was – his woman.

"So, I need you, Alex." He moved his hips, not a question but a demand, and she scowled up at him. Matthew brushed his nose against hers, his leg already wedging itself between hers. "I need you so very, very much." His tone softened her face and when he pressed himself against her again, she widened her thighs.

With a grunt he rolled to the side, releasing her. She got out of bed and he propped himself on his arm to watch her as she washed and dressed. She took her time about it, throwing him the occasional look over her shoulder, and he waited until she was almost done before he beckoned for her to come over.

"Take it off, take it off and come back to bed, wife."

"You wish," she said, and when he rose off the bed she squealed, laughing when he grabbed her, undressed her.

"Does it work both ways?" Alex said once she finished dressing for the second time that morning. She pulled on her stockings and gartered them before looking round for her hand me down shoes.

"Hmm?" Matthew looked up from his shirt.

"You heard me."

"Of course it does," he said seriously.

"Good, I'll hold you to it." There was a challenging gleam in her eyes as she swept by him, and Matthew's toes curled in anticipation.

Once he was dressed, Matthew went to join his wife in the kitchen, detouring by his study to pick up his Bible. She gave him a surprised look when he sat down by the table, flipping through the Holy Writ with one hand, while feeding himself with the other.

"I have to choose a text," he said, "the household will be

in within the hour to hear me read."

"Hear you read?" She yawned, sitting back against the wall.

"Aye, I read, we pray and mayhap sing a psalm or two."

"What? Every Sunday?" Alex sounded hesitant.

"The household expects it, and it's important, no? What better day to read and reflect on God's word than on His day of rest?"

"Ah," Alex nodded.

"Is this new to you then, mistress?" Mrs Brodie broke in from where she was standing by the hearth.

"New? How do you mean?"

"Well, don't you study the Holy Writ where you come from?"

"Of course we do." Alex said, looking quite indignant. It made Matthew bite back on a smile.

"That's good," Mrs Brodie nodded, "and what text will you be wanting the master to read us then? I dare say he'd gladly let you choose, as this is your first Sunday here, no?" She straightened up and adjusted her linen cap.

Matthew eyed her with irritation. Mrs Brodie had the instincts of a badger hound when it came to weaknesses in others, and there was an expectant expression on her face as she leaned towards Alex. His wife, however, surprised him. She stood up, smoothed down her skirts and gave Mrs Brodie a smile that bordered on glacial.

"Why, Mrs Brodie, I think I'd like him to choose. As his wife, I must defer to his judgement." With a curt nod she escaped outside.

Later that Sunday afternoon, Matthew went looking for Alex. He'd seen her set off up the hill after dinner, and once he got to the top he found her sitting on a small outcrop of stone, just at the edge of the moor.

"Beautiful, isn't it?" she said without turning around. She'd been crying, the skin under her eyes bloated and red.

"What is it?"

"Oh, you know; one of those days." She pulled up her knees and rested her chin on them. "I miss my home."

"You are home."

"Yeah, right; you know what I mean, don't you?" She sighed. "It's … I don't know. I just feel so totally useless, and whenever I ask something the cow – Mrs Brodie, I mean – sniffs and says that she's not used to having to teach the mistress everything. And she's right; I don't know how to milk, or gut a pig, I've never cooked over an open fire, I don't even know the bloody Bible!"

He frowned. "You mustn't refer to the Bible like that; it's blasphemous."

"See? Even you think I'm strange."

"You are strange. But you'll learn, all those things that seem new to you now, well you'll master them over time, no?"

"Maybe. But I'm not sure I even want to." She scratched at her head. "I'm used to another life. And today, well, today I miss it. I want to go home, I want to …" She hitched her shoulders.

"Is it him? Is it John you're missing?" He tried to sound relaxed.

"Him too." She gave him a very blue look.

"So if you could, would you go back? If a door through time opened here, now, would you walk through it?" And what about him? Would she just leave him? Plunge him back into loneliness?

"There is no door."

"But if there was, what would you do?" He was close enough that he could feel her exhalations on his face, see the tear tracks down her cheeks.

"I don't know," she whispered. He reared back, she grabbed his hand. "I don't. But I think that if I did walk through that door, I'd spend the rest of my life missing you. Talk about torn in two, hey?"

Something soared inside of him, a fluttering feeling that rose from his gut to tickle its way up his gullet and explode as a smile on his face.

They took the long way back, Matthew pointing and explaining as he led her all over his lands. Every now and then he'd stop for a word or two with one of his tenants, noting with a small smile how they all gawked at Alex. Well, she was bonny, his wife, and when she smiled and laughed it was difficult not to laugh with her.

He detoured through the graveyard and Alex helped him brush the graves free of leaves and debris.

"She died while you were in prison?" She patted Mam's headstone.

"Aye. Of consumption." And grief at seeing her eldest son betrayed by her youngest. "I wish I'd been here for her," he said, "we were very close, Mam and I."

Alex took his hand. "She knew why."

He just nodded, not trusting himself to speak. He coughed, placed a late rose on her grave and led the way towards the water meadows.

"Why aren't we going over there?" Alex indicated the small cottage that stood half hidden some way up the hill. Matthew lengthened his stride and shook his head. "It's yours isn't it?"

"Aye, but I have no interest in meeting that particular tenant."

"Why don't you kick him out if you don't like him?"

"It's not a him, it's a her. I couldn't just throw them out," he said defensively. "It would have been cruel to the bairn. And she has no other family."

Alex came to a halt. "Are you telling me your ex-wife is living here?"

"Aye," he grunted.

"But why haven't you told me before?"

Matthew shrugged. "I forgot." He took her hand and tugged her back into motion. "I don't want you to spend time with her."

"Well I don't want to either, so that's alright then, isn't it?"

"And Luke?" she asked a bit later, "Is he here as well?"

"Not if he knows what's best for him." Matthew spat to clear his mouth of the bitter taste his brother's name always brought in its wake.

CHAPTER 21

Minister Crombie rode his small hill pony down the lane one early Tuesday morning, a somewhat harried expression on his face.

"I'm telling you, no?" he said to Matthew a few minutes later. "It is restless times we're living in."

"Oh aye; have been for all my life."

Minister Crombie nodded, looking very dour. "But now it has all taken a turn for the worse. The Protector dead and gone, and yon Charles Stuart inching his clever way closer and closer to the throne. Anyway, I didn't ride all the way out here merely for a political discussion. I came to warn you."

"Ah."

"They found the body of the man they hanged," Minister Crombie said. "Some well-meaning soul had cut him down and buried him. So now they know, aye?"

"Who knows what?"

"The local garrison," Minister Crombie said. "They know that the dead man wasn't you."

"They do? Who told them?"

"They had the remains carted in," Minister Crombie said, looking rather sick at the thought. "And several people stepped forward to swear it wasn't you." He threw Matthew a worried look. "Luke's friends, most of them." He sighed and shook his head. "Stay away from Cumnock and go canny, aye? It is but a matter of time before they come looking."

Minister Crombie refused Matthew's invitation to dinner, repeated his admonishment to be careful and sat up on his horse, muttering something about needing to make haste back to Cumnock.

Matthew walked him up the lane, shook hands and trudged back down, deep in thought. It took some time for him to react to hearing his name called, and even more to recognise the voice, but once he did he broke into a huge grin, and after helping her dismount, he swept Joan into a wild hug.

"Let go," she protested, half laughing, half crying. Matthew complied, steadying her at the last moment to avoid her falling to her knees. They stood face to face and the exuberance drained away, leaving them grave and sad.

"Three years…" Joan sighed, lifting a gloved hand to his face. "What happened?" She ran a finger over the scar that bisected his brow and continued as a shallow groove below the hollow of his eye.

"Whip." He jerked his head out of reach. "Mam? Was it bad for her in the end?"

"It was awful. And then there was you and Luke … she never spoke to him after your trial. Margaret tried; several times she came by, but Mam refused to see her."

Matthew looked at her in surprise. "She did?"

Joan nodded. "I think she was ashamed. She swore she'd had no idea what Luke was planning, but I'm not sure I believe her – always a glib liar, our Margaret." She patted his arm. "I'm sorry, that there was no alternative than for her to stay."

Matthew hitched his shoulders; he was uncomfortable with Margaret living this close, even more because it reasonably meant Luke was skulking round as well, but it had been his decision, not hers, to offer Margaret somewhere to live when his good for nothing brother couldn't.

At times he wondered what kind of man Luke would have been had Da not thrown him out all those years ago. It had warped him somehow, and the impetuous, fiery lad hardened into a bitter young man with a grudge, simmering with anger that at times he just couldn't control. His jaw clenched; Luke deserved no understanding.

"Have they wed?" he said, motioning for Gavin to take Joan's mare.

"Do you care?"

"No," he lied, "for the lad, aye, but for them… no."

Joan fell into step with him, and he clasped his hands behind his back, strolling towards the house. She looked at him again, stopped him and ran her hand down his face. He laughed, embarrassed, and twisted away from her touch.

"I'm no ghost, Joan."

"So," he repeated. "Are they wed?"

"Aye."

It was strange that it should hurt so much. He didn't want her back, but there was an element of injustice in it all that made him rage. God should have struck them down, not blessed their adulterous union.

Joan came to a stop when Alex appeared in the door. She gaped, blinked and wheeled to frown at Matthew.

"Does she know?"

"Know what?"

She snorted. "Does yon lassie know that she's a spitting image of your first wife?"

"No she isn't," Matthew said with an edge. "Her hair is lighter and her chin is square where Margaret's is pointed and…"

"So you have been making comparisons," Joan interrupted him.

He looked away. "Aye, I have. But I cared for her long before I saw the likeness, and now I care for her despite the likeness, not because of it."

"Will she believe that, you think? Because someday she'll meet Margaret and unless she's blind she'll see it too. And she won't like it, what woman would?" She stopped and grabbed him by the arm. "You have to tell her."

Matthew made despairing gesture. "But how do I do that?"

"I don't know, but do it soon."

Alex liked Joan immediately, sizing her up in silence. Tall and gangly, Joan overtopped Alex by four inches or so, hovering just below the six feet mark. Wide grey eyes, dark hair tucked away under a linen cap, and very neat in a dove coloured skirt and purple bodice that made Alex feel shabby in her brown. She smoothed at the rough homespun of her skirts and looked away.

Joan laughed and shook her head. "Quickly sorted, no? There is plenty of fabric in the chests – I think we have a most becoming green that will make you a right nice bodice, and if I recall correctly there's a bolt or two of blue broadcloth as well." She threw Alex a sharp look. "Didn't Mrs Brodie show you?"

"No," Alex said, "I suppose it must have slipped her mind." And anyway, what was she to do with bolts of fabric, sew her own clothes?

"There's quite a few yards of good linen," Joan went on, "enough for a couple of shirts for Matthew and a shift or two for you."

"Oh." Shit: she barely knew how to thread a needle.

"Tomorrow," Joan said, "we start tomorrow, aye?"

"I can't wait," Alex replied, pasting what she hoped looked like an enthusiastic smile on her face.

Joan not only set Alex to sewing, she also took one look at the overflowing hampers of soiled linens and decided it was time for a long overdue laundry day – this said with a rather irritated glance in the direction of Mrs Brodie.

The chosen day dawned bright and warm, and Alex had her head filled with romanticised images of laundresses, laughing and splashing as they washed their clothes by the river shore, lounging in the shade of an oak for a leisurely lunch.

The reality was far different; it was bloody hard work, was what it was. Her arms felt about to fall off as she lifted yet another heap of steaming linen from the wash cauldron to the wide basket by her side. The skin of her hands was red and irritated with the lye, and she kept up a long string of colourful Swedish curses as she carried the wicker basket over to the stone trough and kneeled to first scrub then rinse the linen clean.

The whole yard was alive with flapping sheets, but there were still two or three more armloads to go, and right now Alex was thinking that she could definitely do without clean sheets – hell, she could sleep in the hay instead. She poured bucket after bucket of cold water over the scrubbed sheets, stuck her tongue out at the waiting pile.

"List of the day; washing machine, toothbrush, huge pizza, hot shower, and a TV." And chocolate, and salt and vinegar crisps and Magnus … she scrubbed at her eyes to stop herself from crying, which only made them sting with lye.

Joan took one look at her red rimmed eyes and chapped hands and shoved her away from the cauldron.

"Why don't you take a walk? You look greensick."

"I'm hot, mainly." Alex attempted to unstick the linen from her sweating skin. "But yes, I'd like a walk" She smiled gratefully at Joan and strode off towards the woods.

It was a relief to get away from all of them. She was so tired of always being on her guard, of noting what words she used. The other day she had spoken dreamily of afternoon tea only to realise that no one in the room had ever heard of that concept before. And she missed Matthew, her time with him restricted to short snatches in bed before he fell asleep, worn out after his long days. She looked for somewhere to sit down, aware of a sudden heaviness in her body. Maybe she had an infection, because for days now she'd been ridiculously tired. She sighed, swamped by a general feeling of irritation.

She counted days as she walked up the hill, and came to a halt when she realised it was the beginning of October. She counted again and plunked down in the grass, not caring that it was wet. No wonder she was feeling so strange! A child… Isaac! She hadn't thought actively of him for weeks, his existence in that other time a constant chafing in her heart that she preferred to ignore. And now… she splayed her hands across her midriff. A child; a baby conceived in passion, a son – daughter? – she would never resent, never eye askance. Oh God; Isaac, unloved in her womb, hated at the time of his birth and so unwelcome afterwards. Her breath came in loud gulps, her eyes filled with tears that she blinked back into their ducts.

"Sorry," she said out loud, "I'm so sorry, Isaac." As if he could hear her, as if he would care, safe in his future world with John and his Offa. She was only slightly more peripheral now that she was gone, than she had been while she was there, always maintaining an emotional distance to the boy that with every single day more and more resembled his damned father. Shit. Alex hid her face against her knees, sat like that for a very long time.

She made her way down the hill, and just as she reached the yard she saw Matthew enter the stable. When he climbed up to the hay loft so did she, her single conscious thought being that she had to be with him. The whole loft bathed in the sun streaming in through the loading hatch, and when he heard her he turned, a dark silhouette against all that golden light. He moved towards her, as wordless as she was, and laid her down in the stacks of sweet smelling hay.

"I'm pregnant," she said between his kisses.

"I know."

"You do?"

"Of course I do." He brushed his nose against hers. "It makes me very happy."

"Me too," she said, and the naked joy in his eyes made her realise she meant it.

To her irritation, Joan just grinned when Alex told her the news, commenting that it had taken her quite some time to realise, no? What? So she was surrounded by wannabe gynaecologists? Joan grinned even more at her scowl, tucked a hand in under Alex' arm and led her off to the parlour, telling her they had mountains of mending to get through. Whoopee.

"Right ," Joan said, once they were settled. "Now I want to hear it all."

"All?" Alex asked.

"About how you met."

Alex looked down at the shirt she was mending for Matthew. She had to her delight discovered that she was quite good at sewing, her small, even stitches complimented not only by Joan but also, miracle of miracles, by Mrs Brodie .

"Didn't Simon tell you?"

Joan raised her brows in derision. "Had you been the victim of moss-troopers you'd be dead or working in a brothel." Nice; some things never change. Alex sighed and rubbed her collarbone, wondering how to explain.

It was obvious her cover story was much better than Matthew's half baked attempts, even if Joan still regarded her with some scepticism afterwards. But a freak thunderstorm, a disappeared father, a burnt foot and, for some days, no idea of who she was, was in some aspects almost true.

"Matthew found me," she finished. "And, well…"

Joan uttered a soft grunt. "You bedded with him there, on the moor?"

It was difficult to deny, so Alex just nodded.

"And you knew him to be a fugitive? A man who might still hang?" The subtext was very clear, making Alex hide a smile.

"Well, I didn't take him for his money," she said, rather gratified by the red stains that flew up Joan's face.

"So why then?"

Because his hands drove her crazy and his smile warmed her gut. Because of the glint in his eyes and the heat in his mouth. But mostly because with him there were no secrets, no subterfuge.

"I love him."

"Truly?" Joan's grey eyes were only inches from Alex' face.

"Truly," Alex answered. "But don't tell him that, it might make him quite unbearable to live with." Joan burst out laughing and promised she wouldn't say a word.

CHAPTER 22

Hector nodded a thank you to the serving maid and attacked his stew. Awful; tasteless, full of gristle and with very little meat. But it was hot, and the bread served with it was edible enough. He downed his beer, signalled for more, and went back to his food, all the while keeping an eye on the men in the small, smelly room.

He'd had no major problems adapting to his new environments. Breeches and clumsy boots, hats and cloaks he'd worn before, and he was more than adept at using a sword – or a knife. After several weeks in Cumnock he was therefore the proprietor of a heavy pouch, lying snug against his thigh. His victims had mostly escaped unscathed, except for the fool that pulled a dagger on him and so... well; at least he'd died quickly, if somewhat messily.

Hector shoved the bowl away from him and frowned; a month of keeping eyes and ears open for any gossip that might lead him in the direction of Alexandra Lind and so far nothing. He had no idea, he reminded himself, she might have ended up somewhere else entirely.

Hector chewed his lip and studied the depressing little inn in which he seemed to spend most of his evenings. In three hundred years or so the Merkat Cross would no doubt be a quaint little pub, complete with historical interiors and an interesting past, but at present it was dirty, damp, full of far too many smelly men and with a complement of furry things that darted hastily from one dark nook to the other.

He knew for a fact there were mice in his mattress, he could hear them rustle through the straw, and only by paying extra had he managed to get a clean set of sheets. Hector scowled. He wasn't meant for this squalor! No, if nothing came up in a fortnight he'd leave, make for

Edinburgh or London, maybe even try to find a ship bound for Spain.

And then he had his first stroke of luck. The fat little lawyer sitting beside him was conversing with the innkeeper, a casual sharing of this and that, when the innkeeper leaned forward with a gleam of interest in his eyes.

"Is it true then? That Matthew Graham has wed a foreign lass?"

"Aye, Swedish," Simon Melville confirmed.

"Swedish?" the innkeeper shook his head. "Is she heathen, do you think?"

"No," Simon said, "nor does she foam at the mouth or in any way look different from us."

"Oh, aye?" an unknown man put in. "She had no hair, did she? All cut off."

"Really?" Hector asked.

Three faces turned like one towards him, three sets of eyes narrowing suspiciously. For all that he'd been drinking here for several weeks, he was definitely a stranger, and strangers did best not to meddle in local matters.

"What is it to you?" Simon demanded.

"Nothing. I was just wondering what a woman might look like without her hair. Bare, no?" Hector dragged a hand over his own, still very short, hair.

"Not that short! More like this." Simon waved a hand somewhere just below ear level. "Sick," he said for the benefit of the innkeeper. "Alex had the fever, Matthew said, and so the healer up Lanark way cut her hair off."

"Ah," the innkeeper nodded, seemingly not that interested. "No dowry? No land?"

"None, but what good would it do Matthew to have a parcel of land in Sweden?"

Hector had heard enough. A Swedish woman called Alex with short hair, who could it be but the elusive Ms. Lind? He was bursting with questions, but recognised that to ask any more tonight would be to draw undue attention to himself. After yet another beer he bade the men goodnight and pretended to stumble up the stairs to the bed he paid double rates for to sleep in alone.

A few discreet inquiries, several beers, and he had a pretty good picture of this Matthew Graham. A stouthearted Parliamentarian, a man who'd fought for the Commonwealth but then betrayed the cause – even if quite a few of his respondents were doubtful as to how true that was.

"His brother," the innkeeper confided, well into his cups. "That Luke Graham set him up, aye? Matthew is no royalist, but now he lingers in gaol, convicted for treason."

"He lingers in gaol?" Hector asked, looking up from his pipe in surprise.

"He should, but he didn't like it much, and as we hear it he escaped, aye? A fugitive, one could say."

"Oh," Hector nodded.

The innkeeper gave him a bleary look. "He has been keeping well to the ground, aye? No need to let the local garrison know he's back."

"I won't tell," Hector said, "but I dare say his brother will."

"Yon Luke is elsewhere at the moment." The innkeeper glowered in the direction of his kitchen. "He isn't welcome here, not after nearly burning my place to the ground."

"I don't like it," Simon said to the innkeeper a couple of days later, following Hector out of the room with his eyes.

"How so?" the innkeeper yawned.

"We don't know him, and for all that he speaks effortless English, he's definitely not Scots, is he? He may well be a royalist spy."

The thought had clearly not struck the innkeeper before, but now that Simon mentioned it…He pursed his mouth into a narrow spout and poured himself and Simon yet another tot of whisky.

"Aye, he asks a lot of questions."

"Far too many," Simon nodded.

"Hector? A Hector Olivares you say?" Matthew frowned and shook his head. It couldn't be, could it? Nay, such must be impossible, it had to be an eerie coincidence no more. "No, I can't say I collect such a man." He threw a discreet look at Alex; she'd sunk her hands into her skirts, eyes locked on the floor.

Matthew stood and stretched. "And he's been asking questions?" he said in an uninterested voice.

"Aye; about your wife as well," Simon said, scrutinising Alex. Matthew frowned; wee Simon was far too adept a lawyer not to react to her frozen stance.

"About me?" Alex said. "Why would he want to know about me?"

"I don't know," Simon said, "but mayhap it's because you're a foreigner."

"Well, so is he," she snapped and Matthew closed his eyes.

"How would you know?" Simon said, but nodded all the same.

"His name," Alex said, "not exactly the most Scottish of names."

"There are plenty of Hectors up here," Simon said.

"But not that many Olivares; that's a Spanish name."

"Spanish, you say?" Simon mulled this over.

"A spy?" Matthew offered.

Simon grinned. "That's what we told the garrison commander, and now Hector Olivares is on his way to Edinburgh. I dare say it won't help his case when they find out he's Spanish, and no doubt papist to boot, hmm?" Alex visibly relaxed, and when Joan called for her from the kitchen she hurried off.

Simon studied Matthew for some moments, his eyes very serious.

"I didn't like it that he asked around for you, and when I saw yon Hector conversing with Luke I decided to nip that friendship in the bud."

"Ah. So Luke is back, then?"

"Unfortunately. You know he'll come here, no?"

"That would not be wise." Matthew injected his voice with menace.

"Hmm." Simon threw a look at where Alex had left her shawl. "She knows this Hector Olivares, doesn't she?"

"Aye," Matthew said, "it would seem so. I'll ask her."

"It might not be him," Matthew said a few hours later, watching his wife pace up and down their bed chamber.

"No," Alex said, "but it does seem probable it is, no?"

Aye, Matthew sighed, however inexplicable, he'd hazard this man was the same man who'd orchestrated Alex' abduction. She did another turn; he grabbed her and pulled her down to sit beside him on the bed.

"I don't fucking believe this," she muttered, more to herself than to him. "How on earth can he be here? And yet here he is, having somehow left the twenty-first century behind." She stuck her hands in under her thighs and sat swinging her legs back and forth. Matthew kneeled before her, his hands cupping her face.

"You're frightened."

She nodded, scuffed at the floor with her toes. "And I don't understand. How?"

Matthew half smiled and drew her close enough that he could kiss her brow.

"A thunderstorm?"

Alex shook her head: too improbable.

"Aye," Matthew agreed with a sigh. He sat back on his heels, regarding her thoughtfully.

At times it struck him that he didn't really know her or the world she came from, he had no manner to verify if her story was true – she might be a full-blooded witch that had enthralled him through magic, or something as mundane as a lass fleeing from the long arm of justice. All he truly knew was that he'd found her, concussed and burnt on the moor, and that now that he had, he had no intention of relinquishing her – ever.

"What?" she said, and Matthew realised he'd been staring at her.

"He won't hurt you."

"But what does he want?" Alex said hoarsely. "Why is he here?"

CHAPTER 23

Alex had been at Hillview for more than a month before she met either of them. She sometimes walked in the direction of the isolated cottage, drawn by a curiosity she couldn't fully explain, and on this October morning she'd sat down under a rowan tree to look at the landscape spread out below when the sound of a breaking twig alerted her to the fact that she was no longer alone. She knew who he was immediately and slid up to stand while she studied him.

Where Matthew was tall and solid, Luke was fluid like water, long hair the deep red of a fox pelt, eyes a vivid, sharp green. With his colouring and strong facial features, he was catwalk material, drop-dead gorgeous. He was also very young, Alex noted with some surprise, before remembering that he was only twenty-three, five years younger than Matthew.

"Well, well," Luke said, giving her a bow. "My new sister-in-law, I believe." His eyes travelled over her with interest, stopping at the too short hair, registering her breasts and hips. He laughed and shook his head, sunlight dancing in his hair.

"Poor Matthew, he'll never get over her." He looked at her again. "Remarkable, absolutely remarkable."

"What?" Alex smoothed down her skirts.

"You could be sisters, twins almost, you and Margaret." Luke tilted his head and studied her with frank curiosity. "Your hair's lighter, and you're not as narrow around the waist as my Margaret, but apart from that …" He laughed again.

Had Matthew been there Alex would have torn into him on the spot, demanding an explanation. Seeing as he wasn't, she decided to save that little spurt of anger for later and studied Luke as openly as he had studied her.

"Have you changed your name yet?"

Luke gave her a blank look.

"It should be Cain, shouldn't it?" she said, very pleased with the red that stained his cheeks.

"Cain killed Abel," he said icily.

"Well, bully for you, how unfortunate the sentence to hang was commuted to one to rot in prison. But I'm sure you attempted to find ways round that, didn't you? You probably bribed the prison guards to give him hell."

He paled and turned away.

"Oh my God! You actually did!" She stepped up close. "Have you any idea what they did to him?"

Luke hitched a disinterested shoulder. "He should've been dead."

"Why?" Alex demanded. "What has he ever done to you to deserve that?"

"Done to me?" Luke echoed. "Has he not told you then? Of how he had Da throw me out?"

"Matthew had nothing to do with that. Your father threw you out because of finding you with Margaret, not ..."

"He asked him to, aye? Matthew had taken a liking to Margaret already then, and he made Da throw me out."

"That's not what he says," Alex said. Had he? Her Matthew?

"No, but he wouldn't, would he?" He was standing far too close, brittle eyes boring into her. No warmth, some interest, and Alex backed away. It seemed to amuse him. He took a step towards her and she retreated. Two quick steps and he had his hands on her and when she backed away again she slammed against the tree, with him far too close.

"A kiss for your brother-in-law?"

"Go to hell! Go home and fuck your two-timing wife instead." She winced at the pressure on her wrist bones.

"I love my wife," Luke hissed, a fanatical gleam in his eyes. "And he, that bastard brother of mine, tried to take her from me."

"Really? As I heard it, she eagerly led him on."

"Led him on?" Luke's voice climbed a register or two.

"What lies has he been telling you? He forced her! He violated her, dishonoured her, and then what was she to do? What could she do but wed him, all alone as she was in the world? For that he deserved to die, for all the pain and sorrow he put my Margaret through, you hear?" He twisted his hands into her skin.

"Ah!" she gasped, tears springing in her eyes. "Let me go!"

"I will, soon. Once I've made my own comparisons between you and Margaret. After all, he probably already has."

"You heard her; let go of her." The quiet voice cut through the clearing and Luke wheeled. Matthew was standing only feet away with his dirk in his hand.

"I should have killed you that afternoon in my bedroom," Matthew said, "and I am of a mind to do it now. I won't, not this time. But if you as much as lay a finger on my wife again – any wife of mine – I swear, on my blood, that I'll have your balls off, you hear?" He took two long strides across the clearing, raised his knife and slashed himself across the palm, holding up the bloodied hand to Luke.

"My word, brother. And now, get off my land." He motioned with his knife and waited until Luke disappeared up the hill before moving over to Alex.

"What were you thinking, coming up here alone? I told you to stay away from her cottage. And why didn't you kick him, like you did with those men on the moor?"

"He got too close, okay? And I wasn't under the impression that your brother was going to behave quite as erratically as he just did. You never told me he's a total wacko."

Matthew blinked in incomprehension.

"He's insane," Alex explained impatiently.

"Ah no, he's not insane. He's twisted and dangerous, but very sane." He muttered a quick prayer and held out his hand to Alex. "Come, lass, let's go home." She turned and stalked away, her arms crossed over her chest.

"Is that why you don't want me to see her?" she

demanded a couple of minutes later. She was seething inside, wanting very much to hurt someone.

"See who?"

"Her. Margaret." She turned towards him. "Luke just told me that we could be sisters she and I, is that true?"

He didn't reply, keeping his eyes on the ground.

"I asked you a question!"

"Aye, and I'm not inclined to answer."

"Fine. I'll go and check for myself." And just like that she was off, running back the way they'd come.

He caught up with her and tried to grab her. She wrenched herself free, gripped his forearm, and with a twisting motion sent him flying to land on his back. He lay staring at the sky for a long moment, his breath coming in loud, choked gasps.

"I'm sorry," she said, made as if to help him up, but he waved her away. He moved his legs, rolled over on his side. "I didn't mean to." She stood a distance away, not quite sure what to do. "I'm sorry, do you want me to …" She swallowed down the rest. He looked at her with blank eyes as he got to his feet. She could see he was bleeding from just below the ear and her stomach turned with shame.

"I'm sorry," she repeated.

He wiped his face with a shaking hand and spat into the ground. He was bleeding from his mouth as well, and she wanted to rush over and try to make things right again, but the look on his face was cold and forbidding.

"You wouldn't defend yourself against him, but me you throw like a sack of barley," he said, pushed through the closest thicket and walked away.

"Fuck." She sat down, "*djävla skit*, bloody hell, fuck."

"Well, you have a tongue on you." The voice was soft with amusement and Alex swivelled towards it, not seeing anything much with the sun in her eyes.

"I'm a bit upset."

"Aye, I gathered."

Alex could hear someone moving and stood up, fists

balling. This time she'd send whoever got close flying first and ask questions after.

"So you're his new woman then?" The disdainful tone cut, and Alex drew herself up straighter.

"His wife, I'm Matthew's wife."

"The foreigner," the voice laughed. "But I had him first, aye?"

"Oh, you're Margaret. Lucky me, first your lowlife husband and then you. What else could a girl want?"

The disembodied voice stepped out from the trees and a dark haired woman walked towards her. Alex inhaled noisily. Luke was right; this could have been her sister. Margaret seemed equally surprised and stopped an arm's length away, her eyes amazed.

"You look just like me!"

Alex just stared. Where she had brown, curling hair, this woman had a straight blackness that hung down her back, uncovered except for a most nominal linen cap. Margaret's eyes were several shades lighter than Alex' dark blue, but the shape was the same as were the brows, dark and elegantly arched. It was like looking in a flawed mirror; the same nose, the same mouth, although Alex' lower lip was fuller and no one had ever broken Margaret's nose. And where Margaret's face ended in an exquisite point, Alex' chin was square.

"Well," Margaret said, having completed her own inspection, "it would seem he hasn't forgotten me." She smiled and brushed at her hair. "Does he talk much of me?"

"No, not really, but he's mentioned your name."

Once she got home she was going to flay the bastard. Luke was right; the resemblance was eerie. Make comparisons indeed! And it didn't exactly help that while she, Alex, was attractive enough, bloody Margaret was absolutely ravishing. She was quite glad she'd sent him flying, except that the look in his eyes as he'd stared up at her still cut her to the bone.

"Mentioned it, aye? I think it would be somewhat more."

"Well, let's say that what I've heard hasn't been to your credit."

"No," Margaret said, and there was a tinge of sadness in her tone. "I suppose it wouldn't be." She sat down and patted the ground beside her in an inviting gesture. Alex hesitated. "I won't harm you," Margaret assured her, making Alex raise an amused brow before sitting down.

"I never loved him," Margaret said. "It was always Luke for me."

"Oh good; nice to have cleared that one up. So, you married a man you didn't love, you fucked his brother on the side, foisted him with a cuckoo child and... let me see, have I forgotten something? Oh yes! You contrived to have him convicted for crimes of treason of which he was perfectly innocent. I sincerely hope that any resemblance between us is only skin deep because the world doesn't need more than one conniving bitch of that calibre."

Margaret was staring at her with a gaping mouth, and Alex had a sudden urge to stuff it full of grass.

"You don't like me much, do you?" Margaret said.

"I don't know you. But what I know of you doesn't have me hoping for a long and mutual friendship."

"It wasn't quite as simple as you describe it."

"Simple? There's nothing simple about this whole mess, is there?" Alex glared at her and Margaret shifted away.

"They threw him out. He was my whole life and they threw him out, telling him he was never welcome back again." She glanced at Alex. "You've heard, no? Of how his father found us in the hayloft, and us only fifteen."

Alex nodded.

"I took Luke to bed when I was not quite fourteen. We couldn't help ourselves." Margaret smiled and picked up a bright yellow rowan frond, running it through her fingers. "We loved each other, and had Malcolm only asked, we would have wed the next day. But to Malcolm what we did was sinful, and he was disgusted by us, but mainly by Luke whom he called rotten to the core."

"Good description," Alex said.

Margaret frowned. "He was but a lad. Wild and high-spirited, aye, but rotten?" She shook her head, and Alex muttered a vague agreement. It still struck her as excessively harsh to boot your son out for sleeping with a girl he loved.

"Malcolm gave him a horse and some funds, and with those Luke rode north and spent the following years trailing the king on his progress. Took a liking to him, the king did, and even more after Luke took a blade for him in a skirmish just over the border."

"There is no king."

"Ah but there is!" Margaret said. "King of Scots and soon to be King of England as well. He will prevail, aye? He's only five or six years older than me, is Charles, and already a king and a fine man says Luke."

"Oh, and Luke would know?"

"Mayhap." Margaret looked like a smug cat at the idea of her Luke being confidant to the king.

"I was rather referring to the fact that Luke wouldn't exactly be a reliable judge of character – given his own."

Margaret sniffed but continued with her story. "I missed him so much it hurt, every day I woke and missed him yet again. I was so lonely, and Joan and I were never close, so I turned to Matthew. He'd not noticed me much before, but I changed that right quickly, aye? After all, he's not bad looking, and stood to inherit all this – the only home I'd ever known."

"Callous." Alex exhaled, relieved to hear there'd been nothing going on between Matthew and Margaret before Luke had left.

"I was only fifteen. And I was good to him, to Matthew I mean." She gave Alex a coy look.

"I don't want to hear this." Alex got to her feet, but Margaret grabbed her skirts.

"But I want to tell, aye? You've only heard his side, haven't you?" She refused to let go until Alex sat back down.

"If I'd thought there was even the slightest chance of Luke coming back, I swear I'd never have married him, and as long as Malcolm lived, that was never going to happen. So I wed Matthew, and five months later his father was dead and Luke rode into the yard. I thought I was going to die." She fell silent, fingering the rowan frond.

"I did try to hold to my marriage vows, but I ... just to see Luke again, to have his hand touch mine ..." She looked away, gnawing at her lip. "It was unbearable, and Luke ... well, he was so angered, accusing me of being false." She hitched her shoulders. "But I wasn't, not really; in my heart there was ever only Luke."

Alex rolled her eyes at this somewhat melodramatic statement.

"And I suppose you told him that, right?"

Margaret ducked her head, her fingers tearing the rowan frond to shreds. "Aye, I did."

"So how did you explain it to him?"

"Explain what?"

"That you'd married Matthew, seeing as you swore Luke undying love."

Margaret brushed the crumbled leaves off her lap and shrugged.

"I just said I had to. He understood my predicament."

Alex raised her brows; not quite as simple, and in particular given Margaret's piggy pink hue. And it definitely didn't tally with Luke's version of events earlier. No; Margaret had concocted a heart pinching story, starring herself as victim and Matthew as the beast.

Margaret fidgeted under Alex' eyes. "In the end I couldn't help myself, and you know the rest, no? How Matthew threw us out naked, threatening to kill us both." She dropped her eyes to her lap, fiddled with her waistband. "I didn't mean to hurt him so badly, to leave his heart permanently scarred."

"That he'll get over; in fact, I think he already has." Alex smirked. "But the rest..." She shook her head.

"I did try to stop Luke, but he'd heard that the Commonwealth men had information about a royalist spy, a Graham just like the Montrose, God save his soul, and so he gave Matthew up. He had to, for the sake of the cause."

Alex stood up and spat at Margaret's feet.

"That lie has probably saved you from many sleepless nights, but isn't it time you admit what you did – at least to yourself? You were sending an innocent man to hang! And how convenient, no, that in the case of his death his heir would've been the brother who denounced him."

"I'm sorry," Margaret said. "I truly am."

"And that doesn't help, does it?" Alex said and walked off.

She wandered through the woods for hours, piecing together what Margaret had told her with what Matthew had said about the whole business. She avoided the house all day, wondering what she could possibly say to Matthew that would wipe the look of astounded hurt from his face, and at dusk she slipped in to the stables to delay a bit further the confrontation with those cold hazel eyes.

She rubbed Samson over his back and fed him a small apple before sinking down to sit on a pile of hay by the door. She sat there for a long time, watching how candles were extinguished one by one and the house before her went to sleep. He hadn't come looking, and she had hoped he would.

Alex was hugely embarrassed when Sam shook her awake. After a muttered good morning she rushed over to the house, and taking a big breath walked inside.

Matthew was sitting by the kitchen table but gave no sign of having noticed her entry, so she hurried through, grabbing at some bread on the way, and disappeared into their bedroom. She could hear Matthew talking below, even heard him laugh. He hadn't worried about her, the bed very obviously slept in. On the floor he'd left a discarded pile of linen and dirty stockings, and she kicked it into a corner. He could do his own bloody laundry!

She spent the morning helping Joan make preserves, a strained silence between them. Alex wondered how Matthew had explained her disappearance, somehow she suspected he would never admit to having been thrown to the ground by his wife. When she saw the men return from the fields, Alex escaped, mumbling something about taking a walk. She darted out below Matthew's arm, her face averted from his. He didn't come after; she wished he had.

Matthew stayed outside for as long as he could, only reluctantly returning to the house. She wasn't there, and the reply to his casual question indicated that she'd been gone all afternoon. She didn't appear for supper, and when a quick inspection revealed that she was neither in the stables nor the barn, a small coil of unease snaked through his belly.

He'd been so angry with her yesterday, humiliated by the ease with which she'd wheeled him to the ground, but even more upset by the fact that she'd done that to him but not to his accursed brother. So when she'd not come in for supper, he had put out the candles and locked down the doors, assuming that she'd either come knocking or find a pocket of hay in which to sleep. And he'd been right, hadn't he, seeing her come in this morning with hay in her hair. But now... He walked through the stables again, he climbed up to the hayloft and she wasn't there, and he stalked through the nearby woods, calling her name but she didn't reply.

For a giddy second he contemplated the terrible possibility that maybe she'd been thrown back to her time and he would never know his bairn or see her again, and the anguish made him bend over in pain. For another second he considered that she'd just left, taken what few things were hers and walked off. The thought brought him up cold, and he rushed to his study to retrieve his little strongbox. It was gone; John's ring, her necklace and the ring her father gave her.

"She can't have gotten very far," Joan said, "she's on foot, Matthew."

"But where would she go?" He threw a saddle on Samson, brusque in his haste.

"To Cumnock I imagine, where else?"

"To do what?" Matthew said. "What can she do there, a woman all alone?"

Joan shrugged that she had no idea. "Why did she go? What did you quarrel about?"

"I'm not even sure we had a quarrel, we had a silence, aye?"

"Ah," Joan nodded.

Matthew threw her a quick look; for all his expansive nature, wee Simon was a master at cutting silences, days when his gregarious self would disappear and be replaced by a stranger. It would seem that at times those silences were directed at his wife.

"And she found out about Margaret and her being alike."

"Really? How?" Joan shook her head. "I told you, no?"

"Luke."

"Luke? Was he here?"

"Aye. I came upon them by the large rowan, Mam's spot, and he was trying to kiss her, making interesting comments about wanting to compare for himself."

"What did you do? Please tell me you didn't do anything daft!"

Matthew scowled at her. "The one daft thing I've done with my brother is to not have killed him when I found him in bed with my wife. That's something I fear I'll live to regret many times over."

He tightened the girth one more time and led the horse over to the stable door. "But I told him; I warned him that if I ever catch him touching a wife of mine again I'll geld him." He ignored her shocked exclamation and swung himself up into the saddle. "Will you light a candle? In case she should come back and not find her way?"

She patted his leg. "Of course I will."

He found her sitting just off the road, a couple of miles from Cumnock. By then he was worried sick, imagining one scenario after the other, all of them ending with her being carried forever out of his life.

If it hadn't been for the horse's little sound he might have missed her, a dark shape against a slightly less dark background. She was sitting just off the verge, shoulders hunched against the drizzle, and when he approached he saw her stiffen. He dismounted and dropped down beside her, arms propped on his knees.

"Why did you just go?" he said, breaking an endless silence.

She had no idea, she muttered; it definitely had something to do with coming face to face with Margaret and discovering herself to be a faded copy of a glorious original, but just as much with the shame she felt at having turned her anger at Luke on him, letting him pay for his brother's intimidation. Most of all it was because he hadn't cared enough to come looking for her last night, hadn't even bothered to say something to her this morning.

"I was so angry with you, that you would toss me like that…" Matthew said, feeling shamed.

"I told you I was sorry."

"And why did you stop here?" No cover from wind or rain, it made a dismal spot to spend the night.

"I…" she bit her lip. "I just felt like it."

"Oh, aye? You like sitting out in the rain?"

"I don't have anywhere to go," she mumbled, and he could hear how she hated having to admit it. "I was thinking of going to Edinburgh or London, but what was I to do there? How would I earn my living?"

"On your back, in all probability," Matthew said harshly, frightened by the image of her disappearing into the teeming underbelly of a city the size of Edinburgh. "But you're not going anywhere, are you?" he added, softening his voice.

"Not much choice, is there?"

"Alex," Matthew sighed, "you're my wife. You don't need anywhere else to go, because you belong with me, no?"

She turned back the hood of her cloak and faced him. "I'm not used to being so dependent on one person."

"Neither am I," he said seriously.

By the time they got back home, Alex was stiff with cold, no matter that Matthew had wrapped her in both their cloaks. She stumbled into the kitchen, dropped cloak and shawl onto the floor and at his urgings sat down as close as she could to the fire.

"More," she said, waving her cup in the direction of Matthew.

"Not too much more," he warned, replenishing her cup with hot milk before spiking it with brandy and a dollop of honey. He added an extra dash of brandy to his own cup before coming over to sit with her by the kitchen table. The small strongbox lay on the floor, its contents removed to be hidden elsewhere, with his father's secret cache. Her wide-eyed look at the sight of the gold and the small pieces of jewellery had gratified him – at least she need no longer think it was her wee trinkets that he was after.

"I didn't see it."

"See what?" Alex yawned.

"The likeness."

Alex raised a sceptical eyebrow. "Poor you; you need glasses."

"I didn't see it from the first, if I had, I wouldn't have gone near you with less than a six foot pole between us." He smiled at her. "It would have made it difficult to bandage your ribs, no?"

"Huh. Sometimes I wonder if my ribs really needed bandaging, or if that was just an excuse to have me undress."

"An excuse," he said, laughing when she swiped at him. He grabbed her hand, gathered her to sit in his lap. "Once I did notice, well then it was a bit late in the day."

"Hmm." Alex regarded him thoughtfully. "She's very beautiful."

"Oh, aye. That she is. Very beautiful." He felt the ice splinters bury themselves in him, but decided to add a bit more fuel to the flattering fire of jealousy he saw burning in her. "Like an angel, no?"

"You think?" It came out very cold.

Matthew buried his nose in her cleavage and exhaled. "A fallen angel, while you..." He tickled her with his hair.

"... am not an angel." She squirmed on his lap.

"No, too hot blooded by far." He nuzzled her neck. "A handful."

"Somehow I don't think you mind," she said, twisting so that she straddled him. Now it was him that fidgeted.

"No," he breathed, "I don't think I do."

Over the coming days Alex gravitated in the direction of Margaret's cottage, overcome by an instinctual need to size up the competition. Sometimes she saw her, mostly alone but at times with a child. They never spoke, at most nodded before going their different ways.

One day she heard someone laughing, a high happy burbling, and Alex smiled in return, detouring to see who was making the sound.

A sturdy little boy sat by the running stream and dropped acorns into the rushing water, and every now and then that contagious laughter just bubbled out of him. When he turned his head she bit back on a surprised exclamation. This must have been what Matthew had looked like as a child; dark, tumbling hair, wide hazel eyes and a small cleft chin. Nothing at all of Luke, she mused, eyes narrowing as she grasped at a half baked thought that whizzed through her brain. Several years bonking the daylights out of each other, and only one child? Hmm.

"What do you want?" Margaret planted herself to shield the boy from her. Alex looked at her and peeked round the side to smile down at the child, who readily smiled back, an exact copy of Matthew.

"What do you want?" Margaret repeated belligerently.

She flicked a strand of black hair off her forehead and sank her eyes into Alex.

"I was just passing by." With an ironic nod Alex sidestepped her. She threw one last look at the child. "He looks just like his father," she said, very pleased by the way all colour drained from Margaret's face.

CHAPTER 24

Every Sunday, Simon would ride in well before noon, slide off his horse and rush to embrace his wife. They made an odd couple, she an ostrich, him a strutting pigeon, but anyone not blind couldn't help but notice the tangible attraction between them.

"Why isn't she living with him?" Alex asked Matthew, watching with astonished amusement as Simon swept Joan off her feet and carried her inside.

Matthew's features darkened. "He had some misfortune some years back, after my trial."

"Misfortune?"

Matthew sighed and looked away. "They found him in a close, aye? And they beat him and promised they'd do the same to his wife, closet royalist that she must be." He fisted his hand and punched it against his leg. "She's safer here."

Joan laughed disparagingly when Alex confronted her about all this.

"It's none so bad, and once you're settled in, I'll be going to live with Simon – now that he's finally found us acceptable lodgings."

"You don't need to stay for my sake, I'll manage." Alex heard Mrs Brodie snort behind her back, and considered throwing the contents of the slop pail in the housekeeper's face, but decided it would be unnecessarily antagonistic.

"I'll stay some weeks more," Joan said.

"Have you heard any more of yon Hector?" Matthew asked after dinner. He moved his rook, grinned at Simon's responding move with his knight.

"No, but he hasn't come back, has he? They hang spies at present." Simon threw them both a worried look. "And you'd best be careful, Matthew. They hang escaped convicts as well."

Over Simon's head, Alex met Matthew's eyes. He smiled and stretched out his long legs, his toes nudging hers.

"They must catch me first, no?"

"Aye, there is that," Simon agreed, "and you may be a bit weak in the arm but you run like a hart."

"Weak in the arm? Come here, you, and I'll show you, aye?"

"Do you think he's dead then?" Alex said, interrupting their horseplay.

"Who? Oh, Hector Olivares. Probably," Simon said, smoothing down his rumpled coat. "Does that make you feel better?"

Alex attempted a disinterested shrug. "Why should it? I don't know the man, do I?" But it did; however awful a person it made her, she was glad Hector Olivares was dead.

"So; are you a royalist?" Alex asked Joan some days later. Joan gave her a disapproving look, and tilted her head in the direction of Mrs Brodie.

"You shouldn't ask," she said once they were alone. "It's not an easy subject." She sighed and shook her head. "One brother a puritan, the other a wild eyed royalist. It's enough to make your head burst, no?"

"Puritan?" Alex bit back on a smile. "Matthew?" Definitely not in bed.

Joan rolled her eyes at her and held out her hand.

"Let me see that," she said, and inspected the rip Alex had just mended before going on. "Matthew was only a lad when the Covenanters defeated the king that was, and when the Scottish Army rode south to fight he begged Da to let him go. When Da said no, Matthew tried to sneak off but was caught and given the belting of his life, and he already fourteen. He wept when he heard of Marston Moor, telling Da that it was his fault that he, Matthew, had not been there to fight and win against the king." Joan smiled, shaking her head. "It was Mam, no? Egging him on with all her talk of all men being equal in the eyes of the Lord."

Joan broke off, eyes straying to the window. "It was always Mam and Matthew, it was always Da and me, and for Luke it was Margaret – he had no one else. Always alone, Luke was, until the day Da brought Margaret home."

"Poor him," Alex said, not even attempting to sound sincere.

"The fighting was far from over, and one day Matthew disappeared and went to fight against the royalist rebels, against Montrose." Joan stabbed her needle through the coarse linen and worked in silence for some minutes. "He was a lad, Alex, and he came home after the battle of Philiphaugh, shocked by what he'd seen and done. It was the murder of the Irish, I think."

"Murder of the Irish?"

Joan hitched her shoulders. "They surrendered, the Irish soldiers, and were promised their lives. Instead they were killed – them and their camp followers, down to the smallest bairn."

"Anyway," Joan went on, ignoring Alex' shocked exclamation, "a few days after Matthew returned, a troop of Horse rode in, and one of them recognised Matthew. They told Da he must be very proud of his son, and then they hauled Matthew onto a horse and told him he was coming with them, for hadn't he signed up with the Horse? Matthew didn't want to go, he was weeping, big lad that he was, and Da tried to make them let him go, but the officer just shrugged and said it was easy; come with them or hang as a deserter. So he rode south with them, and when he came back four years later he had changed from a lad with romantic notions of equality among men, to a man with the firm conviction that all free men rule themselves." Joan sighed, an inward look in her eyes.

"He came back in June of 1649, a lean, tanned man with his buff coat hanging open. I scarcely recognised him, and in many ways he was a stranger, the lad who'd ridden out all those years ago permanently gone. Instead here was a man, a man whose eyes regarded the world with a hint of caution, who no longer smiled and laughed quite as readily as he was wont to do." Joan smiled at Alex. "But he laughs now, no? I hear him laughing in your room, your bed, and every time I do, I wonder what you might be doing."

"Umm," Alex said, extremely embarrassed.

Joan chuckled and bent her head to the buttonhole she was stitching.

"Mam was so glad to have him back. And Luke, well Luke was not yet fifteen, and he followed Matthew like a wee dog, asking him about the war, and had he ever been wounded, and what was it like to kill a man. He was too young to understand that Matthew wanted to forget, and Matthew was too young to explain. He just ignored him, became close-lipped and hard-eyed whenever Luke was close, until the day when he exploded and told Luke to leave him be, to stop nagging at him like an old wife and that he had no time for untried laddies that knew nothing of what it was like to fight or die."

Joan handed a new shirt for hemming to Alex and folded the finished shirt in her lap.

"Luke never went near Matthew again, and a year or so later Luke was out on his ear and as far as I know they've never since spoken properly to each other. Well; now I suppose it's too late, no?"

"Probably," Alex nodded.

"Luke was always..." Joan frowned. "... unpredictable, aye? As a child he threw tantrums, as an adolescent he'd be smitten by huge rages and the only one who could reach him in these black, destructive moods was Margaret. He's still like that, very dangerous once he loses control."

"Tell me about it." It had taken days for the imprints of his fingers on Alex' wrists to fade.

Joan didn't seem to have heard. "She lied, I fear. Margaret wasn't entirely truthful when Luke came back. God knows what fanciful stories she told Luke, but I don't think they painted Matthew in a favourable light."

In Alex' opinion, Luke wouldn't have been willing to

listen to any story not casting his brother as an ogre, and to be fair Margaret had probably not quite understood the consequences of spinning together this little yarn in which Matthew figured as a cross between Bluebeard and a particularly disgusting Orc . She threw a look out of the window and folded together her work.

"I'm going for a walk, want to come?"

"Walking with you is far too exhausting."

"Exercise, Joan. It's good for you."

"Hmph," Joan produced yet another garment from her work basket.

"Suit yourself." She was sick of sewing, and the autumn day was far too bright to waste it sitting indoors.

Matthew sank back behind the trees. In front of him Alex was singing, arms extended as she swung her hips this way and that, and even from here he could see how she peeked down at the way the skirts swirled.

She growled out the words, bending over at the waist in a series of quick, jerky movements that made her hair stand wildly round her head. He smiled, recognising the song as something she'd sung for him on the moors, all about her being made for loving him.

She sang on, making some lewd pelvic movements that had Matthew laughing, before dropping to lie on the ground with her eyes closed, one hand on her belly and a wide smile on her lips. She looked so achingly happy, and a rustle of premonition ran up his spine. He went over to her and her smile widened into a grin.

"Enjoy the show?" she asked, without opening her eyes.

"You knew I was there?"

She just nodded.

"So that's why you were doing those…" He made some thrusting movements himself. "… and you do them right well, you do."

"Well you would know, wouldn't you?" came the floating reply. She'd undone the top of her bodice, and her breasts swelled against the linen below. She lay in a pile of autumn leaves, russets, golds and faded greens, and in her hair he saw the red of a cluster of rowan berries.

"You look like a wood sprite," he told her and kneeled down to scatter a handful of leaves over her skirt.

"Really? Then you must be Pan, all curly haired and wild." She opened her eyes fully, dark and promising, and lifted her hand to his chest.

He pillowed his head on her lap afterwards, enjoying how her fingers combed his hair.

"Do you love me?" The question burst from her.

He was glad he was lying as he was, his face hidden against the folds of her skirts. Love her? He laughed, bit her through the fabric of her garments. Love her? He buried himself deeper into her lap, inhaled her scent.

"What could possibly make you think I do?" He sat up and cupped her cheek. "You're a wee fool to have to ask me that, Alex."

"But you've never said it. It's only me who tells you… when we're, you know." She hitched her shoulders expressively. "When we're in bed and when you hold me I tell you how much I love you, but you …"

He cleared his throat and looked away. He'd told Margaret repeatedly; he'd whispered 'I love you' into her black, black hair, he'd kissed 'I love you' down her front. And she'd taken the gift of his heart and ripped it apart.

"I show you, don't I?" He kept his eyes on the curl of hair he was winding round his finger. He released it and watched it bounce into a corkscrew before meeting her eyes.

"Yes, but I'd very much like to hear it. Sometime."

"Sometime," he promised, and got to his feet.

* * *

After weeks in the Tolbooth, Hector was so filthy he could barely stand his own scent. His cheeks bristled with heavy stubble, his skin itched, and when the door opened the shaft of light cut like laser across his cornea.

"The captain wants to see you," the warden said.

"Finally!" Hector replied. "He took his time about it, no?"

"I dare say he has other things to concern him than the fate of a spy."

Hector eyed the warden with dislike but held his tongue and shuffled after him in his chains.

"A mistake!" Hector gasped, drawing in air in long, steadying gulps. Jesus! He raised his dripping head in the direction of the officer. "How many times must I tell you? I'm no spy!"

The officer nodded, and Hector's head was yet again pushed into the barrel of water, his hands flapping ineffectually in their chains.

"I'm a man of God," Hector gargled when he was let up for air.

"A papist, I know," the officer said.

"No!" Hector reared back against the hands that were pushing him towards the scummy water. "I'm not a spy, I have no interests in the petty squabbles between king and commons."

"What?!!"

Once again Hector was held below the surface, and at one point he actually thought that he might die, and then he remembered that he wouldn't – he couldn't – no matter that his lungs were burning, that his nose and mouth filled with this foul, oily water. This time he surfaced angry and desperate, and he wrenched himself upright, fixing burning eyes on the officer.

"Beware, you're tampering with things you don't understand." He planted his manacled hands on the rim of the barrel, coughed to clear his lungs. He was struck by inspiration and shaped his right hand into the age old sign for evil.

"See?" He raised his hand as far as it went so that the lantern threw a shadow image of a horned head on the wall behind him. The officer took a step back and Hector smirked; superstitious idiot. "I'm a witch hunter," he said, inclining his head in a slight bow.

"A witch hunter?"

Hector nodded; well, it was the truth, no?

"And you think there's a witch at large in Cumnock?" It came out with a derisive edge.

"As yet I don't know. There are definitely witches here in Edinburgh though, I can smell them." Hector sniffed theatrically before realising what he'd done, closing his eyes at his own stupidity.

"Really?" the officer said, trying for an uninterested tone, but Hector could sense the excitement in him. He clapped his hand together and had Hector unchained. "Let's see, shall we?"

The officer led a soaked Hector down a badly lit passage to a small, dank hole. No light, the floor was damp as were the walls, and sitting in a corner was a girl. She shielded her face from the light with trembling hands, and at the officer's curt command got to her feet.

Dios mío! Hector was washed by an unfamiliar wave of compassion. The girl had been tortured, her face was a mass of bruises, her fingers hung twisted and deformed.

"Who's done this?"

"Why would you care?" the officer said. "She stands accused of witchery."

"Amateurs," Hector said. "Whoever has been in charge of her questioning has not known his trade."

"Then how fortunate that you're here now, no?" The officer indicated with his head that the girl was all his. Hector resigned himself to the inevitable; he'd have to condemn an innocent woman or two before he was left to pursue his own business. He nearly laughed; full circle, right?

"Bring me a brazier, two six inch nails, a marten hair brush and some heated oil," Hector said. Two hours later the girl admitted to everything, words tripping over her tongue in her haste to condemn herself.

"Well done," the officer said with some admiration. "Welcome to Edinburgh. We have a lot of work for you to do here, Mr Olivares. Ample opportunity to prove your skills – and your rectitude of faith."

To that, all Hector could do was nod in acquiescence.

To his surprise it stuck in his craw. Age must have mellowed him, because how else to explain the disgust he felt over the coming months as one woman after the other was led before him. Old and ugly most of them, dirt poor and unprotected, and at least three of them feeble in the head – no great loss to humanity, in fact one could almost argue he was doing society a favour by getting rid of them.

Impassively he stood in a corner when they were questioned, on occasion he'd do the pinpricking just to prove himself capable, but in general he oversaw, now and then inclining his head, thereby committing the wretched female to more torture in the hope of wringing a confession from her.

They generally succeeded – well, some things never change, and a red hot needle under your nails is most persuasive – the woman in question admitting to long lists of sins, from putting the evil eye on Janet Cameron to nights of debauchery with the devil himself.

Hector was bored; no doubt some of these women had dabbled in dark arts, but witches... no, they fell well short of someone like Mercedes. She jeered at him; through his nights he dreamt of her, during the days he imagined her everywhere, a lithe elusive woman with dark hair. He heard her laughing whenever he caught a glimpse of his own reflection, a soft, mocking sound that increased in volume as he studied his rapidly aging face, his hands.

But sometimes it was Dolores who came to plague his nights, the bright girl with the burnished hair he'd seduced and bedded, even loved, in a far gone Seville before his whole life turned into an impossible nightmare, an everlasting quest to find his way home.

CHAPTER 25

The sound of galloping hooves disturbed the peace of the Saturday morning, and when a lathered horse with a rotund shape perched on top appeared, Alex knew exactly who it was and why he was coming.

"Run!" Simon gasped as he fell off his horse. "Matthew, run!" Matthew didn't wait, he flew, his shirt flapping in the breeze, towards the hill.

"My wife," he called. "Take care of my wife."

"I'm going with him," Alex was already moving in the direction where he had disappeared, but Joan stopped her.

"Nay, Alex, you'd hinder him. He'll be fine up there on his own."

"No he won't! He needs me, and I ..." she broke off and stood silent as a company of soldiers rode down towards the house. She recognised one of them as Watson, the man with the hangman's rope, and just the thought of seeing Matthew die like that had her throat constricting.

"We're looking for Matthew Graham," the officer said once he'd halted his horse. He took off his hat and bowed in the direction of Joan and Alex. "Ladies, Captain Leslie, at your service." Alex had an overriding impression of a very grey man; grey hair, grey clothes, rather grey skin – unfortunately – and intelligent, grey eyes.

"Sir," Joan curtseyed, indicating with her eyes that Alex should do the same. "I'm afraid Mr Graham is presently not at home," Joan went on, "in fact he hasn't been home for quite some time."

"No? And here I have a copy of a wedding contract made on the last September twelve between said Matthew Graham and Alexandra Lind. Would you say it was a marriage by proxy?" The officer looked with interest at Alex' hands spread over an as yet relatively flat belly.

"But that was quite long ago," Alex said, "more than

two months. And since then, well, I'm sorry to say we haven't seen much of him." She suppressed an urge to raise her skirts and take off, run until she found Matthew. Instead she smiled at the officer.

The officer let his eyes linger on Alex. She shifted on her feet.

"Ah well, it only takes the once, no?" he said with a shrug and swung off his horse. "You'll not mind us looking, will you?"

"Of course not; go ahead, be my guest."

The officer looked slightly puzzled, but bowed and gave Alex a pleasant smile, sending his men off to search the buildings, trudge up the wooded slopes, swords in hand that they used to prod thickets and heaped leaves. Please don't let this be happening, Alex prayed, don't let these soldiers find him and cut him down, or even worse cart him off to languish in jail and then hang.

In the end all they carted off was an indignant Simon, his voice squeaking as he protested this high handed treatment. His fine, reddish hair stood all ways, making him look like a Cabbage Patch doll. A pale Joan watched him ride off, her lower lip held between her teeth.

"I'm sorry," Alex said. "Will he ... will they hurt him?"

Joan hitched her shoulders. "Nay, they won't. But they'll make him sweat a bit."

They sat waiting for Matthew until late, but finally Joan sighed and stood up, extinguishing the candle on the table.

"He won't come back tonight. We may as well get to bed." They stopped halfway to the stairs, both of them alerted by a sudden movement down the lane.

"It's the soldiers!" Joan said. "Oh my God, it's the soldiers come back to search for him again." Alex peeked out. Several dark shapes were moving towards the house. No horses, no lanterns, and from what little she could see no attempt at formation.

"Those are no soldiers."

Joan squinted, and then she whimpered. "Moss-troopers!"

Alex gave her a confused look. "Here? Aren't they more like highwaymen?"

"Mostly," Joan shrank back against the wall. "Shh, perhaps they'll think the house is empty."

"No," an amused voice replied, "we know it isn't."

Joan made a dash for the stairs. Useless, and she was dragged off in the direction of the kitchen. When one of the men made as if to grab Alex by the arm she shrugged him off.

"I can walk on my own." The passage was too narrow and too dark to allow her much room for manoeuvring, and once in the kitchen she and Joan were backed into a corner while the men tore through the house in their search for valuables. Six; no, seven men, making it all very crowded when they returned to the kitchen. Alex rose on her toes; could she? No; the odds were overwhelmingly against her. Too many men, too little space, and she doubted Joan would be much help. She glanced in Joan's direction; what was the matter with her anyway? Ever since they'd entered the kitchen Joan had been mute, eyes never leaving the men.

"I thought you said there was gold," one of the men whined to the apparent leader. "But all we found are some silver spoons."

"There is gold, have you checked the master's desk? He has a box there." The speaker was leaning against the further wall, his face and upper body in shadow. Alex frowned; there was something vaguely familiar about the voice.

In reply the first man held up the little strongbox, shaking it to show just how empty it was. Thank heavens he moved it, Alex thought, forcing her eyes to keep on staring straight ahead, not at the loose stone at the back of the hearth.

"Where is it?" There was a thread of steel in the dark voice and Alex felt a snaking fear run down her legs, making her want to sit down.

"It's gone." She repeated that stubbornly for the coming half hour, even when one of the men put the point of his dagger to the tender skin under her eye.

"Give us your baubles then," one of them said.

Joan pulled off her rings and handed them to him.

"You too," he said, nodding in the direction of Alex. She had no intention of giving this little arsehole the only thing she had left of her father so she just shook her head.

"No."

"Alex!" Joan hissed. "Do as he says."

The man waved his knife in Alex's direction and she brought her hand down in a swift motion, sending the knife spinning across the floor.

"Make me; try, you stinking son of a bitch and you might just find you've taken on more than you can handle." Why, oh why couldn't she just learn to keep her mouth shut? She'd angered him, and the man laughed nastily as he advanced towards her. She kicked, was hampered by her skirts, and he grunted in surprise when her foot caught him just below the sternum, not in his head as she'd intended.

"Stay back!" she threatened. "Get too close and I'll kick your balls off." They regarded her warily, edging towards her, and she lunged for a knife, a cleaver, anything to brandish against them, but all she got hold of was a stirring spoon.

"Do as you're told." A cold voice cut through the dark. "Hand over your ring or I'll slice your sister-in-law's hand off." Joan made a muffled, whimpering sound and Alex turned towards the door, where the man previously lounging in the shadows was holding Joan's hand against the frame with a knife at wrist level.

"You!" Alex launched herself across the room. "Why you..." she brought the wooden spoon down on her brother-in-law's head, ignoring Joan's warning sounds. "What kind of a bastard cuts his own sister, what's wrong with you?" Alex was stuttering with rage, she whacked Luke again, was vaguely aware of how silent the men around her had fallen, and then her wrist was wrung, the large spoon dropping with a clatter to the floor.

"Ow!" She tried to tear her hand free, glared at Luke, and the green ice in his eyes made her swallow down a sob. She chopped at his arm, hard enough for her to gasp with the impact. Luke grunted but held on.

"Luke... please," Joan said, grabbing at her brother with her uninjured hand. He shrugged her off, wiped at his bleeding brow and then he hit Alex, straight in the gut. She opened and closed her mouth a couple of times, tried to force air into her lungs.

"No woman raises her hand to me, and definitely not my brother's foreign slut," Luke slurred, and once again he drove his fist into Alex' stomach. Time stopped. Pain exploded, up her spine, down her legs.

"Agh!" Oh my God, the baby! She struggled to breathe, tried to back away. She wrenched at her arm. He laughed. He pulled his arm back, fisted his hand. He met her eyes. Another blow and her legs buckled, small stabbing points of black swimming in front of her eyes. Again. Air rattled its way up and down her windpipe. Again, and again. Wet; something wet down the inside of her thighs.

Joan was crying, pleading with him to stop. Yes; please stop. Alex collapsed to her knees. The kick sent her sprawling. Someone picked her up. She couldn't stand, she fell to her knees. He kicked her again. She crawled, keening. She could taste blood in her mouth. A hand in her hair and she was dragged to stand. So quiet. All she could hear was her own breathing, her own pulse. Yet another blow. Son of a bitch! A spark of anger flashed through her brain, spluttered and died. So much pain. Her baby.

She was half dragged, half led out of the kitchen and up the stairs. She heard Joan scream her name, was aware that she should try and do something, but the hand in her hair tightened its hold and then she didn't remember, no, please, she didn't remember ...

Matthew made his way cautiously down the slope. He was

cold after his night out on the moor, had hoped for a warm welcome and hot food. Instead, his home seemed deserted, sunk into a silence that made his skin prickle. He stood for a long time hidden under the trees, surveying his yard, his buildings. No smoke belched from the chimneys, no bustle in the yard. A trap? He hesitated, uncertain as to what to do.

He moved stealthily along the fringes, trying to understand what had happened. Horses – several horses – but they were gone now. In the barn and stables the beasts stood unharmed. He met Gavin who'd been to milk the cows and asked him if he'd seen anyone at the big house yet, but Gavin shook his head, saying that as it was Sunday he'd thought they had given themselves a bit of a rest after all that business yesterday, what with Mr Simon being carried away by the soldiers and the master himself running like a fox.

Matthew nodded but felt his shoulders tense. Mayhap the lad was right, but half the morning was gone, the November sun almost at its zenith, and Joan would be worried blind for Simon.

He armed himself with a pitchfork and approached the house. In the kitchen he found Joan, sitting unresponsive against the wall. There was a deep gash on her right forearm, and she looked at him with no initial sign of recognition, grey eyes focusing and un-focusing. She held out her tied hands to him in a supplicating gesture.

"What did they do to you?" Matthew asked, loosening the makeshift gag.

"Nothing too bad," Joan said, eyes sliding away from his. "Alex?"

"Upstairs, he took her upstairs, and I haven't heard a sound from her since … oh God, since she stopped screaming."

"Who?" he asked, forcing the words through a mouth filled with gravel, but he already knew, had his answer in Joan's shocked face.

"Luke." She frowned. "Someone left the door unbolted. It must have been Mrs Brodie. Rosie was off to visit her Mam, and it seems Mrs Brodie is gone, no?"

At present, Matthew couldn't care less. All of him was focused on the heavy silence from upstairs.

"You think she's ..." Joan whispered, grabbing hold of his arm.

"I don't know," he said, making for the stairs.

Alex was on the floor. Alive, thank the Lord, alive and lucid enough to start weeping when she saw him. He helped her to stand, and her skirts were stiff with dried blood.

"I'm sorry," she said, "I'm so sorry, so sorry ..."

He hushed her, blinking his eyes free of tears. Time for that later, aye? Now he had to be strong and reassuring for this woman who had problems standing, who wouldn't meet his eyes. What had he done to her, that bastard brother of his?

She held her soiled clothes to her, cried that she didn't want him to see, didn't want to see herself, but he insisted, calling down to Joan for hot water and towels – many towels.

One garment at the time, and she wept and sobbed, gasping now and then as he undid lacings and buttons. Merciful Father; her front, her back, her upper thighs. Carefully he washed her, and she recoiled from his touch.

She breathed, he breathed.

He rinsed the towel, and in the basin the water was a dirty brown. A clean shift, her bed jacket and he carried her over to the bed, cradling her in his arms as if she were a wee bairn. His wife; his throat clogged with grief and anger.

"Joan will come and sit with you," he said, brushing at her hair. "I have to find Simon, aye?" And Luke. She nodded and rolled over on her side.

Matthew was gone all of the following week. He rode like a madman across the surrounding countryside looking for his brother, but of Luke there was no trace. Margaret swore she hadn't seen him for weeks when Matthew appeared at her door, but he could see she was lying, her neck mottling red.

Despite Joan's worried entreaties that he not put himself at risk, he rode into Cumnock, walked his way through all Luke's haunts but there was no sign, not even a whiff of him.

"Are you sure?" Simon panted, trotting after Matthew towards the Merkat Cross Inn. "Was it really him?"

"Joan says so, no?"

"But... no Matthew; not even Luke would so harm a woman, would he?"

Matthew shrugged, shared a look with him. They'd both seen Luke in one of his rages, seen him lose all control. He turned to look at Simon with despair.

"My brother, Simon! Abusing my wife, aye? And she pregnant and hurting and begging him to stop!"

"Maybe he didn't know – about the wean, I mean."

"And that's an excuse?" Matthew spat in the gutter, wiping his hand hard across his face. "I swear if I find him, I'll kill him."

Simon paled at his tone. "He's in Edinburgh."

"And now you tell me?" Matthew glared at him from under his wide-brimmed hat.

Alex retreated into silences and blankness. Mostly she avoided him – all of them – disappearing for hours on end to walk the woods or sit alone in the hayloft. The bruises faded, but her eyes remained sunk in her face, wary and dark they would but rarely meet his before she averted them, hands fiddling with her apron, her skirts.

"It's my fault," she said one day. They were sitting in the parlour, and Matthew closed the book he was reading and looked at her. There was a strained set to her mouth, and she'd pulled back her hair into a tight little braid. It didn't become her, her hair should float and fall around her face, not be tamed this brutally.

"Of course it isn't," he said. His gaze strayed to her waist and then away.

"You don't sound as if you mean it." She took a long, steadying breath. "I shouldn't have provoked him, but I guess I didn't think. It sort of got to me, to see him sawing his way through Joan's wrist."

"Oh, Lord…" Matthew hung his head, torn apart by the fact that it was his brother, a man he could – no should – have killed that had done this to his wife. He was at her side in seconds, tried to take her fisted hands. "Tell me, don't carry this alone, lass."

"I can't." She wrenched herself free and fled the room, and behind her Matthew sank his face into his hands and groaned; how was he to help her, help them both, if she wouldn't let him?

He tried. God knows he tried to talk to her, prise a description of that night from her, but every time he did, Alex just shook her head and escaped him, leaving him to imagine one sequence of events after the other, each of them successively more cruel, more degrading.

"She needs time," Joan said when he came to her, "and she's right, isn't she? You do think she is to blame, at least a little."

"I blame him, accursed bastard that he is."

"Aye – and her, for not handing over her ring." She sighed and patted at his arm. "It wouldn't have mattered if she had. Luke didn't come to rob you of what little gold you may have. He hurt her to hurt you. You know that, don't you?"

That didn't help, he told her, if anything it made it all so much worse.

"My Alex, and her so damaged and I can't help her."

Joan clasped his hand and gave it a little shake. "You love her, you really do, no?"

Matthew muttered something and looked away. Loved her? Oh aye, he most certainly did. That's why all of this was like ingesting ground glass, leaving him torn and bleeding on the inside.

He woke to her muffled sobs, his heart breaking at each of these low, desolate sounds. His hand moved of its own accord, stroked her back, her arm while he made shushing noises, anything to stop her hurting. And then she was there, in his arms, her mouth was wet on his neck, on his mouth, her whole body demanding that he love her, hold her. And he wanted to, oh dearest Lord he did, his body arching under her touch, his mouth seeking hers. He rose above her, he kissed her, and there, unbidden, came the images of his damned brother making free with Alex as he had done with Margaret, and everything in Matthew shrivelled at these far too explicit pictures.

With a groan he fell back beside her. Not the same, he reminded himself, not at all the same – but it didn't help.

"Nay." He shifted away, disentangling himself from her. She froze, eyes huge in the pale oval of her face, and flipped over on her side, her back stiff like a board. Matthew wanted to stretch out his hand and pull her close, mayhap kiss her hair, comfort her but more than that... no, he just couldn't, not when his brain was invaded by disjointed pictures of Luke with his Alex.

"When I come to you with my need you won't deny me," she whispered into the dark and he could hear how much it cost her to keep her voice steady. Matthew moaned, twisting his face to hide himself against the soft, worn linen of his pillow.

"You said it worked both ways, and now... well, now I come to you with mine." She rolled over again, her face only inches from his. He reared back and put a hand on her shoulder. To draw her close? To keep her away? He didn't know.

"I can't, lass. Not like that. But I can hold you, aye?" He gave her a weak smile and held up his quilt to invite her in.

"That's not enough." She slipped out of bed and left the room.

"Will you stop doing this?" he said next morning, rubbing his hand hard across his face in a futile attempt to wipe away his exhaustion.

"Do what?" she asked mildly, in total contradiction to the expression in her eyes.

"You know what I mean! You get out of bed and then you don't come back, and I spend the night looking for you, to make sure you're safe."

She banged his plate down in front of him. They were alone in the kitchen, Joan having decided that she needed to inspect the smoking shed.

"Well I'm here when you *need* me, aren't I?" She glared at him. "There's food on your plate when you *need* it, clean clothes when you *need* them, warm water when you *need* to wash. All your *needs* I make sure are adequately cared for, right? And here I was, thinking it was supposed to work both ways." She slammed the door on her way out. With a resigned sigh he got to his feet to follow her.

He found her where he knew she would be, in the stables. As he walked down the length of the building towards Samson's stall he heard her voice, a hushed monologue in a language he didn't understand. She started when he appeared in her line of vision and ducked under Samson's massive neck to hide her tearstained face from him.

"It's been over a month, and unless we talk about it, this will fester, poisoning every aspect of our relationship. It already is, no?" He gave her a crooked smile. Whatever it was she wasn't telling him, it couldn't be worse than what he was imagining.

She met his eyes over the horse's back. "I don't want that," she said, eyes so dark the pupils were deep wells only faintly ringed with blue.

"Neither do I." He extended her cloak to her. "Walk?"

They didn't talk, they just strode side by side, holding hands. By the time Matthew led them in the direction of the little graveyard, her fingers were tightly braided round his. He stopped at the gate and swung it open, brushed some wet leaves off the bench and invited her to sit.

A weak December sun filtered through the bare branches

of the rowan, long extended fingers of shadow thrown across the faded grass. Their breath came in soft puffs, and Matthew slid to sit closer, pressing his thigh against hers. He could feel her relax, a slow softening of muscles that for weeks had been rigid with fear and grief. He didn't push, he just sat beside her, every now and then sweeping his thumb in a caressing movement over the back of her hand.

"I can't stand it," he finally said in view of her continued silence. "I can't … I see these pictures in my head of you with him, and I can't wipe them away, and I want to … Sweet Lord, Alex, I'm so sorry!"

"Of me with him?" Her confusion was apparent, and he turned to look at her. Her eyes widened. "Oh my God; you think he raped me?"

"Didn't he?"

Alex made a slow negating movement with her head, and Matthew's shoulders dropped several inches.

"He… well, he just lost it, you know? He punched me and hit me, he swore at me, hit me some more, and I begged for him to stop, but he just went on and on about you and Margaret, and how would you like it now, when he did to your wife what you'd done to her, and…" She threw him a look and came to an abrupt stop. "It isn't your fault."

"Aye it is, I should have been there to protect you."

"Well, he made sure you weren't, didn't he? And had you come back, what could you have done alone against six men?" She shivered when the sun disappeared behind fast moving clouds. "I don't think he was fully aware of what he was doing."

"That's no excuse."

"No; it definitely isn't." Her hand drifted down to knead at her abdomen. "Our baby."

Matthew took both her hands in his and knelt before her.

"We'll have other babies, lass."

"But not like this one," she replied, tears hanging off her eyelashes.

"No, not like this one."

"He would have had your eyes," she breathed.

"She would have had your mouth," he whispered.

Slowly she toppled towards him, and he released her hands to wrap his arms round her, hold her safe against him while a flurry of wet snow danced around them.

CHAPTER 26

Mrs Gordon inspected the kitchen, did a quick stroll round the house, hemmed and hawed as she inventoried the pantries and the storing cupboards, and then sat down on the single kitchen chair, folded her arms, and began a long and heated negotiation with Matthew. Half an hour later they were in agreement; Mrs Gordon would come to work for them, replacing the disgraced Mrs Brodie.

It had been Alex' suggestion to ask her, insisting even when Matthew muttered something about her living very far away and being a midwife to boot, but in the end he'd agreed to send and ask. The reply had come in person, Mrs Gordon riding in on a hired horse, arms clenched tight around its groom, and now she sat by the fire as if she'd always belonged there, her bright, black eyes studying Alex with open curiosity.

"How's your knitting?" she asked, tongue-in-cheek.

"Progressing," Alex said, deciding to ignore Matthew's muffled laugh.

"Ah well, that's good, no?" Mrs Gordon said. "Have you finished anything yet?"

"Umm," Alex said and hastily turned the conversation to the upcoming party.

Five days later, Alex sat down with a thud on the kitchen bench and groaned.

"I'm dead on my feet and the party hasn't even started yet."

Joan pulled yet another pie from the oven and plunked it down on the table. The whole kitchen smelled of kale and cabbage, there were pies everywhere, and currant cakes and bread and legs of smoked lamb and an awful lot of things that quivered in jelly. Alex intended to keep well away from those. Mrs Gordon and Joan sank down beside her and in silence they studied the heaped foods before them.

"We're done," Joan said, eyeing the fruits of their labour.

"I sincerely hope so," Alex said, "this should feed an army."

Joan laughed and stretched, grinding her knuckles into the curve of her back.

"You'd best eat a bite before, unless you fancy fighting for it later on."

Matthew stood at the barn entrance to receive his guests and tenants, slapping men on the back, bowing to the womenfolk before offering them a drink. Alex stood beside him, smiling and curtseying to what to her seemed an endless line of unknown people. For the first time ever it was Matthew that was the host at the Hogmanay dance, and she could see he was nervous, wiping his hands down the fine cloth of his new breeches – made by yours truly, no less.

There was plenty of beer and cider, and it didn't take long for a general spirit of cheer to settle on the crowd, further augmented by all the food. It was like watching a swarm of biblical locusts; one moment the plates were overflowing, the next there were at most crumbs left.

Mrs Gordon bustled over to ask whether Alex wanted her to replenish the plates.

"Do we have anything left?"

"Oh aye," Mrs Gordon grinned, "but they don't want more food, they want whisky."

"I would never have guessed," Alex said, thinking that in some respects things were pretty much the same no matter what century you were in.

After the first few dances she didn't see Matthew except in glimpses. He danced and laughed, so obviously in his place, with his people, that it had made Alex feel even more alone. It cut her to the quick, the way he melted in to belong with her on the outside, wrong footed in the dances, excluded from jokes and the buzz of conversation by accents that broadened as the evening went along. But she smiled and laughed, danced with everyone who asked, drank far too much cider and laughed some more, before the effort of it all became too much and she settled herself in a dark corner to watch.

"Everyone wants a piece of him, no?" Simon said, materialising with two brimming mugs in his hands. Alex nodded, her eyes tracking Matthew on the dance floor. He was flushed with exertion, dancing in shirt and breeches only, and as she watched he lifted his blonde partner in a high arc, her wide skirts falling to reveal pink silk stockings. That was the third time he danced with that particular girl.

"Who's she?" She'd never seen the woman before, of that she was sure, and she couldn't remember her coming with his Graham cousins. But maybe she had.

"Her? Oh that's Sarah. They were sweethearts once, before..." Simon broke off and looked at Alex with amusement. "She's married, aye? And it was nothing but a childhood fancy."

"I suppose he must've had quite the string of sweethearts, what with him being the master's eldest son."

Simon considered this and grinned. "He had no luck with the lasses, Matthew. It was always me they wanted." He expanded his considerable chest and preened, looking very smug.

Alex laughed and shoved at him.

"Of course; you must have had them swooning over you."

Simon winked and stood up, extending his hand to her. "You don't believe me, I can tell. Let me show you, dearest good sister." He swept her off to dance, and Alex found to her amazement that not only was he by far the best dancer there, but he was right; as he danced and jumped and twirled her round, he was followed by many, many female eyes.

It was almost midnight, or at least she thought it was, and Alex picked up her cloak from where it was thrown across a bench and stepped out into the cold night air. She knew exactly where she was going, hurrying across the yard and over the water meadows, her eye set on the bare patch of hill that rose before her.

The night was clear, with a half moon hanging like a slice of lemon in the sky and the stars spread out in twinkling fields around it. She heard the distant baying of a dog, the rustling of things she startled as she walked through the woods, and from well behind came the sounds of fiddles and song.

Alex stopped for an instant to look back at the manor spread out below; candles in the windows, a muted square of light that spilled from the open barn door, and shadowy shapes that even at this distance moved unsteadily on their feet. She wondered briefly if one of them might be Matthew, but then turned back up the hill. She had an appointment to keep.

All day she'd been thinking of them; of Isaac and John but mostly of Magnus. New Year had been his and her thing, because Mercedes hated this marking of time and would lock herself into her studio to paint, refusing to join in any festivities. So Magnus and Alex cooked and spent the hours counting down to midnight talking about the year that had been. She wondered if he'd be alone this year, or if he'd be with John, but deep down she knew that he'd be as alone as she'd felt the whole day.

All their New Year's Eves had ended the same way; they'd go out into the garden and stare up at the sky, looking for the North Star. Even when the sky was overcast they'd still go out and scan the skies. And on the stroke of midnight Magnus would toast the star, visible or not, and smile down at his daughter.

"*Skål, lilla hjärtat,*" he'd say and she'd reply in Swedish as well.

"*Skål, pappa.*"

Alex reached her high point and craned her head back to look at the carpet of stars. Like diamonds, little points of glittering ice in a dark, dark sea. She located the North Star, closed her eyes and pretended; in her hand a champagne flute, by her side her father, and from the open door behind them streamed electrical light and warmth. In her head her father held out his arms and she walked into them and knew that she was safe, because he would never let anyone hurt her again, no one at all.

"So, who do you miss the most tonight?" Matthew's dark voice made her jump, but she remained standing where she was, shivering in the cold. He moved over to her and placed a warm hand against her cool cheek. "What are the things you need the most, tonight on Hogmanay?"

"Need or miss?"

"Both."

She looked up at the sky again. "I miss him so much."

"Who? John?"

She smiled at the edge in his voice. "Magnus, it's him I miss the most." She felt ashamed saying that, after all, shouldn't she be missing Isaac the most? "And I hate it that he'll be so alone, without me."

"But he has Isaac, no?"

"Yeah, he has Isaac. A three year old boy."

"A child of his blood, lass."

She liked that; and anyway, no doubt John would be there for Magnus as well, and so would Diane. A spike of jealousy flared through her gut. Magnus had always liked Diane – too much in Alex' opinion.

Matthew's arm slipped round her waist and gathered her close, and she rested her ear above his heart, listening to the steady, strong beat. It trickled into her ear, it flowed through her brain and down her spine – his pulse, reverberating through her. She rubbed her cheek against his coat and his hand came up to stroke her head.

"So," she said, clearing her throat. "In reply to your question; I miss them all at times, but there's only one person that I truly need and want, and that's you, Mr Graham." She laughed at herself; pathetic, Alex Lind, totally pathetic. But true.

This woman of his was breaking his heart, he reflected, all

of him throbbing with joy at her last comment. He had to give her something back, and he nudged her face off his chest to see her.

"It's a new year," he said, "and I'm standing here with a woman I should never have met." Alex shook her head in agreement; no, she said, she shouldn't be here, but here she was.

Matthew closed his eyes and tore the following words from his heart. "I love you, Alexandra Ruth; I love you so very, very much." And please God, don't let her hurt me like the other one did, don't let me know that pain again, now that I've bared myself to her. He opened his eyes to find her looking up at him.

"I need you," she said. "I need you now."

He held her hand all the way back down. He held it and it scorched him, her skin burning into his and leaving him short of breath. He ignored the revellers out in the yard, except for a peremptory wave, and then they were inside, and he was following her up the stairs, his hands already under her skirts.

His cock twitched with irritation; take her now, on the stairs. Take her on the floor, just take her, goddamn you, before I burst at the seams! So he did, and she was as eager as he was, shoving her warm, warm self against him, and he thought he would die, at least a little, but he didn't, and she stood on her knees in front of him and he took her like a rutting beast.

Matthew got to his feet and helped her up, and all of him was still twitching and aroused, and he wondered if it was all the beer that made his cock still stand. He threw the door of their bedroom closed and leaned against the cool wood, panting as he watched her.

"Undress yourself," he said roughly. "Undress and come here, come to me." He fumbled with his lacings, tore at his shirt and coat, and fell onto the bed with his stockings on. He didn't care. He just had to, and there she was under him, over him, everywhere and he had to, oh God, he had to, and so did she.

* * *

In his garden, Magnus welcomed 2003 in silence. He raised his glass to the unclouded sky, with a half moon hanging among the hazy stars, and toasted his lost daughter.

"*Skål, lilla hjärtat,*" he said, and in his head he saw her come into his waiting arms.

"*Skål, Pappa,*" he heard her whisper, and a shiver ran up his spine. She was alive, he told himself, alive and well in another time and another place.

CHAPTER 27

It was an early March day, the shrubs were beginning to show a promise of green and the hazels hung decorated with yellow tails. At present Alex was oblivious to it all; to the catkins on the willow, to the odd whites and blues of early anemones, to the cheerful chirping of robins and tits. She was too tired, too wet and far too angry, scowling in the direction of where a weeping Rosie had disappeared only moments ago.

"Thanks a lot." PMS, she decided and went back to the huge washing cauldron. To really make her day it soon after began to drizzle, a soft rain that soaked through every piece of drying linen on the clotheslines.

"Right," she said crossly. "That's it."

Her black mood lifted somewhat when Simon rode into the yard a few hours after dinner, accompanied by Minister Crombie.

"Matthew's out in the fields," she said. "But if you want, I can send Gavin out for him."

"No, no," the minister said, "we're but riding by."

"Old Mr Williams passed in the night," Simon said, jerking his thumb in the vague direction of their closest neighbour. "So here we come."

"Aye, spiritual and legal support hand in hand," Minister Crombie grinned. But they sat down at the table when she offered, attacking her bread and beer with enthusiasm.

"Luke's back," Simon said as they stood to leave.

"Here?" Alex squawked, having to sit down when all blood drained away from her head.

"In Cumnock," Minister Crombie said. He gave her a look and scrunched up his bristling brows into a ferocious glower. "You should press charges, for a man to ..." He shook his head; he'd seen Alex a week or so after she'd lost the child.

"Matthew does best not to appear before a magistrate,"

Simon reminded him. "However just his grievances, it's an unnecessary risk when you're an escaped convict. He won't be coming here," he continued, directing himself to Alex. "Even Luke Graham has some modicum of basic shame in him."

"You think?" Alex replied with an edge, but was relieved all the same.

Matthew was tired to the bone when he led the oxen in from the fields. After months of winter lassitude, his body protested at the punishing pace he had kept up for the last few weeks, and there were several more such weeks coming if he was to complete the harrowing and planting before the lambing began in earnest. He grimaced and unclenched his frozen hold on the leather reins.

"Here," he said to Gavin. "Rub them down."

Gavin looked harried. "I must be milking. Rosie isn't here, and the cows are getting restless."

Matthew looked down towards the cow stalls and frowned. "Where's Ewan?"

Gavin shuffled his feet, eyes on the floor. "I don't know, mayhap he's poorly?"

Matthew very much doubted that – Ewan had looked in florid good health this morning – but was too tired and cold to care.

"Take the cows then," he said to Gavin, "and I'll see to these."

The kitchen was dark when he got in. Mrs Gordon was off to visit her brother for some days, and accordingly meals had become simpler, even though Alex was making an effort. Now it irritated him to find the hearth fire low, and Alex nowhere to be seen.

"Alex?" His stomach grumbled, and he found a wrinkled winter apple and bit into it.

"Alex?" Far louder now, he wanted to be fed. He stomped up the stairs and flounced into their room. She was fast asleep on the bed in only her petticoats and shift, damp skirts left in a heap on the floor. He shook her awake.

"Haven't you cooked?"

"Apparently not," she said, trying to burrow herself back into bed. "I'm sure you'll manage, right?"

"I'm tired, I'm back from a day in the fields and I want something to eat, aye?"

"Order in, call a pizza delivery service, whatever. Just don't bother me."

"Alex! Will you get out of bed and make me something to eat?"

"Why? Surely you can fry something up. Or ask Rosie. I'm done in. Look, I can barely lift my arms." She waved an arm in his direction.

"Rosie isn't here." Matthew sank down on the bed.

"She isn't?" Alex struggled up to sit. "She took off halfway through the laundry, crying her eyes out. Maybe she's ill or something."

Matthew made an incredulous sound. "Her and Ewan both. Will you please get me something to eat? I have to wash." He yawned and looked down at his dirty hands and breeches. He yawned again, swaying with the effort of remaining upright. She gave him a long look and with a little sigh got off the bed.

"I'll bring up some hot water," she said, kissing his temple. "And then eggs and toast up here. Okay?"

"Okay," he agreed and began to strip.

"Simon came by before," she said later. "They dropped by on their way to the Williams place."

"Ah," Matthew nodded, "Samuel told me old Williams died."

"He said Luke's back."

"Aye, I heard."

She slipped out of bed to move the tray. She wandered over to the small window, struggled to open it wide and hung on her elbows, staring out at the night. The air was rich with the scents of spring, of newly turned soil, of rain, but she wasn't registering any of it.

"Alex?" he materialised by her side. "He won't hurt you again." He propelled her back to bed, tucked her quilts into place before sliding in to join her.

"I'm more worried that you'll do something stupid like challenge him to a duel or something."

"Oh, are you? And don't you think I'd win?"

"I have no idea, but Luke Graham doesn't strike me as a man that fights fair so I don't want you to do anything rash, okay?" She propped herself up to sink her eyes into his.

"I won't," he promised and they moved on to discuss other things. They did that a lot, long hours spent in the dark, hands lazily travelling down each other as they talked about anything and everything.

"I've never spoken so much to anyone before," Alex reflected as she moved closer to him. Matthew spooned himself around her with a satisfied rumble.

"I like talking to you," he said to her nape. "I like having you this close, knowing I can tell you all my thoughts." He fondled her breasts, fitting her to him. "Didn't you talk like this with John?"

"No." The evenings with John had been so full of other things; work and e-mails on their respective computers, housework – and the presupposition that there would always be time to talk; later.

"Do you miss him?"

"Sometimes. Do you mind?"

"Nay."

Alex laughed and twisted round to hug him close. "Liar. There's no competition, okay? And you know that, don't you?" She brushed at his hair, rested her hand for an instant against his cheek.

"Aye," he smiled, "I do."

Rosie reappeared in the morning, bedraggled and red eyed. Matthew took one look at her and cursed under his breath.

"Tell me." There was no disobeying that tone, so Rosie

stood in front of him and wept as she admitted that she was with child.

"You wee idiot," he said viciously, ignoring the surprised look from Alex. "Do you at least know the father?" Rosie twisted her hands hard into her apron. Her Da was going to kill her, she sobbed.

Matthew closed his eyes. "Oh Merciful Lord; he's married."

She nodded unhappily.

"Who?"

Rosie tried to avoid his eyes.

"Who?" he repeated, but he already knew; Ewan, the bastard. And now he'd scampered back off home to wife and bairns, leaving the lass to fend for herself. He chewed his lip, mentally listing potential husbands for the lass.

"We'll have to find you a man," he said, pinching the bridge of his nose. "You can't stay here, unwed."

Rosie hid her face in her apron and cried even more.

"Of course she can," Alex said. "We can't just throw her out if she's pregnant, can we?"

Matthew gave her a dark look. "I'll find her a husband. This is not a matter for you to meddle with." He stalked out of the room.

Alex caught up with him halfway to the stable.

"Why can't she just stay? Who'd care?"

"I would," Matthew said, "she can't have a child unwed."

Alex made an exasperated sound. "It happens all the time."

"Aye, but not to my people." He strode down the stable towards his oxen at a pace that had her half running to keep abreast.

"And what kind of a husband will you find her? Who'll want to marry her under these circumstances?"

"An unmarried man." He was already busy with the animals, crooning to them as he harnessed them.

"Maybe she loves Ewan, maybe she'll hate this man you find for her."

"She should have thought of that before no? Before she bedded with a married man." He made a disgusted face. "Had the lad been unwed, then he'd be forced to do right by her, but Ewan's married, and she knew that. Not only a slut but an adulteress as well."

"But she couldn't help herself, she fell in love."

"She shouldn't have done it," he insisted. "And it reflects on us, on you, that she has."

Alex gave him a confused look.

"Her father sent her down to serve at the big house. He was expecting she'd remain untouched, aye?"

"But how can I be responsible?"

Matthew gave a frustrated snort. "You're the mistress. It's you that must ensure the morals of your servants." He sighed and tried to explain. "I'm responsible for the well being of my people, and as my wife so are you. It's up to us to stand in the stead of Rosie's parents and we've been remiss in not seeing and stopping this before it went this far."

"Oh." Alex didn't look overly enthused at this new role as a moral guardian. "So now what happens? You force her to marry, even if she doesn't want to? Isn't there something else we can do?"

"No." He frowned at her. He had no time for this discussion. He took hold of the reins and began leading the oxen towards the door.

"Poor Rosie," Alex sighed.

Matthew was most affronted. "What do you think of me? That I'll purposefully find her a husband who will beat her or harm her?"

"Of course not, but to be married off like that... and what if her husband doesn't like the child?"

Matthew rolled his eyes. "He'll be good to the bairn."

"How do you know, it isn't his, is it? So how can he love it?"

Matthew smiled despite his irritation. "And you ask that?" he said, digging his eyes into hers. It took some moments for her to understand, but when she did, she flushed.

"That was pretty underhand."

"Was it? I was aiming to point out that a man can love a child not his own. Like you said John loved Isaac, no?"

"Loves Isaac."

"Will love Isaac," he corrected and left her standing by the stable, his mind already elsewhere.

Two days later Matthew appeared at dinner with a man Alex recognised as one of his tenants. Rosie gave a squeak at the sight of him and darted out of the kitchen just as the two men entered.

Alex studied him while setting down a plate in front of him. He looked ancient; his hair was streaked in grey, his face lined, and from the shape of his mouth Alex could bet he had teeth missing, a suspicion that was confirmed when he smiled a greeting with his lips pressed together.

"This is Robbie," Matthew said. "He's the tenant of the small cottage just beyond the stream." Alex summoned up a picture in her head – a well tended little garden, a huge apple tree, and a small grey stone house that was relatively well kept up.

"How'd you do?" she said, pouring both men beer.

"Robbie is a widower since five years back," Matthew said, "and it came to me that mayhap he needs a new wife."

Young enough to be his daughter, dirty old man. Alex gave Matthew a disapproving glare; if this was doing the best he could for Rosie then she could but pity the girl.

"How old are you?" she asked, ignoring Matthew's warning look. Robbie finished chewing and swallowed before answering.

"Thirty-eight, I think. Or mayhap forty?"

Alex nearly dropped the pitcher. Matthew was almost twenty-nine, and this man looked as if he could have been his father!

"Do you have any children?"

Robbie shook his head.

"You do know that she's pregnant, no?" Alex pushed on, making Matthew wince at her directness. Robbie nodded, his eyes on his heaped plate. He got plus points for eating the vegetables.

Matthew went to get Rosie, returning some minutes later with a pink, newly scrubbed Rosie, hair combed and plaited beneath her starched cap. She clasped her hands in front of her and bobbed Robbie a curtsey. Robbie got to his feet and bowed, and Matthew gripped Alex' arm and led her out of the kitchen.

"They don't need us there, they'll talk easier without company."

"What if she says no?" Alex said, having major problems seeing pretty little Rosie in bed with Robbie.

"She won't, it's a good match. And she can still work here at the big house, at least until the bairn comes."

"But..." Alex shook her head. "She can't marry him! Look at him!"

Matthew gave her a condescending look. "Is that how you assess people? If their looks don't please you, then you deem them unworthy?"

"No, of course not, but if she marries him she'll have to, you know..." She made an explicit gesture with her hands.

"Aye, I suppose she will, no? A man has the right to his wife and Robbie will have missed someone to warm him over the last years."

"And what will he do if she doesn't want to? Force her? Beat her?"

Matthew turned to look at her and there was a twinkle of amusement in his eyes.

"He'll do like I do when you forget your wifely duties; he'll insist." It happened now and then that she'd pretend that she didn't want to and say no, because those times were so very good; he strong and demanding, she totally possessed.

"It's different," she said. "I love you."

"And mayhap with time she will learn to love him – at least a little."

To Alex' surprise, Rosie seemed content with her intended husband. When Alex offered to intercede with Matthew should Rosie want her to, Rosie just blinked. Question the master's decision?

"Well, he isn't God, is he?" Alex said, making Rosie gape.

"The master knows best," Rosie said, "and I must do as he says, aye? As must all under his care." Including his wife, her tone implied.

Alex chose not to continue this discussion, but spent most of the evening digesting it.

"Matthew?" Alex turned to face him in bed.

"Mmm?"

"What rights do I have? As your wife I mean."

He smiled and scooted closer. "You're mine, Alex, mine to hold and care for, mine to love, mine to get with child. If you misbehave it is I that must punish you, if someone does you wrong I will defend you. But rights? You have no rights, not like a man does. No woman does, unless she's a widow and remains unmarried. You belong to me, Alex, all of you, all your worldly goods belong to me."

He opened one eye and smiled even wider at what she supposed to be an astounded expression on her face.

"But you're fortunate, aye?" he said and kissed her brow. "For there's one thing you own that I can't take from you, nor live without; my heart."

"Huh." Not much of a comfort when you'd just been relegated from human being to chattel – or maybe it was.

* * *

Edinburgh, Perth, Inverness and now Glasgow; Hector regarded his surroundings, taking in yet another sad little town full of grey houses, dirty streets and acrid smoke.

"Not much to see," he said to Minister Weir.

"To see?" the minister gave him a blank look.

"It's very small." Hector dismounted, handed the reins to one of the minister's hired goons.

"Bigger than Inverness," Minister Weir replied with a shrug.

"Anything's bigger than Inverness," Hector muttered. At least it wasn't raining, and soon this goddamn tour of his would be over. He eyed the minister with dislike; months with the small preacher hadn't exactly endeared him to him, in fact rather the reverse.

A bigot, a self-serving runt of a man who enriched himself through a combination of extortion and bullying, Weir had cornered Hector one night in Edinburgh and suggested they work together – or else he'd find himself obliged to inform the authorities Hector was a papist and a spy. When Hector had laughed, the little man had sunk those piggy eyes into him and told Hector that he, Minister Weir, could make life extremely uncomfortable for him, in fact he could make it unbearable, a stretch of days, no years, sitting forgotten in a damp and totally dark cell. And, the minister gleefully added, Hector might be a renowned witch hunter, but he, Minister Weir, had quite the reputation for rooting out papist subversives – and seeing them hang.

Hector recognised a genuine threat when he heard it. As he had no desire to rot away in darkness he had spent the last months traipsing round Scotland in the wake of an enthusiastic Weir, listening to endless discourses on the evil of popery, complete with vivid descriptions of the torments in hell that awaited any Catholic unfortunate enough to die. They made Hector's head ache, these rambling monologues that always ended with the minister professing his willingness to die for his beliefs should it ever be necessary. Not bloody likely; this weasel of a man would recant, give up his friends, his wife, his mother, even his children to save his own skin. It takes one to know one, Hector snickered. Well; he would have drawn the line at his children – at least he hoped so.

"Three," Minister Weir said, interrupting Hector's thoughts.

"Ah, openly?" Hector asked, calculating his share of the potential profits.

"No, no, my dear Hector. A discreet visit, an opportunity for them to make... eh... amends, and once they do we'll be on our way."

"One day someone's going to call your bluff," Hector warned.

"How can they? I have you, a proven witch hunter, to back me up, no?"

Hector had to agree it was an excellent little scam; accuse and allow yourself to be bought off, all the while dripping veiled threats as to the consequences of being hauled into open court on accusations of witchery.

"Sooner or later..." Hector began, but Weir waved him into silence.

"I'm a man of the Kirk," he said – he said that quite often. "Whose word do you think will count the most? Besides, they're surely guilty of something."

"We all are," Hector said.

"Not me," the minister replied complacently. "I am but rooting out sinners."

The only amusing thing in all this was that the little shit was entirely oblivious to his own hypocrisy.

Hector was halfway down the High Street when he stopped. Mercedes! Here! His nostrils flared, he closed his eyes and opened his mouth as if attempting to inhale her presence. But no; he tasted the air carefully. She'd been here, he could feel that, leaving behind an ephemeral impression that she was just round the corner, but it was very many years ago since she'd walked these streets.

"*Bruja*! Witch." He was swamped by a burning rage to hurt someone and do it soon.

"What?" Minister Weir said. For a moment Hector wallowed in the pleasing daydream of venting all this anger on the minister – disembowel him there and then – but he had no doubts whatsoever that the two men at Weir's back would beat him senseless and drag him off in chains to the closest gaol should he do so. Hector smoothed down his coat and managed a bland smile.

"Nothing," he said.

CHAPTER 28

Matthew looked at peace when they left the service, an inward look in his eyes. Alex slipped her hand under his arm and squeezed.

"It must have been a long time."

"Aye, a very long time."

Simon snorted and clapped Matthew on his shoulder. "Didn't you see, then? Half the congregation was waiting for you to sprout horns, terrible escaped felon that you are." Matthew frowned down at his brother-in-law, and Joan stepped in between them.

"You're exaggerating, Simon. Aye, they were looking, but more at his wife, no?"

"His wives," Simon corrected, and Matthew came to a halt.

"Margaret was there," Simon said, "sitting further back. You should have seen the eyes of the old hens as they flew from Margaret to Alex and back."

Alex made a disgusted sound. She could imagine the comments, the suppressed gasps at how alike they were, and the careful assessment as they compared number one with number two. Margaret won hands down, at least when it came to the looks department.

"Did she have her son with her?" Alex said, catching the look that flew between Simon and Joan. They saw it too then, the striking resemblance between the boy and the man who'd formally disowned him.

"I don't think so," Joan replied airily. "But I didn't really look."

Matthew looked from one to the other, and narrowed his eyes at Alex.

"What?" she asked, attempting to sound confused.

"There's something here you're not telling," he said, and she hated it that she could feel the blood rush up to stain her cheeks. Miss Transparent, that was her.

"I have no idea what you're talking about."

"Hmph! You'll tell me later," he said in a low voice, and she could hear he wouldn't take no for an answer.

"And Luke?" Matthew asked Simon. "Is he here as well?"

"Not as far as I know, off to Glasgow, as I hear it."

Matthew gave Simon a sharp look. "Really? Why else would Margaret be here?" He placed a hand on Simon's arm. "You'd tell me, no? After all, I have matters to settle with him."

"Oh, of course," Simon said, before darting across the street with Joan in tow to greet an acquaintance. Matthew muttered something very foul.

"You've promised me you won't do anything stupid," Alex said, "it's not worth it, okay?"

She gripped his arm, threw a look over her shoulder. She didn't like being here, was worried that at any moment men would appear to drag Matthew off, fugitive that he was. She'd said as much, but Matthew had just shrugged, reminding her that the realm at large had far graver concerns than the whereabouts of one escaped royalist.

"It would seem the ground's burst open and we have supporters of the king crawling out from every orifice," he'd said. Nor did it help that Parliament and the Army were at loggerheads, he'd added, a constant internal squabbling leaving the country rudderless.

"Not everywhere," she said.

"No, but here in Scotland it's mostly for the king now, no?" He'd twisted his mouth into an ironic smile and bowed. "I may need to brush up my court manners, for when I'm asked to receive the knighthood due to the great misfortune I've suffered on behalf of the king." His eyes had darkened as they always did when he recalled his days in prison. "Free men should rule themselves, not be told what to do by a man with curls down to his waist."

Having reassured herself that there were no soldiers anywhere close, Alex turned her attention to her surroundings, looking with interest at the small shops – all of them closed, given that today was Sunday, and most of them shuttered as well. She came to a halt halfway down the main street. What? No, it couldn't be! She took a step closer to the small, dirty window, and if she hadn't been holding on to Matthew she would probably have fallen.

"Bloody hell!" She stared at a far too familiar painting. In swirling greens and blues it captured her eyes, whirlwinds of paint that beckoned and whispered, urging her to come closer, lean in and look for that point of blinding light that existed at the end of this undulating tunnel of ultramarine and turquoise.

She knew, even before looking for the telltale scrawled M, that this was done by Mercedes' hand. No; this was just too much. Her brain ached with the effort of trying to understand; a painting, by her mother, here. But Mercedes had been with her, with Magnus, so how …

She set her hand to the thick glass pane. Mercedes. But when? Just the thought of running into her mother – here, where she shouldn't be – had her breaking into a rash. Don't be ridiculous; how can she be here? She set herself on fire for God's sake! Not much of a comfort, really. She squinted; the paint looked cracked and her shoulders dropped. She hadn't been here recently, at any rate.

"Alex?" Matthew's voice made her jump. "What's the matter?"

She just pointed at the painting. Her vocal chords had gone on strike. She coughed.

"My mother," she said, "she painted that."

He dropped her hand as if it were red-hot, and stared from her to the painting and back again.

"But…"

"I know; how?" Oh God, it was true; her mother was definitely a witch, how else to explain this? She snuck him a look. He was staring at the picture, mouth slack, eyes glazed. Alex gave his hand a little shake. He didn't react, swaying on his feet.

"Matthew?" She tugged harder. He jerked, tore his eyes away from the painting and closed his hand hard round hers. Ouch!

"I must have it," she said. He shook his head. She wiggled her fingers against his tight hold. "I have to have it. I think it must burn." She peeked at it; definitely burn it. Their eyes met, he nodded once and turned Alex to hasten after Joan and Simon.

"Right," Matthew said as they were getting ready for supper. "Tell me."

"Tell you what?" She turned guileless, blue eyes on him, making him suppress a little smile.

"Alex…" he warned, "I saw, aye? There's something all three of you are keeping from me."

"Ask Simon."

Matthew shook his head. "I'm asking you, my wife, and I expect you to answer."

Alex sat down on the single stool and busied herself with her hair. He rested his shoulders against the wall, crossed his arms over his chest and waited. None of them were going anywhere until she told him.

"Have you seen Ian lately?" she asked, making him look at her quizzically. Ian? Why would he have seen him? She exhaled and fixed her bun into place with a hairpin.

"He looks just like you," she said, throwing him a look from under her eyelashes. He was very still as he tried to assimilate what she was saying. Then he laughed.

"Well, that's not so strange. I'm his uncle, after all."

Alex gave a quick shake of her head. "I don't think you are, and I think they know – both of them."

Matthew blinked. But no, surely not even they would cheat him of his son? And wouldn't she, well, wouldn't Margaret want her son protected, safe in his inheritance? He made a negating movement with his head.

"No," he said.

"They've been lovers for years. And there's only the one

child – the child conceived while she was married to you. Strange, isn't it?"

Matthew grabbed at his coat, retrieved his shoes from beside the bed.

"Where are you going?" Alex placed a hand on his arm.

"I'm going to find out the truth," he said through gritted teeth. "If I have to beat it out of her."

"No! " Alex stood herself between him and the door. "Don't you see? It's too late anyway. You've disowned him, haven't you?"

He flung her aside. "If he's mine, then I want to know."

"Open the door!" Matthew pounded at the heavy oak planks. "Open the door, goddamn you!"

"What do you want?" The door was flung open to reveal a half dressed Luke, with Margaret hovering in the background, and Matthew lunged for her.

"Is it true? Is he mine?" Luke's arm stopped him from getting at her. "Is he?" Matthew yelled, and now the laddie was there as well, and Matthew knew, just by looking at him, that Alex was telling him the truth.

"You lying, whoring slut," he hissed, spitting in the direction of Margaret. "May you rot in hell, you hear?"

Margaret blanched, backing away from him, and Matthew slammed Luke against the wall, intent on getting at her. A dull pain slashed down his arm, he was shoved sideways and turned to see Luke raise the knife yet again.

At the last moment Matthew evaded the knife. He twisted his brother's hand, and the knife fell to the cobbles. Luke parried a punch, sank his right fist into Matthew's unprotected gut, and Matthew used his elbow to send his brother staggering back, a hand clapped to his eye. Matthew came after, all the pent up rage of years spilling over. He was going to ... aye, his wee brother was finally going to pay for days, months, years of humiliation and despair.

His left arm hung useless, but he took no notice, using feet and one good arm to fend Luke off. He tripped, was kicked and punched, closed his hand on Luke's breeches and succeeded in pulling him down with him. He rolled, for a moment he was on top and then Luke bashed at his left arm and Matthew almost fainted. Luke bucked like an unbroken horse, and Matthew was thrown to the side.

"He's mine!" Luke panted, "he's mine, damn you. I sired Ian, you hear?"

"You lie! She lies!" Matthew's fist connected with Luke's nose with a satisfying crunch. He swung again, and Luke swayed, blood flowing from his lip. There was an explosion in his head, and Matthew lay stunned, all of him swimming in pain. A second blow crashed into his injured arm, and Matthew gasped. He raised his good arm to parry the next blow, succeeded in deflecting it from his face. He saw Luke raise the rock again, knew that the next blow would kill him, and there was Margaret, throwing herself over him.

"Nay, Luke," she pleaded, "don't, please don't." Vaguely Matthew realised she was weeping, her voice shaking as she begged Luke to stop. Somewhere in the back of his head it struck him that maybe she was repentant for what she'd done to him. It made hope flare in his belly until he recalled he didn't want her anymore, he had her, the other one, the one whose name he couldn't quite bring to mind in his present state.

Luke made a disgusted sound, threw the rock away and stalked off. Matthew's eyesight was blurring, he couldn't even lift his mangled arm, but at least he was alive, however much he was bleeding and hurting.

"We're square you and I, aye?" Margaret said, heaving herself back onto her feet. "I saved your life tonight. At what cost to myself and my man, I don't know."

"You shouldn't have told him," Simon took another turn around the room. "It's not safe for him to walk about alone. And now that he's angered, well…"

"I like it how you give me words of comfort," Alex said, "but what was I to do? Lie to him?"

"You didn't need to tell him!" Simon rubbed his hand through his thin hair, making it stand on end.

"He would've found out at some point, no? He'd have run into the boy sooner or later." She threw a worried look out of the window. It was night by now and he'd been gone for hours. "I'm going to look for him."

"You can't walk out alone. He'd flay me if I let you."

Alex glowered at Simon. "How exactly do you propose to stop me?" she asked, making for the door.

Simon sighed, muttered a God help me and pulled on his coat. "We'll go together. But you must stay with me."

Alex nodded, amused despite her worry. If it came to a crunch it would probably be her defending him rather than the reverse.

It was dark outside; as dark as it gets in May, full of strange shadows and greys, creaking sounds and scattering shapes that she knew to be rats. Simon seemed to have some sort of idea as to what direction to take, and led her through a throng of closes and small, smelly streets. She recognised the church and hurried to keep up as they turned into yet another close.

"Matthew!" Simon called out. "Matthew, are you there?" They walked further in and Alex saw something on the ground. A hand twitched and for a moment she was convinced that was the last movement he would ever make, but then he groaned.

Matthew heard her voice and felt her hands on his body, small, strong hands that tried to lift him upright. His head lolled back and he had the strangest vision of his wife hanging upside down from the sky. He groaned again and twisted his head to throw up, grateful that someone was holding him. Simon and ...Alex; aye, that was her name, she was his Alex. But Margaret had saved him, and her black hair had tickled his face, as smooth and glistening as he remembered it.

He tried to protest when they lifted him, because it hurt

so much, but he was already being half-carried, half-dragged. He gasped when he slipped out of a sweaty hold to hit the ground.

"Sorry, sorry, sorry," someone muttered, and he was in the air again, hearing the heavy breathing of whoever it was that was moving him. He was lowered to lie down, his limbs were lifted this way and that and something warm and wet moved over his body, making him yelp at times. The weak light of the candles was agony to his eyes, and every touch made his skin scream. He attempted to speak, but his lip was split, and his tongue was a useless sponge in his mouth. Alex, she was Alex, and he was Matthew Graham, and ... it all went a blissful, soothing blank.

He woke to find Alex sitting by his side. She was asleep, her head resting against the wall. He twisted to see the window, noting with surprise that it was twilight. He moved his legs, his arms and hands, sending sparks of pain through his mangled muscles. His left arm was one throbbing fire and he inhaled loudly when he shifted it. Alex awoke with a start.

"Hi, how are you feeling?"

He swallowed a couple of times to lubricate his throat.

"Poorly," he creaked. "Everything hurts."

"What happened?" she asked a while later. "Who did this to you?"

"Luke, it was Luke."

"He's here?"

Matthew felt it unnecessary to reply.

"Simon says I shouldn't have told you," she said.

Matthew closed his eyes. Nay, she shouldn't; it would have been better never to consider that there was a possibility of Ian being his son. Possibility? He'd had his answer in Luke's white hot rage, in the way those eyes so like his own had glazed into ice.

"I didn't want you to run into him and suddenly see what everyone else has seen for years," she went on, sounding hesitant.

"I wouldn't, I would never have looked at him for long enough to see it."

"But it's better to know, right?"

No it wasn't; some truths were only thorns driven into your flesh, an unnecessary suffering. Once he'd had a son, and now he no longer did. Ian; my wee Ian... He closed his eyes and pretended to sleep.

In the morning they woke to thunderous knocking on the door, and a baffled and protesting Simon was shoved to the side by a group of determined soldiers that hastened up the stairs.

They ignored Alex' heated pleas that they not move an injured man, they just heaved Matthew out of his bed and dragged him down the stairs, informing Simon that they were taking their prisoner to stand court.

"He'll hang before sundown," the lieutenant said with a satisfied smile. "But our Commander has accorded him the right to be heard. Mayhap you should be there – he doesn't seem to have much to say for himself. Ma'am." He bowed in the direction of Alex before following his bound and dazed prisoner out into the street.

CHAPTER 29

Simon saved Matthew's life that day. In his best coat, with his hair smoothed into place, he lined up argument after argument in the defence of his friend who was kept on his feet only due to the two soldiers that propped him up. Matthew wasn't there; he was lying on his back in his secret place, a grassy dell back home, and above him the sky spread a pale, washed blue. He swayed on his feet and wondered why his arm hurt, and when they took him away to lock him in for the night all he felt was relief at being allowed to lie down.

"You know he's no royalist!" Simon glared at Captain Leslie. "You know it was a trumped up charge last time, no?"

Captain Leslie looked away, uncomfortable under Simon's penetrating eyes.

"He was condemned to hang for treasonous activities." This was distasteful to him; hauling an injured man from his sickbed on the whispered accusations that he, Captain Leslie, was allowing an enemy to the Commonwealth to range free. It made him sick to his stomach to see the dazed and feverish man who'd stood blinking owlishly for most of the proceedings.

"Aye, he was, and all because of his brother and his lies. It's Luke Graham you be wanting as an enemy to the Commonwealth, not Matthew."

Thomas Leslie shrugged to indicate that matters were out of his hands. Simon set his mouth and followed him across the room. Leslie retreated behind his desk. He fiddled with the decorative braid on his buff coat and avoided meeting Simon's eyes. Simon brought his hand down hard on the desk.

"He fought for the Commonwealth!" he yelled. "For four years he fought with the Horse."

Leslie gave him a chilly look and rearranged his disturbed piles of dispatches.

"People have been known to change sides. It happens all the time." Like himself; in his early youth an admirer of Prince Rupert – well, he still was – but now a convinced Commonwealth man.

"His sentence was commuted to gaol," Simon said.

"Yes, but then he escaped, no?"

Simon threw his arms up in the air. "And why is that? May it have something to do with his brother bribing the guards to mistreat him? But no, of course not, how can we dare utter the blasphemous thought that even Commonwealth men are open to bribes – all the way, from court officers to wardens."

Captain Leslie frowned and moved over to the door. "We'll continue this matter tomorrow."

"And will you pledge your honour that he'll wake alive and well tomorrow?" Simon's bitter comment brought Leslie up short.

"Why would you fear for his life, here?"

Simon laughed hollowly. "This has nothing to do with Matthew being a royalist, all that know him can vouch that he's not. This is about Luke and his twitching need to have Hillview to himself."

Leslie drew himself up tall and met Simon's eyes straight on. "I give you my word. He lives the night."

"I'm sure that will be a comfort to his distraught wife," Simon said and left the room.

Next morning Captain Leslie found his office crammed. Simon must have done his rounds until late in the night, and turned up with several witnesses for Matthew's staunch Commonwealth stand. Minister Crombie was as vociferous as Simon in his insistence that Matthew had been set up, calling heatedly for new trial, and in the end Captain Leslie gave in.

This was not a time to be seen as too rigid, with London

in upheaval after the Army had relieved the new Protector, that incompetent son of a great father, of his charge only a fortnight back. The messenger had ridden in two days ago, shaking his head at the anxious unrest in the country. No one wanted a return to war, but as things stood now it might well be that the late Protector, rest his soul, would see his inheritance torn to pieces in yet another bloodied feud.

Matthew was pale but coherent when they brought him in. They had put him in chains, and even from across the room the red welts round the mangled wrists were visible.

"You gave me your word no ill would come to him," Simon said.

"He's a convicted traitor," Leslie replied, smoothing down his long, grey hair.

"Nay, he's not," Minister Crombie put in. "Haven't you just agreed to a new trial?"

Leslie regarded these two obstinate Scots with dislike. A small snake of pettiness reared its head inside of him, and he threw Matthew a disinterested glance.

"He stays in chains."

"I want to see him," Alex said, "I have to see him."

Simon shook his head. "I don't know if that's wise."

"But his arm! I have to make sure he's healing properly!" So that he could walk whole and healthy to the hangman's noose. The acrid taste of bile washed through her mouth.

"I don't think he wants you to see him like this," Simon said.

She wheeled away and tightened her arms around herself. "But what if he's condemned to hang? And it will all be my fault." For the last few nights she hadn't slept, rotating like a spitted chicken in bed as she imagined one end worse than the other for him – her man. He'd hang; she'd die. Boom, just like that.

"Nay, it isn't your fault," Joan said. "It's Luke's fault – he's the one who denounced him."

Alex sank down to sit on the floor, her fingers tracing

the sunbeams that filtered through the half closed shutters.

"It's my fault," she said, pushing the words through her drying mouth. "If I hadn't told him about Ian, he wouldn't have gone to find Margaret, and then Luke wouldn't have known he was here."

Joan knelt down beside her. "He already knew. Margaret would have told him when she got back from church."

Alex bit down on a wobbling lip and shook her head. "I don't think she would, for both their sakes." She got back onto her feet and turned pleading eyes on Simon. "I have to see him. Please."

Captain Leslie protested at first, but finally agreed to one visit from Graham's wife. Alex handed over her basket to the sentry, hated seeing those dirty fingers rifle through her carefully prepared foodstuffs and the clean shirt she'd brought for Matthew. With a nod the sentry allowed her entry, and Alex held on hard to her basket as she crossed the courtyard at the heels of yet another soldier, this one not much more than a boy.

She kept her eyes on the cobbles, closing her ears to the appreciative whistles from a group of soldiers loitering in the yard. Her head jerked up when someone screamed, worried eyes scanning her surroundings for Matthew, but her shoulders slumped when she realised it wasn't him, it was an unknown someone, and from what she could make out he was yelling not due to torture or flogging, but rather due to the inspection of his injured leg.

"It'll have to come off," the boy threw over his shoulder. "But he doesn't want them to cut him."

"I can imagine," Alex said.

Alex stood in the door and waited for him to ask her in. The man sitting hunched on the straw pallet in front of her was a stranger, his face shadowed by lack of sleep and contained fear. He motioned for her to enter, but when she made to come over to him he raised a hurried hand, the chains clinking. Simon hadn't thought to tell her, and she drowned a surprised exclamation in a cough. They were holding him like an animal; a pail in a corner, straw to sleep on and… her eyes went to the iron round his wrists and ankles.

"I don't want you to come too close. I stink," he said.

She struggled to wipe her face clean of disappointment, even managed a smile.

"I don't mind, and I want to see how your arm is."

"My arm's healing. You don't need to worry, aye?"

"I don't need to worry?" She shook her head. "Of course I worry, you bastard!" She went over to him, her hands hard around his face, a hasty kiss on his mouth. "And I don't care if you stink, okay?" Which he did, badly. She studied the iron manacles and bent to place her lips against the reddened skin around his fetters. She stood and brushed his hair off his forehead.

"Are you alright? Truly?" Talk about unnecessary questions …

Matthew hid his face against her belly and exhaled when she put her arms around him.

"No, not really."

Before she left he put a hand on her arm.

"Did you buy the painting?"

"The painting? What painting? Oh…" A shiver rippled through her. "I forgot, these last few days, well, I've had other things to think about."

His mouth curved into a faint smile. "Aye; so have I."

"I can imagine," she said, and she just had to smooth at his hair, kiss his cheek.

"You said you had to buy it."

"It sort of calls to me," she muttered.

"I … well, I don't like it, aye? It makes my innards flip. I don't want you looking at it, you hear?"

"I won't."

"If you buy it, you burn it – as you said, aye?"

"Yes, I burn it."

They dragged the proceedings on over a further four days,

but in the end Captain Leslie concluded that the first trial had been an apparent miscarriage of justice. In the continued absence of the key witness at that trial, Luke Graham, and in view of the multiple testimonials as to Matthew Graham's unwavering support for the Commonwealth cause, he could not but find that Matthew Graham had been wrongfully accused and should be acquitted of any charges laid against him.

Once the chains had been struck off, he apologised, hoping Mr Graham would not hold this against him, he was only carrying out his duty. Matthew bowed and assured him that no, of course he wouldn't. But he held his hands behind his back tightly fisted, nails sinking into his palms.

The moment he was outside he turned to Simon.

"Where is he?"

"Who?" Simon said.

Matthew shook his head. "Nay, Simon, not this time. I know you've locked him up somewhere, and you'll take me there. Now."

Simon met his eyes and with a little sigh acquiesced.

"Stand up." Matthew cut the ropes and hauled his brother to his feet. After more than a week locked up in the abandoned stables Luke was a reeking mess, but despite his bedraggled state he drew himself up straight, sneering at Matthew and Simon. Whatever his other faults, brother Luke did not lack for courage.

"Need help, do you? Afraid that I'll beat you senseless?"

In reply, Matthew crashed his fist into his brother's face. Luke reeled, but came back fighting. But this time Matthew had two good arms, and on top of that he was fuelled by an ice cold rage, one savage punch after the other driving Luke back into a corner.

"For Ian," he spat as he landed one well directed blow. "My son, not yours."

Luke parried, ducked. "Mine," he panted, "Margaret swears he's mine."

"Then she lies," Simon said, "but she does that a lot, no?"

"Take that back!" With a screech Luke launched himself in Simon's direction, was brought up hard by Matthew's fist in his gut. "Agh," Luke groaned, all air knocked out of him.

"That's for Alex," Matthew said. Repeatedly he hit Luke in the stomach, standing back to watch his brother crawl on all four. "And for the babe."

"The babe?" Luke stared up at him, wiping at his bleeding mouth. "What babe?" He groaned, clutching at his midriff.

"The wean Alex lost," Matthew said.

For an instant Luke froze, an expression of acute shame flashing over his features.

"A wean?" He was back on his feet. "I swear I didn't know."

"Does it make a difference?" Matthew said, "Would you have stayed your hand, had you known?" Two bright green eyes met his – angry, catlike eyes.

"I…" Luke looked away. "Probably not."

Matthew was so surprised by the honesty of this reply he lowered his guard, and Luke took the opportunity to swipe at him, landing a forceful punch on Matthew's chin. But before he could reach the door, Matthew grabbed him and shoved him to land on the ground.

"The swords," he said to Simon.

"Matthew," Simon said, "this isn't wise. It's frowned upon, you know that."

"Give me the damned swords!"

Simon handed him two rapiers and stepped as far out of range as possible.

"So, brother, do you know how to use one of these?" Matthew asked. He himself most certainly did, four years at war had left him an excellent swordsman.

Luke nodded, and when Matthew threw him one, caught it by the hilt.

"A duel?"

"A duel? I think not. Retribution, more like." Matthew stood at ease, and Luke licked his lips.

"Afraid?" Matthew jeered. "Uncomfortable when you have to see me in the eyes instead of having others do your dirty work?"

Luke cursed and lunged.

They were well matched in size and reach, and for a while Luke held his own, compensating for lack of experience and skill by sheer desperation. At one point Luke succeeded in grazing Matthew with his blade, a triumphant smile spreading over his face.

That was the only blood Luke drew and over the coming minutes Matthew decorated his brother's arms, his torso with a series of cuts. Desperate and cornered, Luke charged. Matthew sidestepped, rapped him over the hand with the flat of his blade, causing Luke to release his sword, and a few moments later it was over, with a bleeding and trembling Luke standing on his toes while Matthew's blade rested against the uncovered skin of his throat.

"I could kill you," Matthew said, "I should kill you; or geld you. Which is it to be, hmm?" He angled the blade upwards, pressing hard enough to break the skin. His hand quivered; so easy, a decisive slash and Luke would be no more. He was vaguely aware of Simon hovering in the background, pleading with him not do anything foolish. But Matthew's attention was focused on the honed edge of his rapier and how it pressed against Luke's throbbing jugular.

"Please…" Luke croaked, "please." The enclosed space filled with the sour stench of piss.

Matthew wrinkled his nose and drew the blade to the side, leaving a shallow, bleeding gash in its wake.

"Get out, wee brother" he said contemptuously. "Get out before I change my mind."

Luke fled. "I hate you, Matthew Graham," he yelled when he was safely out of range, "I hate you, you hear?"

"… and by now he's halfway to Edinburgh," Matthew summarised much later.

"Oh," Alex said. "And Margaret?"

"Margaret? Well, I assume she's still here, no? She wasn't riding with him."

"She can't, can she?" Joan said. "She has her son, no?"

"My son," Matthew snapped and stalked from the room. Alex made as if to stand and go after him but Simon waved her down.

"I'll go, if nothing else I can offer the comfort of whisky and silent male companionship." He winked at her. "Sometimes that's all a man needs – or wants."

"Here." Simon refilled Matthew's pewter cup, sloshed some more into his own cup and sat back. "You should have killed him."

"Aye. But he's my brother."

"Not for long, if Luke has his wishes come true."

Matthew took another sip of whisky. The warmth of it travelled down his innards, calming the snaking anger that just the thought of Luke inspired.

"Why, Simon? Why does he hate me so much?"

Simon shrugged. "Luke's a difficult man to comprehend, no? And God alone knows what fanciful stories Margaret told him when he returned." He paused and swept the remains in his cup. "I suspect Luke thinks you coerced Margaret into marriage, and for that he will never forgive you." Simon cleared his throat and stretched for the stone bottle. "Almost empty," he said indistinctly, refilling Matthew's cup. "You have to evict her, she can't stay on in the cottage, not after this."

"It isn't her fault," Matthew said.

Simon levelled a discerning stare at him. "What is it you want with her?"

"Nothing! It's just … Sometimes I, well, I'd like to lay my ghosts at rest. To not always see her laughing at me in my head." And as long as Margaret remained at Hillview he could hope for the occasional glimpse of the lad.

"You want to bed her?" Simon sounded astounded.

"No! I don't know what I want. I'd like her to plead that I come back to her."

"And would you?"

"Nay," Matthew said, "but I'd like that she should ask so that I could tell her so."

Alex was still awake when Matthew entered their room. He had hoped she wouldn't be, not wanting to talk to her while his mind buzzed with images of himself and a penitent Margaret. He flushed with shame; in his bed was his wife and he had his head full of pictures of that other wife, the one who crushed his heart. And saved his life, for had she not thrown herself across him that Sunday almost a fortnight ago he would've been dead. He became aware of Alex and found himself staring into two glacial blue eyes.

"So, do you?" she demanded.

"Do I what?"

"Do you want to fuck her? You know, to lay your ghosts at rest."

He considered lying to her, or even pretending he had no idea what she was talking about, but some sense of self preservation made him decide to tell her the truth, as well as he could.

"At times." He ignored her colourful curse and went to sit beside her. "I don't love her, but I wouldn't mind the opportunity to humiliate her as she did to me, laugh at her while she begged for me to… well, you know, no?" He snuck her a quick look. So far the truth had not gone down well. "It's nothing I would ever do."

"But you think about it, you and her, fucking."

"And you don't? Don't you at times think of him, John, like that?" He hoped she didn't, that he'd succeeded in erasing his predecessor entirely from her heart and mind.

"And if I did, how would that make you feel?"

"I'd hate it." He caught her eyes. "Do you?"

She shook her head vehemently. "I think of him, but never like that."

"Oh."

"But you do."

He hitched his shoulders. What could he say?

She turned her back on him, shoulders stiff with reproach. Matthew patted her hip and she slapped his hand away. He sighed, stood to undress. He looked down at her still shape, so unmoving he was sure she was holding her breath. For a moment he considered leaving her to sleep. In the end he decided not to.

"I love you," he said as he rolled her over to face him. "Only you. You know that, no?"

"Huh."

He had to work for it that night. Hard. Fortunately, he was both persistent and creative.

* * *

"Really?" Minister Weir's nose twitched.

"Well, I'm not sure," Luke said, "but I find it… coincidental." He touched his swollen, bruised face and scowled.

"How do you mean?" Hector asked from his corner. He was making an effort to stay out of the light, to keep his ageing body hidden – in particular after seeing the undisguised shock on Luke Graham's face when he'd greeted him. He looked down at his hand, closed so firmly round the earthenware mug. Old, but as yet strong, even if he suspected it was but a matter of time before whatever was happening to his outer shell began to attack muscles and tendons as well.

"The man said, no? How he and his friends had attempted to rob a man and a woman on the moor. And the woman…" Luke shook his head. "She's strange, my brother's wife, and she's not from here. Who knows what she might be?" He raised his hand to rub at the narrow scab that decorated his throat.

"A foreigner," Minister Weir nodded.

Hector gave him an irritated look; this man had major issues with xenophobia.

"That in itself is not necessarily an indication of anything, this inn is full of foreigners."

"Sailors," Luke said, "to be expected here in Leith, no?" He continued with his incredible story about a woman in long, blue breeches and the two robbers she'd kicked to death.

"I ..." Luke broke off, twisted his mouth into a rueful smile. "Well, I suppose I fear for my brother – what if his wife and this woman is one and the same?" The hell you fear for him, Hector sneered.

"Of course you do," Minister Weir said, patting the younger man's hand in a paternal gesture.

"I'll make it worth your while," Luke said, producing a velvet pouch. "And even more so should she hang."

Minister Weir gave him a stern look. "Do you think me motivated by gold?"

Hector choked on his beer.

"Of course not," Luke said, "see this as contribution to your expenses, no more, no less."

"Hmm." Minister Weir caught the pouch when Luke lobbed it to him. "I'll get to the bottom of it, but it would help if we could find the witness, no?"

"Aye, not too difficult, I reckon. The man's a drunk, babbles his story to whoever plies him with sufficient whisky." Luke produced a few coins and dropped them on the table. "Down Lanark way," he added before excusing himself, mumbling something about needing to find the captain of his ship.

"Well, well," Minister Weir said, rubbing his hands together. "Isn't this exciting? A murderess, no less, mayhap even a witch."

"Indeed." Oh yes; very exciting, exciting enough that Hector's hands were twitching. Minister Weir grinned slyly at Hector.

"Interesting enough for me to persuade you to come along?"

"Absolutely; after all, how often does one get to expose a murderer?" Finally, he thought, hiding his smile in his mug, at last he'd have the pleasure of meeting Alex Lind face to face.

CHAPTER 30

It was a quiet ride back home, Matthew submerged in his own thoughts. Alex sighed; for the last few days the single subject of conversation had been Ian, Matthew keeping up an intense debate with Simon as to how he should go about to reclaim his son.

Simon had been categorical; the divorce document and the subsequent disowning of the boy would be difficult to reverse – besides, he'd pointed out in a voice so low Alex wasn't supposed to hear it, how would Matthew's new wife feel about having Ian come to live with them?

A damn good question, Mr Melville, a question Mr Graham should perhaps have raised with his wife first, no? Still; she could sympathise with his feelings, and just the thought of a child growing up under Luke's care made her shudder.

"If you want him back I'd do my best to welcome him," Alex said, smiling at his surprised look. She nudged her mare closer. "It's not only me that's transparent at times," she said, reaching over to pat his leg.

"Do you think I should try?"

Alex mulled this over for a long time. If she were to be honest she would be uncomfortable with his son in the house – particularly a son torn from the only parents he'd ever known. Matthew was still waiting for an answer, his eyes resting on her with a look she couldn't quite interpret.

"I think it would be cruel to the mother." She drew rein, waiting until he'd turned and halted Samson. "I would have no problem with Ian living with us, but I'd never accept having Margaret there. Ever." Definitely not after what she'd overheard the other evening, all that crap about wanting to have Margaret beg him to take her back. His intense performance in bed that night had assuaged some of her jealousy, but most of it was still very much alive and kicking.

A slight flush stained Matthew's cheeks. "My son should grow up with me."

"Your son doesn't consider you his father. He'd hate you for wrenching him away from his mother. It would be devastating to them both."

"Mayhap I should let them stay on in the cottage, then I can see him now and then."

"No. She goes."She drove her heels into the horse and left him in the middle of the road.

Once back home, Alex took care of the unloading, shooing Matthew off to inspect his fields or go and scratch the sow, or why not check on the oxen?

"The oxen?" He looked over to where the two placid beasts were grazing in the closest meadow. But he seemed glad enough to be let off the unpacking, leaving satchels and pannier baskets by the door before leading the horses off to the stable. Alex waited until he was out of sight before digging into one of the panniers. Right at the bottom, hidden under bolts of fabric was Mercedes' picture, wrapped in burlap.

She caressed the bundle. It hummed into life, strands of whispering song leaking out of it. Shit! She fumbled and dropped it. It should burn. Burn it now, yes, yes, burn it now. Gingerly she picked it up. She'd tried to destroy it back in Cumnock, but at the last moment she'd pulled it back from the fire, incapable of burning this last tenuous link with her mother.

"Welcome back," someone said from behind her. Alex smiled a bright greeting at Mrs Gordon, loaded her arms to hide the package, and rushed upstairs. She held the wrapped painting at arm's length. She'd burn it. Yes, of course she would. But not today. Hastily she stuffed it into the mule chest.

They threw themselves back into their respective chores over the coming weeks. Alex rarely saw Matthew during the day, and it took some time before she caught on to the fact that he seemed to be avoiding her on purpose.

Once she did, she began to plan for random encounters only to verify that it took him but a couple of minutes before he mumbled something about having to see to the calf, or repair the storing sheds, or do something about the loose tine on his pitchfork.

He'd kiss her, pat her behind before he hurried away, and she watched him thoughtfully, trying to understand what it was he was keeping from her. Not that she didn't have a pretty good idea.

A long walk in the woods confirmed her suspicion. Margaret was still in residence, although she seemed very ill at ease when she saw Alex.

"What do you want?" Margaret was washing her hair, sitting outside in only her shift and a shawl. Even with wet hair the bloody woman looked stunning.

"Why are you here? Why aren't you with your husband somewhere? Preferably very far from here?"

"He's on his way to Holland, to meet with the king, aye?"

"Not king yet."

"No, but soon," Margaret said.

She produced a comb and began to unravel her damp hair, turning her back on Alex.

There was a breaking sound and Ian appeared from among the shrubs. He came to a halt when he saw Alex, a shy smile appearing on his face.

"Hi," she said to this miniature Matthew.

"Mistress," he bowed, both hands cupped tight over something.

"What's that?" she asked.

"For my Mam," he said, "look Mam."

Margaret smiled down at her son who opened his hands to release a white butterfly. She threw Alex a look.

"Still here?"

Alex raised her brows. "This is my home, not yours. And I want you to leave, as soon as possible."

Matthew came to the table that evening with a

thunderous expression on his face. He barely ate, drinking large quantities of beer instead, and once the meal was concluded he told Alex that he wished to speak to her, and stalked off in the direction of his study.

She was humiliated by his tone and chose to remain where she was. If he wanted to talk to her, then he could bloody well sit down beside her, not request her presence in his office as if she were an errant child.

"Didn't you hear?" he sounded very cold, standing in the doorway. Mrs Gordon threw him a look and scuttled off to her own room.

"You wanted to talk to me, or rather tell me off, and you made sure everyone at the table knew that, didn't you?" Alex stood and moved over in the direction of the stairs. "I'm going to bed, if you have something to say, you might just as well tell me now."

"It's not your place, not your right to order people off my land."

"Oh dear, has Margaret been telling tales?" She took a step towards him. "But that would mean that you've seen her no?"

"Of course I have, she came to find me, all in tears."

"Poor, poor, Margaret, did you perhaps hold her in your arms and shush her? Take the opportunity to soothe those restless ghosts of yours?"

"I did no such thing!" He glared at her.

"Really? But a hug perhaps, you know, a comforting little squeeze no more?" Matthew went a dusky red all over. "Yeah; I thought so. It's very simple, either she goes or I do. Take your pick." She pushed by him and up the stairs, slammed the door hard and shoved the bolt into place.

Next morning he cornered her on the way to the privy, took hold of her arm and led her out of hearing distance from the curious audience consisting of Sam, Robbie and Gavin. She had no idea where he'd slept, but assumed he'd bedded down in his study or in the loft. Frankly, she didn't give a shit.

"You won't lock me out of my bed, ever again," he shouted at her, eyes flaming in gold in the early sunlight. "I'll never have my wife do that to me again."

"At least I was alone in there, not like her, screwing your brother! And let go of my arm, you idiot, you're hurting me." He gave her a rough shake and let go, sending her tumbling to the ground.

"Fine," she said as she got to her feet. "I'm leaving."

"No you're not." He pulled her close, wrapping an arm hard round her. "Please listen, aye?"

She shrugged; she really didn't have much choice, pinned as she was to his chest.

"I gave her my word. I promised I wouldn't throw her out."

How touching. Bastard! And how about discussing it with her first, hey?

"Well then it seems you've made up your mind, right? So if you'll excuse me, I'll just go and pack."

"Alex! You're being unfair. I can't just put them out, where would they go?"

Alex thought about that for a moment. "I have no idea. But neither do I care." She felt a twinge at saying that, thinking of Ian. "She has a husband. Isn't it enough that she cheated on you, connived in sending you to jail – no excuse me, to hang, but unfortunately for them someone felt like being lenient – lied to you about your son, do you also have to support her?"

He let go of her and took a step back. "She saved my life that night back in Cumnock. If it hadn't been for her, Luke would have killed me."

"She did?"

He nodded and scratched at his head. "She begged him not to kill me. And he listened."

"Oh." All the anger ran out of her, leaving her drained. She dropped down to sit and Matthew followed suit.

"If you insist I'll ask her to leave, but I ask you to let them stay – not for her sake, but for the lad's."

Alex did not at all feel like being generous. She wanted Margaret gone, she wanted the living reminder of the fact that she'd been Matthew's wife gone. She exhaled loudly.

"I don't like it."

Matthew's mouth quirked; no, that was rather apparent, he told her, and he had to concede she had the right of it. She glanced at him and then away.

"What if Luke shows up? He will, sooner or later, and what if you run into each other?" Or if he walks into me … Her guts tightened into a knot and she closed her eyes, squishing down her lids until all she saw was bright red.

"I'll tell her, it's a condition, aye? She may remain here as long as he stays away."

Alex found that a dubious comfort, but gave a small nod.

"And you keep well away from her, Matthew."

He bowed his head in acquiescence.

Entering the kitchen, Alex was attacked by the scents of porridge and honey, eggs and warm bread. It made her want to throw up and she concentrated on breathing through her mouth. She sat down on the bench beside Matthew and shook her head in a no at the extended plate. Mrs Gordon studied her for a moment and smiled, dark eyes glinting.

"You're breeding."

Matthew looked at Alex, letting his eyes slide over her breasts.

"I think so, but it's early days yet." She hadn't wanted to say anything before she was absolutely certain and gave Mrs Gordon an irritated look. "I was planning on telling him myself." She stormed out of the kitchen before she burst into tears.

"You'd best go after her," Mrs Gordon said, grinning at Matthew. He regarded her calmly and tore off another piece of bread.

"It'll keep, no? I'll go and find her after breakfast."

Inside he was loud with joy, but surprised that he hadn't noticed. The last few weeks of tension around Margaret must have made him unobservant, and it struck him that he hadn't really seen her naked since they got back from Cumnock – not to properly look at.

He found her on the hill, standing with her arms crossed over her chest, her eyes fixed on the endless miles of moor spread before her.

"How far along are you?" he asked, hugging her from behind.

"Two months."

He counted in his head; a January babe.

"It makes me very glad." He turned her in his arms, fiddled with her bodice, her shift, and eased the cloth down until her breasts were uncovered. Yes, they were heavier, and when he breathed on them, her nipples prickled, dark against her pale, pale skin. "I should have noticed," he said, rearranging her clothes. "But I'll take my time with you tonight."

"Tonight?"

He smiled at her disappointment and let his fingers travel up her throat and tease at her earlobes. Her eyes unfocused, her lips parted and he kissed her, a long, warm kiss.

"Tonight," he repeated once they came up for air. One swift caress and he walked off, leaving her burning for him. He liked that.

What to begin with had been something that made Matthew laugh and shake his head in amused exasperation, had become something he looked forward to, whether in winter or in summer.

Every Saturday Alex insisted that they should have a bath, and when Matthew and Rosie protested at the work involved in heating all that water and filling the wooden hip bath upstairs, she had decided that bathing would be done in the kitchen, after supper. In winter, she'd light candles and spread the linen towels to heat in front of the fire, and then she'd wash her way up Matthew's limbs in a way that covered both of them with soap suds before she was done.

But today it was a summer evening, and he saw her make her way down the path towards the little eddy pool. He didn't need to be there to know that she'd begin by finding a willow twig and clean her teeth. And then she would... He hurried his way through the last of his chores, ran his hands through his hair, and strolled off after her.

He liked to watch her swimming. She was like an otter, graceful and fast, diving into the deep end and surfacing a long way out before she flipped on her back to float. She did a backwards somersault, offering him an interesting view of her dark pubic triangle, and swam towards the shore. He stood up from where he'd been sitting and came down to the water's edge.

"Hi," she said and extended the soap to him. "Will you help me wash my hair?"

He lathered her hair into a cap of white foam and towed her out into the deep to rinse it. Then it was her turn to wash him, and somehow things ended up as they often did, with him only half washed but terribly aroused. Her breasts bobbed in the water when she leaned back to float away from him, her lower part anchored to his. He stood on the pebbled bottom and made love to his wife as the summer twilight turned to night, wondering if in the darkness of her womb it was a son that lay waiting to be born.

CHAPTER 31

Simon looked very grim when he and Joan rode in a few weeks later. In his leather satchels he carried letters for Matthew and a new book. Matthew handled the book reverently, turning it back and forth between his hands.

"What? A new Bible?" Alex asked Simon in a low voice. The Grahams were prickly when it came to digs at their religion, and it was a comfort to both Simon and Alex to recognise a kindred spirit in each other.

"Nay, a book of poems." Simon rolled his eyes.

Alex brightened; the few books in the house left quite something to be wished for when it came to light reading, and the thought of reading poems – any poems – seemed a welcome change.

Simon tugged at Matthew's sleeve, the grim expression back on his face, and the two men disappeared in the direction of the barn, leaving Alex and Joan alone.

"What's the matter?" Alex asked.

"Simon heard this incredible story, about how three would be robbers found the tables turned on them. Two died, killed by a lass."

Alex' throat dried up. "Really? Sounds unbelievable to me; how could one woman possibly overcome two men on her own?" Not one single telltale squeak, she noted with some pride.

Joan held her eye a bit longer before nodding.

"The third robber is in the custody of Captain Leslie. He'll hang, but the shadow of the approaching gibbet has made him very voluble, and he has been spreading this tale to anyone who will listen. Many do." Joan slipped her hand under Alex' arm and steered her in the direction of the garden. "It's best you don't come to Cumnock for a while, aye?"

"Me? But ..."

"She was a foreign lass, he says; a lass with hair as short as a lad's and strange, blue breeches."

Alex shook out her full skirts and shrugged.

Mrs Gordon came to find her that afternoon.

"Pie?" she asked. Alex looked down at her basket, full of early raspberries. A pie would be very nice.

Mrs Gordon sat down beside her on the bench and in an affectionate gesture took Alex' hand.

"I heard yon Mr Melville talking to the master, about the robber and his story, aye?"

"Ridiculous, isn't it?"

Mrs Gordon looked at her for a long time. "I hope you burnt them, those strange breeches of yours."

Alex didn't know what to say.

"I won't tell, but the description he gave of a strange lass with short hair and odd breeches, well, we both know, no? And then there's the knife wound in the master's shoulder, just where the robber says it should be. So what happened?"

There was no lying to those glittering black eyes, and Alex told her the truth, twisting with embarrassment at Mrs Gordon's admiring expression.

"You fought them with your bare hands?"

"Mostly feet."

Mrs Gordon chuckled. "You know, the first time I saw you I thought you were a fairy. Then I took you for a gypsy, but you left me payment for what you took, and no fairy or gypsy would do that." She regarded Alex piercingly. "But you're very strange; you can't knit nor spin, you've never butchered a lamb ..."

"Yes, I have! We did it together, remember?"

"Aye, and you looked fit to throw up when you were told to rinse the guts clean."

"Well you know, in Sweden..."

Mrs Gordon laughed and shook her head. "Nay, lass; my brother's a sailor and has been to Gothenburg several times. But never has he told me of girls in breeches and with short hair. They seem to be like us, no?"

Alex attempted a derisive snort. "Gothenburg! That's not really Sweden. I come from the far, far north."

"I don't believe you, I think you carry secrets that you can't share, and I won't push. But you must be careful, lass." Mrs Gordon braced her hands against her knees and stood. "I like you, Alex Graham, and I'll stand by you." She gave Alex a perceptive look. "You had no choice; had you not killed them, it would have been you and the master dead."

"But still," Alex sighed.

"Aye well; they'd have hanged soon enough anyway, vermin that they are." With that Mrs Gordon hurried off, saying something about finding some lard for the piecrust.

Two days later, Matthew was halfway to the stables when Captain Thomas Leslie rode into the yard, looking as if he wished he could be anywhere but there. With him came four cavalry soldiers, a minister, and a slight man in a huge hat. Matthew came to a halt, noting how Alex appeared in the kitchen doorway, neat in sober green and with a linen cap on her head.

Captain Leslie shook his head at the sight of her, and leaned out of his saddle to say something to the minister. Even from where he was standing, Matthew could hear the minister's caustic reply along the lines that the captain should not meddle with things he had no knowledge of, and then the minister man was off his horse, strutting across the yard towards Matthew.

"Master Graham," he said. "There are questions I have to discuss with you regarding your wife." Matthew swept out his arm to welcome both the minister and the captain inside.

"And you," Matthew added, nodding in the direction of the unknown man who for some reason was wearing a full length cloak, gloves and an antiquated lace collar that succeeded in covering most of his lower face.

"This is Mr Olivares," Captain Leslie introduced. "He's accompanying Minister Weir."

Out of the corner of his eye, Matthew saw Alex take a step back. He struggled to keep his face bland, while inside he was churning with questions. Hector Olivares, here? For what purpose?

"Mistress," Olivares said, bowing in the direction of a pale Alex who succeeded in bobbing him a responding curtsey, before flattening herself to the wall to allow him inside.

"He's a witch hunter," Leslie said, "much in demand. He and Master Weir were called to investigate some unfortunate incident in Lanark when they came upon the wretched robber in an inn. The fool was damning himself with every drunken word he uttered." He frowned down at a spot on his grey coat.

"Ah," Matthew nodded, trying to sound unperturbed. Witch hunter; it made his intestines twist.

"Besides," Captain Leslie said, "there seems to be some truth in his unhinged story. One of my men…"He waved in the direction of his mounted soldiers. "… insists he saw a woman in outlandish breeches a year or so ago."

"Really?" Matthew shrugged.

The coming hour was extremely uncomfortable. Minister Weir directed himself only to Matthew and Hector Olivares retreated to stand in a corner, his strange jewel eyes boring into Alex. Matthew frowned, not quite sure what to do. Alex shifted closer to him, clasped her hands in front of her and dropped her eyes to the floor, but every now and then he saw her lashes flutter as she peeked in the direction of Olivares. And Olivares, God curse him, well he continued to stare at Alex in a way that had Matthew seething inside.

"But why?" Minister Weir asked, eyeing Alex as if she were a cow. "Why would you take up with a strange girl?"

"I told you; I found her on the moor, distraught. Was I to leave her there, all alone?"

"And her father, is he dead?"

Matthew saw the trap in time; say yes and they'd be asked to show them where he was buried.

"I don't know, and nor does my wife. She has no recollection at all. One moment she was riding pillion behind her father, the next she wakes up badly burnt and both father and horse are gone."

Olivares' mouth twisted into a derisive smile.

"Hmm," Minister Weir said, "and she's from Sweden?"

Matthew nodded.

Minister Weir wrinkled his nose as if at the smell of something distasteful and leaned towards Matthew.

"Is she of the right faith?"

Matthew drew himself up straight, well aware of how intimidating his height was to men as small as the minister.

"I'm a man of the faith, Minister Weir. Do you think I'd risk my bairns not being properly raised?"

The little man looked discomfited and muttered an apology.

After a hushed little conference between the minister and Olivares, the minister nodded a couple of times, smoothed down his dark coat and cleared his throat.

"Well," Minister Weir said. "It's best you ride in with us."

"Why?" Matthew asked.

Minister Weir gave him a sharp look. "You know, no? We have a man in jail who says he saw a lass kill his two companions almost a year ago – a foreign lass, just like your wife."

Matthew laughed. "And you believe him? Would any woman you know be able to overcome two men on her own?"

Minister Weir insisted, despite Matthew's protestations that of course his wife had not done something like that, and finally Matthew went out to saddle Samson, giving Alex a supporting look as he left.

She was having problems standing straight. Would the moor-trooper recognise her? And if he did, would his word count for more than hers? As she exited the house, Hector jostled into her, his eyes far too close.

"Scared?"

"Why should I be?" she said stiffly. "I've never done anything wrong."

"Oh I would be, if I were you." He sniffed her. "You smell like a witch, Alex Lind. And I'm the witch hunter, remember?" She reared back from him, but he came after. "I bet you'll scream, they all do when we torture them." He snickered and bowed to allow her to precede him.

Alex walked across the yard on sheer willpower. She even managed to smile at Captain Leslie when he offered her his hands to boost her onto the horse, but once on Samson's back she slumped against Matthew, noting how Minister Weir and Olivares were now huddled together, the minister's eyes fixing on her.

"Oh, God."

Matthew's arm came round her like a supporting bracket. "It's him, no?"

"I think so, and I don't like this witch hunter thing. He just told me I smelled like a witch. It scares the shit out of me."

"Mmm," he breathed.

No sooner had they left Hillview behind, before Hector rode up to the minister, a hushed conversation springing up between them that involved many looks in the direction of Alex, who shrank back against Matthew's chest. The minister said something, the two men shared a little laugh, and Matthew decided there and then that this was enough.

"Is it common?" he asked in a carrying voice.

"Common? Is what common?" the minister said, sounding irritated.

"For ministers of the Kirk to consort with papists."

"Papists?" Minister Weir squeaked. "What are you on about?"

"Him," Matthew said, pointing at Hector. Every single head but Alex' swivelled to stare at Hector who fidgeted in his saddle.

"Hector?" Weir laughed. "You must be mistaken, Mr Graham. Hector is a witch hunter of great repute."

Matthew raised his brows. "Really? That's mighty strange, seeing as we had him arrested as a spy last time he was here."

"A spy?" Captain Leslie looked the small man up and down, taking in the broad-brimmed hat, the enveloping cloak.

"Absolutely," Matthew said, "he's Spanish, no? And he asked so many questions that we sent him off in chains to Edinburgh as a royalist spy – and a papist."

"I had no idea," Minister Weir said in a shocked voice, his eyes flying all over the place. Matthew almost smiled; this wee man was a most incompetent liar.

"No, because if you did, you'd have denounced him," Matthew said solemnly.

"Of course," Minister Weir said, looking at Hector as if he expected at any moment to see horns protrude from his forehead.

"Nonsense," Hector said sharply. "All this is nonsense. It's just an attempt to discredit me."

"A Spaniard," Matthew said. "And definitely a papist."

"Prove it!" Hector said.

"We can catechise you if you want, it will be easy enough for Minister Weir here to verify if you're of the faith or not, and I'm sure Minister Crombie will be glad to help – as will I, and no doubt the captain as well." Matthew smiled wolfishly at them both.

Minister Weir had gone the colour of dirty linen, an unhealthy yellow tinged with grey. He sat ramrod straight in the saddle and nailed his eyes into Hector.

"Well? Are you? A papist?" He cringed when Hector rode in so close their thighs crushed against each other, and a little sound escaped him when Hector grabbed him by the arm, effectively putting the minister between himself and the others.

"You know I am," Hector said in an undertone. "After all, that's how you blackmailed me into participating in your little scam, no?" He twisted his fingers hard into the minister's arm. "Fix this, fix it or I'll tell them everything." He rose in his stirrups, menace oozing from every square inch of him.

"A papist!" Minister Weir called out. "Oh my God, Mr Graham is right! Look, he threatens me! Arrest him, I say! Kill him on the spot if need be!"

"What? Why you twofaced little shit!" Hector turned to face the others. "This minister isn't exactly what he..." As if by chance, Minister Weir crashed into him, nearly unseating them both.

"A papist, a papist! Jesus sweet, he intends to kill me! Do something, Captain Leslie!"

Hector opened his mouth to say something, the minister shrieked as if in agony, and the captain spurred his mount towards him, shadowed by two of his men.

"I wouldn't try anything foolish," Hector said, drawing his sword. The soldier closest to him lunged, Hector wheeled his horse, rammed the sword into the side of the unfortunate man and set spurs to his mare.

"Go on! After him!" Captain Leslie waved his hand in the direction of the rapidly shrinking Hector and turned to frown at the minister. "You didn't suspect?"

"Had I done so I'd have turned him over to the authorities immediately." The little man shook his head. "Terrible, no? No doubt he planned to murder me in my sleep."

"Mmm," Captain Leslie said, "although it seems to me he must have had ample opportunity to do so already." He frowned, mouth pursing as he studied the minister.

Matthew caught his eye, nodded; aye, there was a whiff of something rotten in all this. Not that it greatly concerned him – not now, with Hector Olivares no more than a dwindling speck on the horizon.

"I assume this means we can ride back home," Matthew said.

Minister Weir scowled at him. "Assume? What does the papist spy have to do with the two murdered men?" He drew his cloak around him, regaining his dignity in leaps and bounds.

"Well, I thought…"

"You thought wrong!"

Matthew sighed and settled Alex closer to him. "It'll be alright."

"At least you got rid of one of them. For now," she qualified.

CHAPTER 32

Simon was waiting for them when they rode into Cumnock.

"There's a new witness," he said as he helped Alex down. He inclined his head in the direction of a cloaked figure standing a way off. Alex and Matthew stared as Mrs Gordon winked at them from below her hood. "Gavin rode her in; the moment she saw the minister come riding down your lane, she set off."

Once in the makeshift court room, Minister Weir rubbed his hands together, apparently recovered from the incident with Hector. He allowed his eyes to rest for an instant on the audience before looking Alex up and down in silence. A long silence. If he'd expected her to fidget he had another think coming. Alex pasted a bland smile on her face – sort of like screwing down a lid on a can bulging with ugly, hairy worms – the worms in question being her guts.

"You!" the minister barked, pointing at one of the soldiers, and the man jumped.

"Me?"

"Yes, you. You're Isaiah Smith, no?"

"Yes, sir, I am." The soldier straightened up.

Shit; not him again. Alex kept her eyes on her toes.

"Well? Is this her?"

"Her?" Smith sounded bewildered.

Minister Weir sighed, smoothed down his voluminous sleeves and approached the soldier.

"Is this the woman you saw on the moor? The woman with breeches on?"

"I couldn't say," Smith said after having looked at Alex. "I never saw her properly, it was dark, no? And when I rode after her, I mostly saw her... err... well, her arse, begging your pardon. Very snug, those breeches." A titter flew through the room, making the minister frown.

"But it was a woman you saw?"

"Oh, yes, I recognise a good female arse." Smith chewed his lip for some moments. "Now if I were to see the mistress' bottom, then maybe…"

"Smith!" Captain Leslie bellowed, pre-empting Matthew who was on his feet, a dangerous gleam in his eyes.

"I was just saying," Smith muttered.

"And her hair? Was it long or short?"

Smith scrunched up his brow. "Uncovered, it was uncovered and short."

"Was she alone?"

Smith scowled. "No. If she'd been I'd have collared her. She was with a man."

"Hmm," the minister said, looking at Matthew. "And the man, would you recognise him?"

"No. I was mostly looking at …"

"Yes, yes, we know." The minister waved him silent. "Well," he said to Captain Leslie, "your man's description matches that of our other witness, no? A man and a woman, and the woman in outlandish clothes. Do women wear breeches in Sweden?" He swung to face Alex, who took a step back.

"No," she said, wrinkling her nose at his sour exhalations. "But they do in Turkey, and in China, as I hear it."

The minister frowned, clapped his hands together and a man was dragged into the room. Alex struggled to remain calm, hands relaxed where they rested against her skirts, face demurely lowered.

"Is he sober?" the minister demanded of the guards.

"As much as he ever is," the elder of the guards retorted.

"So, is it her?" Weir asked, waving his hand in the direction of Alex.

The man squinted at Alex. His hair hung in a matted mess and even from the distance of a few metres Alex had the distinct impression he was crawling with lice.

"I don't know," the man said.

"So you don't know if Mrs Matthew Graham is the woman you saw," Minister Weir pushed.

The prisoner stood straighter at the sound of the name. "It might be; I can't see her face."

"Show your face, woman," Minister Weir said, "and take off your cap so that he can see your hair."

"I think not," Matthew interrupted. "My wife doesn't bare her hair in public, Minister Weir – not on the say so of you." Matthew smiled at Alex. "Let him see your face, lass." She raised her chin. The prisoner stared and took a step back.

"It's her," he squeaked and the room exploded.

"You're a perjurer," Mrs Gordon yelled, pointing at the prisoner. "All that you've said about seeing a lassie kill your two companions, who'd believe you? You're a murderer, a rapist and a filthy thief!"

"Not a murderer!" the man screamed back over the shouts for order from Captain Leslie. Mrs Gordon waited until the room has calmed down.

"If yon man..." She pointed at Minister Weir. "... if he hadn't let drop that this was Mrs Matthew Graham, would you have known her then?"

Captain Leslie nodded, giving Minister Weir a beady eye. Despite the situation, Alex was somewhat amused by how the minister paled under the captain's scrutiny. Captain Leslie leaned towards the prisoner.

"Answer, man!"

"I don't know, but I do know that I saw a woman kill my friends."

Mrs Gordon snorted. "You're full of the fairies, Tom Wilson. You've been out of your head since you were a bairn up in Lanark. A lassie kill two grown men!" There was a rustle of whispered agreement in the room and Mrs Gordon expanded her opulent chest. "I saw you, Tom. You came down from the moor alone on an August afternoon, and your hands were bloodied."

Tom shook his head and looked down at his hands.

"Nay, I never killed them. Not me, I just knifed the man. It was the woman." He stared about him and stabbed his finger in the direction of Alex. "It was her! She did it!"

"Hmph!" Mrs Gordon expressed. "I saw what I saw, aye? You, Tom, not a lass!"

"No! Not me!"

Captain Leslie got to his feet and told the wardens to take the prisoner away. "This is unseemly, a ruffian casting aspersions on the character of a married woman, with no proof but his own ramblings."

Minister Weir made as if to protest, but at an icy look from the captain subsided on his chair.

"And from what Mrs Gordon has told us, it may well be he himself is the killer of his erstwhile companions, and if so he has done us all a service, no?"Captain Leslie bowed to Alex. "My apologies, mistress, for an unnecessarily harrowing experience."

"Accepted," she said and curtsied, extremely proud of herself for not sitting on her arse while doing so.

Leslie clamped down his hand on the arm of Minister Weir who was sidling off in the direction of the door.

"A word, minister."

"Aye," Matthew agreed, "a word. Or two, no?" Together they frogmarched the protesting minister out of the room and into Leslie's office.

The previously so cocky little man wilted under Matthew's inspection.

"You have some explaining to do," Matthew said.

"Aye," Simon said, "a very elegant little set up. Slip in the name and have him identify her."

"I did no such thing! It was not done maliciously, it was merely a slip of the tongue."

Captain Leslie made a derisive sound. "You're an experienced man of both church and court, Minister. I don't believe you, and would know – right now – who set you up to this and why."

Minister Weir pressed his mouth shut, making him look like a repulsive toad. He avoided the three pairs of eyes, concentrating on packing his papers into his leather satchel.

"Surely you're not thinking of leaving?" Matthew loomed over the smaller man, closing his hands round an urgent desire to slap the wee bastard.

Minister Weir flinched, a small pointed tongue darting out to wet his lips.

"I'm a man of the Kirk, you'd best not harm me."

"Harm you? You disgusting maggot of a man, hiding behind the skirts of your office when it suits you." Matthew lowered his face to stare Weir in the eyes. "I don't know what you were playing at, but the intent was to rob me of my wife no? And I, Minister Weir, don't take kindly to that. So, either you tell us all you know, or you'll need to look constantly over your shoulder for the few days of life that remain to you." He ignored Captain Leslie's protest at the threat and backed the minister into a corner.

"It was Luke?" Alex looked from Simon to Matthew and back again.

"Aye," Simon said, "he put the wee miscreant up to it, telling him how you'd appeared out of nowhere and how quick you'd been to marry Matthew, all to gain the protection of his name." He drank from his tankard and wiped the foam off his lip before continuing. "And he then added a few twists, aye? Like maybe you were heathen, not being from here, and that you might have bewitched his poor brother, and how worried he was that you were out to kill Matthew in his sleep."

"Oh." Alex took a big gulp of cider.

Mrs Gordon bit into her pie and studied it suspiciously before taking yet another bite.

"That minister is not what he seems," she said, "holier than thou on the outside, but a nasty piece of work on the inside."

"You know him?" Matthew asked.

Mrs Gordon shook her head. "Nay. But I'm a good judge of character." She gave Alex a glance and smiled.

"And Hector Olivares?" Alex asked. "Did they catch him?"

"No," Simon said. "And by now it's too late – he'll have taken to the moor."

Alex scooted closer to Matthew.

"He won't come back," the innkeeper put in, "too much of a risk, no?" He hawked and spat, losing himself in contemplation of the slimy globule that now decorated his floor. "A witch hunter indeed... Pah! Superstitious nonsense!"

"Absolutely," Alex said, agreeably surprised by this rather modern reaction.

"Would his word have been enough?" Alex asked Matthew much later.

"Let's just say that it was fortunate Mrs Gordon came forward."

Alex swallowed. "She lied for me, and now he hangs, right?"

"He'd hang anyway." He sat down beside her on the bed, took her hand in his. "I'd never let them hurt you, they would've had to kill me first."

"How romantic," she snorted.

Matthew laughed, dug into his pouch and extended a small twist of cloth to her.

"Here."

"What is it?"

"It's something you should have had a long time ago," he said, shoving a curl off her cheek. "Won't you open it?"

She did, and a heavy gold ring fell into her hand. A dark stone glinted in the candlelight.

"It's your wedding ring," he said and threaded the ring onto her finger. "Sapphire, like your eyes."

She held out her hand to admire it and placed her hand over his heart.

"Thank you, I'll never take it off."

"As it should be," he replied gruffly and kissed her nose.

CHAPTER 33

She woke and knew that today was it, and she wasn't sure she should leave her safe bed – maybe she could stay here, pretend she was sick or something. Coward. With a muffled sigh she rose and stood naked, inspecting herself in the clear light of the morning. She pinched at her waist, slid her hands down to weigh her buttocks, her thighs; no longer as muscled as they'd been. Well tough; it wasn't as if she'd found a gym anywhere close was it?

Slowly her hands travelled over her belly, already visibly round with child. Very round; she should probably cut back on her helpings. Her skin was a milky pale – except for hands, feet and forearms – her hair fell in curls to her shoulders, giving all of her a softer appearance. She ran her tongue over her teeth; still whole. She dressed slowly; shift, stays and petticoats, skirt and bodice. A year ago they'd felt strange, today she'd feel undressed in anything less. Talk about conforming to conventions, hey? She twisted her hair into a neat bun, settled her cap into place and grinned at her reflection. Mrs Matthew Graham grinned back, but here and there Alex Lind still peeked out. Thank heavens for that! She blew herself a kiss and clattered down the stairs.

All through breakfast and her morning chores, images of her lost people populated her brain. As the months passed, that old life had acquired a dreamlike quality and it was only occasionally that her thoughts turned to them, a sudden flashing image of Magnus or John appearing and fading in her head. Isaac she couldn't visualise, not beyond a hazy outline dominated by two dark eyes.

Today though, her head was filled with them, all three. She tried to imagine what it would be like to be yanked back to her own time, leap into her red convertible, turn the key and continue on her way as if this whole year hadn't happened. She had to sit down; that would mean losing him, the man presently leading Samson across the yard. She inhaled and placed a hand on her stomach, caressing the bulge that was her baby – their baby. This was her time now, this was where she was meant to be – with him.

Matthew was splicing hazels into fencing rails and she sat on an upturned bucket, her hands held tight around her knees. All day she'd tagged after him and it was beginning to grate on his nerves. Out of the corner of his eye he studied her, noting how apprehensively she was watching the sky and let his gaze follow hers. Nothing; a cloudy summer afternoon with the promise of a thunderstorm later in the evening.

"Shouldn't you be helping?" he asked with an edge of disapproval, indicating the yard where clotheslines had been stretched from tree to tree. Mrs Gordon and Rosie had been at it all day, and he'd wondered why she wasn't there, instead of nattering on to him about this and that as she'd followed him to the fields and back.

She didn't reply, her eyes darting to the sky, and she looked so frightened that it made him smile. A short summer shower and some claps of thunder, surely she wasn't afraid of that? He stopped halfway through his next axe chop and turned to face her. Then he looked up at the sky and back down at her again.

"It's today."

She nodded and knotted her fingers into her skirts.

"But you can't think … No," he shook his head. "It won't happen again."

"How do you know?"

Matthew dropped to the ground in front of her and placed his hands on her thighs.

"It won't; you belong here, with me. That's why you've been like an extra little shadow today, no?"

She hitched her shoulders. "I thought…" she began, "I thought that if you were close, then maybe you'd be able to grab me and hold me should anything happen."

He studied her for a long time and then stood up and took her hand, setting off for the hilltop. It had begun to rain, a soft pattering rippling through the tree crowns. Alex hung back, but Matthew dragged her along until they stood uncovered below the growling sky. He undid his belt, looped it round their wrists, and raised his face towards the sky. If you try to take her I will stop you, he assured whatever power might inhabit the clouds, I will stop you or die.

On the way back down he kissed her. Kissed her as if it were the first time, tasting her, exploring her, their bound hands caught between them. He tore himself away and listened to his breathing, long, heaving gulps of air. He kissed her again, he buried his nose in her hair and inhaled her scent, and he wanted her to smell of him, no, reek of him, as she'd done that first time, the time he'd had her by the mountain spring. And he wanted to cradle her as if she were a fragile child, but he wanted to pound her and ride her until she merged herself with him, permanently fused together. In her eyes he saw that she wanted it too, here, now, despite the rain that fell from above, despite the fact that the evening was still light and anyone could come upon them.

"Later, aye?" He undid his belt, stroked her cheek, and walked away under the trees.

They didn't speak. He just stood and extinguished the candles, inclining his head in the direction of the stairs. He held the door for her, helped her with her lacings, and sat on the bed to watch as she shed her clothes, his eyes following her rounded shape. She was beginning to show, a bulge just above her pubic bone, and the thought of his bairn, in her, increased his desire.

He sat back as she undressed him, helping her when she needed it but otherwise remaining still. Her touch, the soft pressure of her breasts against his chest, the tickling sensation her hair left behind as she kneeled between his thighs – all because of a rip in the veil of time, a slight shift of fate that let her drop from her world into his.

She lay back at his unspoken urging, she arched herself against his mouth, his fingers, a gust of air escaping her when he entered her. They rocked together, slowly at first, but soon her legs came up to wrap themselves around his hips, her hands pulled at his waist, his back. Matthew pressed himself deeper, harder, faster, and below him Alex was an enveloping warmth, a sinuous strength that urged him to push, to ride her, please Matthew, please.

Just as she came he kissed her, swallowing down her guttural exclamations, and then it was her mouth glued to his when he exploded inside of her. His body lay heavy on hers, and between them, protected by them both, was their child.

"Good, no?" He smiled down at her and twisted a riotous curl around his finger before rolling over on his back. She lay with her hair a tousled mass, her chest still heaving and a slight sheen of sweat on belly and legs.

"It always is." She stretched like a cat, kissed him on his neck. "I love you."

"And I you, my Alex." My woman, my heart.

After dinner next day, Alex came to find Matthew, carrying a stone bottle of beer. He saw her coming and raised his hand in a wave before going back to his splicing, not stopping until she kissed his nape. She extended the bottle to him and he drank, sitting back against the smooth stem of a rowan. She sat down beside him and leaned her head against his shoulder with a small, contented sigh. She slipped her hand into his and they sat like that for some time.

"I'm going for a walk," she said. "Want to come?"

Matthew shook his head. "I must get this done today, aye?"

"Oh." After a few minutes she shrugged and got to her feet. "See you at supper."

He didn't reply, but raised his axe in a little wave.

Alex took her time. It was a beautiful day, a breather in a stretch of weeks of hard work. This farming thing was quite the workout, she reflected, and July had been an endless succession of long, gruelling days, with August so far not being that much better. She frowned; at least the present busy schedule was keeping Matthew at home, not in Cumnock to argue the merits of the Commonwealth versus the king.

It worried her, this open stand against the king and for the Republic. Not only in words, but also in clothing Matthew was stating his opinions, favouring browns and greys with tidy but simple collars and narrow breeches. As the whole country shifted itself towards receiving its potential king back with open arms and garish clothing, Matthew Graham went the other way, distancing himself from gaudiness and frills. Not that Alex minded, still finding the spectacle of men sporting huge sashes round their waists and massive amounts of lace at neck and wrists somewhat effeminate. But now, with Parliament in shambles, he should be more circumspect in expressing his viewpoints – maybe cultivate the low profile she'd expected him to keep given his experiences in jail. Instead, he seemed to find an almost perverse pleasure in voicing his thoughts out loud .

"It's already too late," Alex had said some days ago. "The Commonwealth is dead, and in the wings stands Charles Stuart waiting to be king."

"All the more reason for someone to speak up, no? So that all won't be forgotten and so that this new king keeps in mind that he rules not alone, but with Parliament."

Alex hadn't replied; she had very vague ideas as to what would happen, but suspected that Parliament's say in things would be severely diminished.

All of this was on her mind as she made her way down the steep slope that led from the hilltop to the mill. She stopped in a small clearing to catch her breath, spent a few agreeable minutes sitting on a stone, her face raised to the sun.

She was in a mellow mood when she got to her feet, a state of mind that changed drastically when she turned to find herself eye-to-eye with her brother-in-law. Alex flew backwards, her hands spread across her front. Her breath rasped its way up and down her throat as she studied him, remembering far too vividly the night not quite a year ago when he killed her other child.

"And so we meet again." Luke cut a dashing figure in deep blue and a sash the colour of his fiery hair, complemented by high heeled boots. His eyes stuck on her belly and for an instant Alex thought she could see shame in his eyes. For an instant, mind you, and then his face hardened. He took a couple of steps in her direction and she emitted a yelping sound. A swift movement and he had her by the arm, pulling her towards him when all she wanted was to run, screaming for help. She swallowed, trying to lubricate her throat. Stiff fingers in his eyes, knee him in the balls, fall to your right and use his body weight to flip him over. She tensed in preparation, but he felt that, twisting her arm up behind her back.

"Let go of me!" It came out as a shriek, loud and high. "Get out of here before Matthew finds you." Much better; more controlled, less scared witless.

He released her and stood back. His eyes glinted a pale, celadon green, lingering on her stomach.

"That child threatens my son's inheritance."

"You don't have a son. Matthew has a son that you've stolen off him, but you don't have one. Incapable of siring your own, hey? " She regretted the words the moment they were out of her mouth and backed away. She tripped, fell to land on her bottom, but was up on her knees and crawling as fast as she could, when his hand came down on her shoulder and wrenched her round to face him.

"Slut! You'll pay for that." That was when Matthew barged into him from behind.

"Take your hands off my wife!" This time he was going to destroy this serpent of a man, slice him down in pieces. Luke made choking noises, his fingers tearing at the strangling hold around his neck. Matthew pulled his dagger and Luke's eyes bulged when the blade sliced through his breeches, baring his privates to the August air. Oh, aye; he didn't much like it, did he, when it was him being attacked. Misbegotten cur; today he would pay. Luke screeched, kicked and flailed – all to no avail.

Matthew knocked him to the ground, sat on him and grabbed Luke's scrotum in a brutal grip, pressing the testicles until the skin looked about to burst. Luke convulsed under him, he was begging, crying, his nails digging into Matthew's back, but Matthew was in no mood to listen.

"Matthew!" Alex' voice barely penetrated the rage that thudded through Matthew's brain. He drew the blade of the knife over the bared skin. "No, Matthew, you can't!" A thin line of blood welled forth and Luke shrieked, a wordless plea for help.

"Aye I can," Matthew said, and Alex threw herself forward.

"No! Please don't!"

Matthew shook her off and directed himself to his brother.

"I warned you, I let you off last time we met, no? But this time…"He heaved his incoherent, babbling brother to stand. "It seems my wife wishes you to keep your balls, however useless they may be. I will, however, have my blood." And with that he sliced off Luke's nose and pushed him away.

"Oh, God!" Alex gasped.

Luke keened, squirming like a hooked worm.

"Stand up," Matthew said roughly. "Stand up or I'll do you some more harm."

Luke staggered upright, one hand to his bleeding face, the other attempting to hold his breeches together.

"Get off my land, and if I ever catch you on it again I'll kill you." Matthew shoved Luke in the direction of the woods. "Go."

"My nose," Luke moaned through tears and blood.

"Go!" Matthew screamed at him, and Luke stumbled away.

"He'll never forgive you," Alex stammered, staring at Matthew's bloodied hands.

"I can live with that, aye? I haven't forgiven him either."

"He'll kill you."

"He'll try." The blinding fury was receding, and his hand holding the knife began to tremble. He tightened his hold on the handle and bent down to wipe the blade clean. "I can't kill him, he's my brother."

Alex began to laugh, a horrid sound that made him want to clap his hands over his ears. She sank down to the ground and the laughter became tears.

"Don't expect him to show you any mercy," Alex said. "He'll move heaven and earth to destroy you for what you just did to him."

"I know that." Without another word he walked off.

It took time for Matthew to regain some semblance of control. He spliced and spliced, he worked until his arm shook, and only when the light was gone did he stop for the day. He'd heard Alex come down the hill behind him, had sensed her standing to the side to watch him drive his axe with frenzy into the hazel poles, but he'd pretended he hadn't, not quite sure what to say to her.

She was right; this Luke would never forgive, and while one part of him was elated at having finally made his brother pay, another part shivered with shame at what he'd done. Not that Luke didn't deserve it, bastard that he was, but in one single slicing motion Matthew had forever severed whatever blood-ties remained between them. He sighed, hefted his axe over his shoulder and went in search of his wife.

He found her in the stables, sitting in the straw with her lap full of mewling kittens. When she raised her face to his he saw that she'd been crying.

"Ah, lass," he said. "There's no need to cry, aye? He won't harm us, I won't let him."

That only made her weep all the more, long hiccupping sobs as he shushed and repeated that he'd keep them safe – somehow. She shook her head.

"It's not that." She wiped at her nose with her sleeve. "Well, it's that too, but not only."

"Then why?" He lifted her to sit on his knees.

She rubbed her face against the bristle of his cheeks and sighed.

"I was thinking of Isaac. I never wanted him, I resented this stranger that had been foisted upon me by a man that I hated and feared." She took hold of Matthew's hand and placed it on her belly. "Today our child moved inside of me and I could feel it, and I was so happy to know it was there, alive and safe." She exhaled softly. "I never noticed when Isaac became a real person inside of me. I didn't love him, not at all, not then. Do you think he knew?"

Matthew kissed her ear. He didn't know what to say.

CHAPTER 34

"You look like a pear." Simon grinned down at Alex from his horse. "A giant pear."

"You have a death wish, Mr Melville," Alex said, miming a slashed throat.

"I was referring to the colour of your gown, not the shape of your body." He dismounted and hastened over to help Joan, before turning to greet Matthew. "Minister Crombie was asking for you, he wondered when you'd be in Cumnock next. I told him it would be a few weeks yet."

Matthew nodded. He stretched and surveyed his lands; wherever he turned he saw work calling to him. There was threshing to do, roofs to be mended, fields to be tilled, and … He sighed, kneading at his left buttock. No rest, not for many weeks yet.

Alex had been working as hard as he had lately, returning inside with grubby hands and reddened cheeks after yet another day in the kitchen garden. He snuck a look at his wife, most definitely pear like in her soft green. Now in her sixth month of pregnancy she was blooming, with a constant appetite not only for food but for him. He intensified his gaze, was gratified to see her ears turn pink.

"Captain Leslie has been recalled to ride with General Monck," Simon said over kale and pork. "Word is that the general is thinking of riding south, and Minister Crombie advices you to be careful. Royalist sentiments are running high, and then there's this whole matter with Luke, no?"

Matthew shifted on his chair, shared a quick look with Alex. Dear brother Luke worried him, much more than he cared to admit. He should have killed him, he thought darkly, not sliced off a wee piece of his nose.

"He's telling anyone who'll listen just how he will make you pay," Simon went on, "and I fear it's not an empty threat, aye?"

Matthew frowned, tilted his head in the direction of Alex.

Simon flushed. He cleared his throat and turned the discussion to politics, sharing what little news he had of what was happening in Edinburgh and London.

"I heard General Monck has been approached by messengers from Charles Stuart." Matthew said. Despite having once been imprisoned for his support of the royalist cause, General Monck had proven a capable governor of Scotland, a firm adherent to the principles of the Commonwealth. If he was listening to the blandishments of the would be king, then it was just a matter of time. Well, he knew it was, but he still hoped Alex was wrong.

"Sent them packing was what I heard," Simon sat back and regarded Matthew. "No one wants war. And unless a strong leader for the Commonwealth materialises soon …"

"It could be the general, no?"

"I don't think so; if he hankered for such power he would already have taken it. No; I fear we'll shortly see the Commonwealth revert to a Kingdom."

"Aye," Matthew sighed. "Will Charles have learnt his lesson, do you think? To not meddle with men's faith nor force a common church upon us all?"

Simon shrugged, looked away.

A little frisson of disquiet fluttered up Matthew's spine; this future king was no friend of Presbytery – and in particular not after those long months he'd spent as a virtual prisoner of the Covenanters, king of Scotland in name only- which did not bode well for men such as him.

"I think he'll have learnt the lesson of subterfuge," Simon said. "Steel inside a velvet glove and woe to those on whom Charles Stuart decides to wreak his vengeance. All those that voted in favour of executing the king that was must be passing right restless nights."

Matthew shifted the conversation to other matters.

"I met Margaret the other day," Joan said, setting her sewing aside. They were alone in the parlour, Simon and

Matthew having decided the afternoon was better spent reviewing Matthew's accounts and in general setting his affairs in order. Every now and then the sound of laughter would emanate from the little study, making Alex suspect that more attention was spent on the whisky than on the matters at hand.

"Oh." Alex wasn't that interested. Margaret had made a huge scene about Luke's nose – understandably – been curtly reminded by Matthew that she'd violated the conditions of her lease by allowing Luke to stay, and the next day she'd been gone. Hopefully forever.

"And Luke." Joan shook her head. "It was horrible."

"I know, he has the same effect on me," Alex muttered.

"His nose, Alex; it's gone!"

"I told you, didn't I?"

"How could Matthew do such? To so disfigure someone, mark him like a common criminal."

Alex frowned. "There's disfigurement and disfigurement; I hope you don't consider Luke an innocent victim."

"No, of course not, but still..." Joan sighed. "He was such a bonny wee lad."

Alex chose not to comment. She stuck her knitting needles through the ball of yarn and left the room.

"It's just ... she was very judgemental, you know?" Alex said next morning. Matthew grunted; if Joan had anything to say about Luke, she should come to him, not to Alex. As it was, the little altercation had poisoned the rest of the evening, with Alex retiring to bed much sooner than she would normally do. He sniffed at his stockings and wrinkled his nose; too much wear, he needed a clean pair. He threw the lid of the mule chest open, all but disappearing into it.

"What are you looking for?" Alex asked.

"My ..." He fell silent, hands closing on a burlap wrapped object.

"Your what?"

He didn't reply, instead he straightened up and turned

to face her, holding the swaddled square in his hands.

"I thought you burnt it."

"So did I. Well, no, I didn't think I burnt it, but I totally forgot." She blushed a bit under his gaze. "Maybe I didn't forget to begin with," she admitted at his continued silence. "But then I did. What with everything else happening in my life, I haven't even thought about it."

"Hmm." Matthew was not convinced.

"Well, okay; maybe I did think about it, but ..."

"Mmhm." He closed the lid of the chest and placed the package on it, not wanting to hold this vibrating object for longer than necessary. "But you'll burn it now."

Alex shrugged a yes. "But ... well, before I do, I'd like to look at it once more, and I don't want to do it alone."

"Why?" Matthew had no wish to see the painting again in his life, all of him crawling as he remembered that beckoning square of blue.

"I don't know; I just feel I should."

"I think you should burn it unseen," he told her, but resigned himself to doing as she wanted. "Not here," he barked when she made as if to unwrap it. "Outside, aye?"

They were well away from the house before Matthew told her to stop. She kneeled down and unfolded the burlap, and with every fold Matthew's sense of fear grew. The painting murmured, a seductive whisper that grew to a clamour inside his head, an imperative that he lean forward and look, drown himself in the exquisitely executed heaving sea.

Alex muttered something that sounded like a curse and reared back, banging her head hard against his collarbone. Matthew grabbed at her with urgency, closing his eyes against the suggestive pull exerted by the painting. He breathed through his nose, fighting back waves of nausea, and all along his spine sweat drops formed. His hands shook as he held her hard around her waist.

"We burn it." This was magic – evil, ungodly magic. He groped, found a stone and drove it through the painting.

Once, twice, and all that remained was a mangled mess. He bundled it into the burlap and stood. "Now."

The picture pleaded with him to put it together and look at it, please look at it. He prayed; over and over he muttered the same short prayer, anything to drown this silent pleading. Alex took his hand and they stumbled their way back to the yard. When he made as if to enter she shook her head.

"No," she said, "not inside. It has to be burnt here, in God's free air." She took the bundle from him and he rushed inside to find a taper, just as quickly stormed back out.

She'd moved over to sit on the outdoor bench and in her lap the massacred painting lay uncovered, her fingers caressing its sides. She swayed, made a clumsy attempt to fit the pieces together.

"Nay!"

She started at his voice, raised unfocused eyes in his direction.

"Alex, no, leave it be, aye?" He'd reached her by now, knelt to take it from her. He had to tug it free. The taper died in a gust of wind.

This time Matthew took no chances, taking the bundle with him as he returned to the kitchen for a new taper. Once outside, he made for the secluded area behind the privy, with Alex trailing him.

All of him twitched with the urge to take one last look, one final peek. A deep breath, one more prayer and he set the bundle on fire. Smoke uncurled from the burlap and rose dark against the sky. He sniffed when the paint began to burn, tingeing the air with scents of oil and spices; saffron and cardamom, nutmeg and ginger and the pungent smell of rosemary in the sun. Suddenly it shrieked; Alex yelped at the loud, eerie keening that filled the air. And then it was gone, small wisps of ash floating into the air when he stamped the fire into extinction.

"What was that?" Simon asked, making both of them jump when he popped his head out of the privy.

"Hmm? Oh, the sound, you mean." Matthew hitched his shoulders. "I don't rightly know; a bird mayhap?"

"A bird? It sounded like a flayed cat."

"Well, maybe then it was, no?" Matthew took Alex by the hand and led her inside.

CHAPTER 35

"You burnt it!"

Alex jumped, whirling to stare at Hector Olivares.

"Burnt what?"

"The painting. You stupid bitch, what have you done? Look at me!" He threw off his hat and Alex inhaled noisily.

She'd only seen him briefly, that afternoon back in early July, but since then things had gone downhill for the man in front of her. The last months had torn pounds off an already whippet thin frame, and his skin had converted itself into something resembling an elephant hide, collecting in wrinkled pouches under his eyes and his chin. There were lesions on what she could see of his arms, his hands, his neck, open wounds that leaked blood and pus. And he stank; a cloying stench of rotting garbage.

"What happened to you?" Alex said, surprised into feeling pity rather than fear.

"Age; it catches up with you at some point, no?"He took a step towards her, crowded her back against the stone wall that bordered the higher pastures. She tried to sidestep him, but he grabbed her by the arms and slammed her into the uneven wall.

"Let go."

"Or what? You think you can fight me just because you have a black belt or two? Think again." As if to underline his words he slammed her into the wall again, this time with enough force for her to gasp.

"Have you any idea? Can you imagine what it's like to be imprisoned in a body that's falling to pieces and be denied the release of death?"

Alex shook her head, licked at her lips. He held up a desiccated hand.

"See? A walking skeleton, and still I live on. And it's all her fault, it's all that accursed Mercedes' fault and now you

— you! — have destroyed my last chance to make my way home to my time, my *Sevilla!*"His hands closed round Alex' neck, shaking her like a ratter shakes a mouse.

"Aagh," Alex croaked, trying to prise the fingers off her.

"I hate her! She stole my life from me, witch that she is! *Te odio, Mercedes, te odio!*"

Hector's fingers sank deeper into Alex' skin and all she could hear was the whoosh of her blood, the throbbing of her imprisoned pulse behind her temples. He's going to kill me, oh my God, he's going to strangle me to death! Her arm flapped, she struggled, saw huge circles of black rise before her. Knee him ... yes ... try ... No air, no strength. She clawed at his cheek, tried to draw in air. His face was very close. She was going to die. Her baby! Matthew ... Her vision shrank to a narrow funnel. And then the pressure was gone and Alex crumpled to the ground, sucking air through her mouth, her nose.

She raised her face. Hector was on his feet, backing away from Matthew. His hand went to his sword, and where before Matthew had been advancing, rake in hand, now he was retreating, parrying a flurry of blows. Alex planted one foot on the ground, another, and heaved herself up to stand.

Before her Hector and Matthew were engaged in a silent, deadly battle, and however much of a novice Alex was when it came to sword fighting, she could see Hector was a master at it. Graceful and fast, he thrust and retreated, lunged and danced away, and with every blow the wooden handle of the rake lost in solidity, shredding into an ineffectual defence.

She should do something. Alex took a tentative step in their direction, raised her skirts in preparation. Do what? She was woozy and dazed, her limbs uncoordinated. Kick him; yes, kick this Hector character before he hurt her Matthew. Too late. One well directed thrust and the rake flew from Matthew's hand. Hector slowed his movements, his lips curling into a sneer.

"You'll die," he said to Matthew.

"Aye; but not today." Matthew panted with exertion, his eyes never leaving the by now bloodied sword held so confidently by Hector.

"Oh, I think today." Hector moved swiftly.

Alex gasped, expecting to see Matthew skewered on that flashing sword. But Matthew rose on his toes and instead of retreating he jumped towards Hector. He hissed when the sword sliced down his flank, but managed to clamp his hand down on Hector's wrist. It was like watching someone grab a tiger by the tail. A dangerous, desperate tiger that kicked and punched and bit, twisting like a snake.

A wrench and Hector had his hand free. It all seemed to be happening in slow motion; the sword rose high up in the air, Hector's fingers tightened around the hilt, and then down it came, whistling through the air. Matthew threw himself to the side, but she heard him exclaim and knew the sword had at minimum nicked him.

Up came the sword again, Matthew kicked Hector in the knee. Not enough to throw Hector to the ground, but enough for him to lose his balance. A low tackle and Matthew brought Hector down, using his weight to pin the man to the ground.

Hector screamed him in the ear. Matthew reared back and crashed his fist into the smaller man's face. Hector jerked and went still. Matthew got to his feet, kicked the sword well out of reach, and turned to Alex.

"Are you alright?"

Was she alright? How about him? He was bleeding from gashes all over his arms, his hands, the side of his shirt was wet with blood. She nodded, succeeded in crossing the few yards that separated them.

"…" she said, hands flying over him.

"Don't try to talk." Matthew ran a finger over the collar of sore and burning skin that circled her neck. She flinched, swallowed. Had he not arrived when he did, she'd have been dead by now. She rested her face against his chest for an instant. Warm. Alive.

"…" she tried, pulling her brows into a frown. She turned to where Hector was groaning back into life. "He said I burnt it," she finally enunciated. Jesus that hurt!

"Burnt what?" His hands spanned her belly, as if reassuring himself the baby was still safe.

"Painting."

"We did, no?"

Alex gave him an irritated look. "H …?" she croaked. She swallowed, tried again. "How does he know?"

"I heard it shriek," Hector said, and both of them jumped – Alex away from him, Matthew to more or less land on him.

"Skulking on my land, were you?"

Hector waved a hand at him, as you'd do with an enervating fly.

"No. I was on the moor." Hector attempted to sit, was arrested by Matthew's grip on his neck.

"Don't move," Matthew said. "Don't provoke me into killing you."

Hector laughed. "You can't kill me."

"Would you have me try?" Matthew sounded as if he really wanted to. She wasn't about to stop him.

"Do your best," Hector said, offering him his neck.

Matthew looked taken aback.

Hector's brows rose contemptuously. "Such hesitation could cost you your life." He whipped out the small dagger he'd carried secreted in his boot. Like a viper Matthew's hand closed around Hector's, and the knife landed in the grass.

"Enough of this," Matthew said, heaving Hector up to stand. "I'll have you accused of attempted murder."

"Really? And what do you think will happen when I tell them you're married to a woman born three hundred odd years in the future?" Hector leaned towards Matthew, eyes like ice. "She'll burn, Matthew Graham, burn like her grandfather did, like her aunt did, like her mother should have done all those years ago in Seville!" He cackled, the sound cut short when Matthew's hand closed around his scrawny neck.

"Burn? Why did they burn?" Her voice surprised her, a whispered hoarseness that scarcely carried over the few metres between them. Matthew released his hold on Hector, allowing him to retch and cough air back into his system.

Hector wiped at his wet eyes and sat up.

"Why? They were enemies of the Holy Church." He lifted his lip in a little sneer. "I bet you didn't know that, huh? Just as you didn't know that your fucking mother was a witch."Alex tried to make sense of what he was saying. Her family, burning to death? But no, stuff like that didn't happen … she brought herself up short. Didn't happen? It happened all the time in the here and now.

"I didn't mean to," Hector said, sliding down to sit on the grass. "Such a bloody mess, all of it."

"Mean to what?" Alex tried to catch his eyes, but he looked away.

"Never mind. And anyway, what was I to do? I would have hanged! And they were heretics, false converts. They deserved to burn, both of them! Yes, they did, they did. I was only doing my job."

"Your job?" Alex was very confused; what was he, some sort of inquisitor? He groaned, clutched at himself.

"Dolores, *perdóname*, Dolores."

"Forgive you for what?" Alex said.

Hector didn't seem to have heard, muttering something in Spanish, a rather incoherent rambling where the only thing she could make out was her aunt's name along with a whispered avowal that he, Hector, had loved her – once, before it all went ugly.

"What did you do to her?" Alex demanded.

"None of your business," he spat, reverting to form. He scowled at her, eyes so cold she flinched. "All this is

Mercedes' fault. Damned witch! First she yanks me out of my time, and then she curses me with eternal life unless I make it back. *Bruja!*"

"My mother?" Alex shook her head in mute denial.

"Well she did, okay? And all because I was a good servant of my queen, *Reina Isabel*, and my church."

What? No, she must have misheard. "Isabel? Like in Isabel and Fernando?"

Hector nodded, mouth twisting into a crooked smile.

"But that was ages ago!" Right; her brain just didn't want to handle this. Too much information, far too much information – impossible information. Her mother was from medieval Seville? Her family were heretics? No, shove this away, stuff it into a drawer marked FORGET.

"And the painting is important why?" Matthew asked.

"A portal, one of Mercedes' time tunnels," Hector said.

Alex shuddered. Thank God they'd burnt it!

"And do they all lead to long gone Seville?" Matthew sounded impressively matter-of-fact.

"No, unfortunately they don't. You fall towards what you see in them." Hector glared at Alex. "I saw my Diego, didn't I? And why was he here, hey? He was here because of you!"

"Me?" Alex said.

"I sent him to find you." He narrowed his eyes. "Did he? Find you, I mean."

Alex nodded. "He's dead."

"I know." Hector threw her a black look. "Your fault."

"My fault?" She was getting tired of being blamed for all this mess. "How can it be my fault that you send someone to harass me? And what about Ángel? What about what he did to me? Is that my fault too?" She leaned towards him. "Well, is it?" She was awash with anger, wanted nothing so much as to rip into him.

"Ángel acted outside his instructions," Hector said, scooting away from her.

"Really?" Alex came after. "Now why don't I believe

that?" Matthew grabbed her by the waist, and she was glad he did, needed his restraining hands to stop her from doing something unacceptable – like kick this bastard in the mouth and watch him spit teeth all over the place.

"Well he did, okay?" Hector said.

"You're lying, I can see it in your eyes."

Hector inclined his head in a mocking little bow.

"So many pictures, no? So many explicit photographs of you, and each and every one of them I sent to your damned witch of a mother." Hector laughed. "I don't think she liked them much, do you?"

"Bastard!" she spat, which only made him hitch his shoulders.

"I should just have grabbed her, once I knew where to find her. Not played out that complicated treasure hunt, however fun it was." Hector frowned up at Alex. "How?"

"How what?"

"Mercedes disappeared down there. How did she do that? Did she have a painting with her?"

Alex shook her head and backed away.

"You don't have to tell him," Matthew said, eyeing the white-haired wreck before them with obvious dislike. "Not after what he did to you."

"Oh, yes you do!" Hector said, springing to his feet. "I deserve to know, you hear?"

"You deserve nothing!" Matthew said.

"If you don't tell me, I'll tell everyone she's a witch!" Hector ducked under Matthew's arm, slammed an elbow into Matthew's bleeding side, and there he was, only inches from Alex' face. "A witch, you hear? A fucking witch! Do you know what they do to witches in the here and now?" He laughed, laughter becoming a croak when Matthew flung him into the stone wall.

"You'll die before you do that," Matthew said.

"What is it you don't understand, you moron? You can't kill me! I can't fucking die!"

"She burnt," Alex broke in, "she set herself alight, and

suddenly she was gone." She folded her arms over her chest.

"What?" Hector said.

Alex tightened her hold on herself, swallowed repeatedly. "She just … I don't know. First she was on fire and then 'poof' she disappeared."

"She went 'poof'?" Hector threw his head back and laughed, a creaky, harsh sound that made the hairs along Alex' arms rise in alarm.

"And Ángel?" he asked once he'd calmed down.

"She held him in her arms." It came out a weak whisper.

"Oh." Hector shrugged, indicating he didn't really care. "It must hurt, no?"

"I suppose it does," Alex agreed, warding off the memory of Ángel's contorted face, his mouth open in a soundless shriek.

"But maybe it works," Hector said.

Alex had no idea; she didn't want to talk about this.

"Self-immolation," Hector murmured, nodding to himself. "Burn, like Dolores did; how apt. Will you stay and watch?"

"What?" Alex had problems remaining upright. "You're going to set yourself on fire? But you'll die!"

"Which is exactly what I want."

"Matthew! Stop him, lock him up somewhere!"

"Please," Hector entreated, "please help me die." His eyes flew to Alex, to Matthew, bright gemstones of desperation.

Matthew nodded, once.

"We can't be doing this!" Alex had problems breathing, walking, talking. On the edge of the moor Hector was piling brush and branches into a man high heap. "I can't just let him do this! It's suicide." And she didn't want to see a person burning to death again – once had been quite enough, thank you very much.

Matthew continued with what he was doing, offloaded yet another armful onto the pile.

"It's a sin, to kill yourself is a sin!" she said.

"To curse someone so that they can't die is also a sin," Matthew said, with an edge of condemnation in his tone.

"Oh God." Alex' knees gave way, and she sat down.

Matthew kneeled before her, smoothed back her hair.

"The man can't go on living forever. Look at him, he's rotting away while alive, no?"

Alex peeked at where Hector was applying the final touches to his bonfire.

"But what if he doesn't die? What if he's right about not being able to die, no matter how, and he sets himself alight and burns and burns and..."

"He's willing to try."

"Why not shoot himself? Or slice his wrists? Hang himself?"

"I believe he's tried all that."

"You think?" Alex wanted to throw up. What had her mother done, how could she have condemned someone to this wandering existence? "Maybe she wasn't all good," she whispered in his ear, "because how can you curse someone like that, no matter how big a bastard he is?"

"You don't know why she did it," he said, "and I scarcely think he'll tell you the truth, do you?"

They stood holding hands and watched Hector step into his burning pyre. At the last moment his nerve seemed to fail him, eyes acquiring a sheen of fear, but after several deep breaths he straightened up, squared his shoulders and walked into the fire. Alex crawled into Matthew's arms, refusing to watch as the flames licked higher and higher.

Not a sound did Hector utter, and Matthew stared slack mouthed as the burning shape dissolved before his eyes, leaving nothing but a tang of singed hair in its wake. There was no trace of anything human in the smouldering embers. Not a single bone, nor a melted button, not even that deposit of greasy, half burnt flesh that would generally be found round a stake.

"He went up in smoke," Matthew said, somewhere between awed and downright terrified.

"He's gone?" Alex still had her eyes squished together.

"Aye, lass; he's gone."

"We never talk about this," he said to Alex later.

"Never," she agreed. And they never did.

CHAPTER 36

Despite being as unwieldy as a whale, Alex struggled up the hill on New Year's Eve to toast Magnus, and then made her way back down to the barn where the party was in full swing. She'd danced earlier in the evening, but the wild reels and turns made the baby sink down to press on her pelvic bone, so now she sat to the side and watched, smiling at the people that stopped for a word with the impressively pregnant wife of the master.

The master himself was quite drunk, and made his way unsteadily to sit down by Alex' feet. All evening he had been eyeing the way her breasts seemed on the verge of spilling over the confinement of her modest bodice, noting with possessive satisfaction that quite a few other men were giving his radiant wife appreciative looks.

It suited her, being greatbellied, as it had never suited Margaret. A slight shiver of guilt flew up his spine when he wondered where Margaret and Ian might be, but he pushed the thought away; they were not his responsibility, not anymore. He leaned his head against Alex' leg and her hand drifted down to smooth his long hair back into place.

"Was he there, then?"

Alex made an exasperated sound.

"Of course he wasn't. But I … I guess I just want him to know that I think of him, that I hope he's alright – him and John and Isaac. Kind of silly, given that I'm hoping that long before they've even been born." She sighed and looked over to where Simon was strutting with the best, a rosy, laughing Joan slung this way and that. "Sometimes I wonder if they'd recognise me, I guess I must have changed a lot, no?"

He smiled; aye, that she had, he told her, and in particular in her present state.

"Not like that," she said. "Have I changed as a person?"

He tilted his head to look at her. "You're a good wife," he

teased, "obedient and submissive, you tend to your husband and his needs." He laughed at the scowl on her face. "I never have to punish you…"

"You try, mister, try that once and I'll have your balls in a vice."

He didn't doubt that, he assured her, cupping his privates in mock horror.

"Nay, Alex," he said seriously. "You haven't changed; not where it counts. You're still that magic lass that fell out of the sky and landed at my feet, and there's not a day when I don't thank the good Lord for that." He got up on his knees in front of her. "You were sent here because He knew I needed you. And mayhap He knew that you needed me, no?"

She cradled his head to her as well as she could given her bulk, and kissed his crown.

"Oh God, I do; I need you all the time."

"Insatiable," he mock sighed, making her laugh.

He placed a hand on her belly and smiled at the responding thumps.

"It will be close, aye?"

Alex grinned down at him. "I bet she foals first."

Matthew made a small noise at the back of his throat. His best mare and his wife, neck to neck…He sincerely hoped they didn't go into labour at the same time, for between mare and Alex he would be sorely torn, in the first case being needed, in the second being expected to stay close. Alex even wanted him in the room, but both he and Mrs Gordon had been so scandalised by this, that she had agreed to not raise the issue again as long as he promised that he'd be sitting just outside.

Matthew kissed his unborn child through the layers of cloth and skin that covered it and rose to his feet.

"Dance with me." He extended his hands to her.

"I can't dance," she said, getting up to stand beside him. "I can barely move."

"I'll be gentle with you." He led her out into the middle of the dance floor where she shuffled on the spot while he danced and whirled around her. Towards the end he just stood and held her, an island of stillness in the singing, stamping sea of people that surrounded them.

Three weeks later, both foal and the baby announced their intention to enter the world – at more or less the same time. Alex shooed a harried Matthew off in the direction of the stables and for the first few hours or so found all of this a rather agreeable experience. Even when the intensity increased, she was more fascinated than afraid, aware of every breath she took, every step she walked across the room. Not at all as she remembered it, but then she'd been drugged out of her mind when Isaac was born, terrified at the thought that she'd soon be face to face with the son of the man who'd … well.

Five hours later and it was not quite as much fun.

"How much longer?" she panted. She was glazed with sweat, her legs quivering with the strain of the last contractions.

"Not much," Mrs Gordon soothed, "not much at all." She helped Alex to sit up straighter on the birthing stool.

"Epidural," Alex muttered under her breath. "Or a planned caesarean." Mrs Gordon gave her an odd look and Alex smiled weakly. "Ramblings." And then she was swept by one, two, three… Jesus, how many were they? huge contractions and she had to go to the bathroom, now, now, now, and something hung between her legs and she pressed down with all her might and it was over.

Mrs Gordon handed her the baby; bloody, covered in white goo, face a mottled red and eyes squished shut, and Alex had never seen anything so lovely in her life.

When Matthew was at last let inside all he could see was her, sitting back against fresh pillows in a clean, embroidered shift, hair brushed out to frame her head. Her face was bent in silent adoration towards the wean nursing at her breast, and Matthew felt his knees weaken so abruptly at the joy that rushed through him that he would have fallen if Mrs Gordon hadn't grabbed him.

"A son, a bonny, healthy son. And big – everywhere. Must take after his sire, no?" She chuckled and nudged him towards the bed. "Go on, Rosie will bring you something to eat later."

"Do you want to look at him?" Alex sounded shy.

Matthew didn't trust himself to speak, so he just nodded. Alex disengaged the wean from her nipple and unfolded the blankets around him.

"She's right, no?" Matthew said, a finger hovering just over the dark genitalia. "He's big there."

"Just like his sire," Alex murmured. "I think it looks bigger just after birth – it's all to do with hormones or something."

"Hormones?"

Alex waved a hand at him. "I'll explain some other time. Right now my brain is a mush." She wrapped the wean up, smoothing the blanket tight around the little body.

"Here," she said. "Come and sit beside me and hold him."

Matthew sat mute with his son in his arms. Alex smiled and stretched out a finger to rub the wean softly over its head.

"He's perfect, isn't he?"

Matthew scrubbed at his eyes with his free hand and nodded. "Aye," he breathed.

"What will we call him?"

"Mark, Mark Magnus."

"Mark Magnus," she whispered to the lad, "welcome to the world, young master Graham."

"Next time I want you to be there," she said against his chest. Wee Mark was fast asleep in his cradle and the fire in the hearth was a glowing heap of embers, throwing the whole room in a weak, reddish light that glinted off her hair.

"Mmhm," he prevaricated.

"I need you there," she said, "and I guess there will be quite a few more, no?"

Oh, aye, Matthew smiled, drawing her even closer; five, mayhap even seven.

"Well, unless we give up on sex altogether, but that's not on the books, is it?" she said.

He assured her that it definitely wasn't, and then he just had to pad out of bed to look down at his newborn son again.

"He looks like a wee toad," he said, drawing a finger down the little spine. Alex came to stand beside him, her hands clutching his arm.

"A very hairy toad." A shock of dark hair stood like a halo round the little skull. "From his father," she said, "both the hair and the similarity to a toad. Oh, and the huge... you know."

She laughed as he kissed her, laughed when he swept her off her feet to carry her back to bed, groaning theatrically under his burden. But when he placed his head between her breasts and thanked her for his son, she didn't laugh – she wept.

"There." Alex smiled down at her baby, smoothed down his smock and handed him over to his proud father who more or less pranced out of the kitchen, son held to his chest.

"Crooked," Mrs Gordon muttered from behind her. "Mark my words, the laddie will grow up all crooked what with you leaving him unswaddled." She'd been saying that for the last month or so, and as always Alex just shrugged before sitting down to finish her interrupted meal.

"Is it alright now?" she asked instead, receiving a nonplussed look in response. "To... you know."

"Itching is it?" Mrs Gordon laughed out loud and then leaned forward to pat her hand. "Aye, it's five weeks, no?"

"Almost six," Alex corrected, making Mrs Gordon smile.

"Do you... err... is it, well, should I, or is it him..." Alex stumbled over the words.

"Don't you think he wants to?"

Alex knew he wanted to, but so far he hadn't tried to touch her like that, and she wasn't sure if he was waiting for her to make the first move.

Mrs Gordon gave her an amused look. "If you want to, then you have to let him know that, no?"

Alex was taken aback by this very modern approach and was even more surprised when Mrs Gordon confided that most women, in her considerable experience, were as hot for it as their husbands, and that there was nothing wrong with that.

That evening, Alex carried her replete son over to his cradle and tucked him in, patting the little bum. She sat down at her primitive dressing table and released her hair, taking a very long time to brush it. In the mirror she could see her husband. Naked, he was lying on his side, eyes golden in the candle light. She remained on the stool and let the shift drop off one shoulder, the soft worn linen sliding down her arm.

"Take it all off."

She did, and when his eyes met hers in the mirror there was a command in them that made her insides contract. She walked over to the bed and sat down. Slowly he traced her breasts, her belly. He laid his head between her legs, rubbing his unshaven cheeks hard against the inside of her thighs. He kissed her there, sending shockwaves of tickling electricity through her body, all the way from her curled toes to her heating cheeks.

"I've missed you," she said, which made him laugh.

"I've been here all the time, no?" His fingers were moving in teasing circles that made her breathing pick up, a ragged, demanding sound.

"But not like this." She dragged a nail up his penis, felt him shudder in response, and when her fingers closed around him he inhaled loudly.

"Nay, not like this. But now I'm back."

For a flashing instant it hurt, a straining of membranes that had grown unaccustomed to this. He noticed and held himself very still, waiting until she raised her hips towards him before he began to move. It had been too long, and as a consequence it was over far too quickly. Alex laughed and patted him on his bare bum.

"Is that all?"

"For now." He rose on his arms and smiled down at her. "But if you give me a minute or two, I'm sure I'll have recovered sufficiently to make you squeak."

"Squeak? I don't squeak!"

"Aye you do, but I don't mind. I find it rather sweet."

"Huh." Alex pretended to be affronted. He chuckled, bent his head to nuzzle her neck, the sensitive spot just below her ear.

"Do you want me to make you squeak?" he murmured against her skin.

"I don't squeak."

But much later she admitted she did – sometimes.

CHAPTER 37

It was May, and after months of hard work Matthew had decided he and Alex had earned themselves a few days of lassitude with Simon and Joan in Cumnock. Not that Alex was all that impressed, grumbling that Cumnock wasn't her idea of a holiday get away. But where her mood improved with every day spent in Cumnock, Matthew's deteriorated. Alex sighed, clearly annoyed by his moping. She'd told him, no?

"It's different to hear you tell it than to see it happening." He made a face. "They're all falling over their feet in their haste to welcome the returning majesty to his throne." He placed an arm around his wife and drew her close enough that he could peek at his son, fast asleep in the carrying shawl.

"That's not true," she said, "at most people are relieved, no more." He grunted, but admitted she was right. Cumnock was not a hotbed of royalist fervour, and now that Luke had ridden south taking most of his vociferous companions with him, the small market town had reverted to being what it had always been; somnolent and more concerned with Kirk and business than with the going on's in far away London.

"Do you think he'll be back?" Alex asked, apparently having caught a whiff of his thought.

"Hmm? Oh, Luke. Nay, I think it most unlikely. He has a life to build for himself at the royal court, no?" He stretched, relieved that his brother was gone out of his life – hopefully for good.

"A few days, no more," Simon said one evening after supper.

"Aye," Matthew agreed morosely. Any day now the king would land, returning to take up his crown at the express invitation of the Parliament.

"You must admit it has been skilfully handled," Simon said, pouring them both a tot of whisky.

"Aye," Matthew said. "It's the General. It was him, no doubt, that urged Charles to write the Declaration."

It stuck in his craw to have to recognise that a man he had considered devoted to the Commonwealth cause was the architect of its destruction, all the way from disbanding the Rump Parliament and calling a new election earlier in this the year of our Lord 1660, to this final little masterpiece, the Declaration of Breda, in which Charles Stuart promised to be lenient to all former Parliament supporters.

"Mayhap for the best. A peaceful restoration is to be preferred, is it not?" Simon said.

"You think? I personally think there should be no king, restored or otherwise," Matthew said.

"The alternative would have been war, and that would have been worse all round, no?"

"Aye," Matthew said, but with no real enthusiasm.

"It won't really change things, will it?" Alex said.

"Not up here. The king will have plenty to occupy him in the southern parts of his kingdom," Simon said, "and for all that his grandsire was Scots, I doubt Charles Stuart has any particular fondness for this our corner of the earth. Dour, damp and dirty, he found it, and far too full of Covenanters for his liking."

"Aye it will," Matthew disagreed. "It all changes. We're back to a world where one man's word counts for more than the rest's, a world where blood and birth carry more weight than ability and commitment." He smiled crookedly. "But other than that you're right; nothing will change." He got to his feet and left the room.

"Longing for home?" Alex teased next morning. Matthew grunted and went back to inspecting girths and harnesses. Only once he had repeatedly tested the pannier basket did he allow Alex to place Mark in it, muttering to

Gavin that he'd flay him if he didn't ensure the wean rode safely all the way back home. Gavin gave him a surly nod, looking rather disgruntled after having been torn from a much needed sleep.

They were at the crossroads with the Lanark road when Alex asked Matthew to stop.

"What's the matter?" Matthew held in Samson.

"I'm not sure, I just feel strange." She dropped off the horse and went to sit in the shade of the huge crossroads oak. "Maybe it's the heat."

It was hot, unseasonably so, and she tugged with irritation at her woollen bodice. She was feeling nauseous and her head was banded by pain, making red swirls dance before her eyes.

"I think I need to sit here a while," she said and undid her hat, flapping it to create a cooling breeze. Matthew studied her with some concern and then went over to talk to Gavin.

"I told him to ride on," he said once he returned to sit beside her.

"Mmm." All of her was itching, sweat was breaking out in the most unusual places, and she licked her lips, surprised to find them so dry. She sniffed; there was a strange stench to the air, an acrid top note that reminded her of seaweed rotting under a baking sun.

"You're looking very pale," Matthew said, helping her to sit back against the trunk.

"I feel pale – and thirsty."

He retrieved a stone flask of cider from one of the saddlebags, and they sat in silence, sharing it.

"Better?"

"A bit," she lied. Her eyelids weighed a ton. A nap, a short little nap, and then she'd feel much better. She barely registered when Matthew eased her down on the ground, his coat rolled into a makeshift pillow under her head.

When she woke a few minutes later she was alone. A swift scanning of her surroundings indicated Matthew had led Samson off to graze along the verge, and if she squinted she could make out the general shape of her husband, a few metres further in among the bushes. She needed to pee, and with an effort she levered herself onto her feet, standing like a swaying beanpole before she regained her balance.

God, it was hot! The previously clear sky was now a threatening purplish grey, the heavy clouds lit from within by distant lightning. The crossroads; something was happening to it, shimmering bands of bright greens and blues overlaying the scenery behind. She frowned, overcome by a disturbing sense of recognition.

The strands of blue and green danced around her feet, a crack opened in the road, pouring bright, white light. Alarm bells clanged in her head, huge red alerts screeched at her to run, flee, but her eyes were stuck in that funnel of light, and she took a staggering step towards it.

She peered into the bottomless drop and there were cars, and motorbikes and a bright red phone box, and in her ears noise pounded; honking horns, screeching brakes and snatches of music from various radio channels. Home. She blinked at the familiar faces that swam before her; John, Magnus in his garden, Isaac. One more step and she'd be there, with them, and a hot wave of longing rushed through her. Home… the word bubbled through her blood.

A whispering filled her head, a soft enticing murmur telling her it was time, time to leave all this behind and return to where she belonged. Yes, of course; go home, go home. Below her the road began to churn, and there was a tugging sensation round her feet, her calves, an insistent force pushing her towards that yawning chasm.

Her foot struck a rock, and the flare of pain tore through the whispered promises of home, a life in modern comfort. Home? No! That wasn't home, not anymore!

She shrieked; Matthew, she screamed, but there were no sounds, her tongue an uncooperative piece of swollen leather in a mouth so dry it felt like she'd been eating sand. Her heart thundered and she tried to retreat, but she was stuck in this quagmire of colours, the whole road was spinning around her, drawing her towards the pulsing light at the centre of the crossroads.

"No!" With a superhuman effort she tore herself free, landing on her front. She clawed her hands into the dirt of the road, desperately anchoring herself to the here and now. She was dragged backwards, her fingertips and nails torn to shreds over the grit and gravel of the roadbed, and her legs ... Jesus! They were being twisted off her.

"Matthew," she croaked. He must have heard her because here he came, flying towards her with his breeches still undone. His hands closed around her arms and he pulled. It hurt so much Alex couldn't cry out – she couldn't even breathe. Oh God; she was going to die, stretched until she snapped like an elastic band between this time and that.

Matthew threw himself backwards, Alex an unconscious deadweight in his arms. It was like trying to reel in a trout the size of a horse, with Alex the unfortunate hook caught in between. He inhaled; scorching pitch seemed to clog his lungs and he gagged on the stench of brimstone that permeated the air. He slipped, landed on his backside, and now they were both hurtling towards that bright, bright hole. A heel struck stone, the other found purchase against a clump of grass, and Matthew roared with effort.

Inch by pathetic inch, he dragged them away from the precipice. His shoulders were on fire, he could no longer feel his arms, his hands. He gritted his teeth, he prayed, calling for God to help him. No reply, and Matthew did battle all on his own, refusing to relinquish his wife to the hungry maw that was snapping at her feet.

Air whistled in and out of his nose, sweat dripped off his brows, his thighs were beginning to cramp, and still he held on. A weak scrabble and her feet were no longer dangling in the void. A heave and there was a yard between her toes and the drop.

"You'll not have her," he said through his clenched teeth, "never will I let her go."

As if in reply, a sudden wind sprang up. Rain filled the air and the previously so hot day cooled. The chasm slammed shut with a distinctive, grinding sound. It made him yelp. After a few half-hearted rumbles the cloud cover drifted away, leaving in its wake cool, fresh air.

He didn't dare to let go of her, not yet, not here, so close to where recently it had all been swirling colours and bright light. He pulled them both into the shade of the oak and once there he unclamped his hands from her arms. Alex lolled like a broken ragdoll, and there was an everlasting moment when he thought she was dead, but then she moaned.

"Alex?"

She turned her face towards the sound of his voice. She was one huge bruise and when she struggled to sit, her mouth filled with the taste of blood.

"Alex, are you alright?"

She wound her arms hard around his neck, glad to feel his arms around her, to hear his heartbeat under her ear. His hand stroked her over her head and she slumped against him.

"Is it gone?"

"Aye," he whispered into her hair. "Aye, Alex, it's gone."

She coughed a couple of times, licked at her dirt encrusted lips and sat up.

"Did you see anything?"

He nodded, eyes huge in his ashen face. "Cars, aye? Just as you've described them. And there was so much noise…" He hugged her hard, not noticing when she winced, and buried his face in her hair. "I thought I'd lose you."

"So did I," she said and began to cry.

"Can you stand?" he asked after a while. She tried, but her legs… She raised her skirts and gasped; bruises covered her calves, her thighs, and one of her knees had swollen as if sprained. Her fingers looked as if she'd stuck them into a shredder, and where Matthew had grabbed her there were two perfect imprints of his hands.

He groaned at the sight of her, ran light hands over her mangled limbs in a futile attempt to soothe and heal. She gave him a weak smile, assured him it wasn't too bad. Besides, he was looking rather worn as well, his lower legs and arms almost as bruised as hers. He looked down himself in surprise, studied her bedraggled clothes, her dirty face, and looked over to where Samson was still grazing.

"We fell off the horse," he said. "The girth gave and your skirts caught in the stirrup and dragged us along."

"It was just like her paintings," Alex said once they were back on Samson. "You know, like the one we destroyed."

"A portal, no? That's what Olivares called it."

"Mmm." Alex rested back against him. "An awful lot of portals, in her studio there were hundreds of those green and blue pictures. What on earth was Mercedes thinking of, to litter our home with potential doors through time?"

"Maybe not all of them worked."

"Or maybe she was just painting to remember. You know; how it was to fall through time." Shivers rippled up her leg, her back, and she clenched her fists hard, concentrating on the pain that flowed from her torn fingers. "Crossroads," she said, looking back at the perfect bisection of two roads. "Somehow it has to do with crossroads."

"Aye; exact crossroads – like this one and the one down at the spring where we first met."

She nodded. In the future she was going to stay well away from those.

"Good," he said, and his arm tightened round her waist.

Mrs Gordon listened in silence to Matthew's description of their accident, took a little turn to peer at the girth, raised both her brows, waited, waited some more and then with a little sigh gave up.

"Just so you know, I don't believe a word of it," she said while she set Alex' hands to soak in a basin of fragrant water.

"I didn't expect you to," Alex said with a weak smile.

"Hmph!" Mrs Gordon said, but the general state of Alex, her apparent exhaustion and her poor, poor hands made her refrain from further questioning. Instead she produced linen bandages and tweezers, and for the coming hour she extracted grains of grit from Alex' hands and underarms. It hurt like hell, and Alex kept on refilling her pewter cup with whisky.

"The legs are mostly bruises," Mrs Gordon said once she was done. "And the knee will mend in its own good time. But the hands you must be careful with, aye?"

Alex belched, giggled and waved her packaged hands in the direction of Matthew.

"The Return of the Mummy," she said and giggled again.

"She's drunk," Mrs Gordon sighed. "Get her to bed and make sure she stays there."

"It must have been terrible for the ones you left behind," Matthew said very much later. "To never know. If you'd been swallowed up by the road and me not there, how would I ever have known?" He shook his head. "If you were dead … well, then I'd have a place to go to when I needed you close, just as I do with Mam, but to have you vanish inexplicably …" He gave her an anguished look. "Do you think they know?" he said, lifting a comatose Mark out of her clumsy hold.

Alex sat back against the bed frame, waited until he returned to sit beside her.

"No, of course not; it isn't exactly the first option that springs to mind, is it?" She rested her head against his solid shoulder and inhaled his warmth, the way he smelled of salty sweat, of earth – always of earth and water – of sun and the drifting scent of tender greens. He caressed her nape, holding her against his chest.

"Our Lord gave you to me, Alex, and I won't let Him take you back."

She laughed and bit him through his shirt, shifting to take some pressure of her throbbing knee.

"Good to know." She raised her eyes to his. "If…" she cleared her throat and tried again. "If something like that should ever happen, you'll know, right? You'll know that I fought it as hard as I could, that I didn't want to, because I never want to leave you, Matthew Graham. Not until the day I die for real." She saw a shimmer in his eyes, and settled back against him. "And that, mister, is going to be years and years from now. So you better get used to me hanging around."

He laughed unsteadily into her hair and promised that he would.

Matthew woke in the middle of the night, his heart thumping against his ribcage. So close! He sat up in bed to verify she was lying beside him, that she was real. Her braid had come undone, releasing all those multihued curls to flow over the pillows. He fingered her hair, he traced her brows, her mouth, and she twitched but didn't wake.

He kissed her cheek and drew in her scent, filling his lungs with her essence. He glued himself to her, his long body shaping itself like an outer peel around her, and still she wasn't close enough. His hand slid in to cup her breast, he pressed his lips against the point on her neck where her pulse thudded so reassuringly, and slowly the cramp around his heart abated.

Alex moved even closer to him. "Matthew?" she murmured, and he wasn't sure if she was awake or dreaming. "Matthew?"

"I'm here, I'm always here, my heart."

With a little sigh she relaxed back into deep sleep. She was still here, with him. Nothing else mattered, nothing at all.

For a historical note to this book, please visit my website, www.annabelfrage.com

For more information about the Matthew and Alex books, please visit www.annabelfrage.com

For a peek at book two, *Like Chaff in the Wind*, just turn the page.

The Matthew and Alex story continues in *Like Chaff in the Wind*

CHAPTER 1

Matthew Graham congratulated himself yet again on not having brought his wife Alex or wee Mark along to Edinburgh. Not a welcoming city at its best, Edinburgh was cold and dreary in the icy January winds, the tall tenement buildings hunching under clouds the colour of pewter.

The city swarmed with people; in every window, in every narrow close, spectators crowded together, and for all that Matthew was both tall and broad he had to constantly use elbows and feet to avoid being trodden on. He shivered and pressed his hat down harder on his head in a feeble attempt to keep his ears from falling off with cold. His brother-in-law, Simon Melville, laughed and punched him.

"It sticks in your craw, no? To be obliged to witness the proud occasion of the laying to rest of the Marquis of Montrose."

Matthew didn't reply. He had nothing against James Graham, a noble man and a warrior of great talent and bravery, and he had not liked it that he was hanged several years ago, victim to the double dealing of Charles the Second. He did, however, resent being forced to pay his dues at this mockery of a burial where the Marquis, ten years after his death, was brought to lie in state at Holyrood Palace at the say so of the king who had so cruelly betrayed him.

He shifted on his feet in a vain attempt to escape the pressure of the sharp stone ledge digging into his back. Slowly the sumptuous coffin made its way down from the direction of St. Giles, preceded by banners and blaring trumpets as if it were indeed a whole man lying there instead of all the bits and pieces that had been brought back to be interred together. The bleached skull had been lifted off its spike on the Tolbooth only this morning, and Matthew doubted if anybody knew whether the body parts now lumped together did in fact belong to the same man.

"Do you think he cares?" Simon asked him.

"Who?" he said.

"Montrose. Do you think it matters to him, all this?"

Matthew pursed his mouth. "He might be laughing some, aye? But nay, I don't think it much matters to him how he's buried." He indicated the procession with his head. "It may matter to his wife, though. And his son."

Matthew smiled at the thought of his own son, safe at Hillview – a lad that with every day grew more and more like his sire, from his hazel eyes to the dark hair that fell in soft wisps to frame his face. He stretched as well as he could in his crammed space and closed his eyes, seeing first Mark as he had seen him last, fast asleep in his cradle, then his wife.

His wife; just thinking of Alex sent spurts of heat rippling through him. He had woken her in the dark pre-dawn the day he set out, and she had been a sinuous warmth under him. When he got out of bed, she had propped herself up on one elbow to look at him, hair escaping in curls from her thick night braid. His woman, his heart…

"Look!" Simon hissed.

Matthew opened his eyes only to meet those of his brother. Wearing a splendid fur-lined cloak, Luke Graham sat astride a fiery chestnut mare. The rings on his hands, the golden collar round his neck and the royal badge decorating his hat screamed to the world that this was a man high in the king's favour, an impression further underlined by the fact that he was riding side by side with the Governor. Where Matthew had expected to see a disfigured nose, he saw instead an elegant silver covering that elicited surprised murmurs from the crowd.

Ostentatiously, Luke set a finger to the gleaming metal, letting Matthew know that he well remembered who it was that had so damaged him and had not forgiven, nor never would. He narrowed his eyes, made a slitting motion over his throat and spurred his horse on, all the while turning to stare at Matthew who stood unmoving until horse and rider disappeared.

"The sooner we leave the better," Simon muttered as they hurried away from the crowds. They took a sharp left, having to lean backwards so as not to topple down the slippery, steep close that led into Cowgate. Matthew agreed, still shaken by the naked hatred that shone out of Luke's eyes.

"I want you to do something for me."

Simon looked at him with a certain caution but nodded.

"I want you to draw up a document, today, that makes you the guardian of Mark should anything happen to me."

"Nothing will happen to you."

"Mayhap not," Matthew shrugged. "But unless I draw up such a deed then both Mark and Alex may find themselves in the not so tender care of my brother, After all, Luke's my closest male relative – unfortunately." Matthew's gut twisted at the thought and it was apparent wee Simon agreed, an uncharacteristic scowl settling on his round face.

"I'll do it when we get back to our room, and you can sign it and have it witnessed by the landlord."

When Matthew prepared to leave for the evening, Simon frowned.

"Should you go abroad alone? What with Luke being here …"

"I'm invited to dine with Minister Crombie and his brother," Matthew smiled. "I don't think I'll be in any danger there."

Simon grunted. "Not there, no. But in the going and the coming you might be."

Matthew strapped on his sword. "I'll be careful." And damn if his brother was going to stop him from partaking of the company of men he respected and liked.

It was a long evening, an evening of discussion and far too much wine, and Matthew felt comfortably mellow when he made his way back to the inn. Tomorrow he'd be on his way home, rid of this damp, dark and teeming city, and soon he'd be at Hillview, with wife and bairn around him.

Something clattered against the cobbles and he threw a look over his shoulder, squinting through the dark. He frowned and blinded his lantern, standing very still as he listened. Soft, rustling noises and a cat ran across the narrow close.

Matthew wanted to laugh out loud with relief. Still, he chose to not unblind his lantern and increased his pace. His skin prickled, his pulse thudded loudly. You're being fanciful, he berated himself, it was just a cat, aye? There was a sound behind him and he wheeled, a hand on his sword. He never managed to pull it free. Out of the corner of his eye he saw something and then his head exploded with pain.

Alex woke with a gasp, convinced that something had happened to Mark. From the cradle came snuffling noises and she sank back against the pillows, trying to bring her heart rate under control. For some reason she was still agitated, and after an hour of turning in bed she gave up on sleep. It was just some silly dream, she assured herself, running a hand over Matthew's pillow before rising to pace restlessly up and down the room. She stood by the window and stared out into the dark, arms coming up to cross her chest. Something was very wrong and she had no idea what it was, but her whole body was clanging with alarms.

"Bad night?" Joan, her sister-in-law, asked next morning.

Alex yawned and handed over Mark into Joan's waiting arms.

"I just couldn't sleep." She nodded a good morning to their housekeeper, Mrs Gordon, but shook her head at the bowl of porridge. Her insides were clenched tight around a pebble of nagging concern, and just the thought of food made her queasy.

With each passing day Alex grew more nervous, making both Joan and Mrs Gordon jumpy as well. He should be back by now, and Alex spent far too many hours with her eyes glued to the lane. When she finally heard the sound of horses, she dropped the basket she was carrying, bunched up her skirts and flew up the lane to meet him.

She saw Samson riderless and turned, bewildered, to Simon. Her heart came to a screeching halt before it started up again, and she moved towards the horse, her hands stretched out to touch the man that wasn't there.

"Matthew?" Her eyes nailed themselves to Simon's and the expression she saw in them turned the air in her lungs to lead, a dragging weight that threatened to suffocate her. He was dead, her Matthew was dead and oh my God, how was she to go on without him? "Matthew?" she repeated, hoping that there was another explanation for the haunted look on Simon's face.

"Ah, Alex," Simon said in a choked voice. "I'm so sorry, lass."

She shook her head; she didn't want him to be sorry, please don't let him be sorry. The household congregated around them; Joan and Mrs Gordon, Rosie with Mark in arms as well as Sam, Gavin and Robbie. She didn't see them, she saw only the empty saddle where her Matthew should have been and all she wanted was to die.

"What?" She cleared her thickening throat. "What has happened to him, where is he?" Simon dismounted and Alex flew at him.

"Answer me! Where's my husband? Why isn't he here, with you?"

"He's gone," Simon said, grabbing at her flailing arms. "Dearest Lord, he's gone." He began to cry, and Alex was taken over by a slow seeping cold, a thickening of her blood that began at her feet and worked itself slowly upwards.

"No!" She tore herself free from Simon's hands. "No! No!" She wheeled and fled, because maybe if she ran fast enough and far enough none of this would be true.